CLAY CENTER

CLAY CENTER

A NOVEL BY
PHIL CONDON

EWU
P·R·E·S·S
EASTERN WASHINGTON UNIVERSITY PRESS
SPOKANE, WASHINGTON

Conrad Aiken quote from Selected Poems by Conrad Aiken © 1961,
2003 by Conrad Aiken. Used by permission of Oxford University Press,
Inc.

Published by
Eastern Washington University Press
705 West 1st Ave.
Spokane, WA. 99201

Cover design by Scott Poole
Body design by Daniel Morris & Joelean Copeland

Library of Congress Cataloging-in-Publication Data

Condon, Phil, 1947-
        Clay center / by Phil Condon.
    p. cm.
    ISBN 0-910055-95-5 (pbk. : alk. paper)
    1. Vietnamese Conflict, 1961-1975--United States--Fiction. 2.
Alienation (Social psychology)--Fiction. 3. Loss
(Psychology)--Fiction.
    4. Grief--Fiction. I. Title.
    PS3553.O4869C58 2004
    813'.54--dc22
                                                    2003023955

for two voices long still:

Philip Eugene Condon   1920-1956

Crystal Ann Gould   1947-1967

Saw the people standing, thousand years in chains,
Somebody said it's different now, look, it's still the same.
Pharaohs spin the message round and round the truth,
They could have saved a million people, how can I tell you?

Wrote a song for everyone, wrote a song for truth,
Wrote a song for everyone, but I couldn't even talk to you.

—*Creedence Clearwater Revival*
"Wrote a Song for Everyone"

It was then that I turned back,
and found the past was changed and strange as future—
cliff tree wife and husband changed and strange,
and the same or a different bird flew past my head
saying previous previous, as if I were again too soon.

—*Conrad Aiken*
"Time in the Rock or Preludes to Definition"

PART ONE

1

Miller counted as the bells in the stone tower at Trinity Cathedral chimed nine times. He and Maureena were stopped for the light at Happy Hollow Boulevard, heading west on West Dodge in Omaha, Nebraska. It was January, 1969. Miller stood next to his red '62 Skylark convertible, lowering the canvas top, Monday morning rush-hour traffic on all sides. The two of them had been up all night in the Skylark, driving, talking, making love—cruising from one end of town to the other and back again, like moths batting at the inside of a lightshade. They had burned half a tank of gas in twelve hours.

The sudden winter sun shone brightly all across the bare brown expanse of Memorial Park that sloped up and away for a quarter mile to the north. Except in the shadiest spots most of the night's thin ground frost had already melted. Miller jumped back in and sat down behind the wheel just as the light changed.

"Phone's been ringing, Miller," Maureena said, laughing and pointing to the red plastic phone on the dashboard, their souvenir from the toy shelf in the St. Vincent de Paul store.

"I told you," he said. They pulled slowly up the hill. Miller shifted to second. "When you have a red phone, the President won't leave you alone."

Maureena reached for the phone. She drew her hair over her shoulder and put the red receiver to her ear. The driver in the car next to them was already watching her. Her hair was long, bright, smooth—people usually looked twice.

Traffic slowed again and they pulled even with the same car. Maureena rolled down her window, gesturing with the receiver, stretching the plastic coils. He rolled his window down, too.

"It's for you," she said to him, "person-to-person."

Miller watched the effect of her smile. The guy smiled back in spite of himself. He wore a dark tie and a blue cardigan sweater, and the neat hairline above his ears could have been trimmed within the hour. He couldn't have been much beyond thirty, but that was fifty percent older than twenty. He looked positively rusted out to Miller.

They inched toward the next light, less than a block away, the Elmwood Park entrance to the University of Omaha. Three lanes of oncoming traffic crept down the hill toward them. The engine noises blended until they sounded like a giant factory, dozens of identical machines cramped side by side into long rows. The Skylark stayed even with the Chevy, both cars moving in short jerks. The driver kept smiling at Maureena and the red phone.

"So, who is it?" he asked. He grinned at her as if he wanted to be in on her game. Maureena put the receiver to her ear, pretending to check. Miller laughed to himself. If it was him holding out the plastic hotline, the guy would most likely suggest getting a haircut or a job, the imperatives of the day, but Maureena—not so.

She reached the phone out again. "The Brothers Kremlinozov," she said, laughing. "They want to know if today's a good day."

The driver gave her a longer look then, as if he knew she was being either more serious or more silly than he had first thought and he wasn't sure which. His car dropped back.

Miller watched her playing with the phone, letting the Impala man decide if she might be flirting. She put her feet on the dashboard and tipped her head back, smiling into the cold blue sky. She wore a maroon corduroy jumper, long white knee socks, and worn leather loafers.

The Impala pulled even again, and the guy leaned out toward her.

"Okay," he said. "I'll bite. A good day for what?"

"A good day for what? The gentleman in the Impala wants to know," Maureena spoke into the red phone and then nodded as if she were hearing the answer.

The red light turned green and an empty space opened up in front of the Skylark. Miller heard a short beep behind them, then two.

"For the flash, friend, the last flash at last." She said it in a serious tone, but with a singsong rhythm. Confusing all around. The guy looked from her to Miller and then back.

"It's all up to you," she said, stretching the receiver out even farther toward him. But then he must have seen the obvious. It was nothing but a joke, the blonde definitely had a boyfriend, and they weren't heading to work, weren't heading anywhere. He was wasting his green. His tires squealed. Miller read the Impala's bumper sticker as it raced ahead of them—*Nixon/Agnew '68*. The Skylark's said *McCarthy For President* and *Stop The War.*

Just as Miller took his foot off the brake, he heard a much longer honk. The sign hanging above them in the street said *No Left Turn*, so Miller switched on his signal, its metronome click a steady counterpoint to a whole chorus of horns that immediately rose up behind the Skylark.

They swung left into Elmwood Park. Maureena kneeled in the seat, facing backwards, waving to the drivers behind them with the receiver. Tall pines shaded the park drive. Splashes of sunlight slanted across the pavement like spills of yellow-white paint.

"I guess I'll have to take it, after all," Miller said.

Maureena handed him the phone. He took a deep breath.

"Comrade B at the house of K?—this is Comrade M from Big O, hey—I assure you I speak on behalf of the entire North American continent—"

Maureena laughed. "Wouldn't you just love that," she said.

Miller grinned back and kept speaking into the phone. "Where was I? Oh, yes, absolutely, we demur, we give you sovereignty over the fishes and fowls, etcetera, but personally, I'd rather die in San Diego, at least you can run to the beach when your bones burst into flame, but like they say, people propose, governments dispose. You there? Hey—he hung up on me."

Maureena crumpled back down into the seat, looking intently at him, not laughing anymore, but fallen out of the moment, her eyes blue mirrors of fear. In the most innocuous moments, pure silliness, she could turn desperate. One hundred eighty degrees, from crest to trough in a blink. But even that, her desperation, could be beautiful to Miller.

He put the phone back in its cradle and turned out of the park onto Happy Hollow. A single rusty sycamore leaf drifted across the hood of the car.

"Where to?" he asked, not speaking to the fear. He usually tried to outdrive it.

"SAC?" she said. She combed her fingers back through her hair as if that might sort all her unslept thoughts into straight lines.

Miller stared at her profile, the slope of smooth flesh falling from ear to jaw, and for a second he felt he could see right into her skin—a thin gloss stretched over a bottle of light.

"Strategic Air Command it is," he said, and headed south toward Bellevue.

It was only ten miles away—the center of the Free World—its electronic waves webbing the planet like mushroom roots threading moist soil. Miller looked at the sky and tried to picture the Flying Fortress, the Air Force's command center that refueled in mid-air and supposedly never landed. Somewhere overhead, he was sure, the Fortress circled and banked into cold cotton clouds, full of real red phones and serious, happy people.

∽

The day had turned way too warm for January, false spring in their part of Nebraska, not that infrequent, but to Miller, always ominous, like tornado weather in a later month. On their way to Bellevue, they stopped at Vernon Gardens park. They parked and walked a few steps to the edge of the bluff overlook for a view of the Missouri River through bare branches—oak, maple, hickory, elm. Iowa in the eastern distance.

"Maybe we should go east," Maureena said, "the next time we go."

They had driven back from southern California just before Thanksgiving once Maureena had dropped her classes. They hadn't intended to stay in Omaha, but November had begun its cold gray spiral toward Christmas. And then it was January.

"Maybe it's different in the East," she said. "Maybe the Ivy Climbers were right."

Miller smiled. He had forgotten the name they had teased their high-school friends with who signed on for the finest eastern schools. The two of them had both gone west, Maureena to Pitzer College in L.A., and Miller, to U.C. San Diego.

"Maybe we were fooled, tricked west by the Beach Boys and the Byrds," she said. "All those radio summers."

"Maybe, maybe, maybe," Miller sang it out, way off tune.

But he knew exactly what she meant. In the deep sleep of Nebraska in the early '60s, the radio waves descended like magic, pop culture from both coasts charmed into everyone's front seat and front room by bodiless shamans, the local DJs. They had both fallen for the California myth, three-minute rock-n-roll songs the seductive handbills of the age. And so they went, college-bound teenagers, not looking for work, or a fruit-grove paradise, or gold, but hungry for myth, a frontier of possibility itself, like a seam endlessly torn open and sutured shut to the zipper sound of sand and surf.

"Older is all the East is," Miller said. "Towns closer in the country, houses closer in the towns, people closer in the houses."

He moved toward her until his face was right in front of hers.

"Like this," he said. She laughed and kissed him.

"Older and closer and more crowded," he said. He kissed her back.

Miller had always gone west, hardly ever been east of Omaha. Even in grade school, for him the country split down the middle at the Missouri. He recalled the maps in the encyclopedias his mother had redeemed a volume at a time with Top Value stamps. In the West the highway lines thinned out into blank spaces, odd triangles and trapezoids of the imagination. But to the east, it was all capillaries, a net of lines with a name at every node, meshing toward the Atlantic until it became strings of clumsy knots, grids of ingrown cities.

"Maybe we should go nowhere," Maureena said, walking back to the car.

"What? Get jobs in Big O?" Miller asked. "Union Pacific? Western Electric? Or wait—we're headed to SAC—let's join the Air Force. We could get ourselves hitched up and honeymoon in bootcamp. After the war ends, of course."

"The war won't end," Maureena said as they pulled back onto Bellevue Boulevard, heading south again. "Never ends."

Miller shifted through the gears. He heard the desperate woman again. From far away. They drove on in silence, her words echoing in his head.

It sure did feel that way. Like a deadly graduation present, this war had sprung up just as they escaped high school, full-size and napalm-ugly. And then all the other wars, stretching away in both directions, past and future. The World Wars, neatly numbered, as if anyone might lose track. The civil wars, the hyphenated wars. Viet Nam. A war by any other name. The War of the Roses. The Thirty Years War.

Miller thought of his father's three years in the South Pacific, his wound and shellshock, and the bounty he brought home. Jungle rot, malaria, nightmares in the daylight. A decade of breakdowns and shock treatments, beer binges, jobs lost and found and lost again. Then in '56, on the wagon and the upswing, working as a traveling accountant in rural Nebraska, he had flipped his Ford Fairlane at seventy.

Miller's mother and the newspaper called it just another lone-vehicle car accident, and at age eight Miller believed them both. But later he found out more. It was high noon, a bright Monday in April, a flat road in the middle of Clay County, no cars around. You might as well say that noon itself was an accident. Or Monday. Or April.

Just past Bellevue, Miller pulled the Skylark off the highway near the outermost gate to Offutt Air Force Base and parked in a gravel turnaround.

"Shall we crash the party?" he asked, pointing at the distant fences and security gates.

"I took a tour once with my folks when I was in grade school," Maureena said. "They took us as far as Level Two underground. They said there were six more levels. I kept asking where the windows were."

Miller thought of the long shadow this place had cast across his childhood, too. While he was sleeping under his Davey Crockett bedspread, playing Sidewalk's Poison on the way home from school, fishing in the park lagoon in summer or skating on it in the winter, all those years and hours, SAC was out here, humming with lethal intent. Miller stared at the barbed perimeters and the cold gray towers in the distance. When the abstract idea that the world was insane sank down inside you and became a sick feeling in the pit of your stomach, what were you supposed to do? Throw up? Grow up?

"Check those out." Maureena pointed as three identical black cars with U.S. Government plates turned slowly into the base drive.

"I don't see any red phones on their dashboards," Miller said.

As the black cars passed, Miller stared at their shiny surfaces, still thinking of his childhood. And the irony of it—their Omaha, thousands of miles from a border or a foreigner, yet he and Maureena had grown up to the daily rumble of B-52s and their skytrails lacing far above Omaha like the frayed strings on an old straitjacket. They had grown up imagining after each radio song the hypnotic *Conelrad* tone and the infamous fifteen minutes that would follow.

The cars pulled up at the security gates in the distance. Maureena was talking.

"...when I read in the paper about this being one of Russia's first three targets," she said. "I used the article for a report for my sixth grade class."

She pulled her collar up around her throat and slid lower in the seat, tilting her head back and looking at the sky. A lone cloud drifted in front of the sun, and a cool wind reminded Miller it was still the dead of winter. He slid down in his seat, too.

"I made up these display charts," she said, "with little symbols. Red for missiles and blue for bombers. Huh." She outlined her lips with the tip of her little finger. "I'd forgotten."

"Forgotten which?"

"Woody was in that sixth-grade class. I knew him even way back then."

They had gone to high school with Woody Lorfen. In his sophomore year at U.O. he flunked a course and went "out of phase" with the local draft board. Miller hadn't known him as well as Maureena, and she hadn't been as close to him as their friend Durham, Woody's best friend, who had completely lost it at the funeral the spring before and screamed until Woody's uncles dragged him out of Our Lady of Lourdes church. Durham's angry quotes made the city paper. Miller's mother had sent the article to him in San Diego.

Maureena put her hands over her ears as a small jet roared overhead and landed out of sight behind a grassy terrace. Two uniformed guards a quarter mile down the entry road stepped out of a booth and saluted the last of the black cars. At this distance, in the jet's shimmering wake, the guards looked like clockwork soldiers in a toystore landscape. Miller stared at them and saw instead little pieces in a windup machine—all the parts ticking, the cogs meshing, everything tightening around the future one notch at a time like a tourniquet with steel gears.

Somewhere way down below the Missouri River, guys in blue threads were making the decisions for everyone else. Maureena and Miller had to learn to live with that, in Omaha or anywhere else—that's all. Every city had its own variation on the theme, a military base, a defense plant, a communications center—you name it. Throw up *and* grow up.

Numbered wars, buried friends, alphabet bombs, broken-down fathers, remote-control death threats—Miller could see it all as a kind of weather, as extreme and unpredictable as the rest of the weather in the central plains of North America. All he and Maureena were supposed to do was buy a tract home on the edge of town and make the payments and water the lawn and wait for the atomic tornado. That's all. If it came, there'd be sirens. Someone would warn them. Someone had a stake in their survival. But did they?

2

"I want to go to Woody's grave," Maureena said, as they came back into the outskirts of south Omaha. "He's in Holy Sepulchre," she said.

Miller nodded as he gunned through a yellow light at 24th and L. The scream of the low jets was still whining in his ears, and he wondered how many hours it had been since he had slept. Holy Sepulchre. It was his father's cemetery. As if he owned it. The last word in private property—six by three by six—a quitclaim deed made out to Loren Silas.

"You remember the night we got locked in there?" Maureena asked.

"It's the only time I've ever been locked in a graveyard. And the only time I ever will be."

"You sound so sure."

"What I want to know is why they lock cemeteries in the first place?"

"See, you have forgotten. You asked the caretaker that same question when he came and let us out."

"I did?"

They had been locked in on a Sunday night the summer before they first left for college. Miller showed her his father's grave late in the afternoon, and then they started making out in the car. Sometime after sundown, the black steel gates had been padlocked. Miller climbed a fence and called the caretaker on a pay phone. The caretaker hadn't been too pleased.

"Yes, you did," Maureena said, "and he told us it was to prevent vandalism."

"I forgot. All I remember is what happened before." Miller put his hand inside Maureena's coat and under her skirt above her knee. Her flesh felt full and smooth and cool, the living skin of apples. "So, you with the perfect memory, what did I say when he said that?"

"Some wise-alecky question about whether they were worried about people sneaking in to change names and dates to protect the innocent."

"Oh. I talked back to him."

"Exactly. He even mentioned the possibility of calling the police."

"For what? Visiting a grave after hours? Mourning without a permit?"

"Laugh now, but you were backtracking fast then. You explained real solemnly about wanting to show me your dad's grave. You said it was an emotional day for you."

"It was. I told the truth. Just like sometimes. Why the hell do we go to graves, anyway?"

"Because we can't avoid them."

Too simple. To get to the other side. There was no other answer. Miller wished he hadn't asked.

"Right. Next question. Better question. How are we going to find Woody's grave?"

"I'll show you where it is," Maureena said.

Miller turned off Underwood into the cemetery's curving lane. Stone markers and monuments of all different sizes and shapes covered the wooded hills.

"It's on the same hill as your father's," she said, "only farther down. It's easy to spot—there's still a little rumple in the carpet. Just keep bearing left."

Miller thought again of their first summer together, those months when they had called their lovemaking, almost always in the Skylark, "going to California." It all seemed so corny and naive in memory, yet they had given each other their virginity that summer, and in more than one way, Miller believed. He remembered too that he had never asked her what it was like to be left alone in Holy Sepulchre in the dark while he had gone to make the phone call. Why was it people left so much unasked? Unspoken? The vast unvoiced country of all that was never said—there was a real frontier. Still, Miller didn't ask her how she knew where Woody's grave was either.

ભ

There was no snow on the graves, only the thin thatch of last year's grass. They carried their coats as they climbed the hill, wandering slowly from Woody's grave up to Miller's father's.

"Do you think your dad did it on purpose?" They stared down at his name in the stone.

Miller knew he had dropped hints, but he had never really told her anything but the version he had grown up with, his mother's version, a combination of bad road, bad visibility, bad luck. He had never told anyone.

"I don't know," he said, and then he explained what he had learned at the State Motor Vehicle Archives in Lincoln when he looked up his father's DMV accident report in 1967, a visit no one else ever knew about, especially his mother. He told Maureena about the accident of noon. Of April.

"So nobody will ever be sure one way or the other?" she asked.

"I guess not. We wouldn't have received the insurance and V.A. benefits, I suppose, if they'd thought it was suicide. My deferment even."

At eighteen, Miller had been assigned a *4A* deferment—*Sole Surviving Son*—because a VA board had assigned his father's death to war disabilities. Loren Silas was judged dead from the war, as surely as if when he had been shot in the Philippines, it had taken him eleven years to hit the ground in a roadside ditch outside Clay Center, Nebraska. And because Miller had no brothers. Calculated losses. The strange military logic. But it had become the logic of the day.

"I'd still be in school, I guess," Miller said. "Or in Canada, or in jail."

His deferment had made it almost too easy to drop out of school the spring of '68, his junior year, although Miller said he wouldn't go into the service no matter what. To him the military was evil in conception—striking or coiled, still deadly, still vicious.

Yet the decision was never forced on him, and if he was honest, he felt guilty because it hadn't been.

"Maybe that's the test," Maureena said.

Miller came back to the graveyard. He wasn't sure what she meant.

"For a deferment?"

"Sure," Maureena said, "a deferment from life. No, I mean to know if you truly want to leave or not. To ask yourself if you would end your life even if no one would ever know you intended it. It takes the ego out of it. And the pity, and the vengeance."

"And the truth, too?"

"Maybe," she said, "but what do suicides really care about truth? I think one reason people do it is because they can't deal with truth. It's like dust in the house, never-ending. It could suffocate you."

"I would have thought just the opposite," Miller said. "I mean that maybe they care more about truth than non-suicides."

Maureena's laugh rang across the stones, nowhere for the unusual sound to settle.

"Non-suicides. Is that the term for people who don't kill themselves? Who haven't yet? Is that what we are?"

"Survivors? Natural-causers? I don't know. We're talking suicide, standing in a cemetery in January, you tell me what seems right. How about—"

He turned and waved his hand at the city beyond the cemetery, the neat rows of chimneys and TV aerials looking too much like just some other kind of plot markers.

"How about the great un-suicided?"

Maureena didn't answer. She only stared into the knoll above them, as if she could see right into the multi-chambered heart of death itself, asleep in the hill.

Within a few minutes, a chilly wind started up from the northeast, and they headed down the hill toward the car. An oily ozone smell drifted in the air from the Omaha Steel plant a block away. As they curved slowly through the north side of the cemetery that bordered on Howard Street, Maureena said she wanted to make one more stop.

"Look. The waiters."

"The what?" Miller scanned a row of short stones, all a similar size and shape. He didn't recognize any names.

"That's what I call them. They're waiting for each other. See."

The tombstones marked married couples. But the names of the living were carved in them, as well as those of the dead. And the living had no second dates:

MARTHA SWINNEN 1895—1959 HENRY SWINNEN 1899—

"So which one's doing the waiting?" Miller asked.

Maureena didn't answer. Miller wondered what Henry thought when he saw his name. Miller was glad his father's name wasn't his. He tried to imagine reading his own name on a gravestone, feeling time itself loop back and close up, spliced in a single stone name.

There were many others. Why hadn't Miller ever noticed them before? Was it that much cheaper to put two names on one stone in the first place? What if Henry moved to Florida? Remarried? Was lost at sea?

Maureena took his hand. Miller thought of the stone she had shown him years before in Mount Calvary Cemetery on Center Street, the one her grandparents shared at the head of the family plot. Had they been waiters, too?

She pressed his palm to the smooth marble. It wasn't all that cold, but Miller feared if he pulled his hand away, the skin would peel off, a wet pink glove stuck tight to stone. He had the sense that Omaha had finally closed in, or the continent itself had contracted, folding him into real darkness, the center of the earth, where nothing lives.

A city, a country, your girlfriend, your father. When you felt crushed all around, it didn't seem to matter much what was on the outside.

"Let's not wait, Miller," Maureena said.

3

Miller steered into Penroy's service station on Leavenworth Street. He pressed the clutch in, turned the key off, and coasted up to the pumps. Bells rang as the car ran over rubber pressure hoses, and an attendant hurried out, zipping up his overall suit. He shook his head as he came near the car, rapped his knuckle on Maureena's window, and then peered down over the rim of it.

"Far as I know, it's still winter," he said.

Maureena rolled her window down. "That's why we have the windows up," she said.

The attendant laughed as she opened the door and slipped her loafers on and pulled her hair back. She left her coat in the car and walked toward the station. Miller got out, too. He shook his legs out and stretched his arms. His back felt as stiff as steel.

As the attendant cranked the meter to clear it, Miller asked him to put a quart of oil in and check everything else, too—water, tires, transmission—the works. He said they were getting ready for a long trip, which was riding the line between a bald lie and a profound truth, because Miller was pretty sure now that they were only driving as far as the garage at Maureena's parents' house and that was only a mile away.

The man was alone at the station. It would take a few minutes. Miller nodded, and when Maureena came out from the bathroom, he pointed toward the sign for *Evelyn's Bakery* a half block east.

At the bakery they drank weak coffee and ate maple-frosted donuts. The place smelled like molasses, and hot oil bubbled noisily somewhere in the back room. A three-week old New Year's sign was still taped to the door, the standard pink baby and gray Father Time on either side of the standard message—*Happy New Year 1969.*

Miller had been in Evelyn's half a dozen times but never noticed the interior door that connected to the adjoining barbershop, *Tom's Razor Cut*. They started talking about barbershops. Maureena said she loved the sound of scissors. Miller said he liked the heads floating above pale capes in the mirror. By the time they stepped through the door, Miller couldn't have said which one of them had actually suggested the haircuts. Still, going into the barbershop was bold of her. Miller wouldn't have gone into a beauty parlor, but then it often seemed that Maureena was stronger than he was—or so much weaker it was impossible to tell, like when you lose track of the laps in a race.

"Short, just all one length," Miller told the barber as he sat down. "You decide."

The barber nodded and tightened the collar of the cape around Miller's neck, and Miller sensed the barber relishing the decision. A hippie, or at least what passed for one in Omaha, Nebraska, sees the light—a freak takes the cure. It might be the barber's chance to partake in a minor redemption, like a priest in crepe-soled shoes, razor in his hand.

Maureena sat in a chair with a leather seat and curved chrome armrests. Everything looked normal enough, a guy out with his girlfriend, getting a haircut, even though it was a weekday morning and they should have been working somewhere or in class at the University. Another barber sat in a corner watching a TV with the sound off. Both barbers wore sheer blue blousey shirts with short wide sleeves.

Miller stared first at the insurance agency wall clock—ten to twelve—and then at the wall calendar, a fat fresh pad of numbered days with a thin rough edge where only the first few pages had been torn off, the big black **20** staring back out at him as if mocking his age. He smelled Vitalis hair oil and open cakes of shoe polish.

Maureena walked to the chair next to his and climbed up into it. The second barber stared at her without a smile. Miller's barber held his scissors up, blades parted. The fluorescent light glinted on the stainless steel.

"Can you cut my hair, too, please?" she asked.

"I don't usually cut ladies' hair. Wouldn't guarantee much." The second barber stood and laughed as he spoke, reaching for a cigarette from his blue pocket.

"You can cut it like a boy's," she said. "It won't matter how short."

"You're the customer," he said. "It all pays the same." Sarcasm edged both his clichés. He didn't light his cigarette.

In a moment it was so quiet Miller could hear the two sets of scissors, separate, then together, then separate again. The blades slipping by each other sounded like stiff paper shuffling. Miller hadn't had a haircut for a year, and for Maureena it had been much longer than that. Their hair drifted onto the small octagonal tiles of the white floor, his dark and curly, hers bright and smooth. The barbers swung them around to look in the mirror almost at the same instant.

"Short enough?" Miller wasn't sure which one spoke.

Miller stared at Maureena's reflection and caught her mirror eyes staring back at his, a silent cross or double cross of vision and light. He thought of the times she had wrapped her hair around him as they made love, her fingers clutching and braiding at their hair, as if she might bind them together that way. They both nodded in the mirror.

Miller paid at the register, staring at the hair scattered across the floor like a feathery Rorshach. Maureena tried to laugh, mugging in the long wall mirror, kissing his cheek as if they were sophomores after all, maybe just punchy from staying up all night cramming for tests, or out on a dare getting identical haircuts, maybe sent, who knows, by a sorority or fraternity. But it was only an act. As they stepped out the door, Miller glanced in the mirror again, and the couple there looked different than the couple who had walked in, paler and weaker, as if the barbers had been bloodless surgeons and removed something vital from each of them.

Back at Penroy's, the Skylark was waiting, the gas full, the oil topped up, the windshield sparkling—someone had cleaned it inside and out. Maureena used her dad's MobilCard to pay for the gas, something she had never done before. Miller stared hard at the name. Richard Ocear.

Richard and his wife were in Miami for an underwriters' convention and winter vacation. They had been gone since Christmas and wouldn't be back for two more weeks. Miller had nicknamed the Ocear place the Icehouse long ago — Richard and Rona had smiles that looked like they were forced with a wrench. Maybe it was from all Maureena had told him about the silence of growing up there, but the place seemed unbearable even when they weren't home, as if when you shut the door, you gained a mile or two of altitude, the air all at once too thin to breathe.

"So this place we're going, Miller," Maureena asked as she drove out of the station. "On our ... long trip. What should we call it?" She sounded as offhand as if she were wondering whether to take Farnam Street or Underwood Avenue.

"Somewhere way the hell off to the east, I guess," Miller said, remembering the talk on their way to SAC. "How about Nova Nova?" He heard himself as if it were a stranger. Someone going for a sleepy smartass laugh. Someone pretending to play chicken with his greatest fear.

"Monoxide's painless, isn't it?" she asked. No comment on his invented country.

It was the most bluntly either of them had spoken of it, yet from the moment they had left the cemetery, Miller had believed they both were thinking it. Now he was sure.

"I've heard that. I suppose it's all relative. I think it's clean."

He felt like he was reciting lines from a script he couldn't remember memorizing. He looked at his hands. They were shaking. He saw a thin line of dirt beneath one thumbnail. It had to be from the cemetery. Was that important?

"What about your folks? Finding it. Finding us."

"They wouldn't. The garbage service comes Wednesdays. They have a key to the garage. My folks aren't due back till the end of the month. It would just be a phone call to them."

As he heard her words, he thought the unthinkable—he pictured the garbage of both of them dead. He wanted to fight the image off, but instead he played with it. He picked up the red phone and made mock calls all the rest of the way to the Icehouse.

He played the king of coroners, with the kindest, cruelest voice anyone ever heard, pausing each time for the scratchy moment of static before grief and condolences. He wanted to stop but he didn't.

He called Richard and Rona in Miami. He called his mother and his grandfather in Omaha and Grant and Carlila in California. And Durham, cruising town that very moment in his Yellow cab—nothing had to make any sense. He called the Dean who lectured him about quitting college, and the bosses on every summer job he'd had. And of course, Mr. Milhous—why not? There were no delays on the line today, and everyone was taking his calls, even the White House.

Miller stepped out and waved Maureena in as she backed the Skylark into the garage. She said she wanted to see a sliver of sky, as if they could drive there. Miller pulled the garage door down behind them, its narrow window a cloudy rectangle of light.

Neither of them spoke for several minutes. Miller's eyes slowly adjusted to the garage twilight. Maureena's face was pale. They sat in open coats, casual, like Isadora and her unnamed companion, only lacking wind and scarves. The Skylark idled smoothly, the four-speed floor shift rattling in neutral. The fuel needle was nudged past the *F*.

Miller knew he could go back all twenty years then, and maybe should, remembering and rearranging, but he also knew he couldn't count on more than twenty minutes. He put his hands on the steering wheel and looked around the inside of the garage. Its air already looked stale and tarnished. The key wasn't memory. The key was imagination. He turned to Maureena.

"It's a beautiful June day here in the heart of Nova Nova, look at those waterfalls on the mountain." Miller waved his hand around the garage like a bus driver. He motioned toward the shelves of Richard's tools, his jars full of graded nails and screws.

"And the way the clouds linger on the peaks," Maureena said. "Even in summer—why haven't we come here before?" She leaned back and stared at the exposed trusses above their heads, a few pieces of lumber and a ladder spread out and stored across them.

They invented strange shorebirds on the graveled edge of a glacier-fed lake. They pointed like tourists to a wall of long-handled lawn tools, rakes and spreaders and shovels. Miller felt light-headed, or thought he did. Which came first, death or its imagination?

They stopped the Skylark by the edge of a dark pine forest, the air thick with a pungent smell like pitch. Miller stared into Maureena's eyes and kissed her. Their lips were dry. It was like a hundred other times, just the two of them in the car, pushing their bodies together in a crush of damp heat, and it was like no other time.

"I want to, Miller, I do." Her voice was hoarse and urgent. "And I don't."

He wasn't sure which she was talking about. He heard something like passion, but it was washed out with fear. "Don't let go of me," he whispered. He hugged her tighter. The steady thrum of the Skylark's V-8 faded to background, impossible to really hear, like the forgotten sound of the earth whirling in space. Their arms tightened around each other's backs, the warm swell of her breasts flattening against him like small round loaves.

"Anywhere," she said. "Anywhere we want. The country of our choosing."

"Perfect pine," Miller said, "perfect."

He heard a chanting far back in his head, an abracadabra of urban death. "Carbon monoxide, carbon monoxide." Odorless and unpredictable. People died accidentally this way, with or without intent. He and Maureena had worried about it themselves on winter nights, parked for hours with the heater on, making love and talking, falling asleep, sometimes waking with dull headaches. Miller was floating between all those times, his head full of tiny white butterflies, every memory a silk wing. Carbon monoxide. So many people crying out for help underestimated it, went too far, were unable to return.

But it didn't feel like a cry for help, it felt plain crazy, wild and sweet crazy-for-a-day—the big crazy. Images careened through Miller's mind—a gleaming razor blade in noon sun on a green suburban lawn, an empty white school bus at the curb at midnight, two dime-store masks at the mouth of a rocky cave. With twenty-four sleepless hours pushing down on both of them, they wanted to be done with the whole thing and escape from it right there in each others' arms.

Maureena undid her buttons and bra. Miller pressed his lips on her nipple. Her flesh was distant candy. He tasted it behind glass.

They struggled to lie down, their legs entwined. Miller pulled her panties aside and eased and circled his finger inside her. Someone's shoe pressed on the gas, and the Skylark thrummed louder. How fast does the earth spin? Why hadn't he felt it before?

Miller unbuckled his belt and jeans and guided her hand inside his pants. He gasped as she took hold of him. He straightened his legs to pull his jeans down and felt his feet sliding against the pedals and bracing against the floorboard, his bare back bumping the cold steering wheel. They were both halfway into the driver's seat now, Maureena on her back, her skirt riding above her waist and her legs draped around the gear shift. She raised one leg up toward the back of the seat and the gear shift shoved forward and the transmission clanked just as Miller reached both his hands beneath her hips and pulled her toward him. And then the clutch popped and Miller's neck whipped back and sideways and he heard the bark of splintering wood and smelled hot rubber as the Skylark lunged forward into the garage door.

The car lurched to a stop, half in and half out of the garage, the shattered door almost even with the rear fenders. The engine backfired twice and died.

Miller pushed Maureena all the way over into the passenger seat and twisted around to face the wheel, exhausted. His head throbbed, his neck ached. The fresh cold air burned his nose and throat. He couldn't focus his eyes on any one thing. Behind them, from the jagged mouth of the garage, dim bluish air swirled, as if it had been under pressure.

"Breathe deep," Maureena said, "gulp." She slapped him gently, holding his chin with one hand. She did it, too, sucking air in spasms. Two scared kids with hysterical hiccups.

Miller watched her eyes as they cleared, and she almost smiled at him, as if they both knew for that one second who had done what—or what had done what—something that you'd never pin down behind only two eyes, under only one name.

"We're not going there," Miller said, "not ever."

"No. We've gone past it now," she said, craning around to look at the shattered door, her hands cradling her breasts through her blouse.

"Go get your things," Miller mumbled, "please." He pointed at the house. "I don't want you to stay here anymore. I don't want either of us to come here ever again."

He turned the ignition key off. Not until then did he really hear the silence.

"Are you all right? What's going on over there?"

The voice was not his, and not hers.

Miller looked around and saw a neighbor, standing on his porch next door, his hand on an open storm door. A sweater buttoned to his chin. Thick-framed black glasses. Miller pulled up his pants and reached for his shoes.

"Talk to him, Maureena. Wave him off. We don't want cops. Just imagine it."

Maureena straightened her clothes, wiped her eyes with a handkerchief, stepped out slowly, and walked partway across the yard, buttoning her coat.

"Mr. Wenshaw, yes, we're okay, I think we're just fine now. Thank you for checking. Miller was working on his car and it slipped into gear. I'll call my parents about the garage door."

Miller was amazed she had any voice left, how strong she yelled.

And such a good lie. They were alive again.

He put the clutch in and rolled the Skylark forward a few feet, pulled up the canvas top, and picked through the shards of the garage door. Maureena came back and helped. Miller felt sick at his stomach. He tucked his faded blue workshirt back into his jeans and knelt and tied his bootlaces. They pulled three sheets of heavy plywood across the door, propping them against two trash cans full of sawdust from Richard's table saw.

Maureena went inside to write a note for the housecleaners and pack. Miller worked not to throw up in the front yard, sure the neighbors were watching every move. Better than any soap opera, Rona Ocear's wild daughter and her screwball boyfriend just drove through the garage door. They must be on something, those knuckleheads, potheads, acidheads. Miller tried to imagine what it might have looked like to the middle-aged Wenshaws if they had happened to see the Skylark burst through their neighbor's garage door in the middle of a January day. How would they explain a thing like that to themselves? Just another sign of the tightrope times? One more thing to make them wonder what their world was coming to?

He wanted to apologize then, to the Wenshaws and the Ocears, and everyone else. And for everything—for living, for wanting to die, for not wanting to kill or grow up or be quiet. But the apology turned obscene and vindictive in his throat and it was all he could do not to scream it. Screw all of you. You and your garages and graveyards. You and your churches and colleges that play culture like an ice-cream-truck tune to the bass beat of bombs and the nightly electric whining of burning yellow kids.

He gagged, felt vomit rise, swallowed and held his breath. He couldn't believe none of the neighbors had called the cops. He imagined their hands on their phones, only hesitating because they had watched Maureena grow up from their windows, remembered her in rollerskates and bandaids. Him puking in the bushes in broad daylight would do it for sure.

Maureena came back out, carrying a grocery sack full of clothes and her backpack inside a cardboard box. "I was afraid to get a suitcase. Are they watching? You all right?"

"My head aches like I have a lump of concrete behind my eyes, this is the worst haircut I've ever had, we owe your folks at least a hundred bucks for the garage door, I've just driven a convertible back from the bottom of the grave—"

"And you're trying to make jokes out of it?"

"Have you got any better ideas?"

"Did this really happen, Miller? Is it my fault? Should we go to the emergency room? A church? Maybe we should get some help?"

"Yes. No. Probably. But let's not."

"Where then?"

"California," he said, the word still sounding like an antidote to him. Only one word any better. "The Pacific," he said. Peace now. Peace.

They coasted out her drive and down the hill with the engine off, a technique Miller had perfected bringing Maureena home in the middle of the night dozens of times. He remembered the empty feeling after she had gone in the Icehouse and he was left alone in the Skylark, summer or winter, spring or fall, that perfect lonely moment, usually after passion and promises, coasting down the hill with the engine killed and the lights off, alone with the lingering wheat smell of her hair in the dark until the end of the block when he'd jumpstart the car and drive away in the night.

He had kept those moments to himself, not even sharing them with Maureena. That lovely long block of silent, savored loss.

Halfway down the hill, he turned the key on. At the bottom, he jumped it into second. It was early afternoon. Far to the west, thin stripes of puffy clouds stretched in bands across the horizon. It looked like it might snow.

4

The Platte River laces from one end of Nebraska to the other like a wide shallow spine. From South Omaha, if you head west on "L" Street far enough, you cross the Platte twice in a hundred miles as it loops north and then back south across the rolling hills where the Pawnee once lived.

Miller and Maureena made it half-way between those two river crossings that night, a few miles from Rising City, before the snow slowed them down. They drove the two-lane, Highway 92, though the Interstate would have been the logical bad-weather choice. But the two of them had sworn off the Interstate several years earlier, numbed out by its homogenous landscape and its endless commercial corridors, where everything was always for sale—or would be in just a few more miles.

For the first half hour after the storm really set in, they stayed close behind a state snowplow, but then Miller couldn't even see well enough to keep up with that. They were down to about twenty miles an hour, not too far past Rising City, when a semi passed the Skylark slowly, its huge double sets of wheels grinding by their windows. As the truck pulled ahead, Miller saw the snowy stickers on the back of its mudflaps—red, white, and blue above the surly admonition that he always took too personally: *America—Love It or Leave It.*

"Can't even try to keep up with that," Durham said from the backseat. He read it aloud. Nobody said anything for a long moment.

When Maureena and Miller had gone back to Miller's room at Drake Court to clean up that afternoon, Durham was asleep inside. Miller didn't lock the door, and Durham often napped there after he picked up his taxi at the Yellow Cab barn just across 20th Street. When Miller's shrieking garage headache finally began to clear and he and Maureena started packing things up, Miller offered Durham the apartment for the rest of the month—it was paid up. But Durham said he would like to come with them. He even suggested they take the old cab he had checked out for the day, but instead they had talked him into coming in the Skylark.

"Should I try to slipstream it?" Miller asked as the semi vanished in the snow ahead.

"Slipstream through the snowstorm," Maureena said, half-singing new lyrics to the old tiptoe-tulip tune. She turned to Durham.

"Hey, good thing we brought the convertible, see? We couldn't roll the top down in your cab, could we?"

"One hundred percent on that one," Durham said. "But on the other hand, the Skylark doesn't have a meter. Can you imagine what the fare to California would be?"

"And who in the world would pay it," Miller said.

"Why is it all the really big trucks have that sticker, anyway?" Durham asked.

"Most of the people they pass are probably reassured," Maureena said.

"Simple," Miller said. "Because America has eighteen wheels."

"Not to mention fourteen forward gears," Durham said.

"And she stops at every greasy spoon," Miller said, getting into the riff, "where a cook with shadowy jowls tosses you a raw burger and says…?"

Miller held his hand out. Durham shrugged. Maureena gave him a blank look, too.

"Eat it or beat it," Miller said. They both chuckled, but not much. Miller cringed inside—it was a crude but almost too perfect image for Mr. Milhous.

"You don't let up too much, do you?" Durham said. "You just ruined truckstops for me." He laughed as he leaned forward between the seats until his face was almost even with theirs. "God, the snow is so beautiful. We'd freeze for sure if we took the top down. You want to?"

"Absolutely maybe," Miller said.

"America is whatever we say it is," Maureena said, still playing off of the mudflap slogan. "A hijacked yellow cab." She looked at Durham. "Or a *Laugh-In* tricycle."

"Two hundred million tricycles," Miller said. "Wobble, wobble."

"Or a convertible full of snow," she said.

Miller looked out into the storm and saw an image of the Skylark, snow drifted from the dash to the tops of the doors. It was as clear as a dream. Durham said something he didn't hear.

"Let's do stop," Maureena said, "let's celebrate the snow." She pressed Miller's hand.

The tires crunched louder as Miller slowed down, and then it was silent except for the hum of the engine, and then the wind seemed to suck even that sound away. As a concession to the regular reality of the highway, Miller put the warning blinkers on. But the patriot trucker must have been the last traffic, anxious to get near the snowplow and bust on through to better weather. And those did seem the only options. Outrun the storm. Or celebrate it.

Durham and Miller rolled the top down and Maureena grabbed the flashlight from the glovebox and pointed it straight up into the falling snow like a beacon. Snowflakes stuck to the seats and the dash. Maureena laughed as they melted on her face and coated her hair white-gold. Durham laughed, too, opening his mouth to catch snowflakes. When Maureena blinked the light off, the world hovered at the edge of a white-tinged darkness.

"I'm cold," she said into the dark. "And glad we're alive."

Miller couldn't see her face. He thought of how close to the alternative both of them had been a short twelve hours before. It already seemed a season back.

"Me, too," Durham said, "on both counts."

The white world flooded around them again the instant Miller turned on the headlights. But somewhere in the moments of no light, they had made a decision. Durham and Miller rolled the top up, and then Durham and Maureena waved Miller away from the drifts as he reversed and pulled forward six times, slowly turning around in the narrow lane the snowplow had made.

It took most of the night to get back to Omaha. The Pacific would have to wait.

CƷ

Since Thanksgiving Miller had been living in Drake Court, three square blocks of rundown maroon brick buildings and small ivied courtyards at the low-rent edge of downtown Omaha. The dark narrow hallways gave off the stale smells of an empty refrigerator left unplugged. The single window in his room opened onto a brick wall of other windows.

Miller had rented the room because it was cheap, and because when you opened the window, you could inhale the thick wheaty smell from the Butternut Bakery a few blocks away. But what clinched it had been that the rental office lady said it was the same room that Johnny Carson had lived in when he worked for WOW radio in the late '40s. Everyone knew Carson had lived at Drake Court, but Miller wasn't sure whether to believe her about the room. Still, he liked the notion—what a perfect patron ghost for 1969. The evening news was filled with freaks and pigs and gooks and grunts, but Carson, a crewcut happy-go-lucky kid from Norfolk, Nebraska, had the flat clueless voice that America listened to more often than any other.

The double daybed in the room pulled out of the wall like a two-foot-high drawer, and sometimes Maureena and Miller would lie there in the dim single-window daylight and make up droll Carson-like one-liners, imagining J.C. holed up there twenty years before, planning his ascent to the throne of American TV.

By the time the three of them returned to Johnny's old digs that morning, they'd dreamed up a dozen strategies for trying to make the best of what was left of the Omaha winter while they saved money for spring in North County San Diego—plus whatever it cost to repair the garage door. Durham didn't know how much longer it would be until the draft board got fed up with his shifting addresses and declared him an evader, but Miller and Maureena promised to help him any way they could. And he gave them the low-down about the Family Equipment Company out past Carter Lake where they assembled cut-rate lawnmowers and snowblowers and were always hiring minimum-wage workers. Maureena came up with a scheme to avoid dealing with their parents, using fake long-distance phone calls and California postmarks from Grant's place in Del Mar.

Keeping each other awake all the way back from Rising City, they convinced themselves they were a threesome as urgent as a legend, destined to survive—at least another month or so—as long as they stuck together.

CZ

By February they had a routine. Maureena and Miller headed out in the Skylark every morning for Family Equipment and worked seven to three putting together riding lawnmowers. Durham drove his cab at night and slept at Drake Court during the day.

Over dinners lit by candles that Maureena hand-dipped in juice cans on the two-burner stove, she and Miller would tell Durham about their day at the mower-blower factory and he would relate his metered adventures from the night before. The three of them even talked about writing something for Omaha's on-again-off-again underground paper, *The Buffalo Chip*, making their work stories up into some kind of cartoonish parables about everything that was wrong with Omaha, America, the war, the world.

And what was wrong seemed easy enough to find. Maureena and Miller drove home from work each afternoon along North 24th, the commercial strip through Omaha's ghetto, most of which had burnt to the ground in riots the two previous summers. For ten blocks, only a few stores owned by residents and a barber shop that doubled as the local Black Panther office were left standing. Posters of black fists clutching black rifles wrapped every telephone pole.

During their evening meals they compared notes, trying to find a common ground where everything might mean something, or something more, at least, than the regulation sound and fury. From Durham's discovery that poor people were consistently the best tippers, he roughed out a taxi story called "The Meek Shall Inherit the Cabs." After watching thousands of lawnmowers roll off the assembly line, Miller tried to sketch out a piece about an army of suburban guys with Saturday-morning smiles wading ashore from the South China Sea and pull-starting their lawnmowers on command.

Although they never actually took any of the ideas to the *Buffalo Chip*, it seemed to Miller, in the short run at least, especially with the daily talks and laughs over supper, like one small piece in the big puzzle of a real education—as opposed to the high-powered, high-dollar college BS he had dropped out of. Plus, they were making and saving money—Drake Court was sixty-five bucks a month, split three ways—and anyway, escape was just around the corner, like always. Down the block. Up the alley. On the highway. Miller kept the Skylark tuned up, and Durham rated all his cabs for cross-country travel. Maureena encouraged him and kidded him, talking about how she could cover the yellow up with spray-paint flowers and mandalas.

She also tried to encourage him about his draft problems, something she knew quite a bit about once she began volunteering on Saturday mornings at the makeshift Draft Resistance Center in an Old Market downtown warehouse. She counseled guys who were thinking about *not* taking the big step—about which were the easiest border crossings in North Dakota, about where to move to get the most liberal draft boards, about what kind of references to get to make a case for conscientious objection. She was the same age as most of the guys were, with a cheerleader's face and figure, and yet she told them it was all right, that caring about killing and being killed didn't mean they were cowards or traitors. She told them she respected them.

And Miller respected her. Maybe alone among everything. He damn sure doubted his own head, his motives, his path. But her, no—even though he knew very well that on the inside she was as unsure as anyone else every step of the way, still, from the outside, to him, and he believed, to the other confused guys who waited to talk to her on Saturday mornings, her every step looked graceful, assured, and free.

If it hadn't been for her, it might have been more obvious, even to Miller, how aimless and angry he was. He might have nosed the Buick into the recruitment office's plate-glass window, or answered the ads he saw for the Cuban sugar brigades, or bought a few five-gallon buckets of cow's blood from a guy he'd worked with at Armour's one summer and poured them over the parked police cruisers that lined North 24th Street.

But no, Maureena was with him. Following him. Leading him. Sometimes the landscape, sometimes the sky. Both his figure and his ground.

5

On Valentine's Day, Durham made two fresh loaves of stove-top bread, and Maureena gave Miller an album Carlila had sent her—*It's a Beautiful Day*. Miller gave her a silver bracelet from the import shop in the Old Market. Durham had traded a crosstown fare for an old toboggan, and that night he checked out his cab early, picked up the toboggan, tied it on top of the cab, and they all went sledding on St. Mary's hill in Spring Lake Park, something Miller hadn't done since junior high. Flying down the slopes, laughing and yelling in the cold night, Miller felt like he had crested the long hill of winter itself. Now maybe he could coast through the rest.

On the way back, they stopped at a phone booth in a Mr. Donut parking lot and called to tell Grant they were coming to California as soon as money and the weather allowed—maybe another month or so. They took turns on the phone, and Carlila, Grant's girlfriend, came on the line, too. She had been Maureena's friend at Pitzer and had met Grant through Maureena a year before. She and Grant had since dropped out of school, too, and now they lived with six students in a big weatherbeaten house across from the Del Mar race track, a half block from the ocean.

Grant told Miller about failing his third draft physical. For the first two, he had downed four aspirin with a bottle of Pepsi every few hours for a week prior, and as expected, his blood pressure and urine samples were off the charts. But they rescheduled him both times, so he went in straight finally, only then he actually flunked because of his flat feet. He and Miller joked about how hard it must be to pull a trigger with flat feet.

Maureena told Grant and Carlila about Drake Court and the lawnmower factory and the Yellow Cab Company. Grant said what they were doing sounded downright crazy—and therefore good. Maureena told them she had just sent a money order—for damages to her folks' garage—in a letter to be posted from out there. When Miller came back on the line after that, Grant asked him if he'd thrown a tantrum, tried to tear down suburbia singlehandedly, one split-level at a time. Miller managed not to answer directly, but he did agree it didn't sound like such a terrible idea.

When they were about to hang up, Carlila wanted them to hear the breakers on the beach. It was high tide, and she stuck the phone out the window for what seemed like five minutes. They had to put more quarters in but the three of them kept taking turns, listening.

Miller wasn't positive he heard the ocean, standing there in the frosted-up phone booth on South 13th Street with his gloves and scarf on and his pants crusted with ice, but the possibility alone made him want to keep listening. Even when he hung up, he wasn't sure. It could have been sand and surf, and it could have been static.

After they warmed up with more coffee, they decided they might as well each make their obligatory call home. It seemed much easier to pretend they were in California after talking to Grant and Carlila.

That night, like the other time Miller had called his mom after he said he left town, he was haunted by the mock bereavement calls he had made on the toy phone in January. He had long since tossed the phone in the trash, but sometimes he couldn't shake the memory. He wanted to ask his mother to forgive him for them, and for what might have happened in the garage, yet she wouldn't even know what he was talking about. And that was all to the good.

He did tell her that he was making money with lawn mowers, a half-truth of some sort, and he let it slide when she said the weather maps had been showing heavy rain for Southern California. He was glad she didn't ask more, and glad, too, she didn't mention his grandfather, Everett Miller, whose last name had become his first through some twist of family politics. Everett lived on a freight agent's pension from fifty years of keeping Burlington trains running on time, and with it he helped Miller's mother out a lot. Usually though, part of her repayment involved listening to his precision pronouncements about how or where her life—and more recently Miller's—had run behind schedule or off-track.

After he hung up, Miller went inside the shop again and watched Durham and Maureena make their calls. It turned out that Durham's parents had received his official induction notice. They marked it *No Forwarding Address*, the way he had told them, but they were still anxious to know where he was. Durham didn't want to tell them something they might have to lie about.

The snag in the calls was when Maureena talked to her folks. She told them Miller had sent the money for a replacement garage door and that she was doing fine, but after two minutes, when she said she was out of change and tried to hang up, they told her to call right back collect. Miller talked a waitress from the donut shop into coming out and faking a long-distance operator voice, and then Maureena's dad must have lectured at her for about five minutes straight. Miller stared through the plate glass of the shop window and watched her nod her head over and over.

They left the waitress a big tip for her help with the phone. All the way home, Miller kept hearing the ocean, the waves against sand like long smooth kisses, each breaking off with a slow, salty sound, over and over.

❧

Durham parked on 22nd Street, at the far side of Drake Court. As they walked single file through the snowy courtyards with the toboggan over their heads, Miller was thinking of the Dostoevsky novels he had loved in high school—all those voluble, apoplectic characters and their wild passions and fiery principles. And the feeling in those books of being in the provinces—how it always had to do with deep snow and narrow streets, with chimneyed brick buildings and an oppressive mix of weather and distance, and all of it hemmed in by horizons that only the railroad or imagination could ever reach.

As they reached the third floor, struggling to twist the toboggan around the turns on the landing, Miller woke up from his fictional St. Petersburg daydreams. He heard Maureena and Durham talking intently about Woody. About Viet Nam and Holy Sepulchre.

"He's buried in the same cemetery as Miller's father," he heard Maureena say. Miller remembered his January calls on the toy phone again. As he walked into the room behind the two of them, he caught himself hoping he might see Johnny Carson himself, sitting at Miller's orange-crate desk, ready to disarm this or any conversation with his trademark grin and wink.

Maureena put *Beautiful Day* on the stereo. They changed clothes and sat on the floor with the fresh bread and a tin of honey. The steam radiator whined when Miller opened the valve, and it seemed to fit into the sound of the electric violin, sweeping across the room in waves.

"Where'd you get this?" Durham asked, checking out the album cover. "I've never seen or heard of them."

"Carlila," Maureena said. "She knows them—they're from Washington State near where she grew up—it's not released yet. It's some kind of demo."

"I'd like to meet Grant and Carlila," he said. "They sounded cool on the phone."

"They're wild," Miller said. "Grant's my best friend out there. I met him my first week at UCSD. His parents are from Palos Verdes."

"Verdes as in green," Maureena said. "Green as in rich."

"In a way almost nobody in Omaha is," Miller said. "But Grant's gone past all that."

"Why in the world did you two ever come back from California?" Durham asked. "I think if I ever made it out of this place—" He pointed out the dark window. "Really made it out—I wouldn't come back."

"It's home," Maureena said.

"The four-letter word that won't let go," Miller said. "We didn't plan it this way. When Maureena quit school, we just drove back for Thanksgiving. Then there was Christmas, etcetera,

etcetera. Plus, you saw for yourself what happens when you try leaving Nebraska in January."

"The great white whirlwind," Maureena said. "Like in the Bible."

"Moses never saw a Midwest winter," Miller said, guessing at her reference.

Durham sliced the bread with his pocket knife. "I loved Woody," he said, staring at the knife, and then Maureena. She touched his wrist with her fingers. Miller sensed the conversation from the stairwell wasn't finished.

"Like a brother," Durham said. "Maybe more."

The tone-arm hovered between cuts, and the click of the needle made the wind outside sound even louder. Durham stared at Maureena's fingertips and bracelet.

"How'd you know where he was buried? You two weren't in town, were you?"

"No, we were still in California," Maureena said. "But Miller read the article his mother sent him." She pointed at Miller. "And last summer I went out and found Woody's place."

She paused and looked out the window. Miller thought of their visit to Holy Sepulchre only weeks before. He realized how hard he had been trying to put that whole day out of mind.

"I always want to know where people went, where they ended up," she said. "Even if it's not really them, just the place, just the placemarker."

Durham gave her a questioning look. "I've never even seen his grave," he said. "After I was hauled out of the church that morning, I just decided to let the big black parade go on without me. That's what I'm still doing, I guess."

"I get this vision sometimes," Maureena said. She raised her slender hands up as if she were holding something breakable and then dropped them slowly back to her lap. "It's hard to express. Like the whole world was a giant book crammed with bookmarks, each carefully arranged, each holding somebody's place, somebody who's never going to read anymore."

"A soil-book," Miller said, picking up on her idea, "with granite bookmarks."

She almost laughed. "Kind of," she said. "But it's true, they should mark the places people die. The exact places where they disappear, like the exact page and word where they've looked away and known—this is as far as I'm ever going to read."

"That would be messy, though," Miller said. "And way too upfront. The one thing you can say for cemeteries is that they're clean and well hidden."

"That's what I mean," Maureena said. "It should be reminding us. It should be vivid."

"What should be?" Durham asked, shaking his head. "You guys are losing me."

"Death," Maureena said.

"You know though," Miller said, "you probably couldn't take ten steps in Nebraska without standing where a Native American died." He thought of his grade-school trips with his best friend's parents through the Omaha and Winnebago reservations on the way to South Dakota lakes. "Every culture builds its homes on top of graveyards," he said.

Ever since the war had made Miller look harder at the government and he had seen so many lies and so much viciousness in the name of honor and truth, he had felt himself pulled backward through a thick web of lies. All the white, black, red, and yellow lies that passed for history in school. It felt like falling into a giant skein of tangled string. Every time you worked a knot loose or pulled a snag free, you ran the risk of falling further. Miller was pretty sure he hadn't reached the bottom yet.

Maureena stood up and took a cube of incense from the little wooden box where she kept her jewelry and letters. She put it in the sink and lit it.

"Maybe one reason you and I are good for each other, Miller," she said, "is because we think in opposite directions. You almost always think from the little up to the big. From the personal stuff to the political stuff. My mind moves the other way."

Durham stared at the wall as if he could see the winter night right through it.

"The personal stuff is hard to talk about," he said. "Even with you two."

"The important things are always the hardest," Maureena said.

She seemed relaxed, open, able to say or hear anything. Not for the first time, Miller pictured her with children of her own, their own. He wondered if children might protect her from the silence he'd seen her drift into so easily, the silence they had both almost gone all the way into in the garage. But Miller didn't want to say what he was thinking. He didn't know what to say.

"Do you two want to smoke some weed," he asked.

Maureena looked surprised. They both had pretty much given it up. Miller, especially, had smoked a lot before he quit school, but since then he felt like he had to stay alert, ready to move fast and think quick. Still, he kept a small stash, a few numbers, nothing that couldn't be flushed or eaten on a moment's notice.

"I don't want to," Durham said. "There's enough confusion going on in here already." He pointed at his head. His bushy hair looked orange in the candlelight.

"Me either," Maureena said. "Sometimes, I feel like I've had enough, period. It's like walking in thick fog on the beach—for awhile you're fascinated, but then you're just lost. It was great for a couple of years, every weekend—"

"And every weekday," Miller said, laughing.

"Speak for yourself, you. I never did know how you stayed in school."

Miller realized he didn't know either. But then he hadn't.

"I've only tried it a few times," Durham said. "Mostly wild ditch weed from along the railroad tracks out in Sarpy County, so maybe I don't really know. But ever since Woody died and I got on Local Board Five's bad side, I haven't had room for anything that makes things weirder. They're weird enough."

"How about we save it for a special time then," Miller said, holding up a wheat-straw joint. "Maybe on the road to California."

"A New Mexico sunset," Maureena said. "Remember that place outside Silver City?"

"I couldn't forget," Miller said. It had been on a little side trip on the way back to school in September '67. They had hiked halfway up a mountainside and then smoked number after number as the sun sank. It took them hours to find the way back down.

"You two really seem so together," Durham said. "Both ways."

Maureena laughed. "If you only knew." The way she said it made Miller wonder if he did.

"Not all that together," Miller said. "Do you want to know the real story on how her dad's garage door got shredded, Durham?"

Miller took a slice of bread Maureena had spread honey on. They had only told Durham the same lame lie they passed off on neighbor Wenshaw and the Ocears.

"I've been wondering," Durham said. He pressed the lid back down on the honey tin with his thumbs. "I guess you were high?"

"Not how you mean," Miller said. "What would you say, Maureena?" He wound up for a run at it before she could answer. "Graveyard psychosis? Barbershop hypnosis?" He heard himself sounding almost as if he wanted to get a laugh out of it.

"We visited Woody's grave—among others—in Holy Sepulchre that very same day, Durham. Right before Tom's Barber shop." Miller patted the cowlick that had come in as his hair grew back. He realized there was no way to laugh about any of it. "It was a very odd day. Maybe the oddest of my life."

"I'd try to say the truth," Maureena said. She looked directly at Durham, talking slowly, a calm smile on her face. "We were trying to kill ourselves. And trying to make love. And we weren't sure which to do first. So we managed to do neither. The only casualty was the door."

Durham's face went flat. "That same day we all took off in the snowstorm that night?"

"The same," Maureena said. "Miller here doesn't know it, but he's a quick-change artist. Of the soul." She looked over at him as lovingly as ever. She rolled her bracelet on her wrist.

"I like that," Miller said. "It's a bit on the romantic side, but I like it."

"Now me, I'm a different story," she said. "I have a twin nobody knows about."

Miller caught her eyes at the edge of her smile. They were deep and full, walking her words right out into the space between them, as if something way inside her essential self was opening like the leaves of a camera shutter in dim light.

"Except Mr. and Mrs. Ocear, of course," she added. Her eyes still held Miller's in a thin blue stream of light.

But Miller knew what he knew. Maureena had two older brothers and no twin.

"Suicide? Why?" Durham asked. "What for? Why you two?"

"There's accidents and there's accidents," Miller said, finally looking from Maureena's eyes and then seeing a sudden picture of his father, thrown from his car and tumbling through the air in Clay County, a tired man with broken wings, or maybe just no wings at all. Miller shook his head to lose the image.

"We're only twenty years old," Durham said. "Suicide. I just don't get it."

"No easy answers," Miller said. "I guess it's all a question of degree—like homicide. There's first, second." Miller counted off on his fingers. "Willful. Negligent. Vehicular."

"Woody died in an accident," Durham said. "He fell from a helicopter."

Nobody said anything for a moment. *Beautiful Day* was playing a lush, stoney instrumental, and the third-floor room felt like it floated on space and wind. If he opened the door, Miller might be anywhere. And anyone. He saw the two earnest faces near him and then sensed the third, his own, drifting in a hazy triangle with them. They weren't exactly children and they weren't exactly adults, and that nervous break in the big drama, like a landing in a long flight of stairs, made anything seem possible. Suddenly Miller felt glad about his life, about everything— glad he'd dropped out, glad he'd smoked pot, glad his mother and grandfather didn't have any more of a clue about his life than he did, glad that he didn't know anything about anything for sure. If he went far enough outside everything he'd ever expected, maybe he would stumble onto an inside he'd never imagined. Swim into a seacave. Surface on another side.

"Until Woody went to Viet Nam, I didn't even know where it was," Durham finally said. "And I didn't care." He pressed his thumb and finger against his temples. "I just wanted to be an accountant and have a cool car and end up like my parents, I guess, watching TV and raising more kids like me who wanted to go to college and heaven and then raise their own kids sometime between the two. That's as far as I figured it."

"Weren't we all dreaming that way?" Maureena asked. "Did you ever see a flock of birds, spaced out across a bare patch of ground, standing still, as if they were all asleep with their little bird faces turned away from the wind?" She smiled and closed her eyes, drawing her arms and elbows behind her like wings. "American dreaming."

"With an Omaha twist or two, of course," Miller said. He kept hearing himself trying to lighten up the conversation between Maureena and Durham. "More elm trees, corn taller than your car, fresh steaks in every restaurant, and mailmen who stop and talk like they have all day."

Durham did laugh a little. "You must have grown up in my neighborhood," he said. "Woody did. He and I were best friends—all the way up. In the summers, we would sneak out of our houses and climb the elm trees that arch over 52nd Street and stay there half the night, hanging over the pavement with cars gliding below us. We pretended we had given them permission to pass. And then when the wind waved the leaves, we would see stars and make-believe they were the lights on spaceships headed our way."

"My father said once that stars were the eyes of dead people," Maureena said. "They watch us while we sleep. He said when a star disappeared, it was someone who had grown tired of watching and closed their eyes."

"What about shooting stars?" Miller asked.

"That's when somebody leans too close and wants too much to change things down here. They fall and burn away. Their eyes are the last thing to flame out."

"I never dreamed your dad ever had that kind of imagination," Miller said.

"Only about the dark," Maureena said. "Only about nighttime things."

"Woody wrote to me," Durham said, "once a week. I even climbed a tree one night—I was a college sophomore if you can believe—and tried to see him on the other side of the world, high in a jungle somewhere, safe in his own tree."

"What were his letters like?" Miller asked. He realized he had never had a male friendship as close as Woody and Durham's. Except maybe with Grant.

"They were like watching somebody disappear," Durham said. "Woody died before he ever got on the helicopter."

"Most people do," Maureena said.

Durham gave her another confused look before he went on. "Woody changed," he said. "At first the letters sounded like him—the Omaha him, the elm-tree him—but by the end he was somebody else. He sent me photos of bodies. Postcard-type landscape photos with dust clouds and black-red globs flying in the air or hung up in trees that he—or somebody—had circled and labelled—'gook arm or gook head.'"

Maureena winced. Miller put his hand on her shoulder. He had seen pictures something like that, too, sent from friends of friends overseas, showing what a Claymore or a rocket had done to human bodies, but never with captions. You had to guess—what's wrong in this picture?

"Woody turned into someone else," Durham said.

"Maybe he had to, to survive," Miller said.

"But he died, anyway," Durham said. "I don't know what it was really, what they turned him into, but they'll *never* do it to me." He clenched his fists and his eyes were bright and wet.

Miller felt that, too, and yet he wasn't even sure what the feeling meant. It was as if his life had turned into non-stop shadowboxing—trying not to turn into something he couldn't even name, while trying to keep alive a chance for turning into something else that was equally unnameable. The last few months of his life made about as much sense as someone bobbing and weaving, alone in a ring, for hours on end. He didn't want to be knocked down, and he didn't want to land a punch.

"What happened at the funeral?" he asked.

"When I made a fool of myself in front of half the town?"

"I thought you were a hero," Maureena said. "Real heroes look like fools."

"Huh. Well, thanks for that vote. Anyway, at the funeral Woody's father and brothers wouldn't say anything more than what the Army told them," Durham said. "Quote, killed in combat in a raid over enemy territory, unquote. Something about that sent me over the line."

Miller remembered how the newspaper article had described Durham's outburst in the church—"disrespectful and deranged."

"Because before the funeral, his mom had invited me over and told me what she'd found out from one of Woody's friends who'd called her—he hadn't been shot or blown up. He had fallen out of a helicopter at fourteen hundred feet. She and I were sitting next to each other, crying over the dining room table. Then she showed me the letters and pictures he sent her, and they were totally different from mine—they were fake. But I couldn't tell her that. I was the one he told the truth to."

"And the one who has to live with it," Maureena said.

"About a week afterward, I got his last letter. He told me how he and his buddies pushed gooks out of helicopters rather than take them prisoner—which was a waste of time—or shoot them—which was a waste of munition. He wrote how they'd plead and wrestle and grab your boot when you kicked them in the chest and shoved them backward. And then I knew how he fell. Someone he was pushing pulled him down."

"You don't know that," Miller said.

Durham stared at the wall and nodded his head several times.

"The same way you don't know how your dad died?" Maureena asked.

The record changer clicked off. The homemade candles flickered low. Miller wasn't sure exactly how the talk had turned so far this way. He wanted to turn it back.

"The light's about had it," he said. "I know I can't ever know how you feel, Steve, losing your best friend. You do have a real friend now though, two of them, right here."

"And the same way I don't know whether my twin lived," Maureena said.

She put her hands out between her and Miller, and he took hold of them with his eyes closed. He had no idea what to make of her mentioning the twin again. He had read an unfinished poem she wrote once about a girl whose twin sister died before either of them were even named. But he didn't think she was still working on it.

Durham took hold of their hands, too, and they sat like that for a minute, a circle with six clasped hands at the center. Miller felt how rare it was for three unrelated people to simply hold hands. Most love was so limited—a small, timid, battered thing.

Maureena broke away and turned the record over one more time.

"I think we will all make it," she said. "I think we're getting stronger this winter. I'm loving better and deeper."

Miller felt something like that, too, and wanted to say so, but he didn't.

"Are you going to hit the streets tonight, taximan?" he asked Durham instead. He put his hand on his shoulder.

"No, if it's all right, I'll stay in tonight." Durham arranged the floor pillows on the toboggan and stretched out on it in his sleeping bag.

Miller pulled the big drawer bed out of the wall, and Maureena snuffed the candles. They all lay down in the dark.

Sometime after the record ended, Miller heard the wind blowing hard between the tall brick buildings. It shrieked and whined like a distant fire engine or an ambulance, one that should have been too far away to hear, as if someone was coming from a million miles away with help.

☃

A dim glow of light came from the window, the moon on snow. Miller kneeled on the bed and looked out and saw fresh untrodden snow everywhere from one end of Drake Court to the other, wet snow clinging to the horizontal brick lines on the north side of the nearest building, as if a hundred white fingers had stroked across it in the night. All over the narrow wedge of downtown that he could see lay only the black silence of new snow and the white hush of no motion. He imagined himself in a tall brick ship that had sailed inland for a thousand nights on a sea of ice.

Maureena was awake, too. She put her hands on his shoulders.

"It's really beautiful when the wind stops," she whispered.

She was kneeling on the bed behind him. Miller turned and kissed her and touched her, and they lay back down and he felt her hands under the covers. He wasn't sure at all what night it was until he was already between her and among her and she was making the most beautiful sounds in the world. Then in a race of images, Miller saw the toboggan in the snow and the ocean in the phone booth and Durham and Woody in their trees and a mother crying and a father dying and boys' bodies falling out of the sky and Maureena's twin, all of it so much like a dream except that the edges were just rough enough to make him sure it had been real. He thought of Durham and the loss in his voice. What would Miller do if he ever lost Maureena? He looked at her face in the shadowed light and felt a sudden grief inside himself. For a moment it was as real as any organ.

He heard a sound across the room. He looked over toward the toboggan. They had never made love with anyone else around, much less in the same room. He saw what he thought might be Durham's open eyes in the moonlight from the window.

Maureena's voice rose and fell again, and Miller felt like he was a wave about to break and crash across a wide warm shore. He looked in Maureena's eyes as if to tell her that Durham was awake and might hear, and she looked back in his eyes, and Miller knew that she knew, and that her knowing was a kind of friendship and love, and she went on then and pulled him apart onto the beach of her knowing, and then Miller didn't know anything until after she was asleep and he was staring at the dark ceiling, drifting through the snowy Omaha night in Johnny Carson's ghostroom with Maureena and Durham and all the thousand jostled memories they each carried to and from their sleep, like water with no container.

6

Three weeks later, around 6 P.M. on a Thursday afternoon in early March, as the last daylight streamed through the window as gray and thin as smoke, Miller heard a noise that didn't fit into Neil Young's "String Quartet from Whiskey Boot Hill," their Drake Court dinner music that night. The second time he heard it, an extra two beats, a flat hollow sound like a leather shoe falling on a dried-out drum, he knew it was someone knocking on the door. He turned the music down.

As he and Maureena and Durham looked at each other, Miller saw it dawn on each of them that nobody else had been to the apartment all winter—no neighbors, no friends, no police, no parents—just the way they had wanted it. If the unfamiliar sound at the door had only been a little friendlier and lighter, Miller might have been able to joke that it was J.C. himself coming to check out his old place. But he couldn't joke, even to himself—against the backdrop of hiding out in your hometown, the sharp, sudden sound at the door was menacing.

"Maureena?" It was Richard Ocear's voice.

Maureena jerked like a roped calf at the rodeo. Durham stood up. Maureena stood up, too, touched her hair, and then dropped her hands to her sides like a puppet with tangled strings. Durham put his palms out with his fingers up, looking at Miller. Miller did the same.

"Who is it?" Durham asked.

"Richard Ocear. I'm looking for my daughter. Let me in."

Miller picked up their plates and stacked them in the sink without a sound. Maureena moved out of sight of the door into a corner, staring at the dangling chain next to the lock. Miller remembered her saying that her father had never allowed locked doors in his house.

"Just a minute." Durham stood near the door, still looking at Miller for ideas.

Miller looked at Maureena, but her eyes had clouded up with something he couldn't name. She shook her head. Miller looked at Durham and shook his too.

It was a weird pantomime, giving silent directions in the small room. Miller's mind was racing, wondering how the hell Ocear had found out they were in town—and where. He looked around the room for Maureena's things. All her clothes were in the closet. Yet he couldn't make Maureena vanish. He flashed on the movie scenes when somebody hangs out a window by their fingertips while the police search the room and question the accomplice who keeps nervously eyeing the ledge. But then Miller didn't want to talk to Richard either. It was something he had avoided pretty well for years—with plenty of help in return. When Maureena lived at home the first two summers in college, her father always managed to be busy in the basement when Miller picked her up. Miller had the feeling he pretended Maureena never had a boyfriend. She had a social life. She went on dates. But not a boyfriend, not a lover. Now he was standing outside the room where Maureena and Miller slept together. Wake-up time all around.

Durham ended the long silence. "This is Steve Durham, Mr. Ocear. The last I heard, Maureena was going to school in Los Angeles."

"Don't lie to me, Steven. I'm not accustomed to standing in dark, cold hallways. I want to talk to Maureena. I know she stays here."

Durham turned around. Miller motioned to keep talking. He moved closer to Maureena. Maybe they were due for a showdown with Ocear. They were both twenty years old. They could live where they wanted, and together if they wanted. He didn't have to like it. Or Miller.

"I think you've got your information wrong, sir," Durham said. "I live here alone. I got a letter from Maureena in California just last month."

When Miller reached for Maureena's hand, it was limp. She mouthed the word "No" over and over at him. He couldn't understand what she was so afraid of. Of course he wouldn't have been too pleased if his mother, or worse, and more likely, his grandfather Everett, had come to the door, but he wouldn't have panicked like this either. She was shivering.

"I asked you not to lie to me," Richard said, knocking harder. "I have plenty of information—all of it correct. Open this door or I go straight to the Induction Center in the Kresge building and tell them where you are."

"They're closed," Durham said. He turned toward Miller and rolled his eyes. There wasn't much more time for pantomime.

"They'll be open first thing in the morning," Richard said. "Let me in. I demand to talk to my daughter."

Maureena moved across the room and lay down on the bed. She pulled the covers up around her chin, motioning to Miller. At first he thought she wanted him to get under the covers and hug her, as if that might make them both transparent. Then he realized she wanted him to roll the bed into the wall.

"Look, she does live here," Durham said, still improvising, watching Maureena and Miller. "But she's not here now. She's at the Family Equipment Company out on North 16th. She works the swing shift. If you know so much, you ought to know that."

Miller grabbed a bottle of salad oil from the kitchen shelf. He dripped it on the bed's four rollers and capped it. He pushed the bed into the wall as slowly as he could.

"Wonderful," Richard said. "My daughter, a straight-A student, spends the winter of what would have been her senior year in college assembling snowblowers in Carter Lake."

"Lawnmowers," Durham said. "There's a production lag."

"Regardless. Let me in. I have something I want to leave for her."

"Are you alone, Mr. Ocear?" The bed drawer rolled flush with the wall. Miller moved a floor pillow in front of it and put the oil back in the kitchen cabinet.

"I am for now," Richard said. "If you make me come back, I won't be."

Miller picked up their glasses and put them in the sink. He didn't see anything else that might reveal Maureena's presence.

"First, I should tell you that Miller Silas lives here, too, sir," Durham said. "He's here now. We don't want any trouble."

"I don't doubt it," Richard said. "Troublemakers always say that about the time their lies come home to roost." His voice went louder when he heard Miller's name. "Are you going to unlock this door? Or shall I go to the rental office and call Mrs. Silas and then your parents? And tell the manager that there's an unmarried couple living in apartment 315C while I'm at it?"

The door wasn't locked. Miller knew it. Durham knew it. But apparently it hadn't occurred to Richard Ocear. Durham reached up and put the chain lock on in one quick motion. The bright brass chain glinted as he moved it. Such a small thing, Miller thought, so weak and brittle, like everything they relied on to hold the world away.

The doorknob turned immediately and Richard pushed at the door. The chain went taut. Miller stepped in front of Durham. He could see Richard's eyes glare above the links of chain.

"Mr. Ocear. Durham told you. She's at work. Do you want me to have her call you?"

"If she's not here, why can't I come in? How did she get to work? She doesn't have a car."

"She used mine. You can see the whole room through the door. Go ahead, look, she's not here."

Miller stepped back and Richard pushed his face as far into the open door as he could. His eyes roamed the corners of the place. It was clear he wasn't impressed with their quarters.

"Satisfied?"

"So, my daughter supports two able-bodied men now?"

"We all work," Miller said. "I called in sick today. Steve works nights." He lied as fast as he could think.

"Listen, I haven't told Mrs. Ocear anything yet, and from the looks of this place, I see I'm going to have to keep this from her. It would break her heart to hear such things. Maureena's given her such a hard time. She's a disappointment to her. All you kids are a disappointment."

"Us kids are disappointed, too, Mr. Ocear."

"She had enough problems before she got involved with you, Miller. I warned her when she said you'd dropped out of school. You have absolutely no sense of responsibility. The acorn never falls far from the tree."

"Oh Jesus, it's aphorism time. What the hell do you mean by that?"

"You're in no position to swear at me, Miller. I've talked to people who knew your father. He never got much farther than a city block from a barstool. Surely, you must know that."

"Why don't you get the hell out of here," Miller yelled at him. He had his gloved hand on the edge of the door, and Miller felt like slamming it in the jamb. Durham grabbed Miller's shoulder, but he kept talking. "I'll be sure and let Maureena know you dropped by—no doubt, she'll be elated. Maybe she'll call you and maybe not."

Richard stuck his shiny black wingtip in the door.

"Get this and get it clear, Silas. I'm driving out to Family Equipment and retrieve Maureena right now. And if she's not there, I intend to fix both your wagons. The Army will know how to deal with you two. They have experience in making men out of boys."

Miller stared at the door trim where the lockplate was screwed in—it looked like it might pull away from the wall any minute. He remembered Maureena telling how Richard had gone overseas in '43 and spent two fairly comfortable years in England guarding an airfield. Of course he preached the army brand of discipline and responsibility. Why not? They'd paid off for him as good as government bonds.

Suddenly Miller heard a sound like a baby crying from an apartment far down the hall. But they didn't allow kids at Drake Court. It was Maureena. Richard heard it, too.

"Where is she? I hear my daughter. What have you done to her? I'll call the law, I swear it. My company writes insurance on city vehicles. I have friends." He pushed harder at the door.

Durham stepped back in front of Miller.

"Look, Mr. Ocear. I'm sorry I lied to you, but Maureena said she didn't want to see you. She made us hide her. She's scared."

"Please leave us alone," Miller yelled over Durham's shoulder at the crack in the door. "Maureena's not well. Can't you hear her crying?" His voice shook.

"She'll be fine at home with her mother and myself," Richard said.

"Go away, Dad, go away." Maureena's voice sounded muffled, like someone yelling from a basement full of cotton.

"Look. Just let me close the door," Durham said. His voice was shaking, too. "If you do, I promise Maureena will talk to you. I give you my absolute word."

Through the slot Miller saw Richard's face. Or part of it. He couldn't see his ears. He wore a gray wool winter coat with a black fur collar. He was a narrow slice of a man, standing in the dark, trying to thin his way into the light of their room. For a second Miller felt sorry for him.

"I don't know why I should trust a draft dodger. I'm not going away," he said. "I give you five minutes." He pulled his foot and hand out of the door. He raised his arm and ran his coatsleeve up and looked intently at his gold watch as if all the answers he would ever need were written there. Durham shut the door.

"Holy shit," he said. "This is way too weird."

Miller pulled the bed out of the wall. He wished he could crawl into it and have Durham close it behind him and keep pushing it until he and Maureena came out in another apartment, another building, another town. Ride their bed west all night and appear at the Pacific just as dawn broke over the beach somewhere near Del Mar.

Maureena sat up, her eyes red. "I'm sorry," she said.

"I'm sorry," Miller said. "I shouldn't have put you in there."

"No," she said. "I wanted to stay in there. It's him. Don't let them take me home, Miller. I don't want that."

"You don't have to," Miller said. They were both whispering. Durham was staring out the window.

"I promised him you'd talk to him," he said with his back to them.

Maureena stood up and went to the window, too. She stared down at the courtyard as if she were gauging the depth of the snow for a jump.

"Could we get out the window somehow?" she asked.

"What's with you and your folks?" Durham asked her. "You act like you're facing the gas chamber or something."

"It's not as bad as I'm making it," she said. "It's just his voice sometimes, when he's mad or disappointed. I hate it. I feel like I'm splitting in two."

Miller stared at her.

"Where does that leave us?" Durham said.

"Huh?" Miller turned to him. "Look, there's three of us and only one of him. Let's just walk out. Let him stand out there in the hallway forever."

"You don't know him when there's something he wants," Maureena said. "He'll turn Durham in—he will. He'll humiliate your mother. He'll do anything."

"So why not go on home for awhile?" Durham asked. "We can leave for California in a couple more weeks, sooner even. Maybe you should take the path of least resistance, for now anyway—make peace with them."

"I've made peace, Steve. Over and over. Peace is the worst with them, it's like marking time in a museum filled with mannequins. They're not like real people, they're clammy and lifeless, and when I'm with them, I'm not like normal people either."

Miller thought of all the nights Maureena had dreaded going back into the Icehouse after they had been out together. How most of all she had dreaded waking her parents up.

"Well, then, what do we do?" Durham asked. "Tip a candle over and start a wax fire? Slip away in the confusion?"

"Tell him I'll go to St. Joe's, " Maureena said.

"St. Joe's Hospital?" Miller asked.

"They have a wing, there, the A.P.W.—the adolescent psychiatric ward. Tell him I'll check in there if he'll leave us alone now."

"Honey, you're not thinking this through," Miller said. "Nobody gets along with their folks. But we don't need doctors and nurses refereeing for us."

"It's the only way to get him to leave," she said. "I don't want you to have to face him. I think he'll go for it. I was there once before."

"When?" Miller asked. He looked at Durham, realizing it sounded like something he should already have known. Durham looked out the window again.

"Five years ago. Just for a week or two. My folks put me there. It's not bad. The place is full of teenagers whose folks can't deal with them. They do tests and stuff. It's the only way we can get this settled down tonight."

Maureena stepped into the closet-sized bathroom and washed her face. As Miller watched her, he counted back. It would have been a year before they had started dating, the spring of their graduation. They were both at the Senior Party at Peony Park Ballroom with someone else, but they danced the second-to-last dance together and then he'd called her the next day and they had never looked back. But in all the years since, she had never told him about this St. Joe's time. Then he thought of how much he hadn't told her, too. About the way his dad had looked after the shock treatments at the V.A. Hospital, limp and rubbery, like somebody had deboned him in a couple of quick strokes—the way you fix a trout. Or about his mother paying a shrink two hundred bucks two summers after his Dad died to hear that it was past time to get rid of his clothes in the closet and move his slippers from under her bed. When Miller moved the slippers for her, two dusty pennies fell on the floor, the ones she put there after his funeral, and she started crying exactly as hard as she had the day he died. Life was always years behind itself, the true bloom of past events sucking the moisture out of the moment, vining around the present as if it were nothing but a flimsy trellis.

Miller shook the thoughts away and went back over to the door. "Mr. Ocear? Are you still out there?"

"Two minutes," he said.

"We don't really need a countdown, do we? Look, I'm sorry for swearing before. We're all living together to save money, okay? We're trying to do the best we can here. It's confusing to be young right now, Richard."

"Richard, is it? I don't think today is a good day for you to start using my given name. Not when you're holding my daughter against her will."

"Nobody's holding her. She's frightened. She's upset. I've never seen her so upset. She says she wants to go to St. Joe's."

"St. Joe's?"

"The hospital."

"I know perfectly well. Tell her to get her things together. I'll take her."

"She doesn't want to go with you." Maureena hadn't said as much, but Miller knew for sure that he didn't want her to.

"She's certainly not going with you."

"Will you let Steve take her then?"

"And you stay here?"

"If you promise to leave, yes."

"I'm not anxious to stand in this hallway any longer."

Maureena came over to Miller. She seemed more relaxed as she took his hand.

"Dad? Steve's cab is parked on 22nd street. Between Howard and Jones. You can pull your car up behind it and follow us down to St. Joe's, all right?"

"Maureena, you're not lying to me, are you? This may be the best for you. You need some quiet time, away from these wild boys, to think for yourself."

"I'm not lying. Go wait by the cab. I promise."

"Your mother's heart would break in little pieces if you ever lied, Maureena."

"I promise not to lie."

They heard his footsteps in the hall. Maureena waited another moment and then took the chain down and opened the door. She stuck her head out.

"He's gone."

"Let's get the hell out of here," Miller said. "Let's pack up and leave town right now. Leave the cab where it is. We can get our checks mailed to us."

"I promised him," Maureena said. "Let's go, Steve."

Durham stepped out into the hall. Miller looked at the two of them. He saw they were really leaving. Maureena kissed Miller at the door.

"Don't you want some clothes or some books?"

She buttoned her coat and kissed him again. "I don't want to stay that long. I'll work this out. Trust me."

"I do." He squeezed her hand. "I'm sorry," he said. "I should have seen this coming. Or something like this."

"I think I saw it," Maureena said. "But something's always coming. If you watch for it, it's all you ever see."

She was right. And yet if you turned your back, it could roll right up on you like thunderheads at the front of a squall line.

"You'll be back soon, Durham?" Miller asked.

"After however long whatever this is takes," he said. He tried to smile. "Don't worry, man. This kind of stuff just happens, I guess."

Then all three of them tried to smile, but Miller knew they each knew the other two were faking it. Maureena and Durham walked down the dark hall, holding hands.

When Miller closed the door, he lay down on the bed. It was still warm from Maureena. In the sudden quiet, he could hear the low music playing on. Neil Young was chopping down a palm tree at the end of "Last Trip to Tulsa."

Miller closed his eyes and wished he could roll the bed into the wall behind him, sleep hard, and dream a long, long time. Long enough to fall back into the past and find a different path. Or jump into the future and catch a new one. Long enough for the wars to end, for the snow to melt, for spring to come. Not the usual spring of flowers and buds everyone knew and expected, the one that pleased everybody but really surprised no one. No, not that one, but something different and entirely new that they didn't know. Something it would be up to them all to imagine.

7

Durham returned later that night and told Miller what had happened at St. Joe's. Although no one could legally force Maureena to admit herself, once she signed the form at the front desk, with her father breathing down her neck and with the phone concurrence of a Dr. Marcus Clotter, the consulting psychiatrist for the A.P.W., she was in the hospital's custody for at least one week—with Clotter as her medical custodian.

When Miller went to a booth on 20th Street and tried to call Maureena that night and then again Friday morning, he was referred to the doctor's downtown office instead. After the fourth call to that number on Friday, he was finally put through.

Clotter already knew who Miller was. He explained his custodian role for the A.P.W. patients and that he made rounds Tuesdays and Thursdays, although many patients had other doctors, too. At this point, however, it was his and the Ocears' best judgement that Maureena not see or speak to Miller for the duration of the week. At the end of such period, Miller's contact with her, as well as her further stay at St. Joseph's, would be "negotiable." Miller pleaded with him until he agreed to meet with him over the weekend. He would be in his downtown office briefly on Saturday morning.

Miller walked down Harney Street as the Federal Building clock rang ten the next morning. As he approached the Redick Tower office building, about twenty protestors across the street and a half block west picketed in front of the Induction Center. More than half of them were young women near Maureena's age. The police had banned demonstrations during working hours so it had become a Saturday ritual.

Miller stepped into the Redick lobby and blew on his cold hands. An old black man with copper-colored eyes and a silver mustache was mopping the gray and white marble floor of the lobby. Miller said good morning. The man looked up and nodded. "Say," he said.

The elevator doors were wide open. Miller stepped in, pushed number *18*, and listened to the cables' low metallic purr as they pulled him up the narrow shaft through the winter morning.

"Nice of you to come," Clotter said. His monotone gave no hint of irony. He sat at a large mahogany desk covered with half-inch glass. From the office window Miller could see St. Joseph's a mile to the south and the stockyards of South Omaha beyond.

"I want to see Maureena," he said, sitting in the chair closest to the desk. "This deal with her dad at the hospital is a lot like kidnapping."

"Her father says the same thing about you in reverse," Clotter said.

"Maureena is twenty years old. She's a strong, smart woman. Ask her who she wants to talk to. Ask her where she wants to be."

"She signed herself in."

"Her father pressured her. He threatened me and my friend. He piles guilt on Maureena the way people shovel food on your plate at Thanksgiving. What was she supposed to do?"

"He threatened you physically?"

"Of course not. If you know him, you know he's the kind of guy who wears leather gloves and doesn't touch anything except with the point of a pen. Afraid of germs. But he's the one with the disease."

"And what disease would that be?"

Miller didn't answer. He saw that Clotter was toying with him. Conversation was a cat-and-mouse game to him, a subtle game of patience and attrition, one he'd been well trained in. Miller was full to the brim with doubts he didn't want exploited, and he couldn't begin to imagine where Clotter's might lie. Rainbow reflections played over the glass on the large desk as scattered clouds passed in front of the sun, shining through the window behind Clotter. Miller wanted to put his sunglasses on.

"Mr. Ocear said you yelled and swore at him and that Maureena sounded like she was either gagged or drugged."

"I'm not defending myself against any bullshit thing he happens to think. Maureena was fine till she heard his voice. That's when the trouble began."

"You don't think it's troubling that she was living in Omaha for several months and telling Mr. and Mrs. Ocear she was in California."

"I was telling my mother the same thing."

"And why is that?"

"It just seemed easier." Miller frowned and looked from Clotter's eyes to the ceiling and back. "Maybe it's way too long to explain, at least here and now, okay?" Clotter smiled more broadly but didn't speak at all. His smiling silence sucked Miller in.

"Look, from the time I wake up, all I see is power and money. The people who have it pay armies and police to bomb and firehose and lock up the people who don't. All the rest is for show, as hollow as canned laughter and cue cards. Maureena ..." Miller paused. He'd said too much. It always came out wrong. Or too strong. "Maureena is just about the only person in the world right now I feel much like talking to. There's no law that says you have to talk, to your parents or your parents' shrink or anyone else, is there?"

"And if you don't want to talk, why are you here today?"

"I want to see Maureena. I want her to feel safe enough to check out of that stupid place where she doesn't belong. I want you to see I'm innocent."

"Innocent of what?"

Miller was suddenly sick of the questions. He pointed out the window.

"Why don't you cross the street and psychoanalyze the brown-suit salesmen at the Induction Center who sign up eighteen-year-olds to go halfway across the world to kill yellow people. Why don't you do something real? How much are the Ocears paying you to be their white-collar lineblocker, anyway?"

"So you've come here with your mind made up about me and everything?"

"If I hadn't, you'd probably have me checking myself into St. Joe's in a minute."

Clotter smiled and lit another cigarette. Miller sensed that Clotter thought that wouldn't be a bad idea, but he knew the doctor would make damn sure he wasn't near Maureena. Still, at that moment Miller glimpsed an idea about how he might get to see her. Clotter scooted the brown glass ashtray across the glass desktop. It made a sliding sound like teeth against fingernails.

"What if we just start all over?" he said. He opened a small notebook on the desk and wrote something. "Can I ask you a personal question about Maureena?"

"Which would be?"

"Has she ever talked about killing herself?"

"If you want to know about Maureena's thoughts, you'll have to ask her."

Miller blinked and heard the Ocear's garage door splintering. For a second he imagined the window behind Clotter exploding instead, the glass raining eighteen stories like a shower of ice-cold diamond dust, the frigid air washing the room clean in one blast. Clotter was writing in the notebook again.

Maureena had only mentioned suicide once before the garage day. Late one warm summer night in July of '67, when Miller dropped her off at the Icehouse, she had said "Goodbye" in a voice that Miller had never heard before, one that sounded as if she really and truly knew what that word meant. When Miller called her on it, she had said, way too calmly, that she was going inside to kill herself that night. Miller put the top down on the Skylark, and they watched the stars until the sun came up, talking nonstop for hours, parked in front of her house. The whole thing was so out of the blue, and so scary, that Miller had done a good job forgetting it. Maureena had never mentioned it again, and neither had Miller, not even in the garage in January.

Clotter looked up from his notebook. "Has she ever spoken of a twin?"

"Like I said before, ask her. Maybe if she really likes you, she'll show you her poetry. Until then, it's her business. Not yours."

Clotter closed the notebook and put his cigarette out. He took his stainless steel lighter out of his suitcoat, as if he was ready to light another, but then set it carefully on the desk between them like a chess piece.

"I'll talk to her Tuesday. I'll tell her I spoke with you. In the meantime, I'm sorry, but I still believe it best you not see or talk to her."

Miller looked at the window, intact as ever, still waiting on diamonds. There wasn't going to be a cold breeze in that room, maybe not ever. He would have to settle for bullshit.

"Look, Doctor Clotter, I want to tell you the truth then, and in return, I need to ask a favor. I have to go back to California—I can't wait a full week. Will Maureena be able to receive my letters? Or do you intercept the mail, too?"

"You're a very sarcastic young man, Miller. It's hard for me to imagine what's made you so angry. Of course you can write to her."

Miller ignored the anger bait. He could have spent a solid year telling this guy what made him mad, and all that would come of it would be a neat profile, a case history, something entirely reasonable and predictable—and just as boring.

"I don't mean to be so sarcastic. I'm sure you must have Maureena's best interests at heart. I'm just so completely frustrated. I really wish her folks and me hit it off better. But I have a chance to catch a ride to the coast this weekend, and I don't want to miss it. You might as well know that when I write her, I'll be asking her to join me. We were both happier in California."

"People seem to say so." Clotter stood up behind the desk. "Have a safe trip, son."

"Will you help me out? Will you tell her I'll write her as soon as I get there? Please. I don't want to leave town without her knowing."

"I'll do that, yes, I'll tell her on my rounds this Tuesday, of course. I think this will all work out well." He picked up the lighter with his left hand and extended his right across the desk. Miller leaned across and shook it.

Moments later, alone in the carpeted elevator cube, Miller fell eighteen stories, thinking of his father's outpatient shock treatments and the prescription tranquilizers he swallowed by the handful and his V.A. shrink who tried to date his mother a year after his father died. Miller imagined the elevator smashing into the Redick basement at top speed and him collapsing neatly into his cuffs and shoes like one of those folding camp cups. The elevator cables sang as they unwrapped from spools high above him. They sounded like the ocean from far, far off, like the murmuring sandy sound of something huge coming close and slipping away, over and over again.

When the doors opened, the black janitor was standing at the lobby door, staring out, smoking a thin brown cigarillo. When he saw Miller, he quickly stubbed it in the standup ashcan and began mopping again.

"Is it snowing yet?" Miller asked.

The man shook his head and ran his hand over his short gray hair.

"Will be soon," he said. Miller stood next to him, staring out at the gray street and the gray sky.

"They still at it," the man said, pointing up the block at the people carrying signs across the street. "Every Saturday. They gonna get cold today, yessir." He squeezed the handle on the wringer on the bucket.

Miller zipped his jacket up. "You think it does any good?"

"I wouldn't know about that," the man said.

"We can hope," Miller said.

"We can do that," he said. "With no money down." He laughed and pushed the mop and pulled it back toward him in a quick figure eight as if he were writing and erasing something at the same time.

Miller wondered how many invisible eights that hard marble had absorbed. As he pushed open the foyer door, he turned back. "Take care," he said.

"And I'll leave some for you," the man said, smiling.

As the door closed, Miller wanted to turn around and find Dr. Clotter or Richard Ocear down there on ground level swabbing cold marble and this old man holding court on a glass-top desk on the 18th floor or writing insurance for city vehicles and wintering at the Miami Fountainbleau on a company tab. It wasn't so impossible—all you'd have to do would be turn the buildings upside down and make the elevators fall up.

He hurried down the block and jaywalked. He recognized some people filling coffee cups from a big thermos. Someone handed him a cardboard sign from a stack on the sidewalk. He didn't even read what it said. He had the rest of the day free. He would walk till he couldn't stand the cold and then head up the hill to the Court and pack and talk it all out with Durham.

He had the beginnings of a plan. All he had to do was flesh it out. He and Maureena would be heading west in the Skylark before Clotter ever saw her again.

8

St. Joseph's, a six-story brick hospital built in 1910 atop the first bluff rising from the Missouri River south of downtown Omaha—where Martha Street deadends at Tenth—seemed to Miller like a larger, older version of Drake Court. Instead of tenants, St. Joe's corridors were filled with patients on the walking cure, dragging IV stands like mute mechanical friends. Instead of one-room apartments, there were private rooms and open wards like the A.P.W.—barracks for the platoons of the sick and injured.

That Monday morning, after Miller cruised by Richard Ocear's office and made sure his car was there, and after he called and hung up when Rona answered at their house, he drove by St. Joe's once, parked on a side street two blocks away, and walked to the visitors' entrance. As he approached the old building, thinking of Maureena hidden away somewhere inside it, the place looked as forboding and labyrinthine as Kafka's castle. Miller renamed it in his mind as he opened the door—The Catholic Castle. Complete with Joseph as patron saint—Jesus' other father.

Once inside, Miller hit the first restroom past the information desk and checked the mirror. He had borrowed a dark gray suit from Durham, the same suit Durham had borrowed from his dad for Woody's funeral, which was big for him and small for Miller. And at a costume shop on North 33rd he had bought a man's short blonde wig and a gray felt hat. His hair was still so short that once he shaved off his sideburns, it was perfect. In the mirror, he was a tall blonde man in a suit and hat, and when he went to a nurses' station on the fourth floor and gave them his name for the day, Ron Ocear, Maureena's older brother who lived in Mason City, Iowa, and had just driven in to see his sick sister, the nurse said she would be happy to tell Maureena he was here.

The ward was a long room with six beds on each side, an open double door on one end, and a wide window with metal mullions and small panes on the other. Along the window end, a dozen or so chairs were grouped around a standup ashtray and two coffee tables covered with *Readers' Digest, Family Circle*, and *Seventeen*. Miller didn't look at anyone but Maureena—he was sure everybody was scoping out his fake hair and tight suit. Out of the corner of his eye, he saw three teenage girls talking and smoking in the chairs.

"Hi, Sis. How're you feeling?" he said, as he came near her bed.

Maureena stared at him. Her eyes were filmed, as if she had been sleeping ever since he last saw her. He leaned over and gave her his best imitation of a brotherly hug. She wore a soft blue terrycloth bathrobe with a fuzzy white collar—one Miller had never seen.

"Where'd you get the outfit?" he whispered in her ear.

"What are you doing, Miller?" She whispered back. He pulled away and saw water in her eyes, but she looked like she might laugh.

"Ron," he whispered. "That must be Mom's robe," he said louder, pulling a chair up.

Maureena nodded. "She brought me a whole suitcase full of clothes."

"I drove in from Mason City as soon as I talked to Dad on the phone," Miller said, louder yet. The three girls in the chairs looked away and continued talking—brothers were boring. Beds on either side of Maureena's were empty. A nurse who'd been talking to a girl across the ward walked from the room carrying a manila folder. Miller took off his hat and held it in his hand.

"You didn't need to," Maureena said, staring at the wig. "I'm fine."

"Hey, what are brothers for?" he said. "This is the biggest bucket of bullshit I've ever seen," he whispered.

"Pretty much," she said. "How long will you be here?"

"I have to head back tomorrow. Have you had breakfast?"

"Sort of. I guess I fell asleep again."

"Can you come down to the cafeteria for lunch then, or coffee?"

"I don't know," she said. "I could ask."

"Why don't I? Who would I need to talk to?"

"The wig looks ridiculous," Maureena whispered, and then she finally did laugh. And Miller did, too—just a brother cheering up his kid sister.

"Mrs. Maltin, the head nurse—she's been friendly." She pointed out to the nurses' station.

"I'll be right back, Maureena."

Miller pulled a Kodak envelope full of photos from his suit coat as he explained to Mrs. Maltin that Maureena hadn't seen pictures of her new nephew yet. He said he'd like to take her downstairs for coffee. Mrs. Maltin smiled. Only half-an-hour, she said, and Ron should know that Maureena's doctor had prescribed a relaxant for her and she might seem slightly sedated.

Maureena dressed while he waited near the nurses' station. She came out with her hair brushed to a gold glow. She wore nylons and high-heel boots with a knee-length skirt, an outfit Miller hadn't seen since high school. Mrs. Maltin commented on how nice Maureena looked as she checked her watch and signed her off the ward for thirty minutes. The photos in the packet Miller held were two-year-old shots of him and Maureena at the beach in San Diego. They stepped into the elevator talking about baby pictures that didn't exist.

When the doors seamed shut behind them and they were alone together, Miller felt all the tension of the last three days rise inside him. He looked at Maureena and put the photo packet in his pocket. He kissed her and held her and felt the surge of saving love he knew like Braille. He didn't want to stop, as if all his subterfuge had been about nothing but that kiss.

In the cafeteria, he kept filling Maureena's coffee cup from the self-serve pot. He told her about the meeting in Clotter's office. She said her mother had already told her, via Dr. Clotter, of course, that Miller was leaving, but she hadn't believed it. Miller was mad that Clotter hadn't waited till Tuesday as he had planned, but then he realized Clotter was probably on the phone to the Ocears before Miller stepped off the Redick elevator. Miller told Maureena he had picked up their checks and packed everything into the Skylark. He would go get it, pull up to the outpatient entrance, and then they were solid gone, just like in the old blues songs. Durham was waiting at a donut shop just off the 84th Street exit. They had ten minutes left on Mrs. Maltin's clock.

They were heading down the second floor hall when Miller saw Clotter at the far end of it, standing by the elevator, dragging hard on a cigarette. The green up-arrow was lit. Maureena's bootheels clicked on the tile floor, and Miller was sure Clotter would turn around. Miller saw double wooden doors to the right, dim light shining through painted glass. Maureena stopped when she saw Clotter, and when Miller touched her arm, she stepped with him through the doors.

They entered the chapel, a small room with three rows of pews, a crucifix on the wall, and a figurine of the Virgin Mary, all lit only by candlelight and the March sun through stained glass windows on either side of the altar. An old man in a wheelchair sat near the altar, his bowed head trembling up and down, as if he was answering yes to questions no one else heard. He fingered a string of beads, muttering the same sounds over and over. Maureena and Miller sat down in a pew, their feet on the kneeling boards. Miller ran his fingers over the gold-edged pages of a missal in the rack in front of them.

"Now what?" she whispered.

"I don't know. Let me think."

Miller had never been in a hospital chapel before. He couldn't help but imagine how many suffering or grieving people had passed through there in the last sixty years, people who were trying their best to come to God's hard terms—that they or their most loved ones weren't ever going out the front door again. The air seemed thick and heavy, as if every prayer ever uttered at the altar still floated in the room, emptied of sound, but not weight, not meaning. Maureena took Miller's hand in hers, and he felt as if nothing could ever happen to either of them, or to anybody in the world, as long as they just didn't move and this old man kept praying. It was as if everything outside the chapel, everything else in St. Joe's, Omaha, America, had completely ceased. Maybe even the war was suddenly transfixed—a hot jungle tableau with every bomb and bullet suspended in midair, halfway between each killer and every victim. Suddenly Miller wanted to pray, pray only that the old man would not quit praying—just keep moving his tired thin lips. The beads rolling in his bony fingers looked as fragile as tiny purple eggshells.

But then he did stop. He turned his chair around and rolled toward the door, the beads draped across the lap of his hospital gown. He rolled by without looking at them. When he pushed at the door, Miller stood and opened it. As he held the door, he looked at the hall clock. The thirty minutes was up. Miller heard the elevator bell ring and closed the door to a crack. Clotter and Maureena's mother stepped off the elevator and headed toward the cafeteria as the old man rolled by them. Clotter looked out of breath, and Rona looked embarrassed.

Miller told Maureena they were looking for her. She said maybe in a few more minutes they would figure out it hadn't been her brother and then assume she had left the hospital. It sounded like a plan. They moved into the darkest corner of the chapel and slouched down together in the polished pew as if it were the back row in a dark, empty theater. As they slid down in the pew, Maureena's skirt slid up, and when they kissed that time, they didn't stop. They put their hands between each other's legs. It felt as good and true to Miller as any prayer.

Miller looked around the chapel. The floor was dirty and scuffed and the pews were in sight of the door. He took Maureena's hand and stood up, moving toward the only private place, the confessional booth hidden in the shadows on the chapel's north wall. She stepped in, and as Miller moved in behind her and closed the curtain, she braced herself and pulled her foot from her boot. Miller helped her peel her pantyhose off one leg and partway down the other.

He moved to kiss her again. She pulled back. She stared at him for a moment in the half-dark. "The wig," she said, "Not with the wig on. I don't like that color."

Miller pulled it off and dropped it on the floor. She kissed him. He fumbled at his belt and zipper, awkward and anxious as the first time.

He slumped down in the chair that was built into the corner of the confessional like the seat in a phone booth. It struck him that the only line from that small enclosed darkness was supposed to be a direct connection to God, and as the warm inside of Maureena's thighs pressed down on the cold skin of his legs, he believed he had found something very close. All he heard then were the sounds of her breathing and his own, muffled and mixed and rising in the close booth like a chorus of warm wind.

9

Miller didn't know whether anyone had looked for them in the chapel, or whether anyone came to pray, or whether Maureena had crashed out like he had. He hadn't slept more than four hours out of the previous twenty four, and when he woke, with Maureena still straddling him and her head on his shoulder, his legs felt sandy and his back ached.

They straightened their clothes and Maureena peeked around the curtain. She went to the chapel door while Miller leaned against the confessional, waiting for his legs to work again. She came back smiling. It was almost eleven-thirty. They had been in the booth half an hour.

The sun was bright as Miller walked to 12th Street to get the Skylark. He pulled into the outpatient entrance, left the car running, and went back to the chapel. Maureena followed him out at a safe distance. She looked nothing like a patient. They saw no one they knew.

They caught I-80 at 13th and headed straight west for the Bakers' Dozen Donut Shop where Miller hoped Durham would still be. When they pulled into the lot, the cab idled in the parking lot. Durham was spread out across the front seat with his feet up, reading a newspaper.

"I'll guess you'll tell me what happened," he said, as he threw his backpack and a cardboard box into the Skylark's trunk.

"We fell asleep," Maureena said, laughing as if she'd just stepped out of a funny matinee instead of three days in a psych ward. For just a second Miller wondered if she actually did have a real twin, a perfect twin, and they kept switching back and forth when he wasn't looking. But then, maybe he did, too. Maybe everyone did. How in the world would you really know? Every time you woke up, there could have been some kind of switch. Or every time you blinked.

Durham called in on his radio and told the dispatcher that Cab Number 29 had broken down and wouldn't start. He gave them the cab's location.

"What about your pay?" Miller asked.

"I'm paid through yesterday," he said. "A good chunk of which I think I've spent on donuts and coffee this morning." He flipped the red flag on the meter down and left the cab running with the keys in it. "I promised myself I'd do that," he said.

He grabbed a sack of donuts from the dash of the cab and hopped in the backseat of the Skylark. Miller's albums were stacked on the floor, so he had to stretch his feet across the seat. As they pulled away, he opened the bag and held it out. Miller couldn't remember eating a donut since that January day, between the gas station and barbershop. He grabbed a glazed longjohn.

Still accelerating, they passed the Omaha city limit sign just after they merged onto the Interstate. Miller pushed his foot down harder on the gas and felt he could fall all the way from there to the coast, the gray oil-stained pavement carrying the Skylark down to sea level as easily as the Redick Tower elevator sinking to street level in downtown Omaha.

Maureena looked over at him. "You left the wig," she said.

He remembered it on the floor of the confessional. "Damn. It cost seven dollars. It might have come in handy some other time."

"It's just as well," she said. "You're good at disguises, I guess, but you're a creepy blonde. Except for the eyes, you really did remind me of my brother." Her voice trailed away as she looked out the window. "My father even."

Miller couldn't shake the falling elevator feeling.

"Speaking of disguises," he said, "I met a janitor in Clotter's building this weekend who made a lot more sense than the wise doctor. A man who truly didn't waste words."

"Speaking of not wasting words, I decided what I want to do with the rest of my life," Durham said. "I thought about it all morning sitting in my cab."

He pointed to the fields opening on every side of them as they left the outskirts of Omaha behind, fields plowed under last fall, the dark soil wet with snow melt, just turning light green with the spring's cover crops.

"Farm," he said. "Grow something."

They went on like that, wasting words as easy as miles, talking about disguises and farming and janitors, and everything in between. They stayed on the Interstate until York, when they cut off and turned south. At Geneva, on Highway 81, Miller saw a sign for Clay Center—twenty-four miles west. He had passed that same sign once before on the way west. And he did again, although he stared at it in the rearview mirror until it disappeared. He didn't look at Maureena to see if she noticed the sign, but she had.

"Not with us, Miller," she said, when we had gone about half a mile past it.

"Then against us?" Durham said, laughing. "What are you talking about?"

"Some things a person only does alone," Maureena said.

"Part of the problem, part of the solution," Durham said. "The Black Panthers' golden rule. I don't buy that simple slogan stuff, do you?" He sounded high on the highway, happy to be heading west and far away from Omaha for the first time. "No, there must be some middle ground," he said, still thinking out loud. "Or high ground. Isn't there?" He wasn't waiting for anyone to answer. "Anyway, you know what Mr. B.D. said about problems?"

"Sometimes. I hope so. What did he say?" Miller asked. Durham had all seven or eight Dylan albums.

"There aren't any, according to him. Problems."

"There has to be more to it than that," Maureena said. "What's the rest?"

"There are only tears," Durham said.

They were all quiet for a minute. Miller felt everything receding behind them—Omaha, the Ocears, SAC, the Induction Center, Dr. Clotter, St. Joe's. And now, Clay Center.

"Then there must not be any solutions either," Maureena said.

Miller grinned at both of them, and they were both grinning back.

"No," he said, "only smiles." They were almost to the Kansas state line.

$\mathcal{CB}$

Durham's dad's gray funeral suit was binding Miller under the arms and in the crotch, but he kept driving well into the afternoon. Somewhere they changed drivers. Somewhere Miller shed the suit—a gas station restroom in central Kansas, maybe. Somewhere Maureena changed her mother's handpicked high-school outfit for jeans and sweatshirt. A coffee shop in the Texas panhandle, maybe.

And somewhere Miller slept. Maybe. The towns slipped by like placemarkers in a thirty-hour American dream, like the last words of verses to a song Miller only half heard: Hebron, Concordia, McPherson, and Pratt. Liberal, Hooker, and Guyman. Texhoma, Tucumcari, Vaughn, and Benson. Alpine, El Cajon, and Del Mar.

Just after midnight on Wednesday morning they parked on the deserted beach between Torrey Pines and Del Mar, a lone car, an old red convertible with Beef State plates. They abandoned it like it was on fire. Miller couldn't roll up his pants fast enough. He had his shoes and socks in both hands and ocean froth up to his knees.

It was still March, and the water was cold. Maureena and Durham looked like tired dancers down the beach. Miller stood knee deep in the water as a thin mist rolled out on the beach from the estuary. He watched the moon rise. Against the rising fingers of fog, it was only a vague smear of light above the bluffs and chaparral desert that stretched inland, back toward Nebraska and the dozens of ranges and rivers and plateaus they had crossed.

Maureena waded out to stand next to Miller for a moment, and then the three of them walked slowly back toward the Skylark

hand-in-hand, shivering, laughing, and breathing fog into the
fog.

PART TWO

10

"We can't stay here forever," Maureena said.

Miller sat up in his sleeping bag. The sun barely crested the Santa Rosa mountains. Was that east or west? Daybreak or nightfall? Everywhere around him the ground was littered with eucalyptus bark shredding to a dry sandy soil, and the light dry spice of the trees drifted in the air.

Maureena pointed to the sky, and Miller felt the boom before he realized he had been hearing a jet. Twice a day, early morning and mid afternoon, they felt them, Navy jets from Miramar Air Base, twenty miles northeast, outrunning their own sound, miles above the earth. Inside the university buildings, window glass would flex and you could watch your reflection shimmer, as if a thin mirror was on the verge of melting. Out in the woods, the leaves rustled like dry newspaper, small birds squawked and switched trees, and then it was gone, like the part of a dream that makes you jerk in your sleep.

For the first week, they had used them as an alarm clock. Miller said they could adapt to absolutely anything if they could fit sonic booms into their daily routine. But for five days in a row now, Maureena had awakened moments before it happened.

"You want to move into one of the dorms?" Miller asked, pulling his jeans on inside the bag. The birds had switched trees. The world had settled back down around them.

He had friends in the Revelle College dorms, and nobody checked who came and went or who lived where. But Miller didn't like spending too much time around those friends. They reminded him too clearly of what he was supposed to be doing with his life. Senior Year. Liberal Arts. He was supposed to be doing Liberal Arts. Like looking for an honest man. With a book instead of a lantern.

Maureena didn't answer. Miller lay back down. It was already warm. He felt he could fall right back asleep. The air was perfect, the morning was perfect, the weather was perfect. He closed his eyes. For three whole weeks the weather had been perfect—highs of eighty, lows of sixty—any hobo's dream. Each day the sun hung just a little higher in a cloudless sky like a blank unblinking eye.

The two of them were camped at the head of a shallow ravine in the eucalyptus groves and chaparral canyons east of UCSD's Third College, the fringe campus that had sprung up as an alternative to the mainstream either-or of Revelle and Warren, the Liberal Arts and Science Colleges. They stashed their sleeping bags in bushes during the day and built twig and bark fires late in the evenings. They checked the college job board to line up cash daywork whenever they could, often in La Jolla Shores—Miller, landscaping and mowing lawns, and Maureena, cleaning houses. They ate most meals in the dorms and kept their clothes in the Skylark.

The days passed for Miller in an unsteady rhythm like the breakers at Black's Beach. One day he felt completely carefree, giddy because the West and the world was so much water, and the next he felt menaced and hemmed in because everything to the east had vanished and they had run out of solid ground. To the south of them was naval San Diego and crowded Tijuana, feeding on each other in daily mercantile exchange, and beyond them Baja, with the drugged dreams of foreign paradise several of Miller's dropout friends from the year before had fled to. To the north was L.A. and Orange County, buffered by Camp Pendleton and its Marine towns. But right at the center was a university on a hill and five sleepy little towns. The names floated by in Miller's mind like banners behind a droning plane—Del Mar, Solana Beach, Cardiff, Encinitas, Leucadia. Five sleepy names and the dozens of beautiful beaches where the sand and spring of 1969 seemed like the day after the second coming. Like the day before the apocalypse. Like both.

Miller jerked awake again. Had there been another jet? He sat up. Maureena was standing now, at the edge of a clearing, half in sun and half in shade, watching the sky.

"Two in a row?" Miller asked.

She turned around. "Just a low plane," she said. "No boom." She walked the few steps back toward their camp. "You were mumbling then," she pointed behind him at the wadded up jacket and shirt he used for a pillow.

"About the dorms?"

"No. You said 'the seconds are coming'—or something. You said it twice." She laughed. "Which makes some kind of sense."

Miller slipped out of the bag and stood and stretched. He shook out his tee shirt and slipped it over his head. Maureena watched him.

"Your voice sounds different in your sleep," she said.

"How?" He brushed his hands through his hair.

"More of a little boy voice. Like the words are too big for your teeth or something."

"Hey, my dreams just bite off more than I can chew," he said. He put his arms around her as he moved to stand behind her. He brought his forearms up under her breasts and kissed her neck. "What were we talking about? Before, with the first boom."

"Where to go next, I guess," she said. She turned around. "How long can we stay here, Miller? The Pacific's perfect, and peaceful, but we sure don't live there. We're stuck on dry land, and the thing we do best is stare away from it. Things aren't the same here, not going to school."

"No place would be. Look, this is just our staging area," Miller said. "We escaped from Omaha. We've saved three hundred bucks already. By summer we'll be ready to go—somewhere. We just have to figure out where, what, and why." He counted off on his fingers, and then held his thumb up. "The how just takes a road atlas and the Skylark. The how we already have."

Maureena smiled and rubbed her eyes. "I guess we do, don't we? As long as we don't get too many more parking tickets. They might tow it away."

Miller had torn up three warning tickets the first week. Since then he parked the Skylark in a different place on campus each night, moving it around like a pea in a shell game.

"No more tickets," Miller said. "No tow."

Maureena smiled. "No tow," she said, "no tow."

They began breaking camp, both muttering it like a mantra—
no tow, no tow. Maureena giggled like a sleepy kid and then so did
Miller. They had to move apart to stop. Maureena piled stones over
the ashes of the fire from the night before as Miller brushed off and
rolled up the sleeping bags. He tied off the bags, watching the sun
glint through the trees off the windows of the library, a four-story
cantilevered concrete-and-glass building in the woods half a mile
east. It looked like a space station stranded on its pod.

Sure, Maureena was right. Camping out on campus did
have the feel of something entirely temporary, even for southern
California, which wrote the ticket on temporary. Maureena called
it SoCal—all the permanence of a new soft drink with a big ad
budget and a zesty taste no one could quite identify. SoCal was
the fastest growing place in the country, but any minute the water
could dry up or the big quake could break loose or the wild fires
could blow through. Yet despite all of it, a part of Miller wanted
to live there under the trees forever. They weren't in the university,
and they weren't out of it—they were on the edge.

Miller watched as Maureena emptied two plastic canteens
into the gallon milk jug they left in camp each day. He looked
around the woods. It was quite an edge they were on. Except for
the glinting library windows and the low distant rumble of I-5
morning traffic a mile or so to the east, there were no signs of
other people at all. Third College was the bastard of UCSD, and
UCSD was a black sheep even in the experimental California
system—isolated, removed, built on the site of old war barracks
on the beach bluffs, above and away from the growing city to the
south. As he thought about it, Miller wondered if the location
wasn't the real reason he had settled on UCSD for college in the
first place, years before. Almost as if he had known he would need
those groves and beaches to hide in someday.

They finished loading up their daypacks, hid their other
gear in the usual spot, and then headed off toward campus. A
loose gravel path at the bottom of the ravine led gradually down
to the remnant of an old military road, abandoned for decades.

They followed that as it wound around the bottom of a twisted arroyo below the southeast side of campus. In the other direction it switchbacked up to meet the coast highway, El Camino Real, the road that split the campus and then headed to the beaches of north county.

From more than a dozen yards away in most places, you couldn't even see the old road. All along its surface, spindly eucalyptus trees sprouted from the buckled, cracking concrete. Everytime he saw them, Miller felt he had more in common with those trees, bursting through pavement, than with anything inside any of the buildings on campus. Those tough little trees were both the future and the past. Only the present moment—one thin century or two—had anything much to do with steel and glass, concrete and copper.

Just east of the Student Union, they took a switchback trail up a steep hill. At the top, the eucalyptus gave way all at once to a manicured lawn, its faultless year-round green maintained by grids of underground sprinkling systems. They stopped and caught their breath at the edge of the lawn. A few yards away Miller saw the guy they had nicknamed the holy boy.

They had seen him every day since they had been living in the groves, usually in the morning, other times near sunset, sometimes both. He wore a pair of shaggy cut-offs and sat half-lotus at the edge of the hill, where on a clear day you could see the open space around Miramar and then the Vallecito Mountains beyond. And he always faced east. It wasn't unusual to see people around campus sitting for hours on the cliffs facing the ocean, but this guy sat cross-legged and shirtless on the east side of campus, facing inland, as if the ocean were a thousand miles away instead of three blocks behind him.

Miller and Maureena had sat down beside him several times. They tried to talk with him, but he only nodded politely and then kept gazing at the distance as if it were a problem he had to solve. His brown hair reached to his waist, and his face looked intense and calm at the same time. Miller figured he was meditating, with or without the help of hallucinogens, but his smile gave no clue as to which. He was so thin Miller wondered if he might be on some kind of hunger strike.

Today they waved to him like every other morning, and in his slow deferential nod, Miller saw more of a smile of recognition than ever before. He reached in a wooden bowl in front of him and held up a handful of magenta bougainvillea blooms. Maureena walked over to him and took the flowers. The guy put his hands together and bowed from the waist as she took them.

"I guess you have an admirer," Miller said as she came back. They walked on. Maureena didn't say anything. She looked back over her shoulder once and waved.

"And/or a secret," he added. He wondered if she had talked to the guy sometime.

Maureena smiled and handed him two of the flowered twigs. "No secrets," she said. "Let's just all admire each other." She raised the flowers to her nose. "All the time."

As they went around the corner of the Union building, Miller looked back. The holy boy hadn't moved from his spot. Miller turned to Maureena. "Sounds good to me," he said. "Even though I'm not quite sure what you mean."

"I mean I'm hungry and thirsty," Maureena said, laughing. She pointed to the Union.

In the Union courtyard, they sat at a round wooden table and drank orange juice and coffee and split a small yogurt, planning the day and reading an abandoned newspaper. They copied phone numbers from the job board and then stopped in the dorm and washed up. They found bread and butter and jam in a fridge. Almost no one was around—morning classes were popular because the waves were better after noon.

This morning the Skylark was parked in a lot at married students' housing halfway down the road to Scripps beach. They hiked down to it from the dorm, and ten minutes later Miller dropped Maureena at a house in La Jolla where she had a morning of housework arranged. A mile or so away, he mowed and edged a lawn in two hours for four dollars cash. Easy money. Then he went to the beach at the Shores to wait for Maureena.

He sat on the warm sand and watched the ocean happen. Tide was low, the surf smooth and even, and the air crisp and clean. He sensed this little perfect springtime in the beach woods, in their lives, was already coming to an end. He had known it ever since he woke up. And he didn't have any very good idea about what came next yet, except that they had decided over breakfast to drive up to the Del Mar house to see if anyone there knew of a place to stay. Or maybe they might even have room there at the house itself now. After the long trip from Omaha, he and Maureena had stayed over for two days, but the place had seemed way too crowded, and when a friend of Carlila's had told them about the groves behind Third College, they had left.

The day was heating up quickly. Miller took off his shirt and felt grains of sand in the wind like pinpricks against his chest and the morning sunshine like a large warm palm on his back. Miller opened his eyes as wide as he could and stared away from America. He wished he could look beyond the blue-on-blue horizon, as if through will or discipline he could reel it closer. In fact, if he tried hard enough, maybe he could see the silhouette of Viet Nam, maybe smell the war's dirty petroleum fire so far off. Instead, only an image arose in his mind—smoke rising from the flesh on the bony spine of an old man, curled up with his back to the South China Sea.

In the foreground, terns traced back and forth above the breakers. The sharp angles of their wings drew patterns, like some kind of broken alphabet in the salty sky. Miller gave up on guessing at what lay beyond the horizon. Instead he watched the terns swoop and dive and rise and then hang motionless for long moments. As if poise itself might be a warning.

11

For ten bucks a month, Durham rented a child's playhouse in the backyard of the house Grant and Carlila's friends leased at the north end of Del Mar. Grant called it Alice's Little House from the line in the song about the pill that makes you smaller. Miller had never been in it before.

The Little House had a bunkbed mattress in it and a child's rocking chair and two car speakers wired up to the stereo in the house. You could lie down inside it and touch three walls with your hands and reach the ceiling and the door with your foot. Small louvered windows on each side offered slatted views of the hill behind the main house.

That afternoon was the first time all five of them had been together in weeks. Grant stacked *Electric Ladyland* and both of Hendrix's other albums on the turntable, and Durham brought his homemade hooka from the refrigerator in the main house. They arranged themselves so they could all hit on the pipe without moving.

He had only been in California for three weeks, but to hear Durham tell it, he was "riding the wave and catching on fast." Grant had turned him on to some good Mexican pot, and after a few days of burning his throat, Durham made a hooka from a half-gallon apple cider jar, three wine-bottle corks, two feet of surgical tubing, and a carved wooden pipebowl he found on the beach. He kept the hooka filled with cheap red wine. And from what Miller could see, he was staying high pretty much all the time.

When they squeezed out of Alice's Little House, Miller felt like he had been riding triple in the back seat of a VW bug. Carlila grabbed food from the house before they all walked down to the beach to see the sunset. Grant and Miller made a driftwood fire.

There on the beach, in the afterglow of Hendrix's guitar and Durham's hooka, they celebrated and then recelebrated everything they could think of—the big escape from Omaha, Durham's first full year of avoiding the draft, and the real surprise, Carlila's pregnancy.

She had only confirmed it two days before, and although she told everybody easily enough, she also seemed embarrassed, as if she wasn't quite sure how to be proud about it yet. Miller watched her, trying to see if she looked different, but he wouldn't have known. She had the same narrow waist and fragile-looking, ivory skin. She was as pretty as ever, but he didn't see the rosy glow people always talked about. Her thin black hair was a little longer than Miller remembered, falling close around her cheeks, framing her face like an old-fashioned painting.

Blue-green flames spit from the driftwood. As the stars came out, they talked about the summer. Grant and Carlila were heading to Berkeley. He was convinced the antiwar movement would crest by the end of the year. Apparently, his SDS friends were in touch with people around the country who were planning a huge mobilization effort, maybe as soon as the summer, the largest marches yet on three or four regional centers at once. And Durham already had his own plans, too. He had answered an ad in an underground paper placed by some guys in Washington State who were building a sailboat—or an ark, he wasn't sure which—and were looking for helpers—or partners, he wasn't sure of that, either. Miller told them about what he had heard from friends on campus about communes in New Mexico and a whole beach-tent town down in Baja.

They collected driftwood as they talked, roaming far from the fire and then building it up again. The tide rose, and by eleven they were near the waterline. A faint glow from the rising moon filtered through high clouds, and Miller was amazed how much more balmy and warm the air felt than it had the last few clear nights in the eucalyptus woods at La Jolla.

When the flames finally died, they sat in a close circle around the embers. Grant rolled five joints, laughing the whole time, but he wouldn't say what about. He didn't laugh all that often, but when he did it was from deep in his chest, an older man's laugh,

Miller thought, as if he found joy in just the laugh itself, regardless of what caused it.

He gave everybody a joint. He pulled his sun-bleached hair back over his shoulders and bent forward and lit his on an ember, and then they each did the same. When all five were going, they started them around the circle.

They all wore broad, uncomplicated smiles. Miller could see theirs in the shadowy light, and his felt just how theirs looked. He sat with his back to the largest ocean in the world and he wasn't afraid. He watched Maureena and realized how much he loved her and how far they had come since that prom dance in '65, not to mention the St. Joseph charade only a month before.

Miller felt like he was in love with four people at once. No, five—himself, too. And there was no reason to stop there. Why couldn't he be in love with everyone and everything in the world? Like always, the small voice whispered—no way, it couldn't be, it can't last, it's as ephemeral as the smoke you inhale or the songs in the wind, but he didn't listen. He didn't care. For a few minutes, he let himself feel it anyway.

When the roaches were too small to smoke, Grant ate them one by one, washing them down with the last of the water in the canteen. He walked back up to the house and brought back their sleeping bags and a jug of fresh water.

Miller fell asleep listening to the waves. Maureena slept with her head on his shoulder, her short hair tossed across his sleeping bag like a cropped yellow wing.

12

In the morning they went back to the house and finished off Carlila's homemade fried granola. Maureena and Carlila drove up the Coast Highway to the People's Food Co-op in Solana Beach, and Grant and Durham and Miller took a bag of oranges and walked south on the beach.

The tide was coming in but still low, and the three of them hiked for a mile below the cliffs. A flock of plovers stayed a few dozen yards ahead, landing and then flying off each time they came too close. The plovers seemed to have a perfect sense of just how close too close was.

"Did you guys catch the poster I put in the bathroom?" Grant said as he plucked a salmon-colored starfish out of shallow water.

Miller watched the plovers land again. He had stared a long time at the poster just that morning—a dried up sea urchin beside a tombstone on what looked like a parched desert floor. And the tombstone had an inscription. "*Death of the Oceans*," Miller recited. "*Circa 1979*. Where in the world did you find that?"

"A friend who interns up at *Ramparts*. They may use it for a cover soon."

"God, it's hard to even begin to imagine ten years from now," Miller said.

"I think the earth will take care of itself," Durham said. Grant handed him the starfish. "Wow. It's beautiful. Is it still alive?" he asked.

Grant smiled. "Live ones are a lot heavier. That one couldn't take care of itself."

"You think I'm naive, don't you?" Durham said. "But everything dies. If we ever managed to stop that, the earth would be in real trouble."

"No, not naive," Grant said. "More like quaint. Things are happening fast now, guys. It's that moment at the top of the roller coaster when you start picking up speed, but you can't see how far down it is or how long you have before it's too late to turn back."

"1969 isn't the first hump in history," Miller said. "People have been thinking that for as long as there have been people."

"Sounds like somebody's parents talking there," Grant said. "Anyway, first hump, last hump, hump all the way home, I don't care. History's over. There's no time for it."

"Without history, we might not even know the oceans were in any trouble now," Durham said. "We wouldn't know the war was wrong or how to stop it."

He set the dead starfish in the surf and watched it drift away with the next small wave. They were all barefoot. The cool wet sand felt good on Miller's feet.

"History's a subject in school," Grant said. "It's a department— a polite, respectable discussion that leaves you stranded in your armchair at the end of a polite, respectable career."

"Hold on," Durham said. "Everything we all want to change depends on knowing history, man. Don't cut yourself off. That's when real craziness comes in."

Grant snorted and looked at Miller. Grant had majored in History before he quit school, and the two of them had had many such talks in the past, often when one or the other was confused or inspired by a lecture or article by Marcuse, UCSD's resident radical philosopher.

"Nebraska dudes," Grant said. "I couldn't see it when I only knew one of them." He pointed at Miller, smiling. "What, do they sell faith wholesale back there? You're at the end of the continent now, gentlemen. From here on out, we have to make it all up on our own." He gestured out to sea. "History ends here at the beach."

"Or maybe it just gets all wet," Miller said.

He jumped on a kelp pod and snapped it under his foot. He picked up a long strand and waved it like a whip. Durham and Grant each picked up a strand, too, and they sprinted, the kelp flowing behind them like translucent green streamers. Grant stopped and twirled his over his head and let it fly, groaning like an Olympic discus thrower. Miller did the same and then threw him an orange. Durham sailed his kelp strand into the air. Miller dodged it and tossed him an orange, too, in a high hook. The sun was shining about a half a mile out on the water, but the beach was still chilly in the shade. It felt good to move fast.

When they moved back together, they slowed down, breathing hard. Miller peeled an orange and tore the peels into pieces and tossed them in the surf. Three gulls chased after them. He looked over his shoulder at the three looping sets of footprints in the sand. They reminded Miller of snow games he had played in Hanscom Park in Omaha a dozen years before.

"Speaking of making it all up on your own, what does it feel like to know you're going to be a father?" he asked Grant.

Grant popped a section of orange in his mouth, and his face turned more serious than it had been when he was talking about the end of history. His blue eyes squinted toward the ocean, taking on its greenish tint.

"Damn, I don't really know yet. You could sure say that it's not what I'd planned on."

"You love her, don't you?" Durham asked.

Grant looked surprised. "Yeah, I do. Sometimes I just sit in the backyard and watch Carlila spin her clay on the wheel and think I've never seen anything so graceful in my life."

"So, what's the problem?" Durham asked. "If a girl like Carlila loved me, I wouldn't ever look back." He smiled and looked at Miller. "Or Maureena, either. They're both amazing."

Durham sounded so earnest and honest it almost hurt. Miller wondered if he ever sounded that vulnerable himself.

"You're all right, Durham," Grant said. "I like you. I'm glad you like Carlila, too. There's nothing wrong with her. It's what's wrong with me. I never saw myself starting a family in the middle of everything like this. Not in the last year of the 1960s."

"She's due in December, isn't she?" Miller asked. "Maybe it'll be late."

"Right," Durham said, "you could turn into a father on us in the first year of the '70s."

"A number by another name," Grant said. "You know I'm not talking about the calendar."

"Anyway," Durham said, "my dad always says if everybody waited till they were ready to start a family, there'd be damn few families around."

"I just don't want it to change us," Grant said. "I don't want it to separate us out. He worked his fingers in the air as if he was kneading bread. "And there's so many kids already here. And over there." He pointed out to sea and shook his head. "Our kids setting their kids on fire."

"But you're not," Durham said. "Miller and I aren't. Maybe the best you can do is make sure you're not piling on. Not adding to the pain or becoming part of the evil."

"That's not enough," Grant said. "I should be working on campus right now. There's some meeting posters I need to copy and post."

"Hey, I should be somewhere, too," Miller said. He suddenly realized it was Friday, not Saturday. He had arranged some work for today. He shouldn't have gotten so high last night on the beach. "I think I stood up two people with lawn jobs today," he said.

"Listen to yourself," Grant said. "It sounds like you're the one who ought to have a kid." He turned to Miller. "You and Maureena are working so hard on the little nest egg. What, are you going to buy a house and settle down next? The 26th Street house is on the market."

"Hardly. But we do want to get out of here. Maureena especially. We quit school, but that's not doing anything, it's only *not* doing something. We have to come up with a real plan. Maybe buy into some land somewhere. Or just travel."

"So how's that really any different from the retirees?" Grant asked. "Travel trailers or VW buses—one's just louder than the other. The ostrich part is still the same."

"Nothing's settled," Miller said. "But roaming the beach can only last so long."

"Come help build an ark," Durham said. "If it floods, we'll be ready. Plus you could learn how to do something real with your hands."

Grant and Miller both laughed.

"Noah Durham," Grant said.

"The simple carpenter from Red Oak, Nebraska," Miller added.

They had walked to a narrow place where large rocks came right down to the water. They climbed a path over them to the head of a cove. Four sun-blond surfers paddled boards beyond the breakers. Miller watched one of them nail a good ride.

"So, Noah, what is it with you?" Miller asked Durham. "In Omaha you didn't even want to get high. Now you have a wine pipe in the fridge and plan to build an ark. You're a walking advertisement for the Southern California headtrip. You haven't started reading L. Ron Hubbard yet, have you?"

"Hey, I'm just experimenting," Durham said. "I spent a year driving rattletrap cabs all over Omaha, just saving tips and hiding out. But that's all dead back there, like Woody, and I'm here, and I want to enjoy it." He raised his arms with his palms open as if the sunlight was something he could embrace. "As the man said, why should anybody turn my spring into summer."

"Thoreau arrives in San Diego County," Grant said.

Miller wondered if Durham had told Grant anything about Woody. He doubted it.

"I'll tell you what though," Grant continued. "And Miller, you weren't so different. Nobody buys into the California trip like you Midwesterners. Us natives just stand back and wait for you all to show us what to do with the place. To me, it's only more of the neighborhood. I started smoking pot at fifteen and surfed my way through high school. I expect the weather to be copasetic every day—what else is it here for? The beach is just another stroll up the block to me. You guys are the ones that make it into something—" He paused and held his hands up and waved his fingers around. "Cosmic." He cracked a big smile. "So, maybe what I should do is head to Omaha. Maybe I could really set the world on fire there. No pun intended."

Miller knew Grant's joke. It was about the article the week before in *ThirdNews*, the underground campus paper, telling how to make street-corner molotovs from beer bottles, siphon hose, and newspaper. It ran under a headline called "The Fire This Time." Miller had listened to an argument about it at a meeting on campus. Miller couldn't shake the memory of the Safeway on North 24th in Omaha in July '67, two days after it burnt to the ground in riots. The store aisles were visible between long mounds of soggy ashes and exploded tin cans. Blackened grocery carts stood among the ruins.

"Oh, brother. Carlila would just love it in Omaha," Miller said.

They sat down on a ledge in the brown rocks. The sun peeked over the bluffs, and the surf washed back and forth across the shadow line. The surfers took turns on waves that were breaking movie-perfect from right to left in long slow swells.

"I've asked her to have an abortion," Grant said.

"Jesus. There's one real good reason not to go to Omaha," Durham said. "Can you do that out here?"

"You can do it anywhere," Grant said. "But it's easier here. There's a clinic down on Mission Boulevard in Mission Beach that does them all day long. You just have to fill out a whole lot of bullshit paperwork. She would, I mean."

"What did she say?" Miller asked.

"She's thinking about it. But she doesn't like the idea."

"I don't blame her," Durham said. "It sounds creepy to me. You can still be the same person with a son. Or daughter."

"Maybe," Grant said. "Anyway, it's her call. I just gave her my thoughts on the subject. It's not like we won't have plenty of time. After things are more settled down."

Miller picked up a handful of wet black gravel and rolled the smooth pebbles around in his hand. He dropped them through his fingers one by one. "Death," he said. "Sooner or later, it always comes to the party."

He thought of Woody and then his dad. For a second, he wondered if his dad had ever seen a beautiful beach like this one. Then he remembered the six beachhead stars on one of the medals his mom kept wrapped in the flag they'd handed her on the hillside in Holy Sepulchre. Miller tried to imagine him, only a year older than Miller was now, storming onto an island beach with a rifle in his hand, so scared of dying that he was ready to kill anyone he ran into.

"Durham was right," Grant said, pointing back up the beach where they had been. "Death's natural. Death's not the enemy." He sounded older than twenty. "Cruelty's the enemy. Cruelty and injustice."

"I'd vote for violence," Durham said. "Violence is the enemy."

"So who's the friend?" Miller asked. He tossed the last pebble into the water and watched its tiny splash disappear in froth. A curlew flew low over the sea right behind the surfers, heading straight north, parallel to the coast.

"You are," Durham said. He put his arm around Miller's shoulder. "And you, too, Grant." He sat between Grant and Miller with his arms around both of them. Grant and Miller put their arms around him, too, and they clasped hands behind his back.

"The three musketeers," Grant said. "Even if two of 'em are Cornhuskers. You guys are all right. Really. Listen, what do you say we all make a vow to stay young for, oh, say, around a thousand years, maybe. Young and strong."

"Young and honest," Durham said.

"How about free?" Miller said.

"Ready to say screw you to the bullshitters," Grant said.

"Ready to say yes to the meek and the silly," Miller said.

"Ready to jump in the ocean on a moment's notice," Durham said.

He stood and stripped off his shirt. He pulled a wad of dollar bills from his cutoffs and tossed them on the shirt. He didn't carry ID.

"Nek-ked as a jaybird," Grant said, stripping bare. "Isn't that how they'd say it back in Neeebrassska?"

"They'd say the last one in has to stay the longest," Miller said, running full tilt for the water in shorts and shirt. He had left his wallet under the seat in the Skylark, and he made it in first, diving into a cold four-foot swell, tasting salt.

When he surfaced, Grant and Durham were underwater and the surfers were too far out to see. For an eerie few seconds, the ocean was quiet and Miller was alone with only his head above water. He felt like he'd dreamed up both his friends—and even his own body—out of thin air.

Then Durham surfaced with a shriek, and Grant came up farther out than both of them just in time to catch a wave and shoot back in toward shore. Durham stood up in shallow water as a wave broke over his shoulders.

Miller heard them both laughing. He swam in and ran to a spot of sunshine farther down the cove and sprawled in the sand, his arms and legs stretched out like a starfish cast up and stranded at low tide.

13

They split up. Grant walked back toward Del Mar. Durham took all but one of the oranges and headed farther south toward Torrey Pines. He said he would hitch home. Miller's clothes were still wet, and he lay half-asleep in the sun for a long time until they were dry.

By the time he started back, the tide had moved in and he had a hard time making it around a few places. The beach was deserted. He climbed on the rocks and was partway up a cliff when he came across two guys smoking a joint on a ledge. They looked like high-school kids. Their brown hair was long and bleached in streaks. One had his tied in two long braids, and the other's was frizzed in every direction as if each separate hair was struggling toward the sun. Miller stopped and said hello. They asked him if he wanted a toke.

Miller hesitated, but the nearest one of them passed him the joint and Miller took a hit. As he exhaled, the ocean sounded louder and farther away at the same time. He smiled and passed the joint back with a roll of his finger. Both of the guys had star tattoos on their palms that looked like they had been drawn with ballpoint pens. One of them had a small leather pouch hanging around his neck on a rawhide drawstring.

"Good weed," Miller said. "You guys look like you're feeling fine."

"We always feel good," one of them said. "My name's Sandstone."

"Miller," Miller said. He shook hands with him.

Sandstone's eyes seemed to focus on everything at once, as if any of a dozen people sitting near him would have sworn he was staring right at them.

"Brother Jack," said the other one. "You from around here?"

"Kind of," Miller said. He didn't feel like telling them much about himself.

"You want to buy some pot?" Jack asked. He offered Miller the joint again.

"No," Miller said, patting the empty pockets of his cut-offs. "Not buying anything today. And no thanks." He waved off the joint. "One hit was just right."

"You got any to sell?" Sandstone asked.

"That neither," he said. "Just out for a stroll on the beach."

"That's a good thing to do," Jack said. "We stroll everywhere. We strolled from San Ysidro to Carlsbad one time. I'll bet you have a car."

"An old Buick," Miller said. "I've had it since high school."

"High school," Sandstone repeated. He looked at Jack and they both doubled over laughing.

Miller watched them and then he laughed, too. Why not? It was a good day for laughing. A killdeer landed at the bottom of the cliff and strutted toward the water. Four gulls chased it off, and it flew over their heads, calling.

Both of them sat up straight and stared at Miller. "You know him?" Jack asked.

"Who?"

"Brother bird." He pointed over his shoulder where the killdeer had disappeared. Miller noticed the skin on Jack's chest and shoulders was peeling off in layers, as if he'd been sunburned over and over. Patches of sand clung to his skin and hair. They had let their joint go out.

"Man, you guys are pretty high, aren't you? You ought to get out of the sun."

"You know another planet?" Sandstone asked, something like earnestness in his voice. "Me and Jack are ready. We're already gone."

"Here." Miller handed him the orange Durham had left him. "You could get dehydrated out here."

"Milner's worried about us, Stone," Jack said. They both laughed again. "We don't worry about anything, man."

Jack pulled open the leather pouch. He dropped the roach into it and drew out a pack of wheatstraw rolling papers and opened it while he talked. He pulled a single edge razor blade from between the papers and began cutting and peeling the orange with smooth strokes.

"See, every time somebody worries, it tightens the universe, it wrinkles it up worse. Everything gets jammed in closer together. I say, just let it float apart."

"Good advice," Miller said. He thought Jack had said his name wrong on purpose, but he couldn't imagine why. "I think I'll float on down the beach now." He stood up. "Take care."

"Peace, bro," they both said.

Miller climbed down the cliff and started along the beach. The two of them skipped up close behind him, eating orange sections, one on either side of him. They were both the same height, almost a head shorter than Miller.

"Hey, you know how you can drink seawater?" Jack said. "You fill your mouth up and let it sit there for about five minutes, until most of the salt settles. Then you swallow it real slow and spit out the salt."

"Where you guys from?" Miller asked. He didn't know whether he felt sorry for them or envied them or what.

"Everywhere," Sandstone said, waving his arm over his head slowly.

"Nowhere," Jack said with the exact same gesture.

"Well, I guess it was lucky you met then," Miller said.

They both laughed a long time. Miller kept walking. They stayed close behind.

"Hey Milner."

"It's Miller." He didn't know which one had spoken.

"We like you. Want to see something nobody else knows about?"

"Like what would that be?"

"A cave. We found a cave. It's got paintings and drawings of animals on the wall. It's from way back."

"Where?"

"Right over there." Jack pointed up at the base of the cliff where a narrow finger of beach wound into the rocks. A knotted clump of washed up seaweed the size of a small car covered the base of the cliff.

"You mean Indian drawings?"

"Dig it. San Dieguitos, man. Prehistoric. There's a big room in under the cliffs. We've been exploring it. C'mon."

They were both grinning as friendly as could be. Miller wondered if two high-school beach freaks could possibly have found a shore cave nobody else had. Not likely. They looked so stoned out, Miller figured the drawings on the wall would say *Patty and Mike '65* or something. But he followed them up between the rocks. They took a turn he hadn't seen from the beach, and then he saw a dark slit between two tall brown boulders. Jack and Sandstone walked right into it and disappeared in shadow. Miller edged in after them. It was cool and smelled like sour seaweed and dead fish. His eyes adjusted slowly. It was so narrow he had to turn sideways between the rocks.

"C'mon, man."

"How far in is it?"

"Everyfar," one of them said.

"Nofar," said the other one. They were both laughing again. Their laughter echoed against the damp stone like chanting.

"I thought you said there was a big room," Miller said, slowing down. He felt afraid and he wasn't sure why or what of.

"There is, but we aren't there yet."

"How do you see?"

"We burn our candles. You like candles, don't you?"

Miller heard the waves pounding outside, like massive stone doors crumbling into pieces, and he panicked. He felt pinned down suddenly, giant rocks on his arms and legs. Someone was burning his hair off. Someone was shaving the skin off his chest with a long straight razor. A hand reached inside him, pinching off his organs and plucking them one by one like ripe fruit. He pushed hard against the damp stone walls of the cave entrance and felt more trapped. He slithered loose and ran back out toward the light.

When he came near the water, he was at full speed. He kept running for half a mile, slowing down gradually and trying to look normal. He felt foolish.

The sun was as bright and gentle as ever. Miller shook his head. He didn't feel high anymore, but in the cave with those two druggies, he thought he'd seen a glimpse of something dark, something bigger and uglier than just his own fear. Whatever it was, he wished he hadn't seen it. For the second time that morning, he decided not to smoke any more pot for awhile.

Half an hour later, he made it back to the Del Mar house. Grant was helping Carlila unload a stack of large cardboard boxes from the back of a purple Econoline van. The boxes were packed full with sections of track for model race cars. Maureena was stretched out in the shade on the hood of the Skylark, reading with her sunglasses on, singing along to the *White Album*. Harrison's guitar was weeping out into the yard from the speakers in the playhouse.

Miller went in the house and took a shower. He didn't say a word to anyone about the cave and Sandstone and Brother Jack. As he stood under the lukewarm shower water, staring across the bathroom at Grant's dead oceans poster, he wasn't even sure they had been real.

14

Maureena drove the Skylark north up the slow rise from the San Lorrentos estuary toward Solana Beach. The top was down, and the Coast Highway at noon felt like a warm river of wind. Maureena wouldn't say precisely where they were headed, though she didn't seem concerned about leaving Del Mar, and Miller knew she didn't want to go back to the eucalyptus groves.

"Carlila and I found a great opportunity posted on the Co-op board."

"That doesn't narrow it down too far."

"Trust me, Miller. I'm excited about this."

"You're at the wheel. I'd ride the Al-Can highway with you."

A shirtless hitchhiker with shaggy hair and a sombrero with a Confederate flag on it leaned against his guitar case on the roadside. Maureena slowed, but when she saw that his sign said *LAGUNA*, she motioned to the right to indicate they were turning soon. After Sandstone and Jack, however real or unreal they had been, Miller was just as glad not to stop.

"So what was the deal with the all the cartons of race track?" he asked.

"An art exhibit on campus this winter," Maureena said. "A friend of Carlila's got money from the Art Department and bought three hundred feet of track and set it up in the men's gym annex. They also had a crawl-through maze of cardboard boxes and ten eight-millimeter movie cameras for everybody to use. They called the whole thing People's Art. We missed it."

"Too bad. I guess. So what's Carlila doing with the track?"

"She offered to store some of it," she said. "Or she was going to. But now Durham wants to set it up in the house. While you showered, he figured out he could use it all if he looped it twice through the dining room around the table and then back into the living room. He's even trying to design a space into the middle of his layout for the couch where Grant and Carlila sleep to fold down into. Carlila's all for it."

"I'd like to see the look on Mitch Kellor's face when he sees that," Miller said.

Mitch was an oceanography student with a full-time internship at Scripps Institute. His personality ranged all the way from serious to studious, to hear Grant tell it. The rental lease was in his name, but Grant said that except for meals, he came in late every night and left early every morning, and he only knew half the people living there. Miller had seen the long look Mitch had given them all just the day before when they had climbed out of Alice's House.

"I'd like to try that track out," Miller said. "I used to be able to ace those."

"Maybe we can come down some night next week," she said as she pulled up close behind an old stationwagon. She waved at two little Chicano girls facing backwards in the back seat. "That is if they really keep it set up that long."

"So we're not headed to Alaska then."

"Not today." She turned at the light in Solana Beach and eased over the railroad tracks and headed up the hill to the heights. The little girls kept waving as the stationwagon went on north. "I've found us a real deal—two jobs and a place to live."

"Does it come with a retirement plan, too? Does it have anything to do with why you're wearing nice clothes?"

Maureena had switched her worn sandals for neat black flats and wore a dark skirt with a rose blouse that she usually saved for special occasions.

"How does three hundred dollars sound? For two weeks with board and room provided?"

"Better than social security. What are you talking about?"

"2020 Los Altos Road," she said, as she turned onto a winding street with beautiful houses on both sides, the architecture Spanish, the yards large and well-landscaped. A block later she slowed more, searching the house numbers. At a wrought iron gate with a swirling letter "A" designed into it and a dense row of oleanders on either side, Maureena turned in the driveway.

"The regular help is on their annual trip back home to Sonora," she said. "Just remember, we're married students at the U. taking the quarter off to earn money. I'm a terrific housecleaner and a whiz with an iron and you know just about everything there is to know about sprinkler systems and grapefruit trees."

They rolled slowly up the driveway. Above the oleanders and a row of dwarf orange trees, Miller caught a clear view of the Pacific. A blue Mercedes was parked in front of the garage next to a shiny garden tractor with a little trailer behind it.

"That one wasn't made at Family Equipment in Omaha," Miller said, pointing at the tractor. "It's quality." He looked around at the grounds. "I don't know about all this. We're married, too?"

"The Silases," she said as she smiled and held her hand out to show Miller a gold-colored band around her third finger. "Carlila gave it to me. It's from a vending machine. Look, we both know we need a place to stay. And we can save as much in two weeks here as in two months of odd jobs in La Jolla."

"I wouldn't argue with that. So where do we stay?"

"Above the cars." She pointed at the dormer windows in the second story of the garage. "Servants quarters, of course."

"You've already talked to these people?"

"Mrs. Allenwhitt. For twenty minutes on the phone. They had another couple already lined up, but they cancelled at the last minute. I told her we're from Nebraska. She said she'd never met anyone from there before."

"At least we won't have any stereotypes to disappoint. But I didn't change my clothes." Miller wore old jeans and a Sears long-sleeve denim work shirt, like almost every other day.

Maureena laughed. "You never do, Miller." She reached over and stuck a finger in a hole in the knees of his jeans. "But you're only the yard man, so it's okay. Anyway, she was really quite friendly. She's a contributing editor for *Sunset* magazine. The hubby manages their rental properties in La Jolla and Pacific Beach. They're expecting us."

"No, they're expecting Rosalita and Manuel."

"After you, Manuel." She turned the Skylark off and handed him the keys.

A tan silver-haired woman wearing a turquoise and silver eagleclaw necklace over a beige sundress waved from the deck of the house. Miller saw two dozen balled-and-burlapped trees, which he guessed to be grapefruit, leaning on their sides in the shade of a live oak next to the garage. Beside them lay a bundle of ten-foot lengths of PVC sprinkler pipe, a maddock pick, two shovels, and a two-handled posthole digger.

As Miller stepped out of the car, the sun glinted off the Pacific below them like a wink. He took Maureena's hand and walked to the porch, gawking appreciatively at the fine house and manicured grounds the way he imagined any earnest, hard-working, married student might.

೫

By the second full day at the Allenwhitts, Miller had raised a good set of blisters. Mr. Allenwhitt told him to put a pair of leather work gloves on his tab at Solana Beach Lumber. Other than that, both Allenwhitts were friendly, but distant. After the initial interview, the main thing either of them seemed particularly interested in were formal pleasantries in the course of quiet compliance with their instructions, and that was fine with Miller. He worked outside all day, and Maureena, inside. They ate most meals together in the kitchen, perched on bar stools pulled up next to the butcher-block island, and then they holed up in the garage attic each night.

Their attic quarters were austere, a bedroom and a bathroom with wood floors and wood walls, and Miller and Maureena's few things didn't change the tone much. Pictures of Jesus hung in both rooms, the one in the bathroom above the sink instead of a mirror. That and the Spanish Bible on the nightstand made the place feel to Miller like some kind of combination knotty-pine motel and Christian College dorm room. Maureena and he agreed about the bathroom crucifix—it was too much to handle—so they draped a beach towel over it the first night. Miller put the Bible in a drawer next to a stack of pre-addressed envelopes to a Sonoran town he had never heard of. Mrs. Allenwhitt had explained that Tomas and Carmen had four children whom they supported with the money they earned in Solana Beach and who lived with Tomas' parents fifty weeks a year. Tomas and Carmen had "been with" the Allenwhitts five years, and the Allenwhitts felt gratified that their employment allowed the family to live well by "Mexican standards."

Maureena took the Bible out and read in it several nights during the first week as Miller dozed off early, exhausted from digging shallow trenches in clay for the orchard sprinkler system. She said it was a great way to bone up on her Spanish, and yet Miller sensed there was more to it. Maureena had gone to Presbyterian church with her parents until she was into junior high school. If asked, she said—pretty much as Miller did—that she was no longer a capital-C Christian, but she seemed to have retained a more gracious attitude toward it than Miller could muster.

For Miller's part, the DeSuelos' picture of Christ on the bedroom wall kept pulling him, back and back, to his childhood. Back to the beatific painting on his father's parents' living room wall. That, as well as the tired crucifix above the altar at the Grace Methodist Church in South Omaha, the only church Miller had ever attended, during his parents' year-long separation, when he was seven and his mother and he had to live in her father's house.

To Miller now, those childhood images stood in for the two ragged strands of Christianity that had been woven clumsily together when his parents married. From what he had gleaned, they fell in love at least partially to escape the numbness of their religious backgrounds: the pale and punitive hands of the nuns that ruled his father's schools, the dull Methodist self-righteousness that smothered his mother's girlhood. And as Miller looked back on it all—the enforced church attendance Sunday mornings with his mother's family, the long Sunday afternoons at his father's parents' house after his father died—as he looked back now, he began to see something deeper working beneath the family conversations—some undercurrent of vindication. As if in first his father's steady string of failures, and then in his actual dying, suffering itself had been strangely reaffirmed for the whole family, and the notion of escape had been laid, once and for all, to rest.

Besides her evening forays into the Spanish Bible, Maureena was working through a dogeared copy of *The Glass Bead Game*. From the UCSD Library, Miller had borrowed a copy of *Five Acres and Independence*, a 1932 back-to-the-farm manual. That, plus *How to Build Your Cabin in the Woods*, and Grant's copy of a Bernard Fall book on Viet Nam, kept him in reading during the quiet nights in the attic after a hard day's work. The Allenwhitts had told Miller and Maureena not to come in after midnight, nor to have any visitors any time, and they looked relieved when they saw either of them with a book, although Miller didn't think they were interested enough to take notice of the titles.

The garage attic seemed a very odd place to be the first place where he and Maureena actually lived together alone, and almost as if man and wife, even if it was only to be for two weeks. They joked about how domestic it all felt, in more ways than one, but beneath the jokes Miller saw how really good it might be to have their own place someday—but a place outside the political and economic web that the Allenwhitts and DeSuelos seemed snared in together like spiders and flies. That part of it—all the politics and economics of it—that part Maureena and Miller agreed not worry about. They would just do the work, count the cash, and plan the summer run. It was like picking a marker for a board game—I'll be white, you be brown—I'll play groundskeeper and husband, you play housekeeper and wife.

On Thursday morning that first week, a thick fog rolled in at dawn. It was still way too wet to work outside by ten, so Miller drove down to Grant's place and spent three hours racing slotcars around the two-room track with Durham.

While they were racing, Grant came home and asked Miller if he could help out with some SDS anti-war work for a few days. They were planning a big rally at the Naval Air Station at the harbor. Miller explained that he would have to pass until the job at the Allenwhitts was over, but he offered to stuff mailboxes in the departmental offices at Revelle that afternoon. Durham worked with Grant sometimes, but he also still kept the hooka in the fridge, spent hours roaming the beach, and now, hours racing model cars around the track on the floor. It turned out that Mitch Kellor had taken a vote, and the house had agreed to leave the track up for one week. Durham said they would have booted it right then if he hadn't invited two of the other renters to take a round at the hooka out in Alice's House first.

Plus, Durham had found a dog, a small black and white terrier he called Psychout. He had found it on campus in one of the Biological Lab buildings. He had been putting up rally posters and took a break partway down the cliff trail to Black's Beach, talking with a woman he ran into at the Union. On his way back, Durham got lost on campus and wandered into a lab building and headed up a back stairwell. Psychout was bellying down the concrete stairs trailing two wires with electrodes taped to shaved spots behind his ears. At first Durham thought he was hallucinating, conjuring a machine-dog from hell, but the dog whined and cowered until Durham found the nerve to pick him up, electrodes and all, and hitchhike back to Del Mar with him.

He had removed the tape and washed off the Vaseline where the electrodes were attached, and Psychout seemed all right, even if skittish—he wouldn't go farther than about two feet from his rescuer. While Durham sat in the middle of the fold-out bed, running the little track cars in and out of the dining room and then back through the tunnel under the bed, Psychout twisted his shaved head and cocked his ears at the whine of the cars. He barked each time one of the cars came out from under the bed.

Before Miller left for campus, Durham told him the best part. The next day he had cut Psychout's electrode wires up into envelope-length pieces and mailed them back to the Biomedical Psychology Research Lab Office with a note he made from cutout newsprint: *I'm free now, and I don't like any of you.*

An hour or so later, while Miller was stuffing the mailboxes in the Anthro department and still laughing about Durham's letter, he had an idea. The Allenwhitts were driving to L.A. to see their daughter at USC over the weekend. Miller still had all the grapefruit trees to plant, so on the way back up to Solana Beach, he stopped and left a note for Durham and Grant and Carlila. He invited them all to come up Saturday and spend the day. If they helped plant the trees, they could all relax and enjoy the oceanview hacienda afterward. He wasn't positive when the Allenwhitts were leaving, so he told them not to come before noon. He also told them not to bring any drugs.

15

Miller left his invitation in Del Mar the day before he found out about Torbay, the youngest Allenwhitt. They met shortly after Torbay came home for the weekend, when Miller was about to pack it in on Friday afternoon. The Allenwhitts had left for L.A. only an hour before.

As Miller made a loop on the lawn tractor around a large palm tree, the boy was standing there, barefoot, in a tie-dye T-shirt and creased beige slacks. He had his mother's tanned California good looks, his face well-proportioned and well-lotioned, his body thin and fit. His trimmed brown hair had three sunbleached streaks in it, and Miller guessed he spent a lot of time at the beach. He motioned for Miller to turn off the mower.

"You're not Mexican," he said when the engine sound died off. He didn't say it with a tone of irony, much less humor.

"You're not either," Miller said.

"I'm just the kid," he said, "the rich kid. Torbay. Everybody but my parents calls me TB. They don't like that. They say it's a disease."

"I'm just the hired help," Miller said.

"I know," he said, pointing at the tractor. "That's why I was surprised you weren't Mexican. Where are you from?"

"Nebraska," Miller said. It still felt strange, even after several years, saying that name while standing in the shade of a palm tree. "Omaha." He paused, but saw no sign of recognition. "It's a lot farther away than Mexico."

"Cool. What tribes were over there?"

"Tribes?"

"You know, Indians. The Sioux?"

"In the western part sometimes." Miller was surprised at the boy's interest. "Where I'm from there were mostly Pawnee. And Omaha, and Oto, and Ponca. Only the Omaha and Winnebago have reservations near there today."

"Is that where that name comes from? My folks have an Airstream," he said. "It's locked up in the shed." He pointed across the driveway. "I love Indians. I wish I had been one. Long ago, before any of us now were here. You know what I mean?"

"Nostalgia for something we've never seen. Yeah, I get it sometimes."

"I like Mexicans, too," he said. "Tomas is my friend."

"That's swell," Miller said. He wondered how Tomas saw it. "Why haven't I seen you before?" It seemed to complete the scenario that there would be a troubled teenager sequestered in some private part of the house.

"I go to the Boys Academy in Rancho Santa Fe," he said. "Monday through Friday."

"I didn't see you last weekend." Miller pictured the million dollar estates he had seen around Rancho. It was always referred to as a rich conservative bastion in the mountains.

"I camped with friends on the beach at Encinitas." He pointed up the coast. "But don't tell my folks. They think I stayed over in Rancho."

"Will you be here till Monday? By yourself?"

"With you and your wife. But don't worry. I look after myself. I'm used to it." He moved a step away toward the house, and then turned back around.

"Tomas doesn't cut it this short," he said, running the bottom of his bare foot across the top of the fresh-cut grass.

"I didn't change the setting on the mower," Miller said.

Torbay nodded and then walked away. Miller hadn't even told him his name.

Miller drove the lawn tractor over toward the garage and then up the driveway. Maureena stood in the shadows near the back of the open garage, staring out the side window, her fingers twisting a strand of hair. She didn't turn around, despite the raucous noise of the engine. Miller turned the ignition off at the door and stepped off and stared at her for a moment. Still she didn't turn. He rolled the tractor on into the garage and put it in gear.

"I'm thinking we should cancel tomorrow's visit from the Del Mar contingent," he said.

"Huh?" She turned toward him. "I'm sorry."

He said it again.

"Why's that?" She looked at the apple-oat bar in her hand as if she had forgotten it was there. She broke it in half and offered Miller half.

He shook his head and held up his dirty hands. "Torbay Allenwhitt," he said. "Fourteen years old and home for the weekend." He pointed down the drive and toward the house. "We're babysitters, too, it appears."

"She told me about him after lunch today," Maureena said. "I haven't seen him yet though. What's he like?"

"Like a Torbay," Miller said, shrugging his shoulders. "Like an Allenwhitt. Except he's into Plains Indians. What kind of name is that anyway?"

"I asked Mrs. Allenwhitt the same thing. It's an old family name. She said they've had some problems with him, but she didn't say what kind. And I didn't ask."

"That may explain the boarding school," Miller said.

"Yeah, he sounds like he might be a pretty strange kid," Maureena said. "But who wouldn't be, living here all your life—or maybe worse yet, all your weekends."

"I thought you kind of liked it here," Miller said. He sat down on the garage floor and began to unlace the hiking boots that doubled for his work shoes.

"Not to live here," she said. "Would you raise a kid here?"

"I guess I wouldn't put myself in a position to," Miller said.

Maureena sat down across from him. She took the laces from his hand, pulled off one boot, and started unlacing the other. It was something Miller often did for her. It felt good.

"So would you raise a kid at all?" she asked.

"That's piling hypothetical on top of hypothetical," Miller said. "If I had one, sure. But what's that have to do with Master Torbay?"

"I think I'm pregnant, Miller. I'm two weeks late. That's a week later than ever before."

Miller watched the second boot slide off his foot. The cool air felt good on his hot feet. He peeled his socks off and pressed his feet against the concrete. In his head he was counting back through the weeks. The concrete felt almost cold.

"It would have been in Omaha?" he asked. It didn't seem like the best thing to say, but it was the thought the counting back led him to. His next thought was an image of the dark confessional booth in the St. Joe's chapel, but he didn't say that outloud.

"I guess so. I don't know if I'm the right one to have a baby. I don't know what to do."

"You do what you did. Tell me. Then we go and find out. Then we talk and decide."

"One, two, three. Easy as that?"

"I don't mean to make it sound easy."

"What I'm asking is, what do you think about it?"

"I think about it—I'm surprised," Miller said. "I can't quite imagine it. It'll take a little while for it to sink in. You haven't talked to Carlila, have you?"

"I haven't talked to anybody."

"She and Grant have talked about an abortion."

"But you and I haven't."

"No, of course we haven't. I didn't mean that."

"Do you want to?" she asked. She still had his boot in her hands.

"Talk about it? I'm not sure I know how to."

"I don't think there are any instructions."

Miller took the boot out of her hands. "Are you mad at somebody? Are you mad at me?"

She didn't answer right away, which told Miller it had been a good question. The soles of his boot were packed with hard reddish mud. He took his pocketknife out and pried it out. He tried not to break the little diamond patterns. He set the pieces on the floor. Maureena moved them around with her fingers. They looked like some kind of heiroglyphic against the concrete.

"No. Not at you. But yes, I am mad. I just don't know who at. My mother?"

"Why her?" Miller ran his hand through her hair. She leaned her head against his leg.

"I just hear her voice in my head, Miller. And his. I've told you they didn't want to have me. I heard them talking about it, more than once. And ever after, my mother never wanted more than part of me, one of me."

"One of you? I don't get it." As usual, Maureena was vague when she talked to Miller about her childhood. Most often she described it in generalities, bleak but blank, as if it had been a boring movie she hadn't payed that much attention to.

"The good little girl. Sweet little M, she called her. Other times, I was Maureeeeeena." Her voice changed pitch as she said it, an angry shriek that echoed around the garage. "Whenever I felt the most real to myself, a real girl with skin and a heart instead of a hollow, plaster doll, I was always Maureeeeeena to her. She told me everybody has a battle to wage to see who wins. That's how I pictured what it was to grow up—a battle. And you weren't grown up till the war was over. Then you were either a good person or a bad person, the two ways they both divided the world. Period and paragraph. I was so afraid of that battle and who might win it in me, Miller. I think I still am."

"I wouldn't like hearing voices like that either," Miller said. "Who would?" He looked out at the grounds of the estate. He was amazed at how much she had said. "Not that they're not blaring all around us anyway."

"And he let her judgements stand. Always. I never saw him contradict her once. And yet behind her back he was the world's biggest hypocrite."

She balled up the little mud patterns she had been arranging and squeezed until her knuckles were white and her hands trembled. Miller didn't look at her face. He stared at her fist and held her and waited. Finally her hand relaxed. She rolled the ball between her palms and set it back on the floor.

"I'm mad at those voices. It's like a stupid song that's stuck in your mind and you're sick to death of it."

Miller picked up the ball of mud. He turned and threw it out the garage door and nailed the palm tree across the driveway. He stared at where it hit the tree. It seemed like every baby had something to do with the war and peace between its parents and grandparents, whether anybody said so or not. Miller wondered what his own mother would think about a grandchild. He had never imagined that before. He thought of girls in high school who had disappeared to go live with "out-of-town relatives." Regina Jensen, Lana Baker. The faces reappeared from nowhere, and even their names seemed old-fashioned. His time in Omaha seemed as far away and outdated as a nineteenth-century European novel. He and Maureena were like escaped characters, temporary tourists in a sunny foreign landscape, without a book of their own.

"Look, let's go down to Solana Beach and eat at the fishhouse. Let's celebrate that we are *not* in Omaha and that we can handle whatever comes. Together—just the two of us. Without any of a million other voices. We have time to think this over. First, we need to get you tested."

"Celebrate sounds good. Not in Omaha sounds good." She began to smile. "Fish sounds good. What about Torbay though? Should we take him with us?"

"I'll make sure he has something to eat. He made a big point of saying he could take care of himself. I'm willing to take him at his word. I can phone Grant later and call off tomorrow."

"Why? You told them no drugs, didn't you? It'll be fun. Carlila was the one who noticed the ad for this place—I'd like to see her. What're they going to do, fire us for having friends?"

She smiled again. She seemed to be back with him. Miller realized how much he loved to make her smile and laugh. And how hard he had to work at it sometimes.

"Ship us back to Nebraska?" he said. "Turn us into immigration?"

She did laugh then. "Really. Anyway, you need help planting that orchard. I'll bet they wouldn't have expected Tomas to get it all planted by himself."

"It'd be fun doing it with friends. That was my idea all along. A tree-planting party. And it would be good for you to talk to Carlila. Ask her where she went to get her pregnancy test."

"I'll see. Don't you bring it up, though. And don't tell Grant or Durham, all right?"

"I wouldn't. You know that."

Miller stood up and grabbed the handle of the garage door to pull it shut.

"No," Maureena said, "don't. Close it from the outside."

She ran out of the garage without looking at him. He followed her out and slowly pulled down the door behind them.

Torbay sat in a deck chair in the yard with his back to them, watching the sun set over the ocean. It dawned on Miller that he could have a fourteen-year-old kid like that by the time he was thirty-five. That seemed unlikely, yet why not as likely as anything else? But Miller couldn't imagine thirty-five. He could put numbers together to add up to it or multiply up to it, and he could count it out, pretending each number was another year the way everybody else seemed to do, but that made it no more real to him. It lay outside the reach of his imagination in the same blank way that the first three years of his life in Cheyenne lay completely beyond his memory.

He turned and looked at Maureena standing against the backdrop of the sloping hills and the wide ocean and the red stripes of sky. He wondered how she would look at thirty-five, but that, too, seemed unthinkable. In truth, he couldn't imagine more than a few months ahead, and even that seemed like just a game, a diversion. The future had to be out there somewhere, moving in, coming closer to them, like the leading edge of light from a newborn star that no one knew about, but even the thought of it vanished in a blue blur like the sea beyond the horizon.

16

A pair of kestrels flitted around a live oak tree as Miller prepared for the planting party the next morning. The air was so light and mild that moving through it felt as good and easy as swimming in cool water. Torbay lit off for the beach right after breakfast, and Miller loaded the grapefruit trees into the trailer and parked it in the shade of a ficus tree near the property line. He laid out the places where the trees would go with string and stakes, three lines of eight trees, twenty feet apart, evenly spaced among the sprinkler heads he had installed.

Around noon Grant, Carlila, Durham, and Psychout pulled up in Grant's pickup, a '59 Chevy stepside with a canvas camper he had built on the back with two-by-twos. It looked like they had dressed out for the day. Durham wore a straw hat and faded Oshkosh overalls from the Pacific Beach Goodwill that were at least a size too big. Grant wore a tie-dyed old-man's ribbed undershirt and his roughout cowboy boots. He looked like Marlon Brando in "Streetcar" had run into Ramblin' Jack and Joe Cocker at the same time. Carlila was barefoot in a white cotton peasant dress with lace on the sleeves.

Maureena made fresh avocado sandwiches for lunch when they arrived. They ate outside, watching the ocean change color as the sun rose higher, and then they played five-corner frisbee, running barefoot on the lawn that looked and felt like a quarter-acre golf green. Psychout wouldn't try to catch the frisbee, but he ran to whoever had it and licked at their feet.

When they were all out of breath, Miller showed Grant and Durham the orchard area and the trees. Maureena and Carlila left to walk down toward the Solana Beach fish market. The plan was to barbecue fresh salmon after the trees were planted.

The three of them devised a system. They dug down eight inches with the posthole digger and then filled the holes with water, letting it drain and soften the soil enough to go deeper. The soil was hardpacked, and without the water, they would have needed dynamite or a jackhammer, both of which Grant suggested as they took turns gouging the toughest holes out with a pick. Working together, they found a rhythm—soaking the rootballs, slitting the burlap wrap, digging and more digging, lowering the trees into the holes, shaking them to remove air pockets from the roots. By late afternoon they had an orchard—or the Allenwhitts did—but as Miller stared at it, he didn't care whose it was on paper. He felt how he often felt when he worked outdoors, a sweat-and-blister sense of ownership, even if nothing but the work really belonged to him.

When they finished, they turned on the sprinklers and tested the system Miller had spent the week installing. One junction leaked, but they turned it off, dug it up, and reglued the PVC pipe. Durham and Grant were as hot as Miller was, and they all ended up running through the whirling sprinklers like kids. Maureena and Carlila were back by then, and they came down and joined in. Every now and then Miller looked over his shoulder, half-expecting the Allenwhitts' Mercedes to pull through the iron gate and put an end to their day of work and fun, not to mention their residency at the estate.

At some point Maureena went up to the attic room and came back with the Spanish Bible. She sat on the grass, her cut-off corduroy shorts and white T-shirt both soaked, reading Genesis outloud in Spanish while the other four of them danced in the sprinkler rain to the Grateful Dead playing on the eight-track in Grant's truck. Psychout sat down right next to Maureena with his eyes closed, listening to Maureena's voice. It all looked like one hell of an alternative landscaping service, for sure, and for a moment Miller imagined them going into business, the five of them, plus the dog, doing contract jobs all up and down the coast from La Jolla to Leucadia.

The ocean gleamed far below them, and they played in their wet new orchard above, children at the end of the continent, and if Grant was right, the end of history. And although it wasn't the conclusion Grant might have drawn from it, Miller could see it as the end of meaning, too. Psychout understood the Grateful Dead as well as Genesis. The gardener's name might be Miller and it might be Tomas. Two babies might be on their way into the world or on their way back to the sea, via the Mission Beach sewage canal. The convertible was full of sunshine or full of snow.

The moment fractured all at once when a sonic boom crashed around them, as if the whole world had redlined at a dangerous resonance. Miller looked up and saw the jet tracing its white line behind it like an exclamation mark. Grant responded first. He staggered backward in the best TV Western shootout style, and then they all fell down, one by one.

There was a quiet space between songs on the tape. The sprinklers whirred and drops splattered in the basins around the grapefruit trees. Miller, Grant, Durham, and Carlila all lay silently in the damp dirt. Maureena had stopped reading, but sat upright, with a stricken look on her face, staring beyond the four mock dead to the sky that stretched away in every direction like an ampitheater. Then Psychout ran over to Durham and bellied up to him with his nose on the ground and bayed as if he had lost his saviour, and by the time the next song came on, Miller couldn't stop laughing because they all couldn't stop laughing.

When they finally did stop, Maureena took the DeSuelos' Bible back to the attic, and they all headed into the house for hot showers. Like a good host, Miller made sure everyone wiped their feet at the door on the earth-tone Welcome mat.

☙

Torbay came home before sunset, a surfboard taller than he was slung over his shoulder. Maureena invited him to join the fish cookout. Before the meal began, he flashed a baggie of weed and asked who wanted to get loaded. Grant and Durham started laughing.

"All right. So we didn't bring any grass," Grant said to Miller. "And the fourteen-year-old heir to the fortune has his own."

"I have plenty," Torbay said. "You guys need to buy some?" He turned to Miller. He didn't seem to have any idea why anyone was laughing.

"No, I don't. But where did you get it?" Miller asked.

"Beach friends," he answered. "They check us for it at the Academy. I keep some outside though. Stashed in a bird's nest."

"You get high in Rancho Republican Santa Fe, Torbay?" Grant asked. He started laughing all over again.

"Every night that I can sneak outside," he said. He gestured toward Grant with the little bag in his hand. "And everybody I smoke with calls me TB."

"How in the world are you going to make it through high school getting stoned every day?" Durham asked.

"Maybe I won't," TB said. "I'm taking off this summer. Maybe I won't be back."

"Your parents let you travel alone in the summers?" Maureena asked.

"I'm going surfing down the coast in Baja—whether they let me or not. I think they will. Anyway, I plan on finishing out at San Dieguito High here in Solana Beach. That's where I should be. That's where my real friends are. Not at Rancho."

"Unreal," Carlila said. "My little brother's thirteen. Amazing."

"How do you know till you try it?" he asked, as he held up the joint he'd been rolling. "It's just plain old Mexican, nothing special."

The five of them looked around at each other. Miller wondered—if the Allenwhitts suddenly drove up, would they possibly believe their son had turned the whole crowd on?

"No," Maureena said. "No thanks. And I don't think anybody else should either." She looked at Grant and Durham and then turned to TB. "TB, you're way too young to be getting stoned all the time."

"Listen to Mother Ocear," Grant said, pointing at Maureena. "Where do you draw the line? We drop out of college. He drops out of high school."

"I don't know," Maureena said. "But I do draw it. Anyway, his folks could come back early. Let's just enjoy the weather and the sunset."

TB put the joint behind his ear and smiled at Maureena. Miller noticed his careful haircut. It looked like it had cost somebody five bucks. Miller flipped the salmon steaks on the grill. Maureena pushed wedges of garlic into the meat and sprinkled it with lemon.

After dinner TB and Grant sat off by themselves behind a clump of oleander bushes. Carlila and Maureena talked on the front porch. Miller played more frisbee with Durham and Psychout. As the light waned, crimson and violet feathers of cloud stretched across the sky. When they gathered together again in the center of the lawn, Miller saw that the joint was gone from behind TB's ear.

"So, you have your summer planned yet, Millerman?" Grant asked.

Miller looked at Maureena. He wondered if she had told Carlila that she might be pregnant. He waited, but she didn't say anything.

"No. Except that we'll travel somewhere."

"Running out on the movement, huh?"

"The movement's bigger than California," Miller said. "Or haven't you heard?"

"It's a rumor," Grant said. He pointed at Carlila. "We're still going to Berkeley, most likely. It's finally happening for real up there. They've taken over a park. People's Park."

"I'd like to go somewhere far from any city," Maureena said. "It's so completely obvious, but I've only really realized this spring that I've spent my whole life inside a city."

"Far away sounds great," TB said. "Hey. I just got a flash, Maureena." He looked at her in a way that made Miller wonder if he wasn't getting an old-fashioned schoolboy crush on her.

"What's that?" she asked, kidding him, "a high-school smuggling ring?"

"You guys take me with you. We all go together."

"Right. Your folks would love that idea," Grant said.

"Miller and I want to go alone," Maureena said, more to Grant than TB.

She hadn't ever said it exactly that directly to Miller, but he knew she did. And as she said it, he knew he did, too. Both Grant and Durham had hinted before about them all taking off together, and Miller guessed they might be about to again, but he had resisted the notion. He wasn't sure if it was more for him or for Maureena though.

"Anyway, we don't have a vehicle for six people," Durham said. "I don't have one at all."

"Oh wow, this is great," TB said. "This is right water. We could take my parents' Airstream. I know where they keep the key to the shed it's locked in. Think of us out there somewhere—Mexico, maybe—riding the highway like a mother wave. I've learned some Spanish from Tomas. And if we took the Airstream, my friend Roddy could go, too. You could say we were your little brothers."

"You know the term A.P.B.?" Durham asked. "You give it a brand new twist."

"The kid's not only a doper, he's a robber," Grant said.

"No. It wouldn't be robbery—it's part mine," TB said. "I'd just borrow it for the summer, and I'd leave my folks a note. Maybe they wouldn't mind me traveling with a nice married couple from Nebraska like Maureena and Miller."

"Oh yeah," Grant said. "It's just too bad we don't have a nice VW bus for the sweet married midwestern folks to tow the Airstream with. Right, Miller?"

"Nothing but hard-working middle-Americans here," Miller said. "Right thinkers and clean livers. But then we would have to hide Durham and Grant somewhere."

"You guys," Carlila said. "You might as well be high. Anyway, I know I don't want to head off into the hills being—" She stopped and looked at Torbay. "Being how I am."

Miller guessed she must have decided against the Mission Beach abortion.

"We could kidnap a doctor," Grant said. He held his hands up as if reading an imaginary headline. "I was held prisoner by five college dropouts and a fourteen-year-old rich kid in an Airstream trailer."

"We could find a commune with midwives," Durham said.

"Really, think about it," TB said. "If you guys do take off, come get me. My parents would never send the police after me, not for anything. They don't like anything messy. That's why I'm at Rancho."

He sounded sad for the first time, but not like he was trying to. For a minute Miller thought that the kid might deserve a midnight rescue. He pictured his own mother and Durham's folks and even Maureena's, back in Omaha, going through their daily lives, an ocean sunset like this one only a distant postcard dream to them. Miller wondered how much they worried about their children out here. He tried to see that thirty-five-year-old couple again, Maureena and him, with a fourteen-year-old who wanted to run away from home.

Psychout raised himself and stretched, his nose pointing at the horizon, and it called Miller's attention back to the sunset. The sun had sunk halfway below the sea line and turned a rich coral like the inside of a ripe peach. As if all the wavy stripes of colored light had fallen backwards across the sky and curled up into half a ball of fire. They all turned to watch it. Finally Miller spoke again.

"Summer's still a ways off," he said. "How about let's do spring first."

"There's no seasons in Southern California," Grant said. "You guys from the interior just drag the past around with you wherever you go."

"We could stash it in the Airstream this summer," Durham said.

"What?" Carlila asked. "The pot?"

"The past," Maureena said, laughing and rolling her eyes at Durham.

"I've never been out of Southern California," TB said in a serious tone. "Except to Hawaii. And except on LSD."

Nobody said anything at all for a minute or two. Miller could see the shock in Maureena's face, and he knew why. He couldn't begin to imagine having dropped acid as a ninth-grader at Central. Who could survive high school after that?

Miller recalled what they had talked about at dinner, Grant's idea for a blowout ceremony of their own the second Saturday in May, the day their class at UCSD graduated. He said he had scored some guaranteed absolutely pure acid and knew a beach in Leucadia that you could only walk to during low tide. He said they deserved a graduation all their own, one that would make the mortarboard and gown affair on campus look as tired and trite as a skit from an old silent film.

All at once, the sun was gone and a light breeze rustled the trees. Carlila suggested they go for a walk in the hills at the end of Los Gatos Drive, and Maureena went in for jackets. Miller scratched Psychout's belly while he lay on his back in the grass, and every time he hit a certain spot, the dog's front paws paddled back and forth in circles. TB went inside to watch television.

Before they left, the five of them wandered down to the new orchard and stood there in the twilight, watching the day's work disappear in the dusk. Miller saw a star, and before he could even think it was silly, he wished. He wished for hard and honest work like they'd done that day—root, dig, and stake work—for all of them, work that didn't trace its way back to the usual economic sources. The metallic machinery of war and peace and crime and punishment. The cotton-candy froth of consumer fantasy.

An owl hooted twice from a thicket on the hill behind the house. The twenty-four little trees looked completely at home— planted, watered, braced. It was so quiet Miller could almost hear them growing already.

17

Three Saturdays later, Maureena sat in a worn cane chair on the porch of the Evans Motel in Cardiff-by-the-Sea, reading aloud from a book of Conrad Aiken's poetry. Miller's chair was pulled close to hers. A few hours after a high-tide sunset, the night air from the sea drifted inland, clean and salty. Miller could make out the dark outline of a long tangled windrow of washed-up kelp, stretching to the north along Cardiff Beach. Thirty feet from the porch, two-inch waves rolled along the flat beach, unfolding like the curled edges of a translucent blanket.

Neither of them had to work the next morning for the first time in six days, and Miller was glad for it. He had been working outdoors with Tomas all day. When Tomas and Carmen had returned from Sonora, Mr. Allenwhitt had asked if Miller would stay on and work with Tomas, expanding the sprinkler system throughout the grounds. Tomas didn't have time to do it on his own with all the regular work, and they had both been impressed by how much Miller had accomplished in the grapefruit orchard.

Pink Floyd had just finished a long instrumental tune on the stereo in the motel room. The record was over, but the music still floated in Miller's mind. He shifted in his chair and stretched his shoulders, feeling the soreness in them. Faint stars and their milky reflections argued back and forth in the dark. From beyond the cresting waves, gulls cried out on the breeze.

Maureena had woven small white flowers into her wet hair. She wore one of Miller's checkered flannel shirts and nothing else. Her legs stretched out in front of Miller.

They had showered together in the motel room's dilapidated metal stall. In the water Miller had smelled the scents of the flowers Maureena worked with all day long. Just as Tomas had accepted Miller as a temporary apprentice, Carmen had taken Maureena under her wing and told her where to find work in the flower fields near Encinitas. Maureena drove the Skylark to the flower fields each day, and Tomas picked Miller up in the Allenwhitts' old jeep. Both of them only made minimum wage per hour—two dollars—but it was paid in cash, Miller liked being outdoors all day, and Maureena loved working with the flowers. It all seemed like the kind of luck you couldn't deny.

And as if to confirm the luck, they had found the Evans Motel, on a tip from TB, no less. You couldn't even see the old five-room motel from the highway, but their room, the end room, closest to the beach, rented for only forty-two dollars a week. Miller felt so permanent he had even moved his stereo and their records and books up from storage in Carlila's potting shed behind the Del Mar house.

They had kissed for a long time in the shower, the weak stream of tepid water washing the heat from their bodies as quickly as it arose. Then they ate fresh bread and abalone while they listened to Pink Floyd and moved out on the porch. An old floor lamp with a cracked, yellowed lampshade cast a sepia glow through the screen door behind them. Their long faint shadows overlapped on the sand.

"That's really beautiful," Miller said. She'd been reading a long poem about a day in the life of a stonemason named Senlin. "The lines roll out so smoothly."

Going through their boxes of books the night before, Maureena had rediscovered her poetry books. She had majored in Literature, yet despite Miller's urgings, she hadn't ever tried a writing class herself. She said she was too self-conscious, but Miller couldn't help remembering something she told him that had happened when she was in grade school. Her mother had found a booklet of little rhymes under Maureena's mattress, each on a separate sheet of pink paper, all ribboned together with a red cover that read, *Daddy Valentine.* Her mother made Maureena tear the sheets up in small pieces and flush them down the toilet where she said they belonged. When Miller asked once what was in the poems, Maureena said her mother's bathroom exorcism had worked completely. She couldn't remember a single line.

Now she closed her paperback copy of *Aiken's Selected Poems*. Masking tape held the binding together. "Perfect evening poem for a perfect evening," she said.

"Do you ever try to imagine being old?" Miller asked.

It was out of the blue, yet it wasn't, too. Besides the sense of aging in the poem, Miller had been thinking about it that afternoon, working next to Tomas and watching Mr. Allenwhitt read on his patio. They were both forty-something, although Tomas looked older and acted younger, and Miller had been struck with the fact that he himself would one day be that age.

"It doesn't work for me," Maureena said. "Nothing comes. I can see the faces of other old women, my grandmothers, someone's grandmothers, but not me. Or if I do think it's me, then I can't picture what I'm looking back on. Like you're on a mountaintop, but there's no view."

"Do you realize we will be fifty-two in the year 2000?" Miller asked.

"I can't even imagine the 1970s."

"For us? Or the world in general?"

"It's hard to separate the two."

"As long as it's hard to separate us two."

Maureena laughed. "I just mean we're in the world. We're just as much the world as the world is. You know what I mean, don't you? Anyway, we've got a summer to plan. That's a bit sooner than the next century."

"Sure," Miller said, "sure, I do." He looked out at the evening. "Do you think Grant's right? If we do take off for the back country this summer, are we running out on the movement?"

"Grant," Maureena said. "Grant's got his own truth. It works for him." She turned and looked at Miller. "You guys are different, you know. Very different."

"Of course. But he's my best friend. Except for you."

"Thanks." She smiled. "I hope so. I ran into him Wednesday when I took off work. I stopped by Del Mar."

"How are he and Carlila doing?" Miller thought that maybe mentioning Carlila's actual pregnancy would help them talk about

Maureena's likely one. She was overdue for her second straight period. Neither of them had mentioned it now for over a week.

"Carlila wasn't there. Grant was going a mile a minute about strategy for the — "she slowed her speech way down, "the movement."

"He's a wild guy. I think what I really like best about him is his audacity."

"Yeah, I guess I do, too," she said. "That's a good word for it. But still." She raised both hands and shrugged. "How many war things have you been to in the last few years, Miller?"

"War things?"

"Against the war." She lifted her hands and counted off with her fingers. "Marches, protests, vigils, sit-ins, teach-ins, actions, demonstrations, rallies, commemorations." She paused. "Have I missed any?"

"I don't know. To both questions."

Miller thought back. He hadn't ever counted. He remembered the first big one on campus in '66, a candlelight vigil after speeches by Dr. Spock and William Sloane Coffin. And then the steady string of teach-ins and rallies and the hard struggle with ROTC before it was officially kicked off campus. And the few marches in San Diego proper, and several in downtown L.A. that Grant and Miller drove up for. And then the ones at the Claremont Colleges on weekends Miller had stayed with Maureena up there at Pitzer. And even one or two in Omaha in the summers, plus a candlelight Christmas march there at Creighton University in '67.

He was shocked at how many. He realized what a big part of his real education they had become, for better or worse—Street Democracy 101. All those speeches and placards and face-offs and chants. All that anger and hope. Fervor. Dismay.

"I really don't know," he said. "Twenty, twenty-five, maybe. Not counting the Black Panther rallies in L.A. and Omaha."

How could he forget those? He and Maureena had heard Eldridge Cleaver speak, in Omaha of all places, before either of them had read *Soul on Ice*, wearing an ammunition belt slung across his black leather coat like a tall black Pancho Villa, in the middle of Fontenelle Park. It hadn't been until that speech that Miller had even known Malcolm X had been born in Omaha.

"That sounds about right for me, too," Maureena said. "And maybe for most of the people we know. But let's face it, Miller, the war's as big as ever, bigger maybe. It may all just be making it worse. When you struggle with something, it may just get stronger."

"Maybe. Sure, a person could see it that way. Or maybe it only seems that way right up until the very moment it disappears. I don't know. What's the alternative?"

"Everything I struggle with just gets bigger," she said in a monotone. Miller heard her starting to sink away all of a sudden.

"But we were talking about Grant," he said. "Not you, not me. It's almost summer, and you and me are about to hit the open road." He pointed to the Skylark parked only a few feet away in the dark.

"I know," she said. "And if we work while we travel, we won't have to use these savings. Maybe we really could find some land to buy into."

"Maybe. Or just keep moving. Watching for signs. The non-road signs."

"It is great when we're on the move," she said, staring at the car. "But it scares me sometimes—how much I like being in the Skylark—when I remember what almost happened in it last January."

"Plenty of other things have happened to us in it, too," Miller said. He laced his fingers through hers. "Freedom and terror. They go hand in hand. The left hand shakes the right, and they both know what the other's doing. The one thing you can say for you and me, baby." He raised his eyebrows and tried to put a cocky swagger in his voice, somewhere between Bogart and Elvis, but really nothing much like either. "Whether we drive to heaven or hell, we'll keep the top down."

Maureena mocked him back. "OK, baby. I can dig it." They both laughed and she waited till he finished to speak again.

"I know what you're saying, Miller. This is a good spring, a great spring. I'm happier than I could have imagined in January. It's just that—" She pulled her hand away from Miller's and stared into it. "We won't take a wrong turn again, will we? Sometimes it feels just that simple—you take one turn that changes everything. You turn into the right person, you turn into the wrong person."

Miller held his open palms up toward her, his gesture of blamelessness, and looked back and forth from her to himself.

"Hey, no wrong people here. None allowed. We left them behind in Omaha. It'll be a good summer. We could do migrant work, pick fruit, follow the harvest. I've been talking to Tomas about it. He's told me places to go."

"I'd like that. I love working in the flowers—fruit can't be all that different. Think of the people we'd meet. Real people. Maybe that's what I was getting at about Grant and all—sometimes it feels like all of us, all of us our age, I mean, aren't really real."

"Because we don't fit in anywhere?"

"That's part of it. You know that line from 'Wooden Ships?'"

She sang it out, although Miller did know it. "*We are leaving, you don't need us.*"

"That's the absolute worst feeling," she said. "Worse than being hated or patronized or argued with. I'm just not sure the world needs me."

"That's what it's all about," he said. "Looking for a new world that does."

"This world we're in has such thick momentum, though. Around here, with our friends nearby—" She waved her hand back and forth, pointing up and down the coast. "Right here and now it looks like it all might slow down enough for us to jump off and make a new start, but I'm not sure that's not a trick. Like relativity. We're like those speed-of-light rocket men in the Physics books who age as fast as everybody else but don't find out until they land."

Miller rolled his head around, as if he was dizzy from following her analogy.

"You're a wise woman. Have I told you recently? I like your mind. I love your mind."

"Do minds make love?"

"Ours do. Sometimes without our bodies. Sometimes with. Maureena?"

"What?"

It was as good a chance as any to bring it up. She had said the weekend before that she wanted to wait longer to see if her period came, but it hadn't. Miller had been waiting for her to pick the time to talk, but maybe she was waiting for him to ask again.

"Why don't you get the pregnancy test? I checked the Yellow Pages. I found two doctors right here in Cardiff. We need to find out so we can decide what to do."

She tipped her head back and to the side and looked through the screen door into the room and closed her eyes and opened them again. In the muted light, her uplifted face was serene. The fine lines of her eyebrows and the fragile curl of her eyelashes looked like finishing touches, delicate brushstrokes on a living work of art. One Miller could reach over and touch anytime he wanted. How had he ever been so lucky?

"Miller, I did get the test. It was negative."

"Huh? When? Why didn't you tell me?"

"I wanted to go by myself. I don't know exactly why. I went to a clinic in La Jolla Wednesday. Anyway, I'm not. And I think I'm going to be starting in a day or two. That's why I didn't want to make love before." She pointed back into the room. "In the shower. I'm achey, like always—right before." She put her hands low on her stomach, her fingers extended down. "It looks like I just skipped a period or something. Maybe whatever Dr. Clotter gave me in the hospital in Omaha messed me all up."

"So when were you going to tell me this? You went by yourself?"

"I was going to tell you tonight."

"Only if I asked?"

"I sensed it would come up. Aren't you pleased?"

"I guess. The truth is, I guess I am. A baby—or the other— either one would be a pretty huge thing to deal with right now. You thought so, too."

"Sometimes I did," she said. "But now there's nothing to worry about."

She paused. For a moment between breakers, the sea was silent. Her eyes were locked on Miller's. So deep. A thousand layers of blue. Maureena looked Miller's face over slowly as if she were reading from it before she spoke.

"My love for you I love."

He took her hand. "Is that part of the poem?"

"No, but it could be. It could all be part of the real poem." She waved her hand around as if to take in everything—Miller, the sea, the night sky, the motel, the car, herself. She looked back down at the book in her lap and tapped it with her finger. "These are just the shadows." She set the book on the porch. "And what about you? Are you going to read to me? We made a deal."

"I will. I'll read you a shadow. But you want to know what I'd like first?"

"What?"

"A starlight swim." Miller pointed out to the shallow beach.

"I think I'll watch. I'll come in up to my knees. Don't go too far out, though. I worry about the riptides."

"You feeling all right?" he asked. She was a great swimmer, much better than Miller was. When it came to water, she usually led the way.

"I'm fine. Cold water might make my cramps worse, is all." She looked away. "It's embarrassing, Miller. I can't believe we're talking about this."

"Hey, you know what you'd tell me? It's the things we don't talk about that are dangerous. Like the riptides."

"Like the riptides," she repeated as Miller pulled off his shirt. He tossed it on the doorknob. "You're gonna freeze, boy."

"Fire or ice."

"Both ends of the piano," she said.

"You're strange."

"I'd have to be to hang around with you for four years."

"Sign on for another term?"

"I'm here until you impeach me."

"I love our congress."

She laughed. "Miller?"

"That's the me."

"Do I seem like the same person to you out here as when we're in Omaha?"

"It's hard for me to believe this is the same world as Omaha."

"You didn't answer me."

"Hmm. Let me see." He closed his eyes and slipped his hand under her shirt between her open thighs. She put her hand on his wrist.

"We're only half a block from the Coast Highway. There's cars."

"Let 'em cruise. I am."

She stood up and pulled him out of the chair. He put his arms around her.

At that moment Miller felt as close to her as he ever had, and yet he also felt a kind of chill down the front of his spine, deep inside, as if he was more alone than ever. You tried and tried to get close to one other person, only to find you'd come so close that it was like being one lone person all over again, trapped inside another single circle. His mother came to his mind, for some reason then, at the center of that lonely circle feeling. She hadn't remarried. It had been thirteen years. Miller wondered if she ever would.

"Have you talked to your parents recently," he asked Maureena.

"I picked up a letter at Grant's Wednesday. It was two weeks old."

"Are they settled down any?

"I think so. I'm out of their orbit now. In some ways they sound as if I'm still there with them and they can just ignore the me who's out here."

They walked out to the edge of the wet sand. The water rolled over Miller's toes.

"Whoa. It is cold. I better take a run at it. Wait."

He ran back to his chair and picked up the book he had brought out to read. Maureena stepped slowly forward into the sea, her ankles appearing and disappearing in thin lips of water that rose and receded around her feet. Miller stood at the edge of the porch and read from Ferlinghetti. He had to yell above the sound of the waves. *Let's cut out let's go into the real interior of the country . . . .*

Maureena rotated slowly toward the east, her palms together. She raised them slowly, pointing inland, smiling.

Another flood is coming, though not the kind you think.

Maureena swept her arms wide. "What kind of a flood do I think?" she yelled.

There is still time to sink and think. I wish to make like free.

Miller tossed the book on the chair and ran to her and took her hand. They skipped out until they were knee-deep. She pointed at him and then waved her arm around underhand and gestured out to sea as if she were directing traffic. He followed where she pointed, running ahead and diving into a four-foot wave.

It did feel like fire and ice all at once. Miller stood up and brushed his wet hair back with his hands. The green-tinted fog lights all up and down the coast highway shone like landing lights on a ghostly foreign craft. Maureena kept her back to the land, her arms open wide, as if she could pull the whole Pacific to her in one big hug.

"I wish," she yelled at the sky.

"To make like free," Miller screamed.

He spread his arms straight out from his shoulders and fell backwards into a rising wall of water. It twisted him forward, and he went with it. He pressed his hands together in front of him, closed his eyes, and let the wave wash him straight back in toward Maureena.

18

Miller and Maureena cleaned out their motel room and loaded almost everything into the Skylark the night before graduation day. When Durham knocked at their door in the morning, it was still dark out. Grant and Carlila were waiting in their pickup with the engine running. Durham decided to ride in the Skylark.

The Cardiff Donut Shop stayed open all night, and they stopped in to buy donuts and fill up a thermos of coffee for the trip to Leucadia. A noisy *Tribune* truck pulled into the lot with the morning papers just as they pulled out. Encinitas, asleep and lit only by the foglights along the winding cable of the Coast Highway, seemed deserted except for groups of Chicano men who stood and squatted along the dark road. Maureena said they were farm workers waiting for vans to take them home to Tijuana and Ensenada for the weekend.

They parked at the public lot in Leucadia. They split up the food Carlila brought, a jug of apple cider, some avocados, oranges, and a fresh loaf of whole grain bread, and then headed up the beach at low tide in the dark. It took half an hour to get to the spot Grant knew, a hidden little cove with a sand and gravel beach not much bigger than a volleyball court, surrounded by steep rocky cliffs. The five of them piled their packs on a shelf of rock and sat in the sand with their coats on, sipping coffee from paper cups. Psychout crawled right into the middle of their circle and went to sleep.

They took the pills the way you take any pills. It was in four lime-colored tabs, flat on one side and half-round on the other. Carlila didn't take one. She said she had read in *ThirdNews* that taking acid might cause a miscarriage.

They were all quiet. It was so early, and he was so sleepy, that Miller felt sure he had forgotten something, something left behind at the motel, something he hadn't done. He went over their preparations. The next morning he and Maureena were heading northeast, inland, to pick fruit and explore the West. Tomas had supplied them with a long list of names and places—lemon orchards in California, cherry orchards in Idaho, melon fields in Colorado, apple groves in Washington. Miller had tuned up the Skylark, they had bought a tent and more camping gear and supplies at a wholesalers in downtown San Diego, and they had turned their seven hundred dollars savings into a wad of twenty-dollar travelers' checks.

All of them would be going off in different directions. Grant and Carlila were driving straight to Berkeley, with one stop at Palos Verdes to tell his parents about their grandchild-to-be. Durham had arranged to meet up with the folks building the boat on Puget Sound, but that didn't start till July, so first he was hitchhiking to the Arizona desert.

As he waited for the sun to rise and the drug to come on, Miller couldn't help but think about where he and Maureena were supposed to be that day—thirty miles down the coast, wearing caps and gowns, stepping up like tasselled penguins to get the paper that would open the doors to the next place that granted another paper to open yet another door.

Miller had talked to his mother for a half-hour from a phone booth in Cardiff the day before, and although she hadn't mentioned that this was the month he should have graduated, he ended up telling her he was sorry that he hadn't finished school. He had been thinking of how she, too, had dropped out of college—to marry Loren before he shipped out to the South Pacific. No doubt she had hoped, when Miller was offered the UCSD scholarship in '65, that her struggling and scheming for his life was all over, that he was on his way out of the morass of money worries she had spent most of her adult life wading through, not to mention the kind of broken dreams she had watched his father's life wander in and out of for years. But on the phone she just said she was confident he would go back and finish his degree before too long, and Miller said, yes, yes, probably so—didn't everybody?

The light was still dim and the beach was still cold and foggy. Miller looked around the circle. Nobody seemed to know what to do while they waited. It was Miller's third time—he had dropped with Grant on campus once, and then once by himself, almost exactly a year earlier, the week he had made up his mind to quit school. He had hiked into a pine grove in the San Diego Mountains above Alpine and spent a day and night alone. It was both Maureena's and Durham's first time, and Miller's first time with Maureena. Miller had a strong sense it might be his last time, too, but he couldn't have said exactly where that feeling came from.

As the sky lightened up, they exchanged graduation gifts. Durham gave Miller and Maureena a miniature slotcar Skylark convertible from a speciality shop in San Diego. It was the wrong color, so he had repainted it, red with white interior. And he had a little pickup for Grant and Carlila with a tiny cloth camper on the back. He had even painted miniature license plates with state logos on them, a cow on the Skylark, and a bear on the pickup. Maureena gave everyone long woven garlands she made from fresh flowers discarded in Encinitas. Grant gave them each an unbroken sand dollar. He had collected them since grade school, and these were four of his finest. Carlila said her presents would be a surprise later.

Miller had worked on his gift in the Allenwhitts' garage, using a high-speed saber saw with a fine-tooth metal blade to carve a starfish skeleton he found near the Cardiff motel into five interlocking pieces. He gave everyone an arm and showed them how seamlessly they fit together.

Maureena sat next to Miller, cross-legged, the little Skylark balanced on one knee and her sand dollar on the other. Miller reached his fingers out to touch her, and his hand looked as prehistoric as the starfish. He could feel the skeleton riding inside it, the bones nestled in his flesh like pearls in the muscles of oysters. In his mouth, he tasted something new, a mix of ozone and sulphur and salt, like vanished electricity.

The fog was lifting. Miller stood up and saw the transparent spears of warmth shining down through the holes in the fog, and then there were no corners anywhere. The space between his feet and the sand was immense. He could feel his cells and organs, bathing and replacing themselves every second. Each second, every blink, was a bath and new flesh.

❀

Before the sunset was completely over, they walked back down to the parking lot in scarlet light. They pulled sleeping bags out of the car and truck, and trudged a couple of hundred yards away from the parking lot again, set the bags out in a row, and lay down to sleep.

Even then, as Miller tried to find sleep, he knew he wouldn't remember. He knew some things that had happened, but knowing them was like listing the names of queens and the dates of battles and calling it history. It was only gloss, a skim on a soup of words—as superficial as the textbook chronologies that tried to index entire centuries with a few numbers and names.

One of the most amazing days in his life was already slipping out of recall, as if each impression had eaten itself clean, down to the bone of the moment. Really remembering it would be like trying to reconstruct a herd of mastodons from one fossilized footprint.

❀

They stare out to sea. When Carlila speaks, each vowel is like a prism melting, each consonant is a wire blade through the cheese of the world. Every time Miller's heart beats he sees twice as far. In less than a minute he sees himself from behind, from the east, one head among five on a beach.

Each wave takes an hour to swell and fall. Miller can decide how long any second lasts. Time is a trick he plays on himself, but it's okay—he's in on the joke. He's the only joke there is. He saws himself in half. He shrieks and claps and bows.

They take turns lying with their heads in Carlila's lap. It's snowing in Miller's mother's eyes as she struggles through the doors of the red brick hospital in Cheyenne, his father's hand pressing the small of her back. Deeper in, the San Dieguito natives walk this beach, fishing with sticks, digging holes at the tideline, their red-brown backs like dark bony drums. They smile at Miller but step right through him. They set food out for him as if he were an ancestor. When he eats an orange, he feels his digestion, as slow as the boa in his freshman biology class, dissolving the white mouse down to the bone week after week.

A rescue helicopter flies north along the coast. Its noise echoes off the water, a thousand people barking up phlegm. Durham pounds his head in the sand, crying. Miller sees all the broken places, the frayed fingernail edges where cruelty leaks out—hands, fists, feet, tongues. Grief is a charcoal flower that blooms like black glass. In the black glass it looks like war across the sea. It looks like napalm death, a flaming monk.

Maureena and Miller stand fingertip to fingertip, seawater washing their ankles. He goes through her eye and floats down the rivers of her blood, a lost baby in a basket. The soles of her feet are cool in the sand, and then he spirals back up through the red turbine of her heart.

Carlila gives them her graduation presents—their names for a day. For Miller, Fall, a sound simple enough he can say it out loud. Miller's friend, the father of Carlila's child, Sea Star, playing in the waves like a fish. Red Oak for the one with the cars in the the sand, the one who laughs and cries the loudest. And Miller's lover Leucadia, the golden-haired woman with eyes like two more seas.

19

The sun rose before Miller did. Carlila and Grant were rolling their bags. Durham was gone. Maureena said he had stumbled over to the public showers. Miller shook his head and wiped at his eyes. He felt sleepy but something else, too, a steady cool pressure behind his eyes, as if his head had been pumped full of dry snow, every extra space filled with something cool and white.

He showered and went back to the parking lot and dried off and changed clothes. They walked up the Coast Highway in search of breakfast. He tried to feel the space between his shoes and the pavement, but it was gone.

They found a cafe and ordered breakfast. All Miller had eaten the day before was fruit and bread. Miller chose waffles and yogurt, which sounded just neutral enough.

Nobody had much to say. Tongue-tied two mornings in a row. While they waited on the food, Grant went up to the counter and grabbed a paper. He stood at the counter a long time, and when he came back to the table, he dropped the paper on the tabletop between their coffee cups with a slap. Coffee swirled out of two cups.

"Easy," Miller said. He wiped up the spill with his bandana. The paper was rightside up to him, but he didn't look at it. Then he heard Maureena.

"Oh, no," she said. "David." She was staring at the upside down paper. "It's the guy we saw in the mornings, Miller. David. The holy boy."

Miller saw the picture next to the headline. He pulled the paper closer and read the lefthand article outloud.

A UCSD religious studies student, David Lindere, originally of Cedar Rapids, Iowa, had drenched himself in gasoline and burned himself alive at sunset on Friday night on the east edge of the UCSD campus. No one had seen it happen, the paper said. The campus had been deserted the night before graduation. The man's identity had only been established late Saturday from dental records and interviews with friends. He had draped a homemade sign between two nearby trees: *Stop Our War*. University officials said Lindere was enrolled, but had not been attending classes. His remains were being removed to Iowa. Lindere's family requested donations in their son's memory be made to the Suicide Prevention Center at Regents Hospital in San Diego.

When the waitress came to the table, she had plates balanced all up and down her arms. Maureena sat with her eyes closed until the plates were all arranged and then walked out of the restaurant without a word. Miller looked at the food for a minute and put a five dollar bill on the table and went after her.

She was stretched out on the hood of the Skylark, staring at the sky. Gulls circled the parking lot like small buzzards.

"There's only one of anything," Maureena said. Her breath was shallow and labored, as if she had run all the way to the car. "And yet there's two of everything."

Miller counted the gulls. There were at least ten. He touched Maureena's hand. He thought of how thin and intent David Lindere had been and how his beautiful hair trailed down his back like a wild mane. He tried not to think of the smell it would have made in flames.

"Do you know what I mean?" she asked.

"No. But I don't have to."

"I think it's one reason we cried yesterday," she said.

"The wars go on every minute of every day," Miller said. "Whether we're high or straight, awake or asleep. Whether we fast or eat." He thought of the plates of food back on the cafe table. He felt queasy.

"Has it ever been any different, do you think?" she asked.

"Probably not. What was that old poem about how suffering always happens when everybody else is just eating or talking?"

"Auden," she said, *"The expensive delicate ship that must have seen something amazing."*

"Yeah. That's it. A man flying across the sun?" Miller hadn't read Auden since freshman year, but he thought it was the poem he remembered.

"A boy," Maureena corrected him, *"A boy falling out of the sky."*

Miller leaned his head back and stared straight up. A sliver of moon floated at the top of the sky, a weak white crescent washed out against the wide expanse of blue. He didn't remember the moon from yesterday. He thought of the way David Lindere sat so still and stared so far away from everything. He pictured him there in the cool mornings. Miller felt suddenly hot and sweaty, lying on the hood of the car. He looked around the parking lot and to the beach beyond.

"It might as well be summer," he said.

"Again?" Maureena asked.

Two gulls flew low and circled near them, looking for handouts. Maureena sat up and turned around, staring through the windshield into the Skylark.

"Flowers," she said. "Let's at least do the least we can do."

She hopped off the hood and unlocked the car and began rolling back the top. Miller helped her. He felt sunburned, even though he was pretty sure they had all rubbed each other down with sun lotion several times during the day before. He remembered the worst sunburn he ever had, junior year in high school, when he had fallen asleep on a sandbar in the Platte River west of Omaha. The backs of his thighs had blistered into two small watery footballs. He wondered how long David had felt the pain before it had knocked him out.

"And maybe the most, too," she said, unrolling her sleeping bag across the back seat, tucking the edges in around the records and books.

Miller recalled then, waking up once, only a few hours before in the dark on the beach, and seeing the sleeping bag pulled over Maureena's face next to him. He had been frightened and for a minute in the dark, he had watched her, afraid to move, like a parent with a sleeping baby, until he saw the bag rise and fall a fraction of an inch with her breath. Life depended on such small things. It was the real game of inches.

ೞ

Grant and Carlila and Durham came along. They drove inland at Encinitas to the fields where Maureena had worked. She showed them the freshest piles of discarded flowers, and they loaded armload after armload into the back seat of the Skylark, piling them up until they were even with the tops of the seats and the rear deck. They filled the open space in Grant's camper, too, though he and Carlila had, besides the regular junk, big cardboard boxes of her pots packed into it.

They had to drive slowly so the flowers wouldn't blow away. It was a beautiful morning. Grant had asked the waitress to bag up a sandwich of Miller's waffles and yogurt and had brought it. Miller and Maureena shared it on the way.

They passed the Cardiff motel. Another car was parked in their spot.

They passed the turnoff to Solana Heights and the Allenwhitts. Miller wondered aloud if he would ever see Tomas or Torbay again. Maureena said she had told Carmen she would write her a letter in Spanish.

They cruised by 26th Street in Del Mar. Grant had told them Mitch Kellor was getting married and had signed a new lease with an option to buy the house. Everybody else had been asked to find another place by June. Miller pictured Mitch's kids-to-be reclaiming Alice's Little House in the backyard—*Sing Oo-bla-de-bla-da.*

The highway ascended to Torrey Pines State Park. The trees there looked like big versions of the twisted trees in Oriental paintings. They clutched at the ocean breeze like gnarled fingers, pinching and wrinkling the sky.

ೞ

The spot where David Lindere died was the same spot where Miller and Maureena had passed him every day during their weeks in the eucalyptus groves. Now it was a rough burnt circle of lawn about ten feet across. A wider square had been marked off around it with red plastic tape strung between lightpoles and trees. Three small bouquets of flowers in vases had been set just inside the tape on one side. One of them was tipped over. Nobody was around. They parked as near as they could and walked closer.

Just burnt grass. Like the postcards of black sand in Hawaii. One of the trees at the edge of the lawn had a few curled leaves, but Miller wasn't sure that wasn't from disease or blight. Wherever David had posted his sign, it was long gone.

After a few minutes Maureena walked to the Skylark and grabbed an armful of flowers. She carried them back, stepping over the knee-high tape, and stood at the edge of the burn.

"I don't want to walk on it," she said. She set the flowers on the ground.

Grant hopped in his pickup, pulled it forward, and then reversed it quickly, jumping the curb and backing across the lawn. The red tape snapped like a kid's ribbon. He eased to a stop at the edge of the burnt grass and pulled the tailgate down. He and Durham climbed into the truck and began tossing flowers out onto the ground, while Maureena worked on her hands and knees, spreading the flowers out ahead of her to cover the circle. Miller went for the Skylark and backed it up next to the pickup.

Psychout watched with his nose on the ground as they covered the circle half a foot deep. Maureena and Carlila took their shoes off and walked on the flowers, fanning them out and arranging them over the black lawn like pieces of colored lace—red, purple, yellow, and white. They left a small black circle open in the middle, a couple of feet across, and at the last minute, Maureena set the bleached white sand dollar from Grant in the center of that. It looked like a monument of some kind.

The sun was hot. Miller scouted around until he found a sprinkler valve box. He took the cover off. With a pair of pliers from the glove box, he reached in and twisted the valve. A row of sprinkler heads popped up and began spraying. An umbrella of mist rained out over the flowers.

He and Maureena got in the Skylark and drove it out onto the parking lot. Grant did the same with his pickup. Durham and Carlila and Psychout walked over toward the lot. As he stood out of the car, Miller realized there was nothing much left to do then but leave, and he almost wanted to drive away without saying anything. Was there any good way to say goodbye?

Durham pulled a pack from Grant's camper, shouldered it, and stood behind the truck. He unfolded a map of the Western U.S. and waved Maureena and Miller over.

"You want a ride to I-10?" Miller asked. "I know a handy entrance ramp in Lakeside."

"I'm too wasted to start today," Durham said. "We're going to hit the beach one more night and leave tomorrow." He looked down at Psychout at his side. Grant jumped out of his truck and came over. They all stood close together between the two vehicles.

"You know what Cape Alava is?" Durham asked, still looking at the map.

He didn't wait for an answer. "It says it right here." He held up the map and pointed to the west side of the Olympic peninsula in Washington. "The westernmost point in the continental U.S." He waved the map. "Let's be crazy all the way," he said. "To hell with halfway."

"After yesterday," Grant said, "I don't think we have to worry much about that."

"Let's set a date and meet at Cape Alava in the fall," Durham said. "Right now. Right here. Pick a date, any date."

No one did.

"What's today?" Durham asked.

"May ninth," Maureena said. "The day after graduation."

Miller looked at them all. Yesterday seemed like it couldn't have been either before or after anything. Durham stared into the distance. The Pacific gleamed like bluegreen fire.

"September ninth," he said. "Four months from now—the five of us and whoever we pick up on the way. Cape Alava. I'll have a general delivery address in Port Angeles by August. Write me.

We can do this. It'll be like an anchor if the summer seas get too rough. You know?"

Maureena looked at Miller and then Carlila. Grant and Miller stared at each other. Carlila leaned over and kissed Durham on the cheek.

"You haven't even started building a boat and you're talking about anchors," she said.

Durham laughed, the first laugh Miller had heard all morning. "Well?"

"Why not?" Maureena said. She looked at Miller again. "Nine, nine. Cape Alava. Port Angeles. Be careful, Durham. Don't get yourself caught. And if you do, write Miller's mother. She'll know where we are. We'll come running. You know her address?"

"In here," he said, pointing to his head.

"It sounds about exactly as likely as anything else," Grant said. "If I'm alive and not in jail, I'll try to be there." He shook Durham's hand.

Durham and Carlila hugged, and Miller hugged them and then Grant, and they all hugged Maureena. Miller heard Grant tell Maureena he hoped she felt better soon. Everybody told Carlila to take care of her baby. Miller shook hands with Grant.

Durham walked away slowly, angling toward the Black Beach cliff trails. For a second Miller half expected to see him hop in a Yellow Cab and drive away. Miller was amazed at how much Durham had changed just since Drake Court, and yet he wasn't sure how much was Durham's change or how much his own. There were so few benchmarks, so many expectations blown away like beach sand, so little left to gauge anything by.

Miller sat in the passenger seat of the Skylark. Maureena coasted out of the lot. Ahead of them Grant and Carlila pulled onto La Jolla Drive that would take them to I-5, L.A., and Berkeley beyond. Carlila waved once and then the truck was gone into the traffic.

The Skylark smelled like a mix between a flower shop and a funeral parlor. Miller looked at the map and the route they had chosen—east into the mountains and then around the L.A.

basin and north to Owens valley and the Sierra Nevada. He had always wanted to see where the water for Los Angeles really came from.

As Maureena shifted into second gear, Miller looked in the rearview mirror, wishing David Lindere could have come with them somehow instead of being shipped back to Cedar Rapids as a shrunken self-made effigy. The flowers behind them on the lawn looked like someone's last spring, cut and pressed for a special occasion.

Miller felt lost then, a dry seasick, an edgy feeling hovering just above his stomach. He thought of his father. He wished he were alive, somewhere, at the end of a phone. It was the first time in a long time Miller could remember wishing for him in that way, for advice, for plain talk. Even the fathers and sons Miller knew who fought, and most did, had that or the memory of that, a simple chat now and then, a few words, whether heeded or not, that left them both feeling linked to something before or after the present moment.

Maureena hummed a slow Creedence Clearwater tune that Miller knew a few words to. *Pharaohs spin the message. Round and round it goes.* He watched murky heat rise above the pavement ahead of the them. The newspaper had predicted the hottest day of the year so far. They were chasing summer, but it felt like it had already found them. Already found them or already passed them, Miller wasn't sure which. He pulled his sunglasses on, took a long slow drink from the canteen, and closed his eyes.

PART THREE

20

The late summer sunlight was thin and golden over the little town of Port Angeles. Miller and Maureena spotted Durham on their first pass by the post office, a little after noon on September Ninth. Although they had sent a postcard from Oregon to the General Delivery there a week before, Miller hadn't been at all sure whether to expect Durham or not. As they pulled over to park, Miller saw Carlila, too, looking pregnant from half a block away.

Miller shook hands with Durham, and Maureena kissed Durham while Miller hugged Carlila. He didn't know how careful to be of her, but when he hesitated, she pulled him closer.

"So the bird's still running, huh?" Durham said, turning toward the Skylark.

"And the top works just as well as ever," Maureena said.

"I know all about that," Durham said. "Especially in blizzards. I still think about that night outside of Rising City."

"And where's Grant?" Miller asked, looking up and down the street. His truck was parked across the street, but nobody was in it. "Wait, let me guess. In the nearest phone booth, calling the underground hotline. Making plans to storm the Pentagon with slingshots."

Neither Durham nor Carlila laughed. Instead she looked away, staring across the street to the gritty sprawl of the Bi-Lo supermarket parking lot and then past it to the green-blue waters of Juan de Fuca Strait that spread away to the north. Durham touched Carlila's shoulder, and she turned her eyes back to Miller and Maureena.

"He said he'd try to make it," she said. "But that was before the Third. I've only talked to him on the phone since then. I can't say whether he'll show or not."

"The Third?" Miller asked.

"Ho Chi Minh died."

"I know that. We read about it on the way up. They published his will to the Vietnamese people in the Portland paper."

"Grant carries a book of his poems," Carlila said, "everywhere. I came up here from my folks' place in Tacoma last week. I've been staying with Steve and his friends since then."

"He could already be on the beach waiting for us," Durham said, pointing toward the Olympic Mountains. "If he has come through town here though, he didn't stop."

Miller followed the line of Durham's finger toward the green horizon. He had looked at the map, but he had only a rough idea where Cape Alava was—still farther west.

"You know Grant," Miller said. "He may drop onto the beach by parachute."

"Who does know Grant?" Maureena said. "And if we figure that out, maybe we could ask them if we should wait here in town for awhile to see if he shows."

"Good question," Carlila said.

"This is too fine a day not to go," Durham said. "I've been here off and on for more than a month, and this is the clearest day so far. Clear as in not raining all day. Besides, I left a message and a map for him, or for you two if you didn't show, with people at the ark."

"How could we not show?" Miller asked. "We've only got two-fifths of a starfish."

"Sounds like you two are all ready to roll," Maureena said. "How far is it, anyway?"

"About eighty miles to the trailhead," Durham said. "Maybe a bit more."

"Trailhead?" Maureena said.

"It's a flat five miles out to the beach," Durham said. "My housemates have been there."

"Are you okay for walking that far?" Maureena asked Carlila.

"Sure. I just can't drive," she said. "The steering wheel crowds me." She patted her stomach. "Us."

Durham turned to Miller. "Follow me, then?"

"To the end of the continent."

Durham nodded. He and Carlila both turned and walked away. Too quickly, Miller thought. Maureena started the Skylark and she and Miller waited. In a few minutes Durham pulled up close beside the Skylark.

"So what about you two?" Carlila said out the window. "Besides that you're still together. Did you find any Edens out there, Maureena?" She pointed behind them.

"Long story," Maureena said.

"Short summer," Miller said.

Durham and Carlila both smiled and Durham pointed a finger down the road. Miller and Maureena followed them out of town and west along the coast toward the mouth of the Pysht River, where the road would turn southwest, heading inland across the peninsula.

The trees on either side of the highway stood tall and thick, and in the midday sun, they steamed with moisture. The wet woods and cool sunshine put Miller in mind of fall, something he hadn't thought much about all summer. Or maybe it was because he had just seen Durham and Carlila—and not seen Grant.

"It was short, wasn't it?" he asked Maureena.

"That wasn't the right place. We'll have a longer talk when we get there," she said.

"No, I mean the summer. Seeing those two, wondering what's happened, where they've been—it makes me wonder where we've been."

Maureena looked down at the gauges, and then mumbled to herself for a minute.

"Four thousand seven hundred miles," she said. "That's where we've been."

"That's a hell of a lot of been," Miller said. "But Carlila got it right—we're still together." Miller thought that's all he was saying, but it wasn't. "Aren't we?" he asked.

For a second, he felt her slipping away from him—a memory? a portent? It had never happened to him, but he imagined himself an older man looking back on a moment that seemed perfectly ordinary at the time but ended up changing everything—the instant he introduced his girlfriend to her future husband at a party, say. Something like that. Something Miller must have read somewhere. Or seen in a movie. He didn't really know what he was feeling. Maybe just the sense that this reunion wasn't going to bring things back the way they had been a few months before. And that awareness made him feel more vulnerable about everything, even Maureena.

She put her hand on his. He didn't know how long it had taken her to answer.

"Miller, I don't really tell you much, do I? Not right outloud, I mean." She laced her fingers between his, one by one. Miller was still staring at the wall of trees. It seemed like hundreds slipped by. "You're the reason for my living," she said.

There was an opening in the canopy where a side road slithered away and vanished. Miller looked at her. It wasn't exactly what he wanted to hear. It was too much. And yet, wasn't the same true for him, too? Maybe that was what he really didn't want to hear. He didn't speak.

"Or our love is," she said. "Look," she nodded at their hands, interwoven between them. "Like this." She squeezed his fingers. "As long as you want."

"I want," he said, "I want." He heard the beginnings from an endless string of songs. *I want you, I want your love, I want a gal just like the gal, I want the world and I want it now.*

"And no matter," Maureena said, tipping her head back and speaking into the blue above as if someone in the sky had accused them. "No matter if we don't know where we're going." She raised both hands from the wheel and turned her palms up. Miller thought of the old *Mad* Magazines. *What? Us Worry?* She dropped her hands and the image faded. But then her words and the wet pine smell in the air reminded him of something else.

"Or where we've been," he said, smiling to cover his new memory—January. But as quickly as the image of that cold garage surfaced, he pushed it right back down. In its place he allowed other uncomfortable car memories, more minor and more numerous.

The three times the car had overheated in the summer. How it lost power on steep grades more than once. Something wasn't right with the cooling system. What if the engine went out? All the money they had saved together would barely buy another vehicle as good as the Skylark.

Winter memories, end-of-summer worries. Miller didn't want to think about any of them.

"Going or been," Maureena said, laughing and pointing at the little car on the dashboard that Durham had given them in May. "Either or both. The Skylark's still a great car to get there in. For as long as it runs."

A half a mile down the road, Durham and Carlila disappeared around a curve, and then the highway ahead was bright and empty.

"It'll run forever," Miller said.

21

The trail was muddy and slick in places. Durham set an easy pace and Carlila walked slowly and watched her footing, but even so, Miller lingered in last place, gawking. Every surface he could see grew solid green with plant life. To look at the tops of the trees, he had to get his forehead horizontal and look straight up. Except for the fact that there had still been no sign of Grant at the trailhead, it felt like the perfect place for their reunion—the complete opposite of San Diego county, and so different from most of the dry West that Miller had seen since then.

Durham said it wasn't real rain forest—the trees were taller and the groundcover thicker in the Peninsula's interior valleys—but that was like trying to tell Miller that the north county beaches weren't really a tropical paradise. He was still from Nebraska—to him, it was rain forest.

It was close to sunset by the time they reached the ocean. A small wooden sign where the trail deadended at the beach told them they were at Cape Alava, the westernmost point in the forty-eight states, and that the island offshore was Ozette Island. By the tip of the arrow that pointed toward Ozette, someone had carved a crude peace sign.

Carlila had her folks' old tent that she had retrieved from their basement. They pitched it at the edge of the woods, where the ground changed from moss to sand within a few dozen feet. It was a large canvas cabin tent that reminded Miller of his Platte River Boy Scout campouts in Nebraska. The canvas smelled oily and mildewed, as if it had been folded up for years.

They collected enough driftwood in fifteen minutes for two days worth of fires. The temperature dropped quickly after the sun sank, and by the time they were eating soy burgers and roasted red onions, they had to huddle close around the fire. Carlila leaned into Durham and he put his arm around her. They talked for awhile, and then as the stars came out, Maureena fell asleep with her head in Miller's lap and Carlila and Durham went inside the tent.

Miller's face felt warm from the fire, but his back was cold. He stretched his legs and Maureena readjusted her head as she slept. Miller looked from her to the flames. He felt as if he had left San Diego only a few days before. How could it possibly have been an entire summer? June. July. August. August. July. June. He knew the months had happened, along with all the towns and states, the rivers and mountains. He could trace every name on a map or a calendar, but there in the dark on the beach, with no light but firelight and starlight, it felt as if he had been nowhere but asleep—drowsing through a syrup of summer dreams to the Buick's drone and the rush of hot air on an unending highway.

He threw more wood on the fire, but soon the wind off the sea made him colder again. When he felt sand stinging his forehead, it was time to go inside. He jostled Maureena, and she crawled into the tent and stretched out in her bag. She mumbled a few garbled words in the middle of a dream, something about a basement in the forest, but she wasn't really awake.

☙

It was hard to sleep, even in the soft sand, because the wind picked up steadily through the night. Miller woke up more than once, and he heard the others moving around in their bags, half-awake, having trouble sleeping, too. A couple of times Miller thought the tent might actually blow down. The night wind felt ominous, like the threat of some much larger restlessness than just his own, and he had the sense of dreams unfinished, lost in the constant snapping of the tent walls and the incessant pinging of sand on canvas.

With the dawn came rain and mist and fog. The landscape looked entirely different to Miller than only twelve hours before, as if he had slept two seasons instead of a few hours. The tent stood less than a hundred feet from the Cape Alava sign, but when he looked out, he couldn't see it, much less read it. They had pitched the tent with the door facing the sea in the calm of the sunset, but in the morning it became clear what a mistake that had been.

They climbed out and pulled the stakes, and each of them took a corner and a guyline as they turned it around. Miller dug a pit in the sand, and Maureena built a small fire in the lee of the tent, just outside the opening. Durham staked the flaps out partway over the fire and sorted through their wood. He stashed the driest pieces inside the tent before they ate breakfast, oatmeal with cutup pieces of fried hotdog on the side. They ate in their raincoats, squatting near the fire.

Nobody else wanted to venture too far out of the tent, except when they had to, but Miller felt drawn to the storm and the forest. The wet woods loomed like an abyss beyond the opening of a cave—tangled, green, labyrinthine. Something dangerous. Something you could fall into. Yet staring into the completeness of rain in the rain forest, he felt the falling had already begun.

He slipped Durham's oversize poncho over his raincoat and wandered into the woods. He kept looping away from camp and coming back when he felt too cold or wet, sitting by the fire again and listening to the three of them talk.

CS

"Those cactus at Organ Pipe," Durham was saying as Miller squatted by the fire. "What a trip. When they die, they leave these bone-dry upright skeletons honeycombed with diamond-shaped holes." He looked out at the rain. "I can't imagine water like this in country like that. It'd all swell up like one of those sponge toys I used to get when I was a kid."

"I remember those," Maureena said.

Miller did, too. He had liked dripping water on them to make them grow, watching the flat wafers swell slowly into miniature landscapes and animals. He shivered and sipped tea from a tin cup. His jeans steamed in the heat of the fire.

"We went through some hot dry country, too," Maureena said. "But nothing that extreme. We picked cherries for two weeks in the Snake Valley in Idaho. We could only pick from 6 A.M. till noon. The cherries turned too soft in the heat."

"What'd you do in the afternoons?" Carlila asked.

"Read books. Took walks." Maureena looked over at Miller. "What did we do? Let's see, we swam in the irrigation canals by the orchards with a couple of Mexican families. Oh, and the free music at night." She laughed. "How could I forget that? We camped for free on a reservoir a mile away, next to an electrical tower that hummed all night. It sounded like a church organ stuck on one long low note. But it was so hot, we had to stay near water."

Miller smiled and threw a couple more pieces of wood on the fire as he stepped out from under the tent flaps. He paused when he heard Carlila telling Maureena about how much Berkeley had affected Grant. He had seen the Guard shoot street people the morning after the bulldozers plowed through People's Park and the fences went up.

"He went different then," she said. "Intense."

"Wasn't he always intense?" Maureena said. "Aren't all of us? Look at Miller, heading straight out into Hurricane Alava."

Miller sensed she had wanted him to hear. He smiled to himself.

"No, this is major," Carlila said. "Something new."

Miller stopped and moved sideways to avoid the smoke from the fire, still listening.

"I think I know what you mean," Durham said. "It's how come we're here. I met plenty of other people this summer, but I'm out here now with you guys. You know why?"

"Nobody else was crazy enough to come?" Maureena said.

"True. But there's more to it. Everybody's changed so fast. Everybody you meet has this new person they're trying out. New clothes, new hair, new head, new heart." He poked a stick at the fire, and it flared up again. "And so do I. But unless you knew somebody before, you don't really know them, right? That's a big reason I wanted to see you, I think. I can see the old and the new. And it helps me keep track of both of me."

"Right," Carlila said. "And that's what Grant's lost. He's all new. He's got his head so far into fighting the goddamn government, that he's lost everything else he had before."

She was crying. Maurccna put her arms around her.

Durham stood up and stepped outside the tent next to Miller. The fire popped and hissed.

"Well? That was pretty clear," Miller said. "We don't need details, I guess."

"Details just murk everything up," Durham said, his voice dropping.

"What you were saying in there, though," Miller pointed to the tent. "I felt like that this summer, too. It is something different with you. And it's always been different with Grant."

Durham squeezed Miller's shoulder. There was the rapid muted wingbeat of a duck, flying just above them and just close enough to see in the mist. Miller twirled to watch it. It landed near the sign at the end of the trail. Durham stared at it, too. It had intricate markings on its head and chest—odd patches and thin stripes and a white circle behind its eye. Then it was gone.

"What kind of duck was that?" Miller asked.

"I don't know. Somebody at the house will though. Remind me to ask."

It was the only bird Miller had seen all morning. Ever since it first occurred to him when he was a kid, he had always wondered where exactly birds went when it stormed like this.

"You know what, Miller? We're running."

Miller thought Durham was going to tell the whole story about himself and Grant and Carlila. But when he looked into his eyes he saw he meant all of them.

"Probably," Miller said, "probably."

They both looked back out to sea. It had cleared enough to see the waves pound at the shore, but in the rain, the spray disappeared into nothing.

Later that month, when Miller was trying to tell Grant about the weather and the day at Cape Alava—what he'd missed, or hadn't missed—for some reason, what came to his mind first was that beautiful duck. When Miller described it, Grant said it was a Harlequin. He said he had seen one on the Sound north of Seattle once.

CR

Pockets of drier air kept moving inland, minor lulls in the midst of a storm that was probably a hundred miles wide. One minute Miller stood in rain so piercing that he had to keep his back to the sea or take shelter behind a giant hemlock, and the next minute a cloud would slide through like one huge exhalation, and then in a few more minutes, the air would go gray with a mist so fine Miller couldn't tell if it was riding in on the storm or welling up from all the life around him.

Slugs of all sizes and shapes appeared and disappeared with each change in the rain. Miller stared for minutes at a low limb, made twice its actual size by moss, before a banana slug four inches long came clear all at once in his vision.

When the wind reached its worst, Miller walked farther into the forest until the air became almost calm. In there he could hear thousands of separate drippings, a steady symphonic sound, like the soundtrack on growth itself.

The smell of wet cedar hovered thick and heavy in the air. When he wandered back out toward the sound of the waves, the cedar faded gradually into salt. And then near the tent, the smell of smoke mingled with the salt.

CR

"They call it Trinity site," Maureena was saying, "and it is eerie. Really unsettled. All the rocks are black—obsidian black—only rough and pocked like some kind of volcanic cinder. You couldn't go out near the actual spot, although Miller wanted to try. But just being that close, you could feel the spirit in it. Like an old house where there's been a murder in the cellar."

"Half of south Arizona is owned by the military," Durham said. "And most of Nevada."

"Not to mention big chunks of California," Carlila said.

"It had rained really hard the night before," Maureena said. "We didn't realize it until later, but it was the same night they landed on the moon. We'd driven through a wild thunderstorm at the peak of some pass on our way into Alamagordo. But there was sure no moon that night. What was the name of that place, Miller?"

He had slipped into the tent again and was sitting crosslegged in the back, inhaling the steam from his tea.

"San Augustin," he said. He remembered back to it. High sparse desert up above the narrow, lush Rio Grande valley. As they had neared the pass, lightning crashed on the peaks all around them, one after the other. They were still somewhere in the White Sands Missile Range, and the blinding flashes of light seemed connected somehow to the atomic age that had been born in the desert so close by. The best minds of a generation, sequestered in the desert like madmen, convinced they were saving the world from one horror—only to open a door on another.

"The sky was so perfectly blue the next morning and those rocks were so completely black," Maureena said. "You can see why they make such beautiful jewelry in that country."

"I was in Crescent City the night of the moon landing," Durham said. "Almost to the Oregon border. People camping on the beach told me about it."

"We'd backtracked down from Idaho after the Fourth," Maureena said, making a circular motion with her finger. "I think. We ended up in the San Luis valley in Colorado."

"Where were you on the moon night?" Maureena asked Carlila.

She looked in the fire. "I saw it on TV at my folks' in Tacoma," she said. "Grant went off to Seattle for a three-day session at U.W. We'd come pretty much straight up from Berkeley early in July so he could be there. It's a new branch of SDS. They make Marcuse and the San Diego people look like dinner guests. Have you guys kept up on it any?"

"A few underground papers," Maureena said. "Not much. There was something about a big splitup. Sounds like a royal mess."

"The Weatherpeople," Miller said. "They're recruiting in the inner city high schools with a real catchy slogan. *Revolution Now.* With emphasis on the now." He thought of Torbay in Solana Beach, remembering how much he had wanted to come travel with them. But that was for Mexican weed and good waves, not for revolution.

Miller sensed fatalism rising inside himself day by day. Nothing seemed surprising to him anymore, certainly not what he had read of SDS. So what if an opposition that began in idealism wore itself down past cynicism, and then finally sank all the way into fanaticism?

"We did have a great few days on the Oregon coast on the way up," Carlila said, smiling. "Between Berkeley and Seattle."

Miller couldn't stop thinking about the war. He couldn't sort out anymore where he stood among the endless arguments about how to fight it. Rent a suit or buy body paint. Block the stairs or knock on doors. Assume the lotus or raid an armory.

"But then Grant got sick drinking from some stream," she said. "And I had to talk two Oregon State Patrol out of busting us for camping outside the designated area. Grant was stranded in the tent, almost completely green." Carlila paused and pulled her sleeping bag around her pantlegs. "But the weekend right before that was beautiful. We hiked over huge dunes, through weird forests growing in sand. It was something like this place, only the trees were much more scattered out, and it was warmer and drier."

"I'm pretty certain anywhere would be warmer and drier," Maureena said.

Miller stared out into the woods. A thick fog swirled around the tree trunks, but it was only headhigh. The forest above it looked ghostly, grounded in nothing, floating on mist. Maureena was talking about the week they had spent near Klamath Falls, working on a potato farm, helping move last year's crop out of metal Quonset huts into semi-trailers. Maureena worked as a culler on an assembly line built from portable conveyor-belt units, and Miller drove a small tractor with a floor scoop on the front, shoveling into mountains of potatoes hour after hour.

He stood up and finished his tea and then went back out into the weather. The cedar smell in the mist reminded him of that potato smell from Klamath Falls, an earthy fleshy smell that had clung to his skin and hair for a long time afterward.

∽

Whenever the four of them spread out more than a few feet apart on the winding trail back to the cars, they vanished in the fog. Water dripped off Miller's borrowed poncho. Off Durham's pack whenever Miller got a glimpse of him. Off strands of Maureena's hair beneath her hat. Then the silences between waterdrops.

Miller tried to picture Psychout with them, soaking wet on the muddy trail. Miller had been hesitant to ask after him, but it turned out he'd found a home. Durham had camped in Montana with some great people from Alberta on their way to Woodstock, and they'd loved Psychout so much he let them take him. He said it was much better for a dog than hitchhiking.

They all laughed about Psychout being the only one of them that made it to Woodstock. Carlila said that Grant had made a big deal about the gory Hollywood murders happening the very same week—he said they were only different sides of a coin. Carlila said the murders haunted her because Sharon Tate had been pregnant. She had nightmares about it happening to her.

Not far out from the trailhead, Maureena lost her footing and fell down. As Miller helped her up, he saw the jagged scar on the inside of her forearm. She had slipped from a ladder in a California lemon orchard in early June, and the scar from an inch-long thorn was still visible. Miller remembered how frightened he had been when she fell. Another time, when she caught her scarf in the conveyor belt at the potato farm, Miller raced over and pulled at her scarf so hard that they both fell backwards into a pile of culls. The tractor he had abandoned stalled out, trying to nose its way into a huge pyramid of potatos.

But she had more than made up for that a week or two later when they camped by an ice-clear lake in Steens Mountains in Oregon. Not long after sunup one morning they went for a long hike and picnic in the high country above the lake. They stepped over a few rivulets that wove through a boggy area near the lake, and then they climbed all morning to a cup-shaped meadow surrounded by snow fields. Dozens of small streams ribboned down the mountains around them.

When they climbed back down to the lower country in late afternoon, they found a rushing creek twelve feet wide. The water from the melted snow flowed as clear as moving glass. They stared at it a long time before trying to cross. But it was either that or wait through a thirty-degree night—with no matches, tent, or bags—until the water receded.

They both took off their boots and tied the laces together and slung them over their shoulders. Miller found two sturdy poles, and they started across, trying to angle down with the current. They were almost across when Miller went down. It was such a surprise and the stream was so cold that he took in a big mouthful of water before he even knew what was happening. He let go of the rocks he had grabbed and was swept downstream, coughing and choking. Maureena had lifeguarded for two summers in high school, and it showed that day. She tossed her boots and stick over to the bank and lay down into the current. With one stroke she caught up to him, grabbed his shirt and held him as she kicked at the bottom, shoving them both out of the fast current.

Back at the trailhead to Cape Alava, a sheet of muddy water fanned out across the hard gravel lot and disappeared into the ground moss at the edge of the woods. Miller sat on the hood of the Skylark, waiting while Durham packed up the truck. He was still thinking about all that water at Steens Mountains and the way it changed completely in the course of a single summer day, how clear and cold it was, and how dangerous. How he had been so concerned to help Maureena and yet she had pulled him across by his collar. Even now, he still couldn't believe it was the same stream they had hopped across that morning without a second thought. He realized how much he had to learn about the mountains. About everything.

Behind him Carlila laughed outloud. Miller turned around. She said she felt her baby moving. She motioned to Maureena as she sat down on the edge of the seat in the truck with the door open. Maureena moved close and spread both her hands across Carlila's stomach, grinning. Miller stepped a little farther away. He had never really known anyone pregnant before, except the mothers of friends when he was a kid.

"I told Grant last spring I wouldn't say he told," Carlila said. "But now it doesn't feel like it would matter. I guess you weren't?"

"No," Maureena said. "False alarm." She pulled her hands away from Carlila.

Maureena had her back to Miller, and he couldn't see Carlila's face. He looked at Durham, who looked away. Maureena got into the Skylark, and Durham closed Carlila's door and went around and sat behind the wheel of the truck.

Miller took one last look around. He couldn't see any of the high Olympic peaks from where they were, yet he was sure they were up there, snowfields melting in the rain, sloping unseen somewhere high above them.

22

"I didn't tell Grant anything last spring when we thought you were pregnant," Miller said.

They were thirty miles from Port Angeles, driving slow in thick fog. The highway seemed to create itself only a few yards ahead of them. Miller hadn't spotted the truck with Durham and Carlila for miles. They picked up a Seattle station on the radio, though it kept fading. The long version of "Hey Jude" played twice in a row.

"I didn't say you did," Maureena said. She was wrapped in two dry towels, her wet clothes spread out across the gear in the back seat. Miller drove in his.

Maureena hadn't said anything about it since they left the trailhead. She had been busy getting out of her clothes and drying off. Then she had closed her eyes. Miller didn't know if she was asleep or not, and he felt half hypnotized himself, watching the highway well up out of the rain. The station faded in again. Lennon and McCartney's voices rose in a wild high chorus.

But he was confused. He hadn't told Grant or Durham. She had asked him not to. And Maureena apparently hadn't told Carlila. But she must think that Miller had broken his promise.

"No, you didn't say it," he said, "but did you think I did?"

"No."

She readjusted the towel around her legs. The heater was on full blast. Miller had his shoes off and it felt good on his feet.

"I figured you might," he said. "And I'd understand that. But I really have no idea how he knew. Christ, maybe he's psychic."

"It's not important," she said. "It didn't happen."

"Things that didn't happen can still be important."

"Yes."

He slowed around a tight curve. He was glad he couldn't see enough to know whether or not there was a dropoff at the edge.

"You don't want to talk about it, I guess."

"My mom was pregnant with me when they remarried," she said.

She had never told him that. All he knew was the bare outline. Her folks had been divorced once and then quickly remarried.

"How do you know?"

"She told me. At the top of her voice. In the basement."

"Oh. One of those."

"One of those. Miller, Grant's no psychic. I told him. I let it slip when we were talking about Carlila, I guess."

"Yeah, then, that explains it. I've been trying to remember if I could have said something to him that I'd forgotten. I just don't want you to think I mentioned it when you said not to."

"Thanks," she said. "Thanks." She looked out the window. "Hey, can you picture two pregnant women slipping around on that sloppy trail back there?"

She changed tone with a laugh. Miller went with it.

"I can imagine almost anything," he said. "That's not the tricky part."

"And what exactly is the sticky part, Professor Silas?" She tried to hold her mouth still and look serious, but Miller could see it was an effort.

"*Trick*-eee," he said. "The tricky part. And they have a lot of little words for it."

"Like life?"

"That's the best one, I suppose."

"In that case," she paused, one hand in the air. "Let's take the ferry to Canada when we get to Port Angeles."

"Canada? Right now. Why?"

"Didn't you hear Steve talking about that place in B.C.?"

"Yeah. The farm his friends want him to visit."

"What a great name—Edgewood. It sounds real. It sounds ideal. Why don't we go?"

"We could. What about Grant?"

"He wouldn't want to come. He didn't want to come here." She pointed behind them.

"Maybe something important happened at the last minute. Maybe he didn't have a ride. I want to see him, at least, and talk to him."

"I believed all summer we'd find a spot to stop," Maureena said, picking up the starfish arm on the dash. She held it close to her nose. "It still smells like ocean." She set it back down. "And I don't care that we didn't. Nothing felt right. But what if we were in the wrong country? Maybe it's been the wrong country all along. Maybe all the suffering and death over there spreads backwards through everything here—like some kind of infection."

"Viet Nam?"

She didn't answer. Miller didn't know why he had asked. Where else could she mean? And he couldn't really argue with her. It was possible.

"I'm okay with going up there," he said. "We'll need to get our act together for the border though. I've heard they're really tough because of all the evaders."

"You're not evading."

"They don't know who is and who isn't though. And I do want to see Grant, maybe check out Seattle, plan things out a little. Seattle's supposed to be a beautiful city. From there we'll definitely have other chances to go to Canada. It's not like it's going to disappear on us." He reached over and squeezed her hand lightly. "It's too big. Where would they hide it?"

Maureena smiled. "I just thought it'd be fun to do it without thinking. And right after Cape Alava. What I'd settle for though, is just to shake this weather. I feel like I can't breathe."

It was raining much harder. Miller turned the wipers on high. A small leak in the top started dripping onto the back deck.

"So it's a run for the big yellow," he said. "We won't stop till we see sun. Grant or no. B.C. or no. Gas or no." The gauge read half full.

"Whichever way we go, let's ride a ferry," she said.

She bent her head down, trying to dry her hair in the heater vent.

"Done," Miller said. "If you'll dry mine." His head felt chilled and clammy.

She took the towel from around her. She smiled as she leaned over and rubbed his head. Miller looked at her, naked except for the towel at her feet.

"Keep your eyes on the road," she said. "You just keep looking for that ferry."

She draped the towel over his head like a hood and stretched out in her seat. Miller smelled her. The musk of potato, a bite of salt spray, the red living leather of cedar—all mixed together in his mind. And always the hint of wheat he could no longer tell if he imagined or not.

They were at least an hour yet from the nearest ferry, and they both knew it, but Miller pretended to look. He could imagine foghorns. Smokestacks. A dock. A bay. Islands. He looked through the wipers into the fierce rain. He could imagine anything.

C**3**

They stood together on the upper deck. Halfway across the Sound between Port Townsend and downtown Seattle, the storm subsided. No sunlight, but the rain stopped and the fog lifted enough to see green hills on every side. They walked to the railing, glimpsing Seattle to the southeast. It didn't look much bigger than Omaha from a distance, but it was much greener and hillier and wetter. Miller caught sight of the space needle. It reminded him of the postcards.

When they had stopped at the Port Angeles house, Grant still hadn't called or picked up the message. Durham and Carlila wanted Maureena and Miller to stay over for a few days, but they would have had to pitch a tent again, and they both wanted out of the rain, so Carlila gave them an address for Grant somewhere in the U. District.

Dozens of gulls chased the ferry, diving and rolling, coming up alongside in case anyone had food to throw. Miller felt the rumbling force of the ferry, its engines thrumming under their feet, yet it moved so slowly and steadily that its huge, stark power felt beneficent. He stared down into the black-green water, rolling away from the massive hull in wide shallow waves. Maureena thumbed through the schedule pamphlet that came with their tickets.

"There are so many of these," she said. "We could ride them for months. We could become the ferry people. Live on them." She pointed into the glassed-in waiting rooms where commuters lounged and slept as if nothing special was happening at all.

"Do they allow fishing?" He flicked his forearm out over the railing as if he were casting.

"We could sell trinkets to the tourists," she said.

"Do beadwork while we sail and then sell it at the docks," Miller said.

Maureena pointed at the four flags, snapping in the wind above the wheelhouse. America. Washington State. British Columbia. Canada. "It's like being in no country at all," she said.

"It's completely in between," he said.

"Enroute," she said.

"Just about to arrive."

"So recently departed."

"In transit."

"I'm convinced," she said.

"That makes both of us," he said. "Damn near a quorum. Feel like a hot coffee?" Even though the rain had let up, it was very windy. Miller was cold.

"Hot chocolate," she said. "See that table?" She nodded toward an empty booth behind the nearest window. "If you get me a cup, I'll meet you in there. I want to stay out here by myself just a little longer. Everything's so quiet and strong and clean. I feel like I could fly." She pointed at two white and black gulls hovering a few feet out from the ferry.

Miller went toward the snack bar inside. As the second glass door closed behind him, he stopped, savoring the sudden warmth. He looked out at Maureena, standing alone with her back to him, the gulls diving around her, appearing and then disappearing below the ferry railing. Even the gold blaze of her hair shone with a slight green tint, and beyond her there was nothing but the green water and the green hills.

23

The address Miller and Maureena had for Grant turned out to be an old three-story house on 51st Street, half a mile from the University of Washington campus. When they crashed in there, fresh from the ferry and the rain, Grant wasn't home, but Drew, the owner of the house, welcomed them like old friends. He fixed a pot of spaghetti as they talked in the kitchen and after they ate, he offered them half the basement to stay in — "if you're okay with Irish wolfhounds," he said. Miller pictured medium-sized Afghan hounds, and Maureena said later she didn't have any picture at all, so they unloaded the Skylark and went right on down, carrying their bags and packs.

Fin and Erin met them at the bottom of the stairs. The top of Fin's shaggy gray head came above Miller's waist. He was the biggest dog Miller had ever petted, which he did quickly after Fin walked up and nuzzled his head against Miller's chest. Erin was the second biggest.

The wolfhounds had rib cages as big as beer kegs and jaws the size of curbside mailboxes, but inside the house they acted like puppies. Within a few days, Maureena was able to straddle Erin's back with her feet on the floor and pretend to ride her around the basement. They both cowered and whined whenever Maureena raised her voice, which she learned to do as soon as she lost a leather sandal to Fin and discovered his one bad habit—he ate shoes. He ate everything but the rubber soles, metal grommets, and the plastic tips on laces, a mixed pile of which sat in one corner of the basement near his other toys.

Fin and Erin had their half of the basement staked out. They each had a giant beanbag chair to sleep on, and Drew fed and watered them in what looked like a chicken trough. Maureena strung a bedspread between the washer and the furnace to separate an area off for her and Miller. The saving grace for Miller was that at least the dogs always went outside for the really important thing—nobody who knew better ever set foot in the backyard. And at least he and Maureena were off the road for a few days.

Which turned out to be three weeks. Drew told them to stay as long as they could stand the basement, and all he would accept in return was their offer to walk Erin once a day. Nobody but Drew could handle Fin outside the house, and even he couldn't handle both of them at once.

Drew was thirty-five and taught in the Poly-Sci Department at U.W. He made Miller feel completely welcome, and to judge from all the changing faces in the house, he did the same for almost everybody who came by. He seemed genuinely pleased with the daily chaos of so many people passing through his house. He would get up early every morning and clean the kitchen, top to bottom, and then take Fin for his morning walk in Ravenna Park, before he went to work.

It turned out Drew had helped a lot of people move to Canada, and the minute he heard Maureena mention going to B.C. he offered all kinds of advice about getting through Canadian Immigration. He suggested they have their folks wire as much money as possible—an idea that didn't sound likely to Miller or Maureena—to have at the border and then send right back. He advised they take the ferry to Victoria for the least border hassle—an idea Maureena loved immediately. He also had names of people in Vancouver to write to for phony job offer letters. Job offers carried weight at the border, he said.

Drew came downstairs pretty often, checking on the wolfhounds or Miller and Maureena, and sometimes they talked for hours. Drew talked a lot like the other profs Miller had known outside of class, as if he were stuck in the lecture mode. He would hold forth as long as they would listen—usually about the war, racism, the '68 election, Hoover. His raps would most often build up to what he called "our moment in history." He always said "our," but then he would put his hands out toward Miller and Maureena as if it was really theirs.

Most of the others in the house were much closer to Miller's age, and several were SDS dropouts—the Weather Vanguard as they put it. They usually moved around the house quietly, looking intent and serious, something like Miller imagined monks in a monastery might look. Yet they wore no robes and half of them were women. And Miller never saw anybody pray.

Grant wasn't much different. He wore a black armband all the time, and those weeks in mid-September Miller ran into Grant so rarely that he assumed he must crash in other places besides Drew's—probably wherever he fell asleep. Every time their paths did cross, Grant seemed enroute or preoccupied, or both, on his way to the copy shop or the library, late for a self-criticism session on the third floor of the house or a secret meeting on campus. The Weatherpeople were planning what Grant called an "action" in October during the Chicago Seven trial, and he was helping recruit and prepare the Seattle contingent for the trip. The only time they talked at any real length was one afternoon in Ravenna Park. Miller tried to talk about the trip to Cape Alava—he described the bright Harlequin duck he remembered so vividly—and about Carlila and the baby, but Grant wouldn't open up about that at all. Instead, he reminisced about teaching Miller to body surf at the La Jolla cove, their first year at college together. They watched kids playing on the Ravenna park swings for a half hour or so, and then Grant had to go.

On the 22nd, Maureena's birthday, she and Miller rode a ferry to Vashon Island, a place Drew told them about, where they hiked in and had a picnic in the wild country on the west side of the island. They found a sunny point, overlooking the Sound, and spread a blanket. They broke fresh bread and drank red wine and celebrated Maureena's twenty-first birthday and the first full day of fall. Miller gave her a pair of leather sandals from a thrift shop in the district. They looked almost new. He had haunted the shops, looking for a good pair in her size. And he gave her a braided leather ankle bracelet. After they ate, they sat and held hands, watching large ships and small sailboats glide up and down the Sound. The hours drifted by in a slow metronome dream. It was an idyllic day, so idyllic that Miller had the sense even as it happened, that he wouldn't really remember it.

At sunset they ferried on into Tacoma, and they spent the rest of the week there with Carlila and Durham, making two trips the long way around the Sound in the Skylark and Grant's truck, helping Carlila move pottery supplies from her folks' house up to Port Angeles.

Miller and Maureena had been back at Drew's only a few days when Grant came down to the basement early on a Friday morning and woke them up. He asked them to meet him at the HUB, the Student Union on campus, that afternoon.

He said he was leaving Seattle in two days, and it was the last local action before the trip to Chicago. He said maybe it would help them understand why he hadn't been able to make it to Cape Alava. He said it might explain why he hadn't been able to stay with Carlila. He said they might even see what the future looked like.

24

Grant's future looked like a cross between a rally, a circus, and a funeral. On the brick courtyard outside the campus HUB, surrounded by large brick buildings and the tall, well-tended campus trees, hundreds of people had assembled. Students sat at long metal tables with petitions against the war and for a long list of other causes, too—things to correct, change, end, or begin—in the U. District, Seattle, America, Cuba, and just about anywhere else.

Grant stood to one side of the microphone with about a dozen dour looking people, each with a black armband. Miller recognized a couple of them from Drew's place. A white cord hung between two trees at the side of the plaza, and at least a hundred copies of the *Time* magazine cover of Ho Chi Minh were clothespinned to it in a long row, fluttering in the breeze like a strange funereal laundry. As Miller stared at the dates beneath the face, he realized what an old man Ho Chi Minh had been. He was born in 1890, the same year as Miller's grandfather Everett.

Most of the crowd sat or sprawled across the plaza in a large uneven semicircle, spilling out onto the thick grass. Wispy clouds floated overhead, and the mid-afternoon light filtering through them seemed clarified rather than dimmed. At the edge of the crowd, people stood with books under their arms, looking curious and unsure, as if they were wondering whether to cut their next class or not. Others danced to music on portable tape recorders. Cream was singing "I'm So Glad." Frisbees flew back and forth. A few joints were passing around.

Miller and Maureena sat close to the front. They had taken Erin for her afternoon walk, and she sat next to them in the crowd, nervous and alert.

Miller didn't see Drew, but the first person to speak introduced himself as a professor of Political Science. He announced dates and times and places of assembly for the local Moratorium Marches planned for mid-October. As the prof spoke, Erin leapt up and took off at a run after a squirrel. Miller followed her and she led him on a chase all the way back to Drew's. He put her in the basement and jogged back down to the HUB, just in time to see Grant walking toward the microphone.

"Things change," Maureena said as Miller sat down next to her, out of breath. "Fast. See the woman behind Grant?" She pointed at a woman with long black hair cut straight across the small of her back. She wore tie-dyed overalls and sandals made from tire tread and leather straps.

"She just spoke," Maureena said. "She talked about the 'struggle' and the 'sisterhood.' She said ending the war was only the first step."

"Before?"

"Ending the wars on women everywhere," Maureena said. Her eyes opened wide and then narrowed. "She said she would off her own parents if it became necessary to the struggle."

"Off? Necessary?"

"Those were her words," Maureena said. "She used them more than once."

Grant stood silently, moving his eyes slowly around the crowd and the campus, his expression as contemptuous as if someone he loved had just died and he knew who to blame. He pulled his pocket watch from his jeans and held it at arm's length and swung it back and forth like a nightclub hypnotist.

"My grandfather gave my father this watch when he started college. And my father gave it to me when I did. I wound it every day for years. Then one day in '67 I just quit winding it." He looked at the watch face. Some people in the crowd laughed.

He stepped aside from the podium and dropped the watch. The crystal broke on the bricks with a small, fragile sound. It was so quiet for a moment that Miller could hear pigeons cooing in the eaves of the Student Union and the chattering of a lone squirrel high in a pine tree.

"There's no more time," Grant said. "Not for the Vietnamese patriots who've struggled thirty years for freedom. Not for oppressed people everywhere." Grant stamped his shoe on the watch and kicked it aside.

"When time runs out, there's action. The Asian peasants choose—sell out to the invaders or oppose them to the death. The Panthers choose—part of the solution or part of the problem. Now we choose. Either we carry candles and peace signs while Nixon and his stooges blow Viet Nam away with the best bombs money can buy. Or we get right in their goddamn way."

Someone yelled "Right on," and then others did, too, in a string of erratic echoes lacing around the courtyard.

"Yeah, right on. And on and on," Grant said, still not smiling. "We've learned the long hard way that right is not enough—and neither is right on." He moved his eyes from one side of the crowd to the other, pursing his lips. "The war is closer than we think. It's the Seattle police kicking freaks on 45th Street and shooting Panthers on the southside. It's right here on this campus where the war research machine ticks on night and day. It's as close as two blocks away at the R.O.T.C. hall." He pointed behind the crowd. "The war's right here in front of our faces."

He cleared his throat and coughed. Four people near the front stood up and left. The crowd was thinning out. The dancers had stopped dancing, or split, and most of the between-class onlookers had moved on.

As Grant glared at the people leaving, Miller remembered what Carlila had said in the tent at Cape Alava. Miller couldn't really recognize Grant anymore either, but yet it was him, Miller's best friend for years, up there talking as if there really was no tomorrow, as if the entire world had turned completely black and white. Miller closed his eyes and saw Grant diving into the waves in Del Mar like a kid, heard his deep full laugh as they worked in the Allenwhitts' orchard.

And other times, too, further back. The Saturday he had taken Miller up to see the L.A. harbor, on their first spring break in school. In San Pedro, they had found a white-haired Mexican man crying on the sidewalk with the dry heaves. Grant took him to a cafe and held a glass of water for him until he could drink and then bought him hot soup. He went with him to the men's room and helped him wash up. They dropped the old man at the Open Door mission, and Grant had gone inside to make sure he found a bed. It was one reason Miller had liked Grant right from the start—he seemed to do the things Miller wished he had done, but not until later, always after he had had time to think.

At the podium, Grant was speaking again, his voice intense, flat, and slow. "No one is free," he said. He clenched his fists. "Until everyone is free." The crowd seemed silent, stunned.

And so was Miller. He knew there was some truth in it. People were dying by the day, by the minute. Things weren't getting better. And if it all really did turn black and white—them or us, now or never—which way would Miller go? Studying Grant, so serious and secure on the far side of his decision, Miller realized that a part of him wanted it all to be as simple as Grant and his group said it was: *either—or*. And another part of Miller wanted to know which one he was.

Grant raised both arms over his head. "I stand with the oppressed. With the NLF and the Panthers. I stand in the way of Nixon"—he paused between each name on his list—"Hoover, Westmoreland, Reagan, Daley. And all the armies and police who do their dirty work for them."

Almost everyone still listening was on their feet. Grant and the woman in overalls and half a dozen others with them walked quietly away from the podium and through the crowd and across the courtyard as people lined up behind them.

Stop the War. Smash the State. Smash the War. Stop the State.

A band of people, six deep and nearly half a block long, marched across campus, winding back and forth between the buildings, drumming their feet to changing chants. Miller was with them. Maureena was walking next to him. All across campus people stared out of windows: the main library, Fisher Dorm, Sprague Hall.

What do we do? Cars honked as they marched across a parking lot.

Revolution. The wind gusted around them, swirling and scattering leaves.

When do we do it? Their voices drifted toward the distant blue blur of Lake Washington.

Now.

25

At Clark Hall, the R.O.T.C. building, three men and a woman marched straight to the main entrance. Grant and several others followed them toward the door.

The rest of the group gathered into a loose crowd by the stone steps in front of the building. A stack of the Ho Chi Minh *Time* photos was passed around. Miller took one and handed them on. He saw men in brown uniforms looking down on them from the second-story windows. He glanced at Maureena. She looked frightened.

"You look frightened," she said.

"I think I am."

"We should be," she said, pointing up the steps.

Two people on each side held the doors wide open as people charged inside. A guy with a short beard and a blue bandana on his head opened his bookpack and pulled out at least a dozen palm-sized cans of red spray paint. Miller stared at the cans as he stepped through the door.

Loud voices echoed in the wide wooden corridors. They had come as far as they could as a group. Hallways branched to the left and right, stairways led up and down, and behind them was the main door they had entered. On the first floor all the doors were closed and no one came out. A woman stuck a Ho photo under a name plaque on a door that read *Lt. Colonel Rathing*.

Miller heard loud footsteps and saw the creased pants and shiny black shoes of ROTC officers, racing down the upper half of the stairs. He counted five of them as they turned on the landing and started down. They lined out across the bottom step, facing at least forty people.

The officer in the middle of the steps had a dark neat crewcut that jutted out in front like the prow of a ship. He smoothed the narrow black tie that was tucked in at his belt. He cupped his hands to his mouth and bellowed at the people only ten feet away.

"This is as far as you go. All of you, out of this building. Now."

"ROTC out of this campus," someone yelled back.

"The police have been notified," the officer said, dropping his hands.

"Campus piggies," someone yelled. "The wanna-be cops."

"The Seattle police are enroute," he said. "Vacate the premises or be subject to arrest."

His fists were clenched. Miller looked around. Most of the people near him had their fists clenched. Then he saw that his were, too. He spread his fingers out. He took Maureena's hand.

"Let's leave now," she said.

As Miller nodded, he heard several spray cans hissing all at once, as if someone had spiked a tire. The front row broke apart in two directions, people running down both halls. A fat red stripe splattered across the five pairs of pants, over the bannister, and then down the wall.

"The blood of Asian children is on your hands," a woman yelled.

Bodies moved all around Miller, jostling, pushing, but he couldn't tell in what direction. A loud voice echoed from somewhere down a hall. "Trash the files."

Miller held on to Maureena's hand. He didn't want to be here.

The officers ran after the painters and most of the crowd followed them. One tall young kid in the center of the lobby flicked a lighter and a foot-long yellow flame flared up from it. Two women screamed and ran outside. Another woman yelled, "torch it."

Grant and two women were spraying on the big back wall of the stairwell landing. It looked like a dance. Miller watched, fascinated, one eye on the door, ready to run, as the big dripping letters formed words. *UW = U of War.*

Another officer leaped down the upper set of stairs three at a time. He tackled Grant from behind and knocked him face first into the wall. They wrestled and rolled on the floor. The two women kicked at the officer's legs.

Miller ran up the stairwell and grabbed the man's belt and yanked as hard as he could. He pulled him off Grant as the women ran on up to the second floor, spraying all the way. Grant was bleeding at the mouth. He was on all fours on one side of the stairwell, and the officer squatted on his heels against the wall on the other side. His black and white tag read "Captain" something, but the name was smeared with paint. They were both panting, and Miller stood frozen between them. Maureena stood halfway up the stairs, pressed against the wall. Miller heard sirens.

"Stop," Miller screamed, "stop." He wasn't sure who he was yelling at.

The captain stood and glared at him. Miller had only been in two fistfights in his life and hadn't done well in either, but he sensed the man was about to strike. He tried to remember what to do. He bent his knees, spread his feet, and raised his hands. He tightened his stomach.

"Let's get the hell out of here," he yelled over his shoulder to Grant.

"Right. You run," the captain said. "You yellow scum don't deserve to crap in the same hole with the U.S. Army."

He stepped toward Miller with his arm cocked.

"My father died for your goddamn Army," Miller said.

The officer jabbed right between Miller's upraised arms and shoved him hard in the chest. He hadn't expected it that way at all. He stumbled backwards and tripped over Grant. As Miller landed on the floor, Grant leaped up and took a wild swing at the man.

"That's what I needed," the captain said as he ducked the punch. He wound up and nailed Grant square on the mouth and knocked him backwards, and then stepped forward and stood right over Miller.

"You or your friend," he pointed at Grant, "or your fine fucking father, for that matter. You couldn't set foot in this man's army." The veins in his forehead were distended and red.

"We don't use fairies and we hang traitors by the balls." He pursed his lips, and Miller turned away just as he spit. "If they have any."

The spit streaked across Miller's ear onto the floor. He lunged for the man's legs. He kicked out, but Miller held on and pulled until he went down on his back. Just as he fell, three more uniforms appeared at the top of the steps. Miller felt Maureena grab his wrist hard, pulling him across the slick floor. He scrambled up onto his feet and they ran down the steps. Grant was right behind them, and the captain somewhere behind him. Miller hurried toward the doors, trying not to slip on the wet paint streaks and the Ho photos scattered across the lobby floor.

Maureena and Miller raced down the steps and across a parking lot into the trees. People fanned out across campus in every direction. Miller lost sight of Grant.

They slowed down to a walk. Miller took off his paint-spattered jacket and wadded it up inside-out under his arm. They didn't have any books with them, but Miller tried to look like any other student on his way to class, worrying about an assignment or a quiz.

26

They walked a long time before circling back to Drew's. The upstairs was silent and empty. Drew was nowhere to be seen, and Grant wasn't in his room.

In the basement, Fin and Erin sprawled on their beanbags. When Miller and Maureena stepped through their bedspread curtain, Durham lay on their mat, reading the book Maureena had left open, Hesse's *Demian*. Miller threw his jacket in the corner.

Before they could tell him what had happened, Durham started talking. He had to find Grant, he said. The transmission had gone out on the truck right as he and Carlila left Port Angeles to bring it to Grant. They had towed it back into town, and Durham left Carlila there and hitched into Seattle. Grant had needed the truck for the Chicago trip, but if Grant didn't show up before morning, Miller would have to break the bad news, because Durham was leaving town.

"Leaving town for where?" Miller asked.

"My dad," he said. "He has two small tumors in his stomach lining. They're operating. I talked to my mom on the phone. I have to go back."

"Omaha?"

"I'm hitching," he said. "Can you give me a ride to the freeway in the morning?"

"Sure. Sure we can. When do you have to be there?"

"They operate next week," he said, "Wednesday. I don't think I should go to the house, but maybe I can meet my mom at the hospital." Durham looked at Maureena.

Miller looked over at her, too. They had walked in silence since they left campus, and she still looked too upset to speak. He took a deep breath. Something was going on inside him, something he couldn't put in words or name. He was still high from the fight, or whatever it had been. He was furious, humiliated, scared. He closed his eyes and saw the captain's mad eyes and then the endless chain of command that stretched away behind them. The real world was ruled by fists, and all the guns and bombs that were squeezed out of them. Hoping for anything else was simply childish. Miller felt like someone had opened his chest and stepped in it, leaving nothing but a dirty footprint. Yet what could he do about it? About anything? He opened his eyes.

"I want to go to Chicago next week," he said to Maureena. It sounded right. It fit. "And we could give Durham a ride as far as Omaha while we're at it."

"I'm not going to Chicago," she said without a second's hesitation.

"Well, take your time," he said. "Thanks for giving it so much thought."

"Miller, I don't need time. Anyone half awake would be completely discouraged. But the way those people—" she pointed up and out, toward the campus, Miller guessed. "The way they want us to become inside, to fight it—no. It's too much about anger, and looking for pain. I don't need to go a thousand miles and stare down Mayor Daley to feel the grief." She looked like she was in pain. She shook her head back and forth.

"But Grant's path—what?—next we'll be wanting our own tanks and planes to stop the war with. Believe me, I have thought about it. I was there today. In case you've forgotten." She raised her voice and almost yelled. "Don't take it out on me. I don't want to go."

Fin whined from the other side of the curtain.

"Hey, what in the world's going on with you two?" Durham asked.

Miller had forgotten Durham was even there. He looked straight at Maureena.

"I'm sorry," he said. "I'm absolutely frazzled, I guess. I know what you're saying—I can see it. And I'm not about to go anywhere without you." He turned back to Durham. "We'll take you across the lake in the morning. We can get you out of town, anyway."

Then Miller started to tell him about the afternoon. Maureena interrupted.

"Steve, I'm sorry about your dad. I know it's hard to go back. But I admire you."

Miller took her hand. "Ditto for me," he said. He patted Durham on the back and let his hand rest there. "Everything she said. I think maybe I just need to get real quiet for awhile."

Maureena told the story. Miller drifted with his head in her lap, his eyes closed, wanting to believe he had dreamed the scene in the stairwell and if he fell asleep he could undream it.

When he woke up, Durham was asleep. Fin and Erin had come in and sprawled out and dozed with their heads at the edge of the mat. Maureena sat still, watching all of them sleep. Miller kissed her cheek. "How long?" he asked.

"More than an hour," she said, "but less than a day." She smiled but Miller thought there were tears in her eyes.

"Honey?"

"They're so ugly sometimes. Too ugly to see."

"Fin and Erin?" It wasn't the right time to joke, not at all, but he tried to anyway.

"The world. The people in the world. The fears in the people. The fears in me."

He put his arms around her and stroked her hair. "You let us all sleep," he whispered, "me, Durham, Fin, Erin." He pointed around the little group. Maureena smiled. "While you stayed awake and kept looking. Sometimes you're so much braver than me."

She rocked in his arms. They didn't speak for several minutes.

"Do you want to take a nap now?" he asked. He pulled his head away from her. Her eyes looked clearer. "I'll watch now. While you sleep."

She smiled and shook her head. "What I'd really like more than anything is a shower."

"Well, I know right where there's one of those."

He stood up with his hand extended. She took it and he pulled her up. Fin shook his head and snorted, deep in a dog dream.

☙

When they came back downstairs after a long hot shower together, Grant sat crosslegged on the floor, talking with Durham in a low voice. He had changed clothes and cleaned up somewhere. He had a fat lip and a swelling on the left side of his jaw, but he looked all right, and in fact, he acted more like the old Grant than the one Miller had heard speak at the HUB.

He stood up when they came in and hugged Maureena for a long time, and then he and Miller shook hands, both ways. Miller remembered the two of them practicing that special handshake in the dorm, four years before, two nervous freshmen trying to get cool with the latest hip fad. But Miller didn't remind him of that, nor did he say anything about what had happened in Clark Hall either. He thought that if Grant began preaching, he might explode, but Grant said nothing at all about the afternoon, except an hour later, right in the middle of dinner, when Maureena and Durham were talking about the recent news from the people at Edgewood in Canada. Grant put his fingers on Miller's wrist and looked him in the eye. "Thanks for the help today, Miller," he said.

That whole night Grant seemed in a better mood than anytime since they had arrived in Seattle. The four of them walked to the district and ate dinner in a cheap Chinese place, sharing from one big platter, splitting a bottle of wine, giving each other endless grief about how clumsy they were with chopsticks, and mostly just laughing. After the violence and anger at the ROTC building, it was like a big time out. Kings X's. Home base.

They walked home through Ravenna park as a half moon rose from behind Mt. Rainer. They talked about what seemed now like old times—California times, college times. They sat on the swings like kids, kicking at the worn clay ruts beneath them, pulling and twisting at the chains.

All night Miller had been expecting Grant and Durham to have words about Carlila, but they had either talked about her when Miller and Maureena were in the shower, or maybe they had seen each other some time Miller didn't know about, because they seemed to get along as well as ever. In fact, it was the two of them who resuscitated the trip idea and tailored it to fit. It could be the solution to everybody's problems, Grant said, and Durham, looking at nearly two thousand miles of thumb-time, seemed to agree, but by the time they returned to Drew's, it was well past midnight, and Maureena and Miller still hadn't decided.

The moon was high in the southern sky, high enough to cast a path of shimmering light across the glimpse of Lake Washington they could see from Drew's front porch. As they sat on the porch alone, after Durham and Grant had both gone to bed, Maureena made only two stipulations, two promises that she insisted they say outloud to each other, before she would agree to their going. One, that she and Miller stay together, and two, that they do no violence. Both of those seemed easy to say. To Miller, both of those were givens.

Less than two days later, by Sunday noon, the four of them were on I-90, crossing the lake, heading east in the Skylark toward Omaha. And Chicago.

27

Fifteen hundred miles and thirty hours later, Miller parked on a dark downtown street in front of the Greyhound bus station in Fargo, North Dakota. He stood next to the Skylark and zipped his jacket up against the cold breeze. A bus engine chugged unevenly somewhere inside the station, and its exhaust rolled out of the open bay and smelled thick and harsh in the air. A bank sign two blocks down alternated the time and temperature with an advertising slogan in quick blinks—*Fargo First National, The Finest and Friendliest.* The temperature was thirty-nine degrees and it was only seven o'clock.

In the dim light from the streetlamps, a few dry leaves scraped along the center stripe of the street. Durham pulled his duffel bag out from the back seat.

"I can hitch," Durham said. "You don't need to buy me a bus ticket. With some luck and one good ride, I can be in Omaha by morning." He pulled his wool cap over his ears. He looked like he was trying not to shiver.

Maureena opened her door and stood up outside the car, too.

"I thought we already settled it," she said. "We said we'd take you to Omaha. Fargo doesn't count. If it's too far out of the way for us to go, it's too far for you to have to hitchhike. Especially in this weather. You're not dressed for this. None of us are."

"She's right," Miller said. "The money's no big deal. Thirty bucks, tops, I'll bet. If you're going to see your folks tomorrow, you might as well not be totally wasted when you get there."

Durham shrugged. "I still don't feel right about it."

"It's beginning to feel like nobody feels right about anything anymore," Miller said. His head was still spinning from the highway. He hadn't wanted to come the North Dakota route either, but he didn't want to go an extra four hundred miles south to Omaha now. Buying Durham a bus ride was the best thing all around.

"Sign of the times, I guess," Durham said.

"Except maybe Grant," Maureena said. There was no humor in her voice.

Miller knew Durham was pissed off at Grant, too, like Maureena, and counting himself, that made all three of them. He looked again at the bank sign. The message hadn't changed, but the temperature had dropped a degree. He locked the car up, and they walked inside the station.

A woman with white hair and swollen ankles sat on one of the wooden benches, knitting the sleeve of a navy blue sweater. A beatup suitcase stood upright in front of her knees. Two longhairs, several years younger than Miller, smoked cigarettes at the far end of the same bench. They flicked their ashes on the floor, though a standup ashcan was within reach.

The long benches reminded Miller of church pews, their polished wood curving gently down and then up in smooth brown swirls. On each wall, a strip of faded Greyhound ads pictured variations on a theme—happy families boarding shiny buses for sunny summer vacations as smiling drivers welcomed them aboard. A young sleepy-looking clerk sat behind a metal-grilled ticket window on the far side of the room. His head was turned sideways, and Miller heard canned laughter from a TV somewhere behind the counter.

They walked across the station lobby toward the window. Except for under the benches, the once white tile floor was stained closer to a coffee color, and it felt gritty under Miller's boots. A sign was taped to the door of the men's room. *Out of Order.*

Miller pointed to a poster next to the ticket window, announcing a big concert at the Fargo City Auditorium. *The Association*, with *Paul Revere and the Raiders*, October 8. "Shall we stay over?" he asked, trying to joke. Durham and Maureena read the poster as the clerk checked the rate to Omaha. "It's this Friday night."

"Cherish is the word," Maureena sang slowly, smiling at him.

"The Americans are coming, the Americans are coming," Durham said.

"I guess those are two no's," Miller said. "We may never get another chance to see a mock rock concert in Fargo." The clerk behind the grill smiled.

The ticket was only twenty-four dollars. Miller cashed two traveler's checks, and Durham tagged his pack and gave it to the clerk. The next bus to Omaha didn't leave until 10 P.M. They had more than two hours to kill.

First they headed for the restrooms. Maureena stood guard while Durham and Miller used the ladies' room. Miller's hands were dusty and stiff from the steering wheel, and his eyes felt stuck open. There was no hot water and no paper towels in the wall dispenser. He washed up as best he could with the cold and dried his hands on his shirttails.

When Maureena went into the restroom, Miller picked up the wall phone next to a candy machine and dialed the number at the truck stop phone booth on the edge of town where they had dropped Grant half an hour earlier. He must have been still standing in it, because he answered on the first ring. Miller told him the bus time. Grant said the people he was expecting from Winnipeg hadn't shown yet, and he hadn't wanted to go into the truck stop because of all the locals. Miller agreed that he and Maureena would be back to pick him up a little after 10 P.M.

They hadn't eaten except rolls and coffee for breakfast in Miles City, Montana—six hundred miles back. The three of them went outside the station and wandered down the street in the direction of the bank sign and stumbled into the first place that was open, Sophie's Cafe. They stretched out in a half-round corner booth near the front window.

"So, has Grant met his mysterious contacts?" Durham asked as he passed out menus from the stand in the center of the table.

The menu had been typed on a bad typewriter. The *e*'s were faint or missing on every entry. A handwritten insert told the special of the day. *Hot turkey with mash potatoes and cranberrey sauce. $1.95.*

"I guess not," Miller said. It hadn't been until they were well into Montana that Grant had even told them about his prearranged meeting in Fargo. Some people were coming down from Winnipeg, but he wouldn't say what it was about. So instead of angling south at Billings toward Nebraska, they had curved back northeast on I-94 all the way across North Dakota.

Miller thought of Grant now, alone in a truckstop phone booth, plotting his revolution one phone call at a time. Miller imagined a camera panning down from high above for a closeup and then pulling back till the booth's tiny light faded out. Their movie. Their generation. A twenty-year-old Californian, stranded in a cold phone booth in Fargo, North Dakota. Winter on its way in from Manitoba. It seemed so absurd and stupid.

"He's waiting," Miller said. "I told him we'd be back after ten."

He put his menu down and slid closer to Maureena and looked at hers.

"What do we want? Are you two as hungry as I am?"

"Hungrier," Durham said. "I'm thinking about the turkey."

"Breakfast served twenty four hours," Maureena read from the menu. "Pancakes sound good to me. A short stack."

"The meal's on me," Durham said. "My thanks for the bus ride."

"In that case," Miller said, "maybe I'll get a fat T-Bone. And hot apple pie ala mode."

"You'll be ready for Chicago," Durham said.

"Just kidding," Miller said. "Turkey sounds good to me, too. God, I'm thirsty. I wish they'd bring us some water."

Miller looked around the cafe. Three men in flannel shirts and farm caps ate at a far booth, near the kitchen. An old man nursed a coffee at the counter. The only waitress was rearranging stale-looking pie slices in the display near the cash register. Miller stared her way for a minute, but she didn't look up.

"I'll get us some," Durham said. "Why don't you plug the box?"

He pointed at the little machine on the wall next to the booth—four metal-framed song menus with levers at the top for flipping and a number and alphabet key along each side. Three plays for a quarter.

Durham walked toward the counter. Miller fished in his pocket for a coin. Maureena flipped through the song titles, laughing to herself. Miller slid closer and looked at them, too.

The selection was strictly small-town midwest. The only remotely current songs were "In the year 2525," and a new Bobbie Gentry song that Miller hadn't heard but Maureena said wasn't too terrible. And of course, "Sugar, Sugar"—even the thought of which made Miller gag. It had been on all the AM radio stations on the way from Seattle, and every time it came on, one or the other of them flicked the dial as fast as possible. It even became a joke to see who could turn it off first. Maureena played "2525" and the Bobbie Gentry tune and left the last selection unplayed.

Bobbie Gentry came on first, just as Miller noticed Durham walking back toward the kitchen. He stopped and talked to the cook for a minute through the order slot. Miller could barely make out the man's face above the stainless steel counter, middle-aged, heavy, maybe sometimes jovial, but that was only a guess. When the man put his arm out through the slot, pointing over Durham's shoulder toward the front of the cafe, Miller saw a large blue tattoo on his forearm. His hands were creamy white and scrubbed clean.

Durham walked slowly back toward the booth. Maureena put her menu down.

"You're not going to believe this," Durham said.

"They're out of the turkey special?" Miller said.

"That's the owner." He shook his head back over his shoulder. "He's exercising the right he reserves." He pointed at a sign on the wall. "To refuse us service."

"No way," Miller said. "That doesn't happen. Those signs are from some other time zone. They're just for show. It isn't legal."

"Those signs are for Blacks," Maureena said. "And Chicanos. And maybe, around here, mostly for Native Americans."

"He said it's anybody he doesn't want to serve," Durham said. "And that if I don't believe it's legal he'll be glad to call the city police to come down and explain it to me. He was kind of fakey polite, but he isn't kidding. Not at all."

"What do we do?" Maureena said. "Serve ourselves?"

"I'll tell you what we do," Miller said. He stood up and walked to the counter. "Excuse me, ma'm," he leaned toward the waitress. "Could we please get some water?"

She wouldn't look at him. The old man a few stools down sipped his coffee and exchanged glances with her.

A rumpled Fargo paper lay open across the counter. An A.P. headline reported a battle near Da Nang that had killed fourteen Americans. Smaller print claimed two hundred Viet Cong dead. Miller folded the paper closed. He raised his voice a notch.

"My friends and I are very thirsty. We need some water over here."

Out of the corner of his eye, Miller saw the three men in the booth staring at him as they chewed. Between the stacked glasses and coffee cups, he caught sight of himself in the dusty mirror behind the counter—hair uncombed, a week's growth of beard, the peace sign patch Maureena had sewn prominently on the shoulder of the army jacket from the Goodwill in Seattle.

He looked back at their booth. Durham's hair was longer and his beard fuller than Miller's. Maureena wore tight faded jeans and her leather birthday sandals with thick purple socks. A turquoise necklace Miller had given her hung outside her sweater. Two thin silver bracelets dangled from her wrist. Miller guessed the three of them must look like something the Sophie's crowd had seen in *Life* or *Look* magazine—laughable, frivolous, yet somehow sinister, too, like clowns from a circus they had heard dark rumors about and didn't want anywhere near their town. The waitress still wouldn't look at him. He didn't move.

The kitchen doors swung open. The owner stepped out, wiping his hands on his apron.

"She just works here," he said. "This is my place. It's my right to decide who I serve. If you cause any trouble, I'm on the phone to the police. They eat breakfast here everyday. You reading me, bub?"

Miller tried to look in his eyes. He worked to not raise his voice. "I'm not trying to cause trouble," he said. "I'm way too tired to cause any trouble. We drove over six hundred miles today and we're hungry."

"I don't care if you're Paul Revere and his silly-ass Raiders just in from downtown Boston," the man said. "You're not welcome here."

Miller saw the tattoo more clearly. A large-eyed woman, her full lips parted, her long blue hair flowing down and over an exaggerated cleavage. Underneath it, the name. *Sophie.*

"Why? Can you just tell me why? Isn't that my right?"

"I don't need to," he said. "See that sign? It don't say I got to tell anybody. It's my private property. I own it."

"Okay, so you don't need to. But will you?" Miller's voice took off then, getting louder with almost every word. "Will you be decent enough to tell me to my face why you're turning three hungry people, with money—" Miller pulled a ten-dollar bill out of his pocket and held it up, "—why you're turning us out of your fine private cafe with its day-old pies and grade-school menus and 1950s juke box. Can you tell me that?"

Durham said something over Miller's shoulder about calming down. Maureena said that they would just take their business elsewhere. Miller turned toward them, his voice still too loud.

"Stay put," he said. "We're not going anywhere until Mr. Private Property here gives us one simple reason." He turned back around.

The man took two steps toward Miller. Both he and Sophie looked bigger with each step.

"All right, hotshot, you want a simple reason? How about this? I don't like your looks," he pointed at Miller, "I don't like his looks," his finger moved toward the booth, "and I don't like her looks. That's two more reasons than you asked for. Now you're not going to eat here, pal. You're not drinking my water or seeing a single stick of my silverware."

He folded his heavy arms over his chest and smiled.

"I got food on the grill, and if you don't leave my store in one minute, I call the police. Right after me and Al and Fred and James throw your hairy asses on the curb."

He said it very matter-of-factly, in a voice lower than Miller's. He looked up at the large clock on the wall. The second hand made a slow sweep past the twelve.

"That would be us," one of the men in the booth said, standing up. "In case you couldn't figure." He wiped his hands and mouth with a napkin and took a drink of water. The other two men remained sitting. A fork clinked against a plate like a cheap bell.

"Oh, I can figure," Miller said.

Suddenly he thought of where they were and what they were doing. Waiting for the bus to arrive to take a draft evader home. Waiting to take another friend to the Chicago protests. Miller took a long breath and concentrated on letting his shoulders ease down. He felt the anger drain out of him like hot water through a sieve. He smiled at the owner as he stared at Sophie.

"Thanks for the reason," he said. "It's all I wanted. Sorry we bothered you at all." Durham and Maureena had already moved to the door. Maureena handed Miller his coat, and he walked back over to the booth, folded up the three menus, and put them neatly in the rack just as they had been. Bobbie Gentry had ended and "2525" was just starting. As he arranged the menus, Miller pushed *D4* for "Sugar, Sugar."

He pulled his coat on. The wall clock's second hand passed the six and started right back up the other side. The kitchen doors swung open and then shut behind the Sophie man.

Jukebox revenge. So feeble, but the best Miller could come up with. He plugged another quarter into the machine and pushed *D4* three more times and headed for the door.

Back on the street, they saw a restaurant a block farther down, The Stockade, but it looked more expensive, and although he knew it couldn't happen twice in one night, Miller didn't feel in the mood to try their luck. He mentioned the drive-through chicken joint they had seen just after the railroad tracks on the way downtown. They walked back toward the Skylark.

"I don't want to even think about getting in the car again right now," Maureena said. "Could you just pick up the food?" She pointed into the bus station. "I'll wait inside."

"I better stay, too, then," Durham said. "This place looks like it's seen better times."

"This whole town has," Miller said. "So, three chicken dinners?"

"Bring napkins," Maureena said. She looked as tired as Miller felt. She pulled her hair back into a short nub and tied it with a ribbon.

"Paper all right?" Miller said as they turned away, but nobody could muster a laugh.

As he sat down behind the wheel, before he even started the car, Miller felt like he was still moving, like the Skylark hadn't stopped. But since when? Miles City? Seattle? Klamath Falls? Alamosa? Boise? Del Mar? Omaha? He shook his head and slapped his cheeks. He combed his fingers through his hair, and then he started the car.

He pulled a U-turn and drove past the blinking bank sign. Its brightness and steady rhythm seemed out of place on the rundown street, as if it was the only thing holding the town together. The temperature was down to thirty-three, and it had taken them almost an hour to buy one ticket and not get served three meals.

28

They sat in a row on the bus pews, eating fried chicken, cole slaw, soggy muffins, and a Pepsi apiece. Miller finished first and crumpled all the trash into the sack at his feet. He pushed it over between Maureena and Durham.

"Miller?"

"What?"

Maureena put her chicken breast down on the waxed paper in her lap. She waited until she was finished chewing.

"I think I'm not going," she said. She put her hand on his arm with her napkin between them. "To Chicago. I just can't. Durham called a friend in Omaha. He has a place. I can go with him and wait for you there."

"On the bus? Tonight?"

Miller looked from her to Durham and back again. Durham was scraping his cole slaw box with a plastic fork. Maureena looked in Miller's eyes.

"I don't want to be apart from you," she said.

Miller tried to think of the last time they had been separated for more than a night or part of a day. When she was in St. Joe's in March. Over six months.

"Me either," he said. He put his hand on top of hers where it rested on his arm. "It might be a week, ten days."

"I tried to go," she said. "I was going to go. But it'd be better if I wait in Omaha."

"Alone in Omaha?" Miller said it as if it were the end of the world. The feeling of menacing familiarity that welled up in him when he thought of Omaha was as sharp as a smell—oversweet, cloying, airless. "With your folks and all?"

"I'll be there," Durham said. "We'll take care of each other."

"You decided this just now?" Miller asked. "While I went for chicken?"

"I think I decided back there in Sophie's," she said. "I don't know. Anyway, I told you in Seattle what I thought. And now this whole deal with Grant and his secret meeting. He could be picking up guns or plans for a bomb, for all we know."

"I'm sure it's nothing that dramatic," Miller said. "The people in Seattle wouldn't even keep grass in the house, much less guns. You heard what he said—he needs to keep in touch with some concerned exiles." Grant's phrase sounded phoney and pretentious, but Miller heard himself repeating it. "You know you could be one of those yourself sometime, Durham."

"We all could be," Durham said. "But if I do go north, I won't be wasting time plotting ways to wreak havoc down here."

"Havoc?" Miller said. "Is that all it amounts to?—trying to stop a horrible war that benefits nobody but defense contractors and oil companies?"

"No," he said. "You know what I mean. Don't get mad at me, Miller. It wasn't my idea. Maureena went over and bought the ticket. I just said she could stay with me and my friend, as long as she's going."

"I'm not mad at anybody. I just don't know what the hell to do. One minute I'm eating chicken, the next minute I'm supposed to know how to say goodbye." Miller paused and blinked his eyes several times, trying to catch up to what was happening.

"You already bought the ticket?"

"I just walked in here and bought it," she said. "Before Steve even knew what I was doing. Before I did, I guess." She stared up at the Greyhound ad strips. "But I don't have to use it. I should have talked to you first."

Miller blew out a long slow breath he didn't know he had been holding in. "No, no. You must know something down deep." He pointed at her Pepsi. "Can I?"

She held it out and Miller sipped from the straw. The greasy food was beginning to hit him, and the bus station air felt hot and stale. He hadn't been able to sleep more than half an hour at a time on the highway. He tried to think clearly.

He had actually considered asking Maureena to stay in Omaha. But that was when he had assumed they would be driving right through there on I-80. He had never pictured a dingy Greyhound station in Fargo. The truth was, he didn't know what to expect in Chicago any better than she did. Grant's friends had said at least ten thousand people would be there. Things could turn very harsh. Miller might get arrested, sit down, go limp—all of those lines he had been close to crossing several times before. And he was worried about Maureena being hurt or arrested. But, just because she was a woman didn't mean she couldn't be as strong as Miller or any other man in the face of whatever happened—that was one thing the women's movement seemed to be showing everyone. And it certainly didn't mean she couldn't make her own decisions.

When Miller had mulled it over on the highway in the Skylark, mostly in the darkness of western Montana, he had realized how much his whole upbringing had made him feel he was supposed to take care of a woman. Yet if he was honest, he wasn't even sure he could take care of himself. He didn't say anything more until Maureena and Durham finished their chicken.

"Can I see the ticket?" he asked Maureena.

She pulled it out of her pocket. Miller hadn't really believed she bought it till he saw it. He stared at it. *Arrive Omaha 7:45* A.M. He would be somewhere in Wisconsin by then, closing in on Chicago. At the bottom of the ticket, he saw the words, *Refundable Only Before Departure Time*. He handed it back to Maureena.

"Look, this is crazy. I'll shine on the whole deal in Chicago. Let's all go to Omaha together, the same way we left it last March. You see your dad and mom, Durham. Maybe I'll spend some time with my mom. Then we leave together."

"For where?" Maureena said.

"I don't know. Wherever we were headed before all this."

"Turkey Flats," Durham said. "I keep telling you Edgewood, B.C.." He smiled at Maureena. "Canada's waiting."

"We don't have to know yet," Miller said. "C'mon, just sell your tickets. We can leave right now. I really don't like the idea of parting like this," he said to Maureena.

"You can't do that," she said, "what about Grant?"

Miller had completely forgotten him for a few minutes.

"Let him shift for himself. He's good at that, better than any of us, I guess. I almost feel like he just used us for this ride anyway. Sometimes I don't know what he's about anymore."

"But you can't just leave him," she said.

"No," Miller said.

"No," Durham said.

"But I could call him. I could go out and talk to him. We could put *him* on a bus, send him to Chicago with the money from these tickets. There's more than one way to skin a cat. That's my grandfather's phrase, by the way."

"My dad says that, too," Durham said.

Miller looked at him and felt tears rising and then sticking inside himself. He turned away from Maureena and Durham and stared at an Indian couple who had just come in the depot and were standing by the phone. They both had long braided black hair. She was short and pregnant, and he was lean and tall. His face was leathery and pockmarked. Miller lowered his head. He couldn't start crying, and he couldn't stop making little choked noises that sounded like he was.

"Miller, what's the matter? Honey?" Maureena put her arms around Miller.

Durham stood up. "I'll wait over there," he said.

"I must just be way too wired from not sleeping," Miller said. "I don't know. I think I'm afraid to be away from you, even for a week. I know that's weird."

"It's okay," she said. "I'll come."

"No," he said. "You made a decision. It's my choice, now. And it's not just that. Everything turns out so damned different that I ever thought it would be. I thought of Durham's dad just now, lying in the hospital, not even knowing where his son is."

"And your dad," she said.

Miller straightened up and wiped at his eyes but they were dry. His nose was stuffed up and he felt embarrassed. He stared over at the old woman, still knitting the same blue sleeve.

"What would he want me to do?"

"I don't know," she said. "Who could know? He fought for his country. He might think we're all completely deluded. He might think we're traitors." She softened her voice. "Or maybe he'd understand."

"Maybe." Miller held on to her hand. He stared at the clock. It was nine-thirty-five.

"Maybe I'll just drive Grant to Chicago and then turn around," he said. "But I can't leave him in Fargo tonight when everything he's been working toward for months starts tomorrow."

"You decide," she said. "I'll be fine. I'll be waiting."

"You know, part of me does want to stand in the way, just like he talks about," Miller said. "I sure don't buy the line a hundred percent, but Jesus, something's got to give somewhere. They can't just keep killing people ad infinitum."

He stared at the concert poster on the wall. The Indian couple stood next to it at the ticket window, counting out dollar bills.

"And my dad. I know if I even say it, it'll sound stupid and maudlin."

"You're not stupid, Miller."

"Durham's going all this way for his dad, right? Taking a big risk?"

"Yes, he is."

"Well, I feel something like that, too. Like it's partly for him."

"I understand," Maureena said.

"He was twenty-one when he enlisted after Pearl Harbor. He wanted to be a radio technician, and he ended up as a combat grave digger. He told my mom the one thing he'd never be able to forget was the sound of a bayonet blade breaking through a chestbone."

Maureen flinched and looked away. Miller stared at the floor.

"He did that. A young bookish guy, driving around Omaha on a Sunday in December, wildly in love with my mother, and four months later, he's collecting the body parts and dogtags of his friends, hating and fearing the Japanese enough to bayonet them. It killed him."

"I know," she said. "It's not just this war. All of them are connected somehow."

"Yes, they are." A bus pulled into the depot. Miller realized Durham wasn't sitting with them anymore. "Wow, I really went off. Sorry."

"You've listened about my parents," she said. "More than listened."

"Have you got the phone number and address where you'll be?"

"Durham does. I'll write them down for you. You'll call? Soon?"

"And often," he said. "Really, maybe I'll just loop through Chicago. I could do a marathon drive and be in Omaha by tomorrow night this time."

They stood up and walked toward Durham, who was leaning on the candy machine. Several other people had come into the station. The air was smokey. From a speaker somewhere, a dull voice announced that the bus had arrived for Sioux Falls, Sioux City, Omaha, Nebraska City, Kansas City, Topeka, Wichita. There would be a ten-minute layover.

Miller and Maureena went outside. As she pulled her pack out of the trunk and collected her things, he sat in the car and signed his half of the traveler's checks over to her—thirty-one twenties. He tore two out of the book and folded them up for himself. They walked around the outside of the station toward the bus that was unloading. Despite all the other stops they had heard listed, the destination above the bus windshield said simply OMAHA.

They checked Maureena's pack next to the bus where the driver was loading luggage. Durham and Miller shook hands. Miller wished him and his dad the best and said he would see him soon. Durham said not to worry, his eyes shifting toward Maureena. He told Miller to be careful. He climbed onto the bus.

People were boarding and leaving their luggage as Maureena and Miller hugged. He double-checked the phone number and address where he could reach her. Before she could argue, he gave her the traveler's checks.

"I don't want to have much cash," he said. He waved the slip of paper she had given him and then folded it up and put it in his wallet.

They hugged again, longer. When she moved toward the bus, he let go of her hand. But then she turned back to him.

"Miller, I can't. I want to stay together. I don't know what's right except that."

"Honey, it's all okay. It won't be long. I'll be careful. Whatever I do, it'll be non-violent. Just like we promised each other on Drew's porch in Seattle." He took her hand.

"And I'm breaking the other promise," she said. "I'm the one who made you say we would stay together."

"No, you're doing what you need to do," he said. "If anyone's breaking a promise, it's me. But we don't have to look at it that way."

"I don't know how to look at it."

"Me either," he said. "Except we're just a couple of people out of millions, getting older fast in the middle of a big crazy storm. Every now and then we're bound to feel like we've been blown out of our shoes."

Miller saw Durham's face in the window of the bus, watching them. The driver slammed the cargo doors and climbed on the bus.

"But we're stronger than the storm," he said. "You go ahead. I'll deliver Grant to Chicago and play it out how it feels when I get there. You help Durham see his dad by tomorrow and stay clear of what you don't believe in. And when I get to Omaha, it'll be Indian summer—I just know it. We'll pop the top down and cruise. Like always. I know we can find the right place. Together. You believe me?"

Miller looked in her eyes. They were wet. Or his were. Or both. He couldn't tell which.

"I believe you."

After she climbed the three steps into the dark bus interior, Miller went back out and sat in the Skylark until the bus pulled out. It turned next to him and he saw Maureena and Durham waving from a seat near the back, just above the lean Greyhound logo. He waved, too. Maureena blew him a kiss.

He watched the bus get smaller and smaller until it turned left several blocks past the Time-and-Temperature sign. Then he started the Skylark. He followed the path the bus had taken for a few blocks before he realized where he was going. Then he turned right on what looked like the first through street, Buchanan Avenue, and headed north toward the outskirts of town where they had left Grant.

Instead of driving across at least four rough sets of railroad track, as they had done on the way in, Buchanan took him underneath a viaduct in a block-long tunnel. There were no lights in it. Halfway through, Miller had a memory of his dad and him, driving in South Omaha when he was six or seven. They had driven through an underpass tunnel somewhere and he had let Miller reach over and turn the headlights off for just a second. Miller didn't remember why he had wanted to. Or what he had felt. Or what his father had said.

Miller flicked the Skylark's lights off just to see what it would be like. The engine echoed roughly in the tunnel, like a stupid iron creature in pain. He counted to five, feeling like he was playing some kind of perverse game with his will, or his fear. He couldn't see anything. Then his eyes started to adjust enough to make out the faint walls of the tunnel, the hood of the car, a double stripe down the center of the road, the empty seat beside him.

He flicked the lights back on. He drove out of the tunnel. He heard a train whistle and saw boxcars passing behind him in the mirror.

In the distance he spotted the tall neon sign at the truckstop where Grant would be waiting. A stoplight hanging in the center of the street swung back and forth in the wind, and the night sky looked more gray than black. It felt like it could snow.

29

Handcuffed to four other men, Miller walked through a basement door into Cook County jail at 4 A.M. the next Saturday. As the door closed behind him, he had a sense that all the menace from some horrible dream had taken shape and descended on his life.

Lockdown in the cells was at 8 P.M. Lights out at ten. Miller slept as much as he could in the daytime, avoiding everyone and everything around him—if you're not really here, maybe I'm not either. He stole fitful daytime naps during the meaningless freetimes the daily schedule allowed. Then at night he would come alive, staring at ceilings, bars, walls, floors, and the shadows that blended them all together.

Thinking, remembering, dreaming. Confined to his nutshell and counting himself king of nothing. King of shadows. King of fear.

When he couldn't think, he would read in the dim light from a bare bulb in the hallway a few feet from his cell. He sat crosslegged in the cell doorway, a World Almanac from the '50s open on his knees, one of the worn coverless copies he coveted as they made their rounds during the day, the only books allowed on the cellblock except for the Bible.

He could hear the jailer's shoes make the entire round of the floor. Stiff black leather against cold gray concrete, pacing off the rectangle of hall that enclosed the cells. Each time the guard approached, Miller would go to his cot and feign sleep. Every morning at three, a new guard would take over the rounds. But the shoes always sounded the same.

A row of inmates marched into a long gray hall with a red line painted on the floor three feet from the wall. Miller stood on it. Like every time he was taken anywhere outside his cellblock, at least twice a day, he waited for the guard's orders and then did precisely as he was told.

He took off all his clothes and stacked them in a pile on one side of the red stripe. He put his feet on the line, facing the wall, leaning forward, his palms flat against it. He waited while the guard poked through his clothes. When he spoke, Miller took his hands off the wall, put them behind himself, and bent over. He looked neither right or left and uttered no sound. The guard moved to the next man, searched the next pile of clothes, and barked the same command. "Spread it."

Sometimes the shoes sound almost friendly. They remind Miller of the day in first grade when his father came to school to pick him up. Miller was sick in the nurse's office, lying on a cot, feverish, waiting for his mother, the one who had always come to school for him before.

As his father walked down the school hall, Miller knew his step, although he didn't know how he knew it. His father put his fingers on Miller's forehead and then pulled his hand away and snapped it down as if he had touched a hot stove. Miller laughed. His father had grinned and picked Miller up and carried him out to the car.

In the dim light Miller whispers the Almanac entries outloud, trying to memorize them.

The national spelling bee champion in 1954 was William Cashmore, age 14. Margaret Owen held the speed record for one minute typing tests—170 words on October 21, 1918, in New York City on an Underwood Standard. Recorded lynchings declined throughout the century from a high of 130 in 1901 to a low of 2 in 1950.

No one was allowed a phonecall. On the second day in, Miller was given a postage paid envelope and a form letter. He filled it out in the presence of a public defender and seven other prisoners assigned to the same lawyer. The lawyer told them that the letter in place of the phonecall was Cook County's option. He advised it be sent to whomever could best help with bail or defense.

Miller sent it to Maureena at the address he had for her and Durham in Omaha, filling in his name, his jail number, his location, his crime, and his bail amount—seven thousand dollars. He wrote the amount he needed to be released—ten percent. He had to decide whether to fill in the address of a Chicago bondsman the lawyer offered or the SDS legal fund address he had memorized before his arrest. He chose the SDS address.

The officer who gave out the forms said if they wrote anything outside of the lines on the form, it wouldn't be mailed and they would not be given another. Besides the allocated spaces, there was one line for a message.

Unhurt. Sorry. Innocent. I love you. Hurry.

❧

Miller waited in line an hour for his haircut. After the fingerprints and mugshots, after the warrant charging him with Felonious Mob Action on the previous Wednesday night had been typed and sworn on Saturday morning, then came the headshaving, so drawn out and ritualized that it seemed to Miller to be the most important reason each of them was there.

It was S.O.P., he was told, depending on the admitting officer's determination on the need for sanitation. There were two ways for it to happen. You walked to the chair and sat still in it, or you were carried to the chair and strapped into it.

Of course, someone had to test that, a thin, muscular guy with a white-man's Afro who called himself Trail. After Trail was strapped down, a small wiry cop, holding a billy club in both hands, pressed it across Trail's neck toward the back of the headrest while the barber's electric clippers moaned through his thick hair.

When Miller's turn came, he sat very still.

The guys like Trail with the longest hair earned the jailers' catcalls, the mewing, the comments. "He's such a pretty girl." Or, "Goddamn, it's a boy underneath it after all."

Miller's was no big deal—only a nine-month growth. He didn't look the barber in the eye. He didn't look anybody in the eye.

The jail barber was a fat man with biceps as big as paper towel rolls and forearms the size of softball bats. Despite his size and his shears, a guard stood on either side of Miller. Hair littered the floor three inches deep. Like almost everything that happened in Cook County, the haircuts took place in a windowless room on a windowless hall, as if the abstract idea of jail had found its essential shape—an endless concrete tunnel.

ငဒ

March 1, 1954. A thermonuclear weapon was exploded on Bikini Atoll. On Kwajalein, 176 miles away, the explosion looked like a northwest sunrise. A Japanese fishing vessel reported 23 fisherman with burns. From islands near Bikini, 31 Americans and 231 natives were removed for burn treatment.

April 1, 1954. The Japanese government formally requested that the U.S. not explode atomic weapons during the tuna fishing season.

Miller hears the shoes. He smells their polish. He hides his book. He hides his eyes.

ငဒ

At night Miller daydreams about the summer. They camped on the Illinois River in southwestern Oregon on the 4th of July, the first 4th in his life when he had not seen or heard any fireworks, not a single flag or anthem. They swam nude in the river pools. Miller watched Maureena, naked on a wet sunny rock. He sat on the other side of the river, his feet dangling in a cold clear eddy.

The rapids above and below them. Ragged clouds floating across the sun. She stood slowly, smoothed her hair, stretched her arms and dove. She swam underwater toward him, the current carrying her downstream as she crossed. The time between her diving and her surfacing could have been a lifetime. Miller was alone and not alone. She was coming to him in the cool green glass between them. She surfaced so slowly. First her hands appeared on a rock ledge downstream. Then her hair bloomed from the river as she raised her head, blowing out the last of her breath with a laugh and inhaling with a grin. Miller walked to her and pulled her up out of the water. She put her arms around him and kissed him, and that, too, was a dive, a submersion, a complete lifetime in a single moment. The jewel within the jewel.

Miller hears the individual grains of dirt on the floor as the steps recede. He stares at the wall and lets his memory run like an unattended movie.

It had snowed from Fargo all across Minnesota and into Wisconsin. The trip took twice as long as it should have, including the wild trial of Wednesday afternoon rush hour as he and Grant finally rolled into Chicago. After two more hours of wrong turns, they found the McCormick Theological Seminary, one of the Weatherpeople headquarters, but police cars were already circling the streets around it, so Miller dropped Grant off and drove a mile away and parked on a side street in the early evening dark.

He hadn't slept more than an hour or two since leaving Fargo, and he hadn't eaten since breakfast. He shuffled through unfamiliar neighborhoods until he saw a hamburger joint and bought a burger bag—five medallion-sized hamburgers for a buck. Back in the Skylark, he downed the burgers with two warm beers left over from the trip, crawled in the back seat with a blanket and his sleeping bag and fell asleep. He woke up the next morning.

A block from the car, he tried the number in Omaha for Maureena from a phone booth in front of a dry cleaner's sign: *No New Wrinkles*. No one answered.

He walked to the Seminary and found out he had slept through a riot. Two people from Seattle had been wounded by gunfire. Grant had his shirt off when Miller found him, and a woman was wrapping his chest with an ace bandage. He had a cracked rib. He suggested Miller join an affinity group, five or six people who would stick together, no matter what, on the street. Miller found a foursome, and they gave him a helmet, a plastic jock cup, a gas mask. They left for a noon demonstration at the Federal Building where the Chicago Seven trial was in progress.

Riding the El, Miller felt absurd—standing like a lost football player, his helmet in his hand, the plastic cup hot and uncomfortable inside his pants, the strange mask dangling from his belt. He read the headline in the morning paper held by a seated commuter. *SDS Animals Rampage.* He looked at the others in the affinity group, two women and two men, each with gear like his. The women had emergency SDS phone numbers scrawled in ink on their arms.

At the Federal Building, lines of helmeted police behind plexiglass visors advanced to within a few feet of him. Miller couldn't see their eyes. He put his helmet on just as a woman at the podium said, "There aren't enough of us here to start a revolution."

It seemed a ferocious understatement. Miller guessed at under a thousand people, most from non-Weatherman factions. Where were the tens of thousands predicted in Seattle? Miller stared at the shaded mirror of a police visor. He remembered reading Thoreau in high school, his plea for John Brown's movement. "So many condemn them because they were so few."

Fred Hampton of the Panthers spoke next. He said the Panthers didn't support "Custeristic" actions, which seemed a bizarre reference by a black radical to a crowd of young whites. But everything was bizarre. Giant blue Chicago Police prisoner buses were parked down the block, their engines running, like school buses from a brave new world. Dozens of police kneeled on rooftops. Miller couldn't see if they had rifles or not.

Through a corridor of riot-ready cops, the march led from the Federal Building to the International Harvester plant to hear more speakers, some from the plant's union. The crowd sang "Solidarity Forever." A Weatherman sneered at them. "Songs are cheap," he said.

At mid-afternoon they rode the El back to the Seminary. Most of the affinity groups separated off, practicing how to deflect billy club blows, how to administer first-aid on the run, how to make street weapons from rolled-up newspapers, how to use the gas masks. By Friday night everyone at the Seminary, acting on the rumor of a bust, had moved to a better place, much farther from downtown, a safe-haven church in Evanston. But before they left, late that afternoon, Miller finally reached Maureena on the phone. And she told him about Durham.

CB

The 1955 Almanac says, War Ends in Indo-China. The fleeting moment of Dienbienphu.

June, 1954. A congressional act inserts the words "under God" in the Pledge to the Flag. The new pledge is recited on the Capitol steps by a group of Congressmen.

September, 1954. A radioactive egg was laid in London by a hen that had eaten protein grown in waste from the Windscale plutonium bomb plant at Sellafield, England.

Miller looks for funny things in the Almanac, but when he finds them, he can't laugh.

CB

Durham had been busted for evasion by F.B.I. agents outside his mother's house the night after his dad's operation. He told his mother that if she bailed him out, he was leaving the country. Maureena visited Durham in jail and wanted to bail him out, no matter what his plans. She told Miller she would use most of her half of the money, five hundred. What did he think?

He didn't see it as halves, he said. Whatever it takes, he said. Durham's our friend.

Maureena was in a hurry. The bondsman's office closed early on Friday. Before they hung up, Miller told her he would leave early the next morning, Saturday, and be in Omaha by nightfall. If she could hide Durham until then, they would all take off for Canada in the Skylark, and if they couldn't wait at the address he had, he would meet them by the belltower at Trinity Cathedral.

Miller drove to the Covenant Methodist church in Evanston. Again he parked several blocks away and walked from there. He helped run off hundreds of posters on the church copy machine. *All the Wars Are One Big War*—and then below it the times and speakers for Saturday's speeches and marches. He didn't see Grant until around midnight. He told him that he was leaving in the morning. He told him about Durham being busted for evasion.

Grant shook his head. "There's no flight," he said. His hands were full of the posters. He was on his way out to distribute them. "Maybe I'll see you early before you go," he said.

Miller sat in the church library around 2 A.M., listening to people talk about why they had come to Chicago. As he was wondering what in the world he would say, he heard a crashing sound that had absolutely no context in a church—something very large breaking. The only memory that came to his mind was the time he heard a foreman on a summer construction job take a sledge hammer to a window panel of glass blocks. But this was more than glass breaking. It was wood, too, and metal, and then a stifled scream, as if a person could break, too.

Miller stood up. It sounded like a football team was running down the hall. He picked up his chair and held the legs out in front of him like a circus trainer. The door burst open and police swarmed into the room, yelling orders, their guns drawn.

Within thirty seconds, Miller stood in the meeting room of the church, his hands on his head and his face to the wall. Close to two hundred people soon stood just as he did, crowded around the perimeter of the room. Miller craned his neck to see the police behind him. One of them yelled at him. Someone else down the line turned around anyway. A policeman clubbed her to the floor, hitting her shoulders and ribs. Three policemen dragged a man named Victor into the meeting room. He had been manning the card-table security desk just inside the front doors. Blood smeared the carpet behind him. Some of the police were out of uniform, several wearing White Sox jackets. They kept their guns drawn as they searched all three floors of the church.

Finally, they set up a gauntlet. Two plainclothes cops stood on either side as everyone walked down a hallway one by one. One officer stared at Miller, and he made the mistake of staring back. The officer pointed at Miller. "She looks familiar," he said.

Miller was shoved left into an office. The woman ahead of him and the man behind him were pushed right, back toward the main meeting room, while the trek in the hallway continued. Miller and about thirty others waited on the floor of the office under the guns of two policemen. Miller knew it had to be random. It was impossible that he looked familiar to anyone in Chicago. The office got hot and smelly. But Miller was shivering, his hands shaking on top of his head.

They were still shaking when the handcuffs clicked shut. Groups of five were cuffed together and herded out through the shards of glass and bits of smashed mullion from both sets of front doors. One door hung aslant from its hinges, two of its panes unbroken. Three blue paddy wagons were backed up onto the sidewalk amid a dozen patrol cars. Two long rows of police stood outside as the new prisoners started down the church steps. Miller almost expected them to start clapping.

He climbed into the wagon with the four others on his chain. The door was locked behind them, and the world shrank to fleeting lights through an iron grate. Nobody clapped.

In British Columbia there must be a high mountain lake somewhere, a perfect crater, a deep bowl that turns the sky to water, and in the lake a small island rises. That's where they'll marry. Their friends who come will stay on the shore of the lake. Their old best friends, Grant and Carlila and Durham. And all the friends they haven't met yet, many new best friends who've lived high in the mountains so long they've forgotten how to envy or compete, feel lonely or anguished, the people Miller and Maureena have wanted to be. The people who make their own clothes and brush each other's hair for hours. Miller and Maureena wave to all of them and climb to the top of the island peak. They see no parents, flags, crosses, countries. Only green trees, gray stone, blue sky, and the endless reflections on the waters of the lake. Their hands twine as they always have. Two voices speak one vow, and then they can do anything. Swim from the island to shore. Watch the sun fall and the stars brighten. Sail away together, soar over stone, rise nearer night. Miller whispers in Maureena's ear. *There is no refuge but love, yet it is endless, wide, and deep.*

ભ

August 24, 1954: President Eisenhower signed the Communist Control Act. The Justice Department intends to utterly destroy the U.S. Communist Party.

The 1953-54 U.S. Budget fits neatly on 2 pages: 40 billion dollars to the Armed Forces. School construction receives 110 million, hospital construction, 90 million. For the Atomic Energy Commission, 2 billion, the FBI, 75 million, the Soil Conservation Service, 60 million.

ભ

"We don't have no strawbosses in this jail. And no rules but the ones we make."

The head jailer had called everybody to the dayroom. It was Miller's eighth day in. The guards had picked up on what some of the SDS were up to—trying to organize the block. Proposing rules about sharing food, cigarettes, the shower. Holding meetings about how to conduct themselves in court. Suggesting demands to present to the jailers.

That same morning someone had taped a note across the TV screen in the dayroom.

7 years today—10-16—If we appear to seek the unattainable, we do so to avoid the unimaginable. Miller saw it before a guard tore it up. He didn't recognize it, but someone said it was from the Port Huron Statement, SDS' founding document. All Miller thought was that he had lost track of the date. He had thought it was the fourteenth.

The head jailer was a tall pale man with large hands and heavy eyelids that made his eyes look half closed most of the time. But they were wide open then, staring around the room.

"Anybody told to do something he don't like, he ask for me. Anybody try to be strawboss or strawboss stooge to organize this place, he got trouble." He laced his fingers and popped his knuckles. "I know what you're thinking," he smiled, "hell, I'm already in some real big-T trouble. See, your captain here's been with prisoners all his life. He understands prisoners."

He pulled a chair out from a table and put his boot on it. He leaned his elbow on his knee. He cleared his throat. "But they gotta understand me, too. Turnaround's fair game. We're standing in my jail. There ain't no lawyers or judges or mamas in here to hold any hands. There's only me and mine." He waved to the right and the left toward the four guards around him.

"So lookee here." He pulled his billy club from its sheath and laid it on the table. Then one of the guards handed him a fat phonebook. When Miller first saw it, he thought they were finally getting their phonecalls, but not so. The head jailer set the phonebook next to the blackjack and lined them up like he was arranging a place setting. Everyone was staring at them.

"That's right. Look 'em over. Just a stick and a wad of paper. But you fuck with me while you're in the steel kingdom and you'll wish you've never seen 'em." He pointed to the outside hall. "You all been up and down the stairs in our resthome, right? We move prisoners up. We move 'em down. To court, infirmary, laundry, the tanks. Now if anyayou don't believe a man can slip and fall on those steps, you just take a better look. I've had to ship men out of here in wheelchairs more than once. See, I'm the one has to write up the paperwork on any accidents."

He picked up the blackjack in his right hand. He whipped it up over his shoulder quick. Everyone in the room except the guards jumped back. He laughed.

"Now I want all you turdbags to reach your hand around and run your fingers along them little bony knobs just above your buttcrack."

Miller did exactly as he said, and everybody around him did, too.

"Them little knuckles wrap up all that keeps you walking, boys. And you hit them bones on concrete steps, and it can sure be wheelchair time." He shook his head back and forth. "Oh, boys, that's an awful thing. Why a boy can't walk, can't wiggle his toes, can't get nothin' up enough to pull on." He held the blackjack upright at his crotch and grinned. Then he frowned. "Can't even shit."

As he said the last word, he lifted the blackjack and swung it down hard against the phonebook. It made a dull heavy sound like a brick hitting a rotten board. The table shook. Miller still had his fingers on his spine. He twitched.

The jailer turned and handed the phonebook back to the guard next to him. He sheathed his blackjack. He smiled. "End of class. You all just chew on it. And by the way," he turned to the guards. "Did any member of the staff threaten any prisoner here today?"

"Not today," said the guards in unison. The jailer smiled and walked out.

For three nights, it rains. Miller hears it above him, thousands of fingertips tapping on a stone skull. The rain makes the shoes fainter. He listens harder for them. He needs their clock of pain. Without them there is no time.

The men who own the shoes don't know Miller's awake. No one knows. The bail hasn't come, won't ever come. The shoes make a hundred rounds, ten thousand steps.

He doesn't want to be dead, yet he finds a calm dark pleasure in knowing he could be. He wants to be asleep from here and now. Here has a concrete heart. Now has leather hands.

The jailers took his bootlaces and belt. When Miller walks, his boots flop like cardboard boxes. He stares at them now in the shadows across the cell. Their tongues loll out like the swollen tongues of two hanged men—cattle rustlers, army deserters, union organizers. Black boys with missing lips. Yellow boys with no ears. These are Miller's last two friends—he'll cut them down from the gallows when the crowd's gone home. They want to tell him something. They want to tell him how.

A sheet around his neck, then tied to the highest cross bar in the door. He thinks it through, pictures each detail. It requires the cot pulled near the door, his pants tied around his folded legs with his knees tight to his chest so he can't stand up.

Or the iron cot, tipped up on end, and his head on the floor face down with his foot stretched to kick the cot down behind him. If the iron leg hits the base of the skull, it could be quick and painless. But noisy and unlikely, too.

Or the sink faucet. It's rusted out and one side of the lip is ragged, almost sharp. Miller could hold a wrist under it and with his other hand pull up as hard as he can and then shove his arm sidewise to catch the artery. Then get back in bed, wrap the arm in the blanket, and hope for the worst—empty by morning.

The shoes shuffle out of the drumming rain. Miller closes his eyes on himself.

∝

On the twelfth day, his bail was cut in half. He hadn't heard a word on the money from Maureena. He had thirty seconds in front of a judge. He asked if he could make one phone call to notify the sender of the new amount. The judge looked bored. He instructed Miller's bailiff to see to it.

In a hall outside the holding tank, standing with a line of inmates behind him, Miller tried Maureena, Collect. No answer. He tried his mother, Collect. No answer. He thought about calling her at work. He thought about calling the Ocears. He handed the phone to the next man.

On the sixteenth day, Miller was assigned new counsel, Mr. Sloane, who arranged for the two of them to talk one-on-one. Miller told him the bail money should have arrived ten days ago.

"And you're positive it was sent?"

"If the letter from here was ever mailed," Miller said. "Maureena had the cash—I know she would have sent it. If I didn't believe that, I'd be raving by now."

"They do mail the bail letters," he said. "I guarantee that. When and where was she sending it? I can try to check on it."

Miller told him the date and the SDS Defense Fund address. Sloane looked at the ceiling.

"Sorry," he said. "I can look into it, but I don't need to. You're not the first one. Checks sent to that address and payee have been pooled and used to get their most important people released first. I would hazard to guess that's why you're still here."

Miller stared at his laceless shoes. He didn't feel important. Not to Sloane. Certainly not to SDS. Not to the shoes on the block. Not to himself.

"Can you have another check sent?" Sloane asked.

"I don't know," he said. "Maybe my mother."

He dreaded asking her, dreaded even telling her where he was. On short notice, she would probably have to ask his grandfather— another one for the account books.

"I have a car," Miller said. "If it's still in Evanston where I left it. It's worth more than three-fifty. Maybe five hundred."

Sloane looked at the papers on the table. "Your trial date's set for ten days from today," he said. "I can probably delay it."

"By the way," Miller said, "I'm innocent."

"I'm sure," Sloane said, looking up. "You were under a moral obligation to run through Chicago breaking glass and throwing bricks at the police. You had to do it to halt the worldwide imperialist destruction of the United States."

"I guess you don't care much for this batch of clients," Miller said.

"I don't support the war," he said. "But I do believe in government. If it makes mistakes, we do something about it short of street rioting."

"Is that what Viet Nam is?" Miller asked. "Five, ten, fifteen years of it? Just a mistake? Like a misspelled word? A low pitch in the dirt?"

"I'm not here to debate politics," Sloane said. "I've been assigned to you to fulfill your rights guaranteed under the Constitution. I trust the irony isn't entirely lost on you."

"And I trust it might be important for you to know I was sound asleep in my car a mile from McCormick Seminary from 8 P.M. on that Wednesday night until daybreak. I never went near Lincoln Park or the Gold Coast."

"Can you prove that?"

"Like how?"

"Then it doesn't much matter. There's no sympathy for you people in the city." He looked down at the papers again, running his fingers across them. "You're charged with Felony Mob Action. A sworn affadavit from Detective Rudolph Ryan alleges you were seen, and I quote, in or near Lincoln Park on Wednesday, 10/6/69, at 9 P.M., in an unlawful crowd of people carrying clubs, bricks, pipes, etc., unquote. Do you know the kind of sentence you're looking at here?"

"On the cellblock they said one to five years."

"Plus one to five thousand dollars. If you have a defense, comrade, we need to prepare it soon, as in posthaste. You need to get out of here so that when you do stand before that judge you look like a college student and not an inmate. Do you own a suit?"

Miller didn't hear him. He was staring deep into the tunnel. A year into it was farther than he could see. Five years was miles below the ninth circle, no light on either end. He thought of the rusted faucet lip in the cell. He wouldn't ever do that, would he?

"Mr. Silas?" Sloane tapped the table with his pencil.

"Sorry. Look, I've been here two weeks, and I can barely see my way through tonight. I can't sleep at all. And you're talking about years? This is impossible."

"Then I strongly suggest you plead guilty to a lesser charge."

"Isn't it my word against this Ryan guy's? What if I could find people to swear I wasn't there?" He thought of Grant. Or any of the others he met Thursday morning at the Seminary.

"It's up to you," Sloane said. "You certainly have the right to a jury trial. But I'd advise postponing it at least six to nine months. And that involves considerable legal fees. Plus you'd have to bring your witnesses back to Chicago."

"What lesser charge?"

"I'll talk to the prosecutor's office. I would think misdemeanor mob action—a maximum of six months. And probably better. The jails are overcrowded with you people. So are the courts. You have no record. I think they might be amenable."

"And the fact that I wasn't even near Lincoln Park that night?"

"I'll pass it on." He stood up. "I'll see you before the trial date. If you get your bail, my office is in the County Courthouse." He gave Miller a card and gathered his papers. "I hope you sleep soon, Mr. Silas."

30

Miller didn't hear the guard's shoes until they stepped into the cell. It was seven in the morning, just before breakfast call. He had dozed off for a few minutes, the '58 Almanac open on his chest. He wouldn't finish it or the '59.

"Silas," the guard said. "Monkey time."

Miller had heard them say it before. He never understood it. He slipped on his boots. Sloane had cut a deal. Miller pleaded Guilty to State Disorderly Conduct, a misdemeanor, and was given time served—twenty-six days and a few odd hours—plus two hundred fifty dollars, payable before release. Miller said he would have the money wired. He called Maureena. Still no answer. He called his mother at work. She said she'd borrow it and wire it as soon as she could. He waited in a holding tank, praying he wouldn't spend another night listening to the shoes. He was amazed when the money came by ten.

His mother had sent fifty dollars extra. The jail clerk cashed her wire, paid the fine, and gave Miller the balance, along with his effects—car keys, his wallet, his coat, and a sand dollar cracked in two pieces. He took a city bus out to Evanston and found his duffel bag in the church basement in a pile labeled "Unclaimed—October." The front church doors had been replaced.

He walked to where he had left the Skylark. It was gone. He called the Police Impound Unit. It hadn't been impounded. Miller figured that either it had been stolen or Grant had it. He had known where it was parked, and Miller remembered Grant showing him how to hotwire it once in California when Miller had lost the keys at the beach.

Miller called the police again. There was no record of an arrest for a Grant Trayn.

He took two buses to the Union Pacific train station and bought a coach ticket to Omaha on the *City of Los Angeles*. He stared at the name on the ticket. It was the same train Maureena and he had ridden from Omaha to L.A. in the fall of '65 to start college—or the same name, anyway. They had made love under a blanket in the back of the observation car in the middle of the night in Colorado.

Waiting for the train, he called his mother again. She wasn't at work. She had called in sick for the afternoon. He called her at home.

"Are you all right, Mom?"

"It's just been such a shock," she said. "When are you coming home, Miller?"

"Tonight," he said, "on the train. The Skylark's gone. I'm hoping Grant has it. I'll get it back. Have you talked to Maureena?"

"No."

"She was back in Omaha," he said. "Before I got arrested. I think she must still be there, but I can't reach her. Did you hear about Steve Durham?"

She hadn't. Miller saw the thousands of circles in each town, most of them never overlapping. He said he would be in on the *City of Los Angeles* at 2 A.M.

"Mom, thanks so much for sending the money."

"You can thank your grandfather. I had to lie to him, Miller. I told him you'd been arrested and fined, but I said you'd been fighting at a party."

"I appreciate it however you got it. I think Maureena sent my money weeks ago but there was a mixup and somebody else used it. You saved me. It was terrible in there."

Evelyn started to cry on the other end of the line.

"Don't, Mom. I'm fine. Nobody hurt me. It was just three weeks. I'll be fine."

As he heard himself say it, he realized he would be. Maybe he could have survived a year. Maybe we were always stronger than we thought. If that was true, it was good. Very good.

"Can I ask you one more big favor?"

"You know I'd do anything in the world for you," she said. "I can't stand to think of you being hurt." She was still crying.

"Call the Ocears and ask for Maureena. Don't say who you are. Say you're from Pitzer College or something. Find out if she's there or if they have a number for her. If I call, they'll just hang up on me. Have her meet me at the station if she can. Please."

"I can meet you, honey," she said.

"That'd be great. But I want to see her, too. Promise you'll call."

"Oh Miller. I always told you it's not right to lie.

"But sometimes you have to, don't you?"

It was what she had taught him through all the years of dealing with her family. White lies, they always called them. Miller wasn't sure he had ever said it back to her.

"Yes," she said. She blew her nose. "Sometimes you have to."

"Thanks. I'm sorry for all this mess. I'll pay grandpa back. I had to come here, Mom. It was a mistake—I know that now, but I had to try. I never wanted the world to be the way it is."

"None of us did," she said.

∞

Miller had a double seat to himself on the train. He stretched out and watched Chicago diffuse and recede in the late afternoon light. The trees had lost most of their leaves while he was in jail. It was November. Miller felt like he had missed a whole season, his favorite one.

He had no real plan for what he would do in Omaha with no car and no money to speak of. But he would find Maureena. Even if his mother didn't have any luck. Probably Maureena hadn't let her parents know she was back. Maybe she had pulled the long-distance phone trick again. Or maybe she and Durham had left Miller a message at Trinity Cathedral. Maybe Grant had dropped off the Skylark in Omaha.

The train hadn't been out of Chicago more than thirty minutes when he fell hard asleep. He only woke up twice. Once when the conductor walked by calling a station and he jerked awake. He thought he was still in Cook County jail. The other time was on the long bridge over the Mississippi when his eyes opened and he stared down into the river. He had been dreaming he was on a train, but with Maureena, and he tried to hold onto the dream.

They were in the observation car with a bubble dome. No one else was in the car, and no one else was on the train at all. Outside, the sun rose and fell every few minutes. Maureena pushed a button and the bubble overhead floated away. The air was warm, and there was no wind, not even from their movement. They were over an ocean.

Where are we going? he had asked Maureena. The sun neared the horizon. Miller blinked and it had sunk. Viet Nam, she said, The war's gone. The stars whirled across the night, thin tracers arcing behind them. A crescent moon shone halfway up the sky. You tunneled too long, she said, The world's changed—everyone's forgiven. Miller's smile felt big and full. It's our honeymoon, she said, And they want to see you. Why me? he asked. You're the last one, she said, Do you forgive? Yes, he said, Sure I do.

Tell them, she said, pointing away from the train. The sun was rising. Crowds of people lined the shore ahead of them. Americans and Vietnamese both. Soldiers, peasants, students, women, men, and children. They were all waving and blowing kisses. Miller recognized a few of them. He waved back, happy to see them. Then he recognized all of them.

Tell them, Maureena said, Go ahead, you're the last one. The train slowed. Miller couldn't see the sun, but there were no shadows on the water.

Yes, he said, Me, too. I forgive, too.

31

"Omaha. Omaha. Omaha, this stop. Omaha. Omaha."

Miller woke up to the conductor's bass drone, heard the door tone of it change as he walked down the aisle and then away. When the voice disappeared in the metallic bluster of the vestibule, Miller sat up. The train stopped.

He stepped down into the half-lit world of the train platform, the yellowish light diffused through dirty air, the worn concrete stained with the stink of hot steel. Open to the night sky on both ends, the platform led toward a long flight of steps and a wide escalator that both rose up toward street level.

Several cars down, his mother and grandfather stood by an upright iron I-beam column, freshly painted bright red. He wore a long dark overcoat and gray hat, his hands behind his back, his shoulders and head straight and high, as if he still scheduled the trains around him and always would. She waited next to him in her highheels, her 1940s hairstyle and makeup still perfectly in place a quarter century after the war whose pinups they mimicked had ended, her right hand holding her signature Lucky Strike cigarette at a casual angle.

His mother saw him and pointed and started to wave with her cigarette hand and then stopped. Miller walked toward them. Only his grandfather moved in his direction. A few other passengers grabbed baggage and quickly headed for the escalator. The train's huge wheels gave off a warm rusty smell, as if iron could sweat.

Miller didn't relish facing his grandfather. He wished his mother hadn't brought him. Would he have to charade through the story of a wild party and a fight? He wished Maureena had been there alone and it could have been just the two of them. His grandfather and mother could have waited until later—much later.

He was taller than Miller, like always. He stuck out his hand, like always. "Miller, hello, your mother wanted me to bring her down to meet you."

"Hi, Grandpa." Miller let go of his hand.

Everett stared at Miller, yet Miller felt him hesitating, as if he was about to ask an important favor, but that was impossible—the flow of favors and gratitude between him and the rest of the family was as rigidly directed as the east- and west-bound trains around them. Miller leaned over for his bag. Everett grabbed it first. Miller looked at his mother, watching them in the distance.

"I can get it," he said.

His grandfather set the bag back down. He still stared.

"Grandpa, I appreciate the help. I'll pay you back as soon as I can."

"You and I can settle our accounts later." He reached for the bag again but then stopped short. "Miller, your mother can't tell you. And you don't have a father."

"Tell me what?"

"Your friend, Maureena Ocear. Well." He paused as an outbound train jerked away from the station. Miller thought he felt the concrete beneath his feet vibrate.

"Well, your mother talked to her doctor. You knew that she'd attempted suicide before, didn't you?"

"Who? Clotter? Why? What's going on?"

"This is a time to be a man, son. It's not easy for either of us here. Almost a week ago. The first of November. Apparently she was successful."

"Successful?"

The smoke and steam from the departing train made the air smell. The light was even hazier than before.

"What do you mean, successful? Why are you here?"

"She's gone. She's passed away. She's dead, Miller. I'm sorry. I'm telling you because you never really had a father and your mother can't." He picked up Miller's bag again and Miller took one step away from him. "I have my car in front of the station. We'll take you home."

Miller started to sway back and forth. He could hear people talking all up and down the tracks, half a dozen conversations clear all at once, unpaired questions and answers swirling and rising from the travelers' lives like debris surfacing in an eddy below rough rapids. There was way too much to sort out. Who kept tabs on it all?

He spread his feet wide apart to keep from falling down. He saw his mother crying and coming toward them now. He held his hand out to his grandfather and looked at it with a blank curiosity. It seemed to be someone else's. The arm was rigid, the elbow and wrist at an awkward angle, as if whoever it belonged to was practicing protocol from some foreign land. Everett looked surprised but grabbed it. They shook hands again.

"Can I have my bag?"

Everett set it down, but Miller didn't pick it up. He felt ten feet above himself, looking down on a body that would never be big enough for him again. Such a little body. Shouldn't it be wailing, scratching at its eyes, pulling at its hair? But it didn't need him. He had trained it well, and now was the time to let it go off on its own. It could go through all the motions. No one would ever know the difference.

"Miller? Miller? C'mon, boy. Don't break down on us."

His grandfather's hand tried to let go, but Miller's hand didn't want to. It squeezed harder, pumped up and down, the same way Everett had always greeted Miller's cousins and him at his house on holidays when they were kids. But his grandfather didn't seem to recognize his own doorway routine, or he didn't think now was the time for horseplay. This was no holiday. Halloween was over and Thanksgiving was still weeks away.

His hand still locked in Miller's, Everett lowered and projected his voice—his best Methodist baritone. "These are the times that try men's souls." Then he added, in his normal voice, the railroadman's. "I know it hurts, and I know there's nothing we can do."

Evelyn came up to them and rushed at Miller and put her arms around him. He rested his other arm around her and kept shaking his grandfather's hand. He felt hot, as if it were a mid-July noon instead of an early November midnight. He inhaled a thick waft of bread smell from the Butternut factory blocks away. His mother cried into his shoulder, into his ear, drowning out all the other eavesdrop din. In her ragged wet breath, Miller heard the Missouri River, lapping at the edge of Nebraska, six blocks away. He saw the dark swirling water, racing away in the night, grazing the skin of the city like a roiling phantom. It kept washing up at the shore of his shoulder, lapping, splashing.

"When was this?" he asked his mother's hair.

"A week. Oh, son. I didn't know where you were when I saw it in the paper."

"You're making this up, aren't you?"

"No. Miller. How could you say that?"

"You talked to Dr. Clotter?"

"Yes, the Ocears had him call me, when I called them."

"So you're all in on it together."

"Let go of my hand, boy," his grandfather said. "Let go now."

Miller looked up from their entwined white hands, looked at his face for the first time since he had said the word—dead. His eyes were strained and confused.

"Don't talk crazy at your mother. She feels bad for you, too."

Miller dropped his hand. He stood back from them both.

"But how?"

"Miller, honey, let's go home. Let's not talk about it here."

"I don't have a home," he said. "I live on the train."

"He's not himself, Evelyn," Everett said. "He's gone into the state of shock." He put his arm around her.

"But how?" Miller asked again.

"In her parents' car," she said. "In her parents' garage." She cried even harder. "Automobile exhaust."

People walked by. From high above, Miller saw them averting their glances, embarrassed for them, the scene too real for this stop in their scheduled lives. Miller wanted to slap them. Every one of them. He wanted to slap his grandfather and his mother both. He wasn't going to buy into any of their bullshit.

"And, I suppose you went to her funeral, Mom? You saw her?"

"No. They had a private service."

Miller tried to smile, but his face felt too brittle. It wouldn't do to break it here, in front of all these people. "Then she's not dead. I'll find her. Nobody can keep us apart with a trick like this." He hiked his bag onto his shoulder. "I'll wait on the train till you tell me the truth." He turned away and walked toward the train wheels. He kept speaking as he walked. "I've been waiting my whole life for the truth. I'll just get back on this train and wait a little longer."

"Miller," his mother sobbed, but his bird's-eye self heard how unconvincing she was. Someone must have threatened her. Miller remembered Richard Ocear slurring his father. And Maureena warning about Richard's anger.

"It was in the *World-Herald*," she yelled after him. "I saw the obituary."

Miller stepped onto the steps of a coach car. He didn't have time for this. Who were these people? How did he know this was his real mother or grandfather. This could have been a setup, going back to the very beginning. He had to find Maureena and it would take every bit of cunning he could come up with. He was just learning the rules of the game. It was all closing down. Cook County was just a warmup. If he didn't find Maureena and get out of the country with her quick … he shuddered. He heard Grant's voice, a terse warning, repeated again and again to the rhythm of the copier's mechanical whisper in the Evanston Church. *No flight.*

Miller held onto the step railing and turned back to them.

"The *World-Herald*," he said. "That's only paper. I don't believe in paper anymore." He laughed. From high above, he saw the little Miller that was left down below again, circling the dangerous whirlpool edges of a bottomless need, while these two old movie actors in period costumes were talking about the newspaper.

"Newsprint," he yelled. "Fishwrap. I'm tired of all these lies."

He couldn't quit laughing. He went into the train and raced down the aisles as if he could find a coach that was still moving, that had never come to rest.

He had to escape. He'd stopped at the wrong place. He'd picked the wrong hometown.

℥

Miller found an empty spot in the last seat of the last car. That way he could be sure no one would come up behind him. He gazed out the window at a string of boxcars moving backwards and stared at them until he was convinced he was moving forward.

He counted the engines. One, two, three, four. How did they work together? If you welded two or three automobiles together and then drove them with all the engines running, could they go three times as fast? Miller had always wanted to see two locomotives hooked together, one forward, one backward, going nowhere, running in place. Total energy, zero movement. Yes, he had been fascinated with trains as far back as he could remember— that was something he could count on. Train—Track—Train. Train—Track—Train. It was a nice little song.

"Miller. You've got to get hold of yourself."

It was his grandfather again. They must not have arrived in L.A. yet. Had they not even left Omaha?

"You have to get off this train. You don't have a ticket. You're back in Omaha now. Your mother is a wreck, son. Straighten up."

Miller listened closely for clues and code. Think through the words. His mother was a wreck, a junked car, like the six-month-old Ford her husband died in. Afterwards, a Hastings scrapyard had paid seventy-five dollars for it—was that enough for a train ticket? And Miller? He needed to get hold of himself, like a TV wrestler, a furniture mover. Bend with your legs, get a good grip. Now slowly pull your self up by the bootstraps. After that, lift the wreck of your mother. Find out who's been pinned beneath her all these years.

"Miller, listen to me. I brought something for you."

He pulled out a piece of paper from his pocket. Miller saw lines of type. He closed his eyes tight. This was too much. He plugged his ears. Was there no mercy on this train?

"I won't look. I won't listen. Anyone can fake an obituary. They do it in Journalism classes all day long." Inside him a voice chanted. The wrong girl. The wrong twin. The wrong train in the wrong town in the wrong world. The chant had cracked the code. The world was a case of mistaken identity.

"No, it's not that, Miller. Just listen to me, now. When I was fourteen, my oldest brother Eldon died. A horse kicked him on the farm outside Atchison. I was the one to find him. The side of his head was swelled up like a cantaloupe." He stopped and stared out through the train window. "He was my mom's favorite child. He was my favorite brother. My father read this poem at our table the first Sunday after he died." He waved the sheet of paper in his hand. "It helped us all go back to the work that needed to be done."

He cleared his throat to begin. "*If you can keep your head when all about you are losing theirs and blaming it on you.*"

Miller recognized the Kipling poem from somewhere in grade school. But all he could remember was the ending that even the first time had made him feel set-up somehow. His grandfather read quickly as if it were one long sentence. He raised his voice for emphasis.

"*If you can meet with Triumph and Disaster and treat those two imposters just the same.*"

Miller opened his eyes and looked at Everett. He had taken his hat off. He was almost bald. As he read, Miller stared at the shiny, freckled skin on top of his head—a blotted, faded map smeared on a dull, clouded mirror. He had his reading glasses on and sat on the chair arm across the aisle from Miller. He wore a tweed coat under his overcoat. The skin of his hands was veiny and loose. The paper shook as he read.

He was a seventy-nine-year-old Burlington man from Kansas who believed in Rudyard Kipling, the poet of the British Empire.

It was the best he could do, and maybe it wasn't all that bad—who really knew? Yet if Miller tried to explain to the old man where he had been the past day, or month, and for what twist of reasons, Everett would have few options. He would think Miller had gone crazy, or been brainwashed, or poisoned by Communist college notions, or finally revealed the rot in the genes from a drunkard father. They were two generations, a few wars, and a thousand years apart.

Miller felt sorry for his grandfather and his mother both, even as they amazed him. They understood nothing and went ahead and lived their lives anyway. And Miller, the deep undergrad thinker, the big college philosopher, Class of '69—Mister Make It All Up On Your Own—yeah, he understood everything and couldn't make a move to save his life. To save hers.

Everett finished, his voice cracking on the last word of the poem. Miller suddenly realized he had been disappointed with only two daughters.

"*And, which is more, you'll be a man, my son.*"

He stood up and folded his paper. Miller looked beyond him, out the window. His mother had walked down to the end of the train, staring blankly in their direction as if at a solid wall, smoking and crying. In her blank gaze, Miller knew she couldn't see them through the windows in the station light, couldn't make out the father and the son who had pulled at either end of life until her own existence had been stretched thin.

In the cramped car, Miller was back in his little body and it hurt all over. He didn't trust himself to be able to walk or talk or think straight. He wanted to believe this was only the latest, biggest, most intricate lie of his life, but how could it be? His grandfather had chased him the length of the train with his wrinkled Kipling poem, his brother's memory, his admonition. His mother stood stranded in the station at midnight with her mascara rinsed by tears, her makeup smudged around her collar like a dirty necklace. Miller moved into the aisle.

"I'm sorry about your brother, Grandpa."

∞

They didn't speak on the way up the escalator and across the marble floor of the station. When Miller saw passengers waiting on wooden benches under the vaulted ceiling, he thought of the Greyhound station's benches in Fargo, and the confusion of that night welled up from his stomach in a bitter bile of regret.

He walked to the drinking fountain and splashed water in his face while Evelyn and Everett waited at the big revolving door. He looked past them to the row of Yellow Cabs waiting in the circle drive beyond the entrance. He drank deep, washing down the acrid taste of the bile. He pulled his bandana out and wiped his face.

He took a full breath. Acting time.

They walked to his grandfather's spotless pale-green '64 Chevy, a chilly wind blowing through their coats. Miller faced the lights of downtown a few blocks away, letting them pour into his eyes without seeing anything. The skyline looked two-dimensional and phony, a fake backdrop in a late-night rerun movie.

"Mom, Grandpa, thanks for coming to meet me. And thanks for getting me out of a bad jam in Chicago. I'm sorry I lost control of myself down there."

He pointed back to the outside steps that led to the tracks below. His mother smiled weakly. Everett had his car keys out. He stood by the trunk.

"But, I don't want to come home. I'm really not sure what I want. But I can't sleep right now. I slept all the way from Chicago. I don't want to be inside anywhere for awhile."

He rolled his head around and raised his hand toward the night sky.

"I have some friends that I can see. Some mutual friends of mine and—mine and hers." He struggled to keep his voice level. If he had to say her name outloud . . .

"Honey, just come on home. You need a place to be quiet and safe."

"I'll come later," he said. "Right now I just really need to walk."

He lifted his bag and leaned and kissed her on the cheek, smelling the familiar powder and perfume of all her expectations and defense. He nodded at his grandfather.

"I'll take you home, Evelyn," he said. "I think the boy's all right now. I talked to him. Maybe he needs some time to himself now."

Miller faked one more brittle smile, turned around, and started walking south on Eighth Street. He waited till he had gone half a block before he looked up from the pavement. They drove by slowly. He waved. His mother put her hand against the glass.

When they turned west on Mason Street and disappeared, Miller wheeled around and went back to the station. He walked to the head of the line of cabs and opened the back door of the first one.

He knew where he had to go. And he knew how he had to get there. None of it had anything to do with words or thoughts. It came from somewhere else, a ragged cave far beneath intention. He was finally winging it. Like a bird in thick clouds on a cold dark night.

"Where to, partner?"

"St. Joe's."

"The hospital?" The cabbie reached for the meter lever.

"What else is there?"

"The church."

"No, the hospital."

Miller saw the disappointment on the man's face in the mirror. It was only two miles away. Miller could have walked and saved himself a buck and spared the cabbie a wait at the end of the line when he returned to the station.

But the color of the cab was right. St. Joe's might not even be where he had last left it if he didn't return correctly. He felt like he had been dropped into an alien country where every single detail was important. Every nuance could be part of a plan to fool him into believing that a landscape he couldn't possibly live in—life without Maureena—was the real and only world.

As they pulled around the circle, Miller gazed at the downtown skyline again, its angular shapes staining a paper-thin sky. He no longer had any idea at all how deep the deception went.

The cabbie cranked the lever on the meter down. Forty-five cents and counting.

32

Miller walked into St. Joe's as if he owned the place. He took the elevator to the fourth floor and walked by the nurses' station for the A.P.W. A young nurse talked on the phone, her back half turned, her manicured finger twisting at a dark curl, her sleepy smile half visible—a sweetheart on the line.

Lights were dimmed and everyone seemed asleep in the ward. Just as they should be? Or every actor on cue? He moved close to each bed to see the faces. He was only as far as the second bed when the nurse ran up behind him.

"What are you doing? You can't be in here in the middle of the night."

He ignored her. In the third bed, he saw bright blond hair on a pillow. He went closer. But it was a man—he was in the wrong part of the ward. He looked across the aisle. Men there, too. Had they changed things? He looked back toward the nurse station and saw the female ward beyond it. Left, not right.

"You aren't allowed," the nurse said in a harsh whisper. "Who are you?"

Miller turned on her. His eyes in the dark room felt as large and blank as half-dollars. She wasn't much older than him, but he peered down at her as if she were a child.

"Mr. Frank N. Stein," he whispered back at her. "Who wants to know?"

It had the desired effect. She dropped back three steps and trailed him at a distance as he stepped into the hall toward the female ward.

"I'm getting security," she said.

"A neat trick if you can pull it off," Miller said.

She went behind the desk, the receiver still open, lying on a clipboard. The sweetheart was on hold.

Miller checked every bed within a minute, but Maureena wasn't there. But of course, that would have been too easy. This was not going to be easy.

He walked back out. The nurse had the phone at her ear again but wasn't speaking, her face crimped and impatient, waiting. He went right toward her.

"I'll call 9-1-1," she said. "Stay away from me."

"Don't do that," he said. "Call Marcus Clotter. Tell him Miller Silas is here. Tell him I'll take this place apart piece by piece if that's what it takes to find Maureena."

She stared at Miller. He felt strong enough to do it, to do anything. Why had he been feigning weakness all these years? He lifted the end of the oak desk just far enough for the loose papers to slide toward her.

"Did you get that?"

"*Doctor* Clotter?"

"That one," Miller said. "Call him." He set the desk back down. He let his eyes relax. "Please," he said. "It's a matter of life and . . ." he paused, waiting for the dark twin word to surface— pepper and salt, winter and summer, night and day. The nurse was waiting. But the well failed. "Life and life," he said. He turned and walked to the elevator. He leaned on its doors.

"Where will you wait?" She called out after him.

He turned to her. Now his eyes wouldn't quit closing. A long breath blew out of him, his chest caving with a breezy groan. It occurred to him that he had been forgetting to breathe. Wasn't someone supposed to keep track of that? He leaned harder against the elevator door. The reliable steel of it felt good against his shoulder.

She stood up, the phone in her hand.

"Where should I tell him you'll be?" She asked again. She didn't sound afraid anymore. The elevator doors slid open, and Miller pushed himself upright before he fell.

"The chapel," he said. He stepped into the elevator and pushed a button. "The chapel downstairs," he yelled. But the doors had already closed.

૭૩

By the time Miller heard Clotter's voice at the door of the chapel, he had completely forgotten that he might even be coming. Miller had been very busy, moving all the pews against the door, slowly, one by one. Then, sweating and secure in the dim fortress he had made, he had turned around and looked up and gone down to his hands and knees when he saw the depthless blue of Maureena's eyes in the face on the chapel cross. He scuttled across the floor to escape the sight of her, suspended behind that grisly disguise, the too-familiar mask of pain and beatitude. It was only luck that crawled him to the light switches behind a red velvet curtain. The room blazed with fluorescent light then, and the crucifix was safely Christ's alone again—nobody Miller knew.

Gradually it had dawned on him that there was only one place where she had to be. And then he was convinced that if he did draw back the confessional curtain and look, he would find her, as dead as they had said, her beautiful face bleached snow white—the color of all loss.

It was up to Miller. He had all the power and it was terrible.

He refused to look in the confessional. He sat on the back of the pew closest to the door, confident in the weight he had assembled against the rest of the world. He counted the pews—six. It had taken all his strength to slide each one into place, and now he surveyed his little church without churchgoers, three tight rows with no space for prayers or penitents between them. Unless someone wanted to break the stained glass doors, they would have to leave him alone with his power now.

But then he was there, pushing once, twice, on the door, pausing, then knocking politely on the glass like a tardy timid altarboy. Dr. Clotter at the door. And Miller had summoned him.

"Miller? Are you in there? What are you doing?"

"Searching."

"Miller, I talked to the nurse upstairs and your mother on the phone. Son, Maureena's not here. She died. I feel absolutely terrible for her and her parents as well as for you. But it's true."

"I can keep her alive."

"Nobody can do that now."

"What do you know about anything? If I think I can, I will."

"Miller, come out and we'll talk."

"We're talking now. I thought this was your forte."

"What?"

"Open phones at midnight. Ledge chat. Talking to people who might kill themselves. Or somebody else."

"Are you going to kill yourself in there?"

"No. I'm not. I wouldn't give you all the satisfaction."

"You didn't take anybody in there with you, did you?"

"Maureena's here. If I look where I know you want me to, I would kill her. I have to stay one step ahead of all of you."

"You're not coherent. I can't talk to you like this. Miller, I'm sorry, but if you don't come out, the hospital people will call the police. We don't want that. I've persuaded them not to so far, but they will. You're in their chapel."

Miller saw Clotter's shadow on the stained glass, a dark specter trying to eavesdrop on salvation. He heard someone else walking in the hallway, too, leather slither steps on stone like the Cook County shoes. What was he doing? How had he been caught again?

He looked down at his hands for help. They rested on his knees like two old friends who had stayed by his side from childhood, always near, always ready to aid and abet. They had never wanted to hurt anyone, never wanted to do anything but ordinary things. Turning pages. Holding a pen. Steering the Skylark. Caressing Maureena. He felt so sad for his hands that he started to cry. And his hands responded, like always. They rose to his face, to help and hold.

"I think that's what you need, son." Clotter's voice sounded almost gentle through the stained glass.

Miller stopped. He pulled his hands back. Far better to stay cool and listen hard.

"Two things," he said. "If I come out."

"What?"

"Don't call me son."

"All right. What do you want me to call you?"

"Don't call me anything."

"And?"

"You tell me the truth. You help me find her."

"All right. I promise I'll do that. I will tell you the truth. I will help you find her. If you'll do something in turn to help me do that."

"I said I will not look in that booth. I'll break a window and get out of here on my own first. I'll crawl right out Christ's eyes—you just watch it happen."

"No. No. Come out the door. Let me give you something to calm you and help you sleep. And admit yourself to the hospital."

"You don't know any other songs, do you? That's what you did for her. No sir, if she's not here, I'm gone. I'll find her in California with my friends and my car."

"Just for tonight," he said. "And we'll talk about truth tomorrow. I came down here myself out of a sound sleep and a warm bed. Doesn't that seem reasonable and fair? Isn't it better than police and broken glass?"

Miller thought he heard a sound at his back. He whirled and almost fell off the pew. The martyr hadn't moved. The chapel was as quiet as an empty cradle. He was alone.

"Truth tomorrow," he said, "truth tomorrow." It rang real, a simple sound, maybe simple enough to be beneath all the code. Like the station song. Maybe this was chorus to the verse. Train—Track—Train. Truth—Tomorrow. Train—Track—Train. Truth—Tomorrow.

"You just come on out," Clotter said. "I'll wait right here."

Miller didn't have to move all the pews once he studied it. He wedged and wiggled a couple back and then pushed the one closest to the door sideways an inch at a time. It slid slow and heavy on the floor, like the lid of a stone tomb scraping open on years of silence.

PART FOUR

33

Whatever Dr. Clotter had, it worked. One small blue capsule. Miller tossed it down the way you swallow any pill, signed a paper twice, and rode the elevator back upstairs, as docile as the frightened inmate he had been a day before. He shook his clothes off, pulled on striped hospital pajamas, lay down and descended into sleep so deep no dreams would ever surface from it. He didn't wake up enough to know where he was for two days.

The second morning after the standoff in the chapel, Clotter pulled a chair up close to Miller's bed. He told him that he had heard from Maureena only once in October, what he called an agitated phone call when she had had to move into her folks' basement after Durham's arrest, release, and flight. Clotter had asked if she would rather to go to the A.P.W., but she said no. She had sounded very upset about Durham's problems, about not knowing where Miller was, and about having to live at her parents' house, but she gave, in the doctor's words, "no indication whatsoever of being pre-suicidal." Roughly two weeks later, Richard Ocear had called Clotter at his office and said they had found Maureena dead in the garage. He was extremely distraught, Clotter said. According to Rona, who had found Maureena, the car ignition was turned off—officially, to the papers and police, it had been termed an accident. Her parents had held a private service two days later and hadn't returned Clotter's calls since.

Subtract the details, jargon, and hearsay, and it was little more than what the bald old railroadman had told Miller in the station. Propped up on pillows, stiff, and sluggish in hospital pajamas, eyes glazed from thirty hours of chemical sleep, numb from the echo of Clotter's words, to Miller the truth—today, tomorrow, or the day after—was just a twist on murderous Macbeth. It was a tale told by and to an idiot.

Miller stayed in the ward for almost three weeks. One tomorrow at a time. In the old brick hospital, the pace crept and felt petty indeed.

It wasn't until Drew called from Seattle a few days before Thanksgiving, and even then, for no exact reason that Miller could name, that his head began to clear. But at least it was a voice from beyond Omaha. From beyond the grave of Omaha. Miller came to himself.

CB

Grant had been back through Seattle and stopped at Drew's house in the Skylark and then left for the Bay area the same day. Less than a week later Durham had arrived, wanted by both the F.B.I. and an Omaha bondsman, and needing serious help to get safely across the border. Drew helped.

Drew wanted to know what to do with all the stuff Miller and Maureena had left in his basement. Durham had given him Miller's mother's name and number. When he called her, she had told him about Maureena and passed on the number for Miller at the A.P.W.

Miller couldn't remember what all they had left at his house, but Drew reminded him—the stereo, all their albums, Maureena's good sleeping bag and Miller's old one, their tent and camp gear, all the books, a few extra clothes, some tapestry bedspreads.

Miller asked if Drew might be able to sell it. He told him he needed money to look for Grant and his car. They didn't speak at all about Maureena after Drew said how horribly sorry he was. He asked how much Miller needed. Miller said he owed his grandfather three hundred dollars, but he knew that everything there probably wouldn't bring half that. Drew said he would send a check now and sell it later. He told Miller he was welcome to come back and stay at the house whenever he wanted. When Miller told him he needed to find the Skylark first, Drew gave him a name and address in Berkeley to check on for Grant.

As Miller talked to him from the dayroom phone in the A.P.W., he was already sketching out what he needed to do. That night he cheeked his pills—by then there were two in the morning and two others at night. He slept lighter and shorter.

He did the same the next two mornings and nights. A day later a letter came from Drew with seven fifty-dollar bills inside a smaller envelope.

Miller signed himself off the ward on a bright Thanksgiving morning. He wasn't exactly sure what his status with the hospital was, or what he had to do to be officially discharged, but his mother had asked him to Thanksgiving dinner, and though he had been reticent about it before, it seemed the perfect time to go now. Clotter had already left a day pass for Miller with the nurses.

He retrieved his duffel from a pile of dirty sheets that he had stashed in the ward's laundry room the night before. He dropped a letter to Clotter in the hospital mail slot.

> Dear Doctor C, I don't really like your pills. Thanks for getting me out of the chapel, but that's all I can think to thank you for. Things happen that oblivion just can't help. As far as $$, I don't have any to spare right now. I'm twenty-one, so please don't dun my mother. Fair enough? Happy Thanksgiving.
> Miller

C3

Miller walked the four miles to his mother's for Thanksgiving dinner. As he opened the door to the apartment building and climbed the carpeted stairs, he smelled several turkeys baking. He heard football crowds roaring from several TVs and the muffled laughter from family gatherings on all sides. The sounds and smells could have been from any year—1959, 1979—what did it matter? To Miller's family, to the people in his mother's building, maybe to most everyone, it was just one more holiday in one more waning year. Miller knocked at his mother's door.

A place had been set for him at the table, but the meal was mostly over. His mother, his aunt and uncle, and cousin Ray were finishing up, and his grandfather had shredded a piece of white bread into a glass of whole milk, the traditional end for every dinner

Miller had ever seen him eat. Miller sat down in the empty chair, immediately wishing he hadn't come, and not understanding at all why he had. He didn't trust the reason he had told himself on the long walk there—to repay his grandfather—no, part of him had wanted to be at this table, with this family, even as he was struggling to breathe now that he was.

Though half dished out, the brightly colored food in the serving dishes reminded Miller of the plastic refrigerator samples in appliance stores, the turkey more real because it was partially carved, the yams convincingly halved in their bowl. He ladled food onto his plate by rote and made small talk. He hadn't seen his mother's sister and her husband for several years, and for cousin Ray it had been even longer. Not until after Miller sat down did he even remember his mother telling him two Christmases before that Ray had enrolled in ROTC out at U.O.

But Ray didn't mention that, and no one mentioned the war. No one mentioned Maureena. No one asked where Miller was staying. He had the strong feeling that he had been a topic of conversation before his arrival. Kid gloves for Evelyn's boy—if he shows.

After a few excruciating minutes of the big three—football, family, and food—Miller stood up and mumbled an excuse about having to wash clothes in the laundry room downstairs. It was lame, and he tried to bolster it by smiling and shaking his duffel bag convincingly as he headed downstairs. They all seemed just as glad to move away from the table. Miller's uncle turned the game up. Miller took his full plate downstairs.

He dumped a few clothes into the washer on quick cycle, although they were already clean from the hospital. Being in the laundry room reminded him of killing time down there on winter nights in high school before he had a driver's license—a refuge from his mom's apartment and the TV that filled it corner to corner. He sat on a plastic milk crate and listened to the rhythmic slush of the washer. Alone, he was ravenous and devoured the meal. He tried but couldn't remember anything he had eaten at St. Joe's for the last two weeks. Jello? Macaroni and cheese? Spaghetti-O's? Or had that been in Cook County?

He heard someone cheering. The Nebraska-Oklahoma game blared from the apartments on either side of him as well as from his mother's upstairs. He put the clothes in the dryer. He counted the money from Drew in his wallet. He remembered a night with Maureena in the laundry room during their first summer. They made out through two full loads of clothes. Wash and Dry. It was that languid country of endless kisses they had lingered in during the long weeks before they actually made love. The memory seemed closer than Cook County or St. Joe's.

Evelyn came down to check on him. She brought a piece of pumpkin pie and took his empty dinner plate as if it were the most natural thing in the world for her son to be eating Thanksgiving dinner in the basement laundry room by himself.

Miller told her he was out of St. Joe's for good and was planning to leave for California to find the Skylark. She said she and his grandfather had talked, and they both thought he should return to school. He could finish his degree and take his mind away from his sorrows at the same time. Miller explained he needed to find the Skylark first, and he told her he had the money from Drew to pay his grandfather back.

He was feeling much better, he said. She was very glad of that, she said.

He knew as soon as he said it that it was a mistake to mention hitchhiking to the coast. She asked him not to, for her sake, she said, and she suggested he take the train. He told her he didn't have enough extra money. She told him to talk to his grandfather.

They heard Ray and his folks on the stairs. Evelyn went up to the front door landing to see them off. They yelled down to Miller in the laundry room.

"Happy Thanksgiving, Miller. Good to see you again. Don't be a stranger."

Miller waved at them from the bottom of the stairs with the dryer tumbling behind him. He felt indulged, demented, ridiculous. He echoed their goodbyes and good wishes.

"Keep your chin up, young man," his uncle said.

Miller finished the pie and stuffed his dry clothes into his bag. When he headed back up, he met Everett on the stairs.

"Can I get a ride with you, Grandpa?"

"Back to the monkey ward?" he asked. It was clear what he thought of the psychiatric facilities at St. Joseph's.

"No. Actually, I wanted a ride down to the train station."

"Lord knows, I know where that is." He opened the front door.

"I'll be there in a minute," Miller said. Everett went on out to his car.

Miller took the plate back to his mother. She was drying dishes. He told her Grandpa was taking him to the station to check on ticket prices. He said he would call her in a day or two. He hugged her.

"Thanks for the dinner, Mom."

"I'm so sorry, Miller," she whispered in his ear. "I want you to be okay. I want you to come out of this okay."

"Me, too," he said, pulling away from her. He felt the familiar press of the damp dishtowel on his arm. He realized how often they had hugged at the kitchen sink. The habits of family. Where did they come from? Where did they lead?

At the door, she put a fifty-dollar bill in Miller's shirt pocket.

"Happy Thanksgiving, son," she said. "Don't tell your grandpa."

"Thanks."

She put her hand on Miller's face and tried to look into his eyes.

"Right before the dawn, you know?"

"Sure. Happy Thanksgiving, Mom."

She followed into the hall. When he reached the foot of the stairs, she called him back. "You didn't even ask who won," she said, smiling. She looked tall and powerful a dozen steps above Miller, as if each step down had taken him a year back in time.

"Who won?" Miller couldn't think what she was talking about. Not the war? He hadn't read a newspaper or listened to the TV since the train had pulled into Omaha. Could it possibly be over somehow?

"We did,"she said.

"How?"

"A touchdown in the very last minute," she said. "The Cornhuskers may be on their way to the Orange Bowl this year."

"I'll keep my fingers crossed," Miller said.

∝

Miller took six fifties out of his wallet and held them out to his grandfather as he drove down 32nd Avenue on the edge of Hanscom Park.

"A friend sold some of my things in Seattle," Miller said. "Thanks again for your loan."

Everett took the bills, but he didn't pocket them. He wedged them under a container of leftovers on the seat between the two of them. "Why are we going to the train station?" he asked. He had the radio on low, tuned to another football game.

Miller looked out the window. It was a beautiful November day—crisp air and blue skies, as if whoever made them had thought them up for the very first time that day. Windrows of red and yellow leaves nestled along every curb. "I told mom I'd check out the prices to Los Angeles," Miller said. "I have to pick up my car. A friend in California has it."

"That same old Buick?" Everett asked. "It's still running?"

"Sure," Miller said. "It overheats sometimes. It may have a head gasket leaking."

"Aluminum block," Everett said. "You have to watch those. I know you may have heard me say it before, but if you want a reliable car, you buy a Chevrolet."

Miller smiled. How many times had he heard that? "Maybe next time," he said.

Everett changed the subject. "Now then Miller, all told, how much do you lack from finishing up on that degree of yours?"

"A year. Give or take a credit or two."

"I'll make a business deal with you." He turned and looked at Miller and then down at the money on the seat. "You give me your word you'll go back to school and finish your education." He paused as he turned onto Creighton Blvd. After he had straightened the wheel, he resumed.

"And I'll forget about this loan. You use it to finish what you started out there."

Miller stared at Hanscom Park where he had spent half his childhood. Leaves the size of small faces floated between the fat limbs of the trees. What had he ever started that he did finish? Certainly not school. Fifteen years and counting. He remembered years back, when he had still been doing well in the philosophy department. He had seen a frightening image of the future that he couldn't shake off—a vision of endless school, being taught and then teaching forever, an entire lifetime niched in the same cocoon that he had begun spinning in kindergarten. But now, what else was there to do? Three bills would be a start. They passed the east edge of the park, Miller's nose against the glass. The city loomed again. So did his grandfather's voice.

"Miller, we both know you have had a tough break. But don't be like your father. God knows, he had a horrid time in the war. But in this life there are those who make excuses and those who make do. Your father—" He lifted his hand and pointed at Miller. "—made excuses. And then he drank his life away. Not to mention your mother's life. Do you know she was valedictorian of her class?" Finally, he dropped his finger.

"Of course I know." It wasn't too much farther to the station, and Miller was glad of it. This was all too familiar. "I want to tell you the truth about being in jail," he said.

Everett stiffened. "I've never been in jail," he said. "I wouldn't know about that."

"Mom lied for me," Miller said. "I was arrested for protesting the war. I was with people who think the government and the military are doing horrible things to people and have to be stopped no matter what." Miller turned to face him, but Everett kept his eyes straight ahead.

"She did the best she could with you on her own," he said. He frowned.

"But?"

It was a given with both him and Evelyn. There was always a but. Spoken or unspoken. Miller had learned that the unspoken ones were the worst.

"But it looks like it wasn't enough." Everett picked up the money and held it. "You're turning my offer down then?"

"I appreciate it," Miller said. "But I won't promise you I'll go back. It didn't make sense a year ago, and it makes less today. I will give it some serious thought though."

Everett pulled in the station and stopped in front of the door. He pocketed the bills. "Thought's cheap, Miller. I'm sure not going to give you hard-earned money to raise hell on." He shifted the Chevy into park, and the transmission clanged like a dull bell.

Miller opened the door and pushed his bag out and stood next to it.

"See you Grandpa." He leaned back in and reached forward to shake hands. He thought of their frantic handshake a few weeks before.

Everett looked in Miller's eyes. He took a fifty out of his pocket and handed it to him. "At least take care of yourself," he said. "And, don't tell your mother about that."

Miller put the bill in his pocket and smiled. Father and daughter.

"Thanks. Thank you a lot. But that wasn't what I wanted."

He stretched his hand out again. He heard a train whistle blow as they shook hands quickly and let go, and then Miller was right back where he had started.

34

Miller talked to a ticket agent. The fare to L.A. hadn't changed much since Maureena and he had taken the train in the fall of '65. He could have bought a ticket and waited till midnight. Or he could have waited and taken the next day's *Frisco Flyer* straight to Berkeley. It was in the station now, on a two-hour layover, but today it was full up with holiday travelers.

But, that wasn't why he had come. He didn't want to get on a train. He had come back to start over, to finally get off the train he had ridden in on. He wasn't sure what it would take, but this was where he would have to do it. He walked around the station awhile, and then went down the steps to the platform and moved toward the spot where he had met them that night.

The station was crowded with passengers and well-wishers. He looked up at the large round upright clock. Three minutes after four. And then he saw her, boarding the *Flyer* at the far end of the platform. Her blond hair disappeared up the steps and into the car. Miller was even sure he recognized the blue dress she wore, the one she had bought on a visit to him at UCSD the spring he quit school. He dropped his bag and ran after her.

She had gone into the first coach car. Miller walked the length of it, and then the next and the next, hoping for a sign of her. He was excited, strong again, fueled by hope alone—he felt its full force, its buoyant power. If he just didn't puncture it with doubt, anything was possible. If this whole thing hadn't been someone's cruel plot, it still might have been a horrible mistake.

He strolled through the diner and then all the other cars, only slowing down when he came to the last one. She wasn't in it either. Is that how it worked? Would he spend the rest of his life chasing half-glimpses in doorways, trailing shadows through narrow hallways? He walked back through the train, lingering in the sleeping car. The future stretched ahead of him just like that corridor, a narrow hallway with dozens of identical closed doors.

On his second pass through, she was in the diner. Only it wasn't Maureena. Just a young tanned blond woman in her early twenties, close to the same height, a similar build. She was looking at the menu, a man not much older than Miller across from her at the table, doing the same between glances at his watch. When they looked up, Miller hurried on. At the next vestibule, he climbed down off the train.

He leaned against the clock post for the next twenty minutes as the train finished boarding. He watched it leave, its iron mass pulling away in a series of snaps and clanks. And when it was finally gone, even the sound and heft of it completely gone, he felt something new. Maureena's absence. He felt the flood of her absence in the stark clarity of everything around him. He saw the world and its ten million details distinctly for the first time in weeks. And that clarity and profusion was exactly the weight of her absence.

He said it out loud. No one in the station could hear him. "The world is here. Maureena is gone." But it seemed like only two thin ways of saying the same thick truth.

೮

Unlike the previous one, this cabbie was pleased with their destination. He took Center Street toward 84th as the meter clicked rapidly toward three dollars. By the time they reached the I-80 entrance ramp, it had neared four. Miller gave him a five and waved off the change as they exchanged holiday greetings.

The donut house was closed, the *Baker's Dozen Special* sign dark and cold beside it. Durham's cab was long gone. As Miller walked up the entrance ramp, he thought he should have asked the cabbie if he had ever heard about it—the old rattletrap taxi abandoned one morning last winter with its meter running.

Traffic was light. Few trucks. Few lone drivers. Mostly cars packed full of family on their way home from reunions. The sun was low in the sky. Omaha spread out to the northeast like a brown November dream. Miller began to count the cars.

He smelled something fresh on the breeze, perhaps a scent of the Platte, winding its wide slow loop around the city a few miles west. He reminded himself to call his mother from a payphone whenever he saw one. He would tell her he was on the train somewhere. He would imagine he was the intent serious man with the blond woman he had followed onto the *Flyer*.

The sun set. Dusk light rose up around Miller like thin gray ether, the feather touch of gloaming. He had all the time in the world. South 84th Street was a good place to start as long as he kept it simple. He was on a quest, searching for Grant, searching to find the Skylark. And then what? As an answer, he counted three cars in succession—that made sixty-four. He had his arm up and his thumb straight out as if he was plugging a dike that kept the twilight from leaking away too quickly. More cars went by, their headlights blazing now. The blurry faces behind the windshields looked sleepy and full, ready for bed.

Miller began to get cold. Waiting. Plugging. Counting. He caught himself preparing to stand there all night in the cold. He caught myself secretly wanting to. He caught himself thinking, if he suffered enough, would she somehow come back?

35

A woman named Kai showed Miller a large old walk-in closet where Grant slept whenever he was there. Miller recognized some books, a mailing tube full of rolled-up posters, a knapsack, Grant's sleeping bag.

"He hasn't been around for about a week," Kai said, pointing to his bag.

Miller had made the coast in three days, but it took him almost another week tracking Grant from the address in Berkeley to a dorm commune at Santa Cruz, to an apartment in Oakland, and then back to this house in Albany, a few blocks from the bay. Grant's housemates were having a meeting the night Miller showed up, a dozen people sitting on the floor cross-legged around a dining room table with the legs cut down to about a foot high, and Kai had been the only one who seemed willing to deal with a stranger. Even in passing, Miller recognized the serious and secretive tones in their voices. It was not unlike one of the endless criticism/self-criticism sessions that had occupied the Weatherpeople in Cook County jail for hours on end.

"He mentioned going to Altamont," Kai said. "Maybe he still gets a kick out of all that bourgeois music."

"The Stones?"

"It's just diversion, isn't it? Something else for sale. They're just salesmen with hair."

She waited for Miller to pick it up. It was supposed to be a free concert. He let it go.

"So how do you know Grant?" she asked.

"From the U. in San Diego. We started school together. And quit together. He has my car. At least I hope so. I was busted in Chicago in October and lost track of him. You?"

"We met last summer. The movement. The struggle. What kind of car?"

"A red convertible. Old Buick."

"Yeah, that's it. You're not Miller? He's always talking about a couple from Iowa or somewhere? Miller and Maureen?"

"Maureena. And Nebraska. Yeah, he and I have been close a long time."

She seemed friendlier. She smiled and coiled her long braid up as she spoke, threading a thin carved wooden stick through it, her arms raised gracefully above her head. A dancer.

"Old friends are a trip, aren't they?" she said. "You can crash here for awhile if you want. No drugs, though. I didn't mean to be unfriendly. Just being careful, you know. Things can get weird. But you know that. If you really were in Chicago."

"I was." Miller saw she still wasn't entirely sure of him. She was testing him. Maybe she had known the right name and the right state after all.

"It's a phase of the struggle—sorting through the paranoia. Measuring out trust. Trust is a weapon they turn against us, you know." She paused.

Her "they" echoed in Miller's head. She said it so casually, as if he would have absolutely no doubt as to who she meant.

"You want to come down and meet some people? Maybe you'll stay around awhile?"

"No, not really. I just want to find Grant and pick up my car. I'm not sure where I'm headed. Maybe San Diego. Maybe Seattle or British Columbia. Maybe—"

She interrupted him, her voice rising. "You can't run from Amerika," she said, the "k" hard, curt. "The Vietnamese can't run. Why should we be able to?"

Miller let her hear herself for a minute, stayed silent.

"Well. Sorry. You look tired. Remember, no drugs in the house."

"Fine. I don't have any. I am tired—I've been tracking Grant around for almost a week. And I hitched in from Omaha before that."

"December's kind of risky for that, isn't it?" She leaned against the doorjamb. She seemed to want to talk, but he wasn't sure.

"It could be. I was lucky with the weather though. And the rides, I guess—only six. One all the way from Omaha to Nevada with a guy named Arlo and his dog, Mix. And only one bad wait, right after that, at the edge of Elko. All day by a giant yellow sign for a rock shop."

She smiled. "Omaha. Pretty name. Another beautiful stolen name." She pointed at Grant's mat. "Well, go ahead and catch some sleep then. I can't guarantee how quiet it'll be."

"I don't really sleep much these days anyway. But I'll rest."

She left the door ajar. Miller pulled the string on the lightbulb off and lay down on Grant's mat. A light shone through a bedroom window. Miller stared at the peeling paint shadows and shapes on the closet ceiling, thinking of the old childhood pastime, imagining what the shapes of clouds are like. Maureena had been able to play it for hours on the road in the convertible, making up long funny fables about the changing shapes. Miller had tried it for awhile alone in Nevada, during the long wait in Elko, but whenever he remembered where Maureena was—or wasn't—the sky felt like a weight above him—as if even the frayed, puffy clouds were made from white lead, as heavy as locomotives.

36

Miller was already awake when somebody in the next room turned a radio on at 5 A.M. It was the Berkeley FM station, broadcasting news of Altamont every few minutes—how it was going to be the west-coast Woodstock, how the location had changed twice in twelve hours, how everybody from the Governor on down was trying to stop it from happening, but it was still on—no matter what. Miller took the pre-dawn radio as a sign. He decided to go.

He probably didn't have a prayer of finding Grant among a hundred thousand people, yet knowing the Skylark was with him helped Miller trust his sudden hunch. And despite Kai's invitation, he didn't feel like staying in one place too long, especially not there with the self-criticism people. He still felt susceptible to their passionate, either-or reasoning. Five minutes with Kai had reminded him of that. But he didn't want to open that door again, not ever.

Survival first, like any good GI. Those few weeks behind bars had brought the war home for him, all right. It was small by comparison to the real thing, but it was war's essential landscape etched right inside his head. Capture. Panic. Confinement.

And loss. The time on the road had helped Miller begin to accept that he would have to accept it. But why had he ever let Maureena board that bus in Fargo?

In the pitiless glare of his hindsight, it all seemed so clear. He should never, never, never have stood and watched her go back to Omaha without him, in fall no less. Late fall in Omaha, that cold gray midwestern claustrophobia, like a torn, dirty windowshade rolling right down over the sky. To a progression of minor chords. *Now look around. Leaves are brown. There's a patch of snow on the ground.* Autumn panic to a Top Forty beat. *All the leaves are brown. The sky is gray.* But that was another song. And another season.

As Miller packed up what little he had brought in, he spied a copy of *Soul on Ice* by Grant's bedroll, hardback. He picked it up.

Miller stared at Cleaver's face on the cover, and it took him right back to Omaha. He opened the cover. His own name was in the corner. It was the copy he had loaned Grant the fall after Miller and Maureena saw Cleaver speak. It was at Fontenelle Park in Omaha on the hottest day of July '68 when he was running for President in the Peace and Freedom Party.

Omaha police had surrounded the park, dozens of squad cars parked on every access street. Cleaver showed up with his armed Panther guards, rifles at the ready, and asked the mostly black crowd to take a look at the white occupation army. He paused and pointed his finger around the whole perimeter of the park, and you could hear a deep menacing murmur growing. Miller and Maureena were way out at the edge of the crowd, with most of the few other whites, and Miller saw real fear on the faces of police, a first for him. That day power didn't seem solid at all. It seemed ethereal, a flick of perspective, as volatile as the shifting glint in hundreds of angry eyes on a sweltering summer day.

Miller thumbed open the book and found something he wasn't looking for, and once he found it he couldn't not read it. And reread it and reread it. And then fold it up and keep it.

It was postmarked October 16, addressed to Grant at Drew's house in Seattle. Someone there had hand-forwarded it to Berkeley. It was from Maureena.

> Dear Grant,   I'm cold in Oh, Ma,
> Ha, but mother's not laughing. Mainly I'm hoping Drew
> knows where you are and you get this. I also hope you
> weren't arrested or got out quick. You would, wouldn't
> you? I haven't heard from Miller since Fargo except a
> phone call and then one letter from the jail. I wired bail
> money to SDS, but no word since. Meanwhile Steve took
> off on bail and I'm broke and, ta da, my parents found me.
> Now I'm the princess under palace watch. So please, do
> you know where he is? I thought maybe you helped get

him out somehow?

It's life in the basement rec room here. I don't even keep the clocks set. Mother wants to enroll me at UO. Father watches the news and me with the exact same frown. Nobody talks down here but me and my shadow. Very quiet twins.

I'll write Carlila next. I guess you must know. She's with Durham—and out of the country, I hope. I'll give you what I have in case you don't. Turkey Flats, Edgewood, B.C. There's a main house there that's supposed to have a phone—604 455 3111.

Not much else. I watch TV with the volume off. Try it. You can sense the '70s coming fast and it's not going to be like any of us thought. You know how it feels when you have a close call in the car? But see, a real accident isn't like a close call at all, it's the one you don't see coming. Did Miller ever tell you about his dad's accident? Am I making any sense?

Sorry I didn't say much of a goodbye in Fargo. I wasn't in a good mood toward you then. But thanks for coming to Mission Beach with me that day though. If you see or hear from Miller, give him all my love and let him know I'm right here where he found me the first time. Tell him I'll be ok or else. Tell him Clotter may be on the case. He'll know what it means. Or please, tell him just to come.

Take care and find peace,
Maureena

∞

A little after dawn Miller waited in a Safeway parking lot next to a cardboard sign where people needing rides to the concert were supposed to wait. There were flyers on the phone poles with an address to write for info on a trip to Cuba the first of the year with the next Venceremos Brigade.

Four people in a pink '61 Valiant picked him up. It was one of those mornings when it seemed like everybody in sight was going the same place, heading the same direction. And that day the same place was a ranch outside Livermore. The folks in the

Valiant—Rain, Levine, Slip, and Dune—offered Miller some pure windowpane doubles that Slip had scored in Hawaii.

Miller passed. He didn't need any hallucinogens. Maureena's death left him feeling wide open to a whole world of dark shapes, as if there was no point in not accepting all the blackness, owning up to it, now that it had happened right in the center of his life. Like an eclipse no one predicted—guaranteed to expand anyone's notions of the possible.

They followed last minute directions on KUBK and arrived by ten. An early sun was shining down on thousands of people milling over pale green hills. The four from the Valiant were coming onto the Hawaiian acid, getting friendly and sweet and harmless, all absolutely positive they knew Miller from somewhere before. They stood together on the hood of the Valiant watching the crowd converge toward a huge grassy bowl, thin morning shadows shifting along behind everyone like tattered black robes. Then the four of them walked into the crowd.

A few months earlier, a year, and Miller would have gone with them—he would have known them. Instead, he walked around the edges of the crowd, looking back and forth in both directions at the quilt of parked cars, scanning for the Skylark.

Musicians played in small groups everywhere, momentary concerts forming and dissolving in the shade of vans or beneath the few stunted pasture trees. Miller listened to a song here and there, turned down drug after drug—some for sale, some free—caught a couple of wild frisbees and threw them on. Around noon he crested the lip of the bowl and saw the biggest crowd he had ever seen, three broad hillsides covered with people, a small city's worth, without a building in sight. Way down at the bottom of the valley a half-circle of semi-trailers surrounded a jumble of platforms and speaker banks and canvas tents.

Miller began tracking the crying guy without even realizing it. He had to be strung out on something intense, a large man, overweight and tall, maybe twenty at most, deep in his own drug terror, wailing like a newborn, and completely naked. Miller imagined there could be many others like him, wandering the crowded hillsides.

The crying guy would settle down and sit still for a few minutes, with someone hugging him or stroking his forehead, trying to talk to him, and then he would rise up again, screaming, thrashing, crying, like a giant baby no one knew what to do with. Miller watched him go through several cycles, stumbling, wiping his eyes with the back of his big round hands, pushing people away who reached out to him, close to violence in the private depths of his public terror.

Miller kept following him through the crowd at a distance. He wanted to help him find one of the tents with the big red crosses in the distance, but he wasn't sure he could go that deep into the crowd himself. He wasn't sure he could help him.

Miller was still following him when he saw, way off in the distance, the Skylark.

When he came up to it, he pulled a beer and an apple from a cooler in the backseat and then sat inside, out of the chilly wind. The Skylark looked the same, except two ignition wires hung loose under the dash, both of Miller's bumper stickers had been scraped off, and there were new California plates.

After he finished the beer, he unlocked the trunk to stow his duffel, and he found his old Nebraska plates near the spare and jack. When he flipped back a folded, shaggy throwrug by the plates, he saw two identical rifles, both with scopes and slings, side by side, nestled end to end.

Miller stared at the rifles. Swirls in the walnut grain spiralled across the polished stocks. Hypnotic, beautiful, out-of-place. Find the flaw in this picture. He slammed the trunk shut. He went back and stretched out as best he could in the passenger seat. People roamed by the car, talking, anxious about when the Stones would really show. Clouds folded quickly across the sky in layers, the lower ones overrunning the higher like herds of fleeing, mutable animals chased by wind. Miller dozed on and off for a few hours. It was the most he had slept in days.

37

The sun was halfway down the southern sky, the clouds were gone, and faint electric music thrummed in the distance when Grant showed up. He looked different, his hair a short neat trim, something like they had both looked way back at the freshman orientation in '65. But his eyes looked much older to Miller, covered and guarded by something new, like a fine-mesh gauze you'd have to work your way through to get down to the person inside. Or the wound.

"Miller, Millerman, how in the hell did you find me? Is Maureena with you? Did she use her voodoo ESP? I don't believe this, man."

"Me either." They shook hands, both ways, the old and new. That wasn't enough. Miller hugged him. His fellow graduate. Friend. Out of the thousands. "I guess I got lucky," he said. "I found the house in Albany and Kai said you might be here—among the bourgeoisie, no less."

Grant nodded. But no laugh.

"Besides, I've got a homing sense for this old Skylark, remember? California plates or no." He pointed at the front bumper.

"That's what we all need, Miller, a homing sense. I bet you want your wheels back." Now he grinned, but Miller didn't. He wanted an explanation, and he knew Grant knew it.

"Look, I let Carlila keep my truck, and I didn't know where you were. Cook County wouldn't even say who was held where. I saw the church the next day. What an ugly scene. It was lucky for me I hit the streets with posters that night."

"Yeah, two sets of glass doors shattering wakes a person right up, asleep or not. Like nothing I've ever heard before. Or maybe only once before." For the first time in months, Miller really heard the sound of the Ocears' garage door splintering. He had thought about it ever since the train station, but he had never heard it as clearly in his mind. And then it wouldn't stop.

"Miller?" Grant's voice broke through the noise.

"What?" He remembered what they were talking about. "So you didn't make it to jail?"

"No, I stayed on the streets the whole time," Grant said. "Light on my feet. And lucky."

Miller told him about the arrest warrants typed up hours after the church raid, the fake affadavits, the form letter in place of a phone call, the botched bail money, the copped plea, his mother, his grandfather, the train ride. Miller was stalling, trying to get ready to tell about Maureena, but the thought of telling Grant, saying it aloud—in what words?—in which phrase?—made it feel reduced and small, like filler from the newspaper, just one more bad-news blurb. One more anonymous life turned public for a minute, a day, with a neat black obit border for context.

And then they're filed. No stop-offs. Directly from anonymous to alphabetical. Keeping track. Ocear, Maureena Ann. Wait one moment, please. We're checking.

Miller felt as lost as the crying guy. Who was it he had been looking for? Who was he supposed to meet? Where?

"Miller, are you here? Are you with me? Did you drop anything? Miller?"

Miller, Silas. Wrong. Silas, Loren. Miller, Maureena. Files out of order. Names of the waiters on tombstones. Knots of naked people with painted faces. The un-suicided. The struggle. "S" is for Struggle, for Suicide, for Silas.

"What'd you take, man? How much? There's some bad acid out here today. Open your eyes Miller, it's okay, it's me, Grant, I'll get you to the first-aid tent."

Grant. That's it. We'll set you free now, Grant. The end of the road. Just a couple of things to settle. Things we have to know before we go.

"No. I'm here, I just haven't slept much. I haven't dropped since Leucadia. I haven't even smoked since Seattle." Miller glared at him. "The only thing I'm coming onto is here and now, man. California. December. 1969. Me. You. What the hell are the rifles for, Grant?"

"Oh, you saw, huh?" Grant looked around them. "It's time to move on, Miller. I'll explain it all once we're on the road. What'd you nose around in the trunk for?"

"It's my trunk. It's my car, damn it. And I don't own any rifles. I don't want any rifles, Grant. Not in my car, and not in my life."

"Easy, Miller. Just a joke. I didn't know if you still had the keys. I had to pick the trunk lock myself. But look, there's lots of crap people don't want, and get anyway. Frag bombs in straw huts. Napalm in the wee hours. I thought we were past that possessive shit, you and me."

Grant handed him a plum from the cooler. He bit into an apple and got into the driver's seat and closed the door. Miller sat down in the passenger seat.

"Look, I don't care that you used the Skylark—what's mine is yours and all that other jazz—but that still doesn't explain the rifles, man. Let me guess. You plan on shooting Mick Jagger?"

"Right you are—dying Jack Flash—one last encore. Hardly, Miller. I only came here because it was a safe place to meet some people, and I did. What's safer than a crowd of a quarter million hippies? Now what do you say let's go. I said I'd explain on the road."

"So will I."

"About?"

"Maureena."

"What about her? You guys didn't split up, did you? She did send the bail money, didn't she? She wrote me, and she didn't sound so together."

"No. Yes. I know."

"Thanks for nothing, Miller. I hate it when you do that."

He started the Skylark with the wires. Miller turned it off with his key. "I'll drive."

"You don't know where we're going."

"What's new? Anyway, I have an idea. If you'll listen."

They switched seats. As Miller started the car, four guys asked for a ride. They were sick and had to go home. Miller asked where they wanted off. They pointed up to the road. They hopped on, two on the hood and two on the back deck. Miller nosed the Skylark across the pasture, around cars and among people walking, dancing, smoking. Many naked people now. The two guys on the hood stretched out like they were on a rack. Whatever they were on wasn't treating them good. Miller heard loud music in the distance. Country Joe and the Fish maybe. Electric music way down in the valley.

"Okay, so what's this idea?" Grant asked.

"Turkey Flats."

"The place in Canada?"

"British Columbia. It's a commune in the Monashee Mountains. The Inanoklan valley. Durham and Carlila are there, I believe. It's quiet there."

"Not for me. I know where I'm going. And that's a good feeling."

One of the guys on the back beat on the fender like a drum. Miller stopped and he came up and gave Miller the handshake while they all hopped free. His eyes were swirling, out of focus, the twist of penny-size kaleidoscopes.

"Good luck, brother," he said.

"Same to you. Be careful."

CB

After a couple of miles the rows of parked and double- and triple-parked cars ended. When they saw a turnoff for Sacramento, Grant said to take it.

"Sacramento? You want to lobby at the capitol? Hustle petitions? Is that why you cut your hair?" Miller took the turnoff. They were sharing a beer.

"Ha. You're still the same Miller. Look, I'll be downright unsharp and trust you, man. If I can't trust you, then—"

The line of opposing traffic roared by, the windy crescendo from each car rising and falling in a jerky rhythm. People were still streaming toward the concert.

"You can't trust anybody." Miller finished the sentence.

Grant looked him over. Miller could see then that it was something Grant had considered. For a second his isolation showed through. One of a thousand brands of loneliness. Plain naivete perhaps, but Miller hadn't ever thought there would be so many.

"So promise me you tell nobody—not a single word—not even Maureena."

There was her name again. Miller felt his stomach tighten. He wasn't ready to say her name. "About you cashing it in and moving to Sacramento? Sealed lips."

"Miller, I'm asking for your word and you're making jokes. There's nobody else in the world I'd even bother to ask that from anymore. I want your word."

"I give you my word I'll never tell anybody," Miller said, staring straight in his eyes.

"His Honor the Governor," Grant said. It reminded Miller of the old movies where the butler announces the arrivals at a formal occasion.

And then he knew, before it was spelled out. But he had to deny it. "No."

"That's who the rifles are for, Miller. Six millimeter, Remington bolt-action with 4-power Leupold sights. December 17 when he leaves town for his ranch holiday. California's going to have one very dead governor."

Miller looked over at him. Grant opened another beer and offered it. Miller searched his face for a smile. But there was none there. Miller took the beer.

"How far to Sacramento?" he asked.

"An hour. Why?"

He drank and passed the beer back. He didn't want to speak till he was sure. He stalled. He tried to think himself away from what Grant was telling him and from what he had to tell him.

Of course, why not? His Honor the Governor was definitely right smack in the middle of it. Reagan had ordered the Guard into Berkeley to bulldoze People's Park and shoot protestors, he was screwing with the U. system funding to turn education into just one more rat-race commodity, he spoke for the war every chance he got, but wasn't he a human being? Kill him? Miller flashed to the first Kennedy killing, his junior year in high school, the President's brains all over his wife's coat, the limousine, the front page. Only the first of a string of public murders that seeped into the living room. Medgar. Malcolm. Che. Robert. Martin.

Sure, Reagan, like Kennedy or any of the others, for that matter, didn't deserve to live any more than any Vietnamese peasant, and they were being killed like flies. But if Grant Trayn from Palos Verdes could do this, it was like Miller doing it, like Maureena doing it, like anybody doing it. Like they had all ended up drafting themselves, brainwashing themselves, hating themselves. A counter-culture Marine Corps. Pigs in place of gooks.

"Miller, don't sweat it." Grant punched him on the shoulder. "Don't sweat it. I told you because you saw the rifles, that's all. It's all planned. I'm not the only one involved."

"I don't care, Grant. You can't kill somebody to stop the killing. It's stupid. It's evil. The Governor's a person. Like Nixon or Daly or Hoover or anybody you could name. He's got a wife, kids, eats dinner, takes a crap. Just like you and me. What in the hell's got into you?"

"Compromise got into me. I'm willing to compromise my ideals for a revolution. Our ideals are a story they taught us in school to keep us calm. We plant flowers in their guns while they spray kids with napalm, man. And then sell shares in Dow Chemical on the open market."

He paused and then pointed toward the car radio. "Or shoot three hundred and forty seven unarmed peasants, for Christ's sake. Did you read Hersh's story on My Lai last month?"

Miller nodded. He was in St. Joe's when the story broke, but he had read about it since.

"See, that's their real world, and let me tell you, it's minus every ideal you or me could ever think of. I don't care about Reagan's kids or his crap. He's just a step in the process."

"Process? What kind of a word is that? What in the hell does that mean?"

Grant stretched his hand out the window. He spread his fingers in the wind. "Picture this for a process—Christmastime in California, the governor and maybe a mayor or two gone, a few million people minus electricity. Freaks pouring out here from around the country. Every campus a headquarters, complete with radio stations."

Grant's voice was getting louder and higher. He kept working his fingers in the wind, as if he was kneading it into the vision he saw. Miller checked the speedometer. A mile a minute.

"We can take this state, Miller, or part of it. Break off a chunk. Declare independence. Call for a U.N. plebiscite—like in the Panthers' ten points. And while they figure how to react, we make it a media show. Negotiate with Mexico. Secede. You name it." He was almost laughing.

"Take over California? My God, you're the one on the bad acid, man."

Grant held his hands up in front of him and looked at his palms as if they were someone else's and he was trying to read them. "This is my life, and I want it to be something besides fiberglass, not just a Ralph Edwards TV show and shit-eating grins while the cameras roll and they tune up the commercials." He spoke more slowly. "I want to struggle for fairness. It's as simple as that."

"Nothing's that simple, Grant. Teenagers believe things are simple."

"Desperate people discover the world is simple. Read the mystics, the lives of the saints. Read Che's diaries. It's an aspect of grace, one of the few I still believe in."

They passed the entrance to the freeway. Another sign for Sacramento.

"You missed the turnoff." Grant pointed behind them.

"I want to stay off the Interstate. How big a hurry are you and this revolution in?"

"As long as I get there today and meet my man. You can drop me off and take the car."

"You were going to use my car? In all of this?"

"I have been using it. I told you. I didn't know where you were."

"Out of sight, out of mind, right?"

"Let it go, Miller. I figured when you wanted it, or me, you'd be in touch. Are you taking it to Canada? Boy, you know it's getting bad when the people with the deferments have to split."

"Or murder."

The word sounded dirty and thick. Miller let it hover between them. Grant didn't flinch.

"Yeah, that could be the plan," Miller said. "I've even thought about school again. But I don't want to stay out here. And I don't want to go back to Omaha. I've been bouncing back and forth as long as I can remember. Canada sounds better every day."

"Jail really freaked you, huh?"

"Educated me. The cops can make the law. They may have to answer for it later, but in the moment, it's their show—kid gloves or lead sticks. I've never felt so out of control in my life."

"They can't take your mind, buddy, they can't take your will."

"They could take mine," Miller said. "But then maybe I'm just weak."

Grant tapped him on the shoulder. "Or maybe you're trying to be too strong. Maybe you just have to let yourself get broken down to find the fault lines and see what remains."

"What if nothing remains?" Miller's voice trembled and broke. "Answer me, I want to know the party line on this, what if not a goddamn thing remains? Huh? What if it all boils down to an ashen face in a satin sideshow?" He tried to picture Maureena's funeral and couldn't. He had no context for it except his father's.

"Miller, where are you at? I thought we were talking politics here. What's going on?"

"Maureena."

Everything seemed to shimmer, ready to collapse. Or explode. The road, sky, fields. There were only two words left now, but he couldn't say them. Grant would have to.

"Maureena?"

"What's the worst thing you could imagine?"

"How should I know?" Grant slapped the dash. "She has a new boyfriend. She won't speak to you. She's crazy." He paused. Miller didn't answer. "She's sick. She's dead."

"Yes."

The wheel felt tiny, a toy in his hands. And then his hands, toys on the end of his arms. "You're kidding," Grant said, but it was in the air. "No, you're not. Jesus H. Christ."

He put his hand on Miller's shoulder. Stupid, real stupid, but Miller thought of Spock on Star Trek, the way he pressed people into instant slumber. Often for the best of reasons. Such tender violence. Stupid as a TV series. Fake as a voyage on the Enterprise. Miller's life. Maureena's. Their ideals. Fears. Love.

"I don't want to drive anymore." Something big and ugly was rising inside him. Like thick nausea, only from behind his eyes. He was afraid of it.

"There, pull over under those trees," Grant said. He kept his hand on Miller's shoulder until the car stopped at a wide gravelly place with a blue trash barrel under two live oaks and a scrub willow. The Skylark dieseled for a few seconds when Miller turned it off, and when it stopped, he pressed his forehead into the top of the steering wheel, his fists tight around the sides, and his whole body shuddered and heaved. He sounded ridiculous to himself, like a wounded elephant in a cheap safari movie, bellowing in leathery pain.

Grant didn't move, just kept pressing his shoulders, with both hands now, his warm palms and fingers Miller's only connection. After a few minutes, he began to hear the word Grant was saying, just one word, softly, "Miller," over and over until it sounded like low wind.

ભ

When they were both silent, Grant stepped out and walked around the car and opened the door. He took Miller's hand and helped him stand up. "Let's walk," he said.

They headed down a gravel lane. The hills on one side were smooth and bald, worn pasture with no cows in sight. On the other side was some kind of row crop. Miller couldn't tell if they were on a rancher's driveway or a county road or both.

"How?" Grant asked, after they'd gone a long way.

Miller told him what he knew. He told him what he thought, and what he would never know. He told him about freaking at St. Joe's and that he hadn't cried until now. He told him about the January day in her folks' garage. About Clotter and the Ocears and how they must all believe it was Miller's fault. About how he wanted to think it was theirs, but it was really his.

Grant cut him off. "Bullshit. Screw them. If anything, she's another casualty of the war. Some people feel the stiletto edges of this world, man, some can hear the screams in their sleep."

Miller pulled the letter he had found in Grant's room out of his pocket. He handed it back to him. Grant recognized it. He unfolded it and stared at it.

"Like I said, she did not sound good." He looked at the letter again, shaking his head. "But listen, maybe it was an accident, maybe that's what she meant in the letter."

"What day in Mission Beach?" Miller asked, pointing at the letter.

Grant kicked a stone in the road. A hawk took off from a fencepost, flew a dozen posts farther down the road and perched again. He folded the letter up.

"I don't know if I should tell you. Even now. Especially now."

"Especially now," Miller said. "Tell me."

Grant stopped and put his hands on Miller's shoulders again.

"She said she didn't want you to have to know," he said. "I went with her to the clinic there. When she was pregnant." He dropped his eyes to the gravel. Then he raised them again.

Miller stared at the sky. Maybe Grant shouldn't have told. But how could it matter now? Miller had lost too much—Maureena had lost too much—for anyone to worry now about something that had never really been. "She told me she wasn't pregnant," he said.

"Well, after that day she wasn't. And until that letter she acted like it never happened."

"Thanks for helping her," Miller said. "I guess."

"I'd have done anything for her," he said, "or you." He put the letter in Miller's pocket. "It was weird the way she asked. She said I was the only one who wouldn't ask for a reason."

"Did you tell Carlila?"

"I couldn't. I said Maureena thought she might be pregnant. That's all."

They sat down on a broad flat rock next to the road, gazing across the kind of California countryside you never saw in postcards—farmy, plain, useful, used-up—worked and worried over by Chicanos in beatup pickups. Nothing to hear them but the hawk down the way.

Grant put his face in his hands and groaned.

"Jesus H. Christ. I'm sick of all this. What the hell's gone wrong?"

"Absolutely everything," Miller said. "I need somewhere to slow down and think or I may break. I haven't slept a night through without a doctor's drugs since she—since I heard about it." Miller thought back. "Or maybe since Fargo. Anyway, why don't you come north with me?"

Grant stared at the hawk down the fenceline and didn't answer for a long time. Dust trailed and rose behind a slow-moving tractor in the distance.

Miller looked at the side of his face and remembered the first weekend he had visited Grant's home, fall semester freshman year. Grant's parents had repeated it slow, one syllable at a time—"Omaha, Nebraska"—when Miller told them his hometown. He spent the weekend trying to keep his jaw from dropping. Wide curvy hillside roads, lush coiffured semi-tropical vegetation, driveways full of cars shiny as colored mirrors, the calm aqua horizon winking in and out of view.

"I don't want to think anymore, buddy. I've thought too much. Miller, I'm really sorry. Maureena had a whole life waiting. But there's nothing I can do now. We'll keep in touch."

A lie. They both stood. They turned their backs on the hawk.

CB

Miller traced his finger through the dust around the lock of the trunk when they returned to the Skylark. A peace sign. Wash me.

"They loaded?" he asked.

"They're all ready to go."

"When?"

"Soon. By Christmas. If not me, then at least one other at one other time. Maybe more. Everything else will follow. Like the crack in the dam."

"Can you trust whoever? What if they don't follow through?"

"What if? What if? Then the house of cards collapses, I guess. Right now I'm just concentrating on my little ace and when to play it."

"I didn't even know you could use a gun."

"I went to my uncle's ranch in Colorado in the summers. And I've been practicing. With that sight I can put five out of five in a six-inch circle at an eighth mile. That's a block and a half."

"Show me."

"Where?"

"Here. Maybe I'll decide to stay. Help out."

"After what you've been through the last two months?"

"Now who's worrying about who? Maybe I want to know what it feels like."

"You never hunted?"

"My dad wouldn't even talk about guns," Miller said. "A carryover from three years in the South Pacific, I guess."

"What did Maureena mean about your dad's accident, anyway?" Grant pointed at the letter in Miller's pocket again. "I thought he died right after the war—I swear you told me that."

"Would you?"

"When you first told me, you said he had never recovered from his war wounds."

"Right. Who does?"

Miller opened the trunk. Pulled out a rifle. Sighted the barrel. Handed Grant the other.

"Can it, Miller, this is serious. A state patrol could come by."

"So, you're in charge of security. Blow him away. Or tell him we're hunters. We'll go hunting. I saw a hawk back there. A farmer on a tractor."

Miller turned and moved quickly behind the trees and down a shallow ravine out of sight of the car and road. There were tin cans blackened from fire, pop tops, a piece of toilet paper, a Q-tip. He raised the rifle to his waist, the barrel level. He waited for Grant.

"Miller, I have to go."

He came around the trees. Miller pointed the rifle at his chest, ten feet away. He checked the safety, slid the tang off and on. He hadn't hunted, but he had fired rifles on Saturday afternoons at a dump outside Omaha with a high-school friend. It would have to do.

"Rifles at three paces, my friend," he said.

The sun was behind clouds. Miller could see Grant's eyes. He hoped Grant could see his.

"Wow, you really are completely goofy. You'll always pick whatever's bound to shock people, given half a choice. That's one of the reasons I always liked you, Miller. But c'mon, don't screw around with loaded guns. People die that way."

He took a half-step toward Miller. Miller slid the safety off again.

"I know how people die, Grant. How about no more preaching today, not from you or me. You want to kill? Here's your chance.

Two rifles in the trunk of my car. Maureena's and my car. It was meant to be. Don't you believe in meant-to-be?"

They stared each other down. Miller's peripheral vision slowly faded and left only a clean bright tunnel between Grant and him.

Grant raised his rifle. He clicked his safety off, too. Miller wondered what the odds were of two bullets hitting each other, of one bullet firing right into the barrel of another rifle. For a second Miller saw battalions of Marines turning their weapons on each other, the Vietnamese waking from their nightmare one morning and finding the entire invasion force dead by their own hands. And the missiles—what if you could program them all to make big U-turns in the sky and home right back in on their launch sites? Is that what it would take?

"What do you want?" Grant asked. "Do you even know what you want?"

"Shoot me. If you can shoot me, then you get to shoot Reagan. Better yet, make it a pyramid game, say, a dozen people. But if you don't, I shoot you. And then head to B.C. with a real crime to my name. Miller Silas, dangerous revolutionary, wanted for killing his best friend for no reason. Suspected of driving his lover to suicide. Armed and dangerous."

"Christ, Miller, you're so far into yourself you can't see daylight, can you? Take your head out of your ass and look around. There's more going on around here than you and your sad stories. Screw you and your self-serving guilt. Take it back to Nebraska where it belongs or run away with it to British Columbia. But you're not getting me to put you out of your misery."

Grant put the safety back on. He took two steps left and leaned the rifle against a tree. He stepped back to where Miller was aiming and sat down slowly. Cross-legged. A half-lotus.

"Lower your sights, Miller. I'm down here."

Miller did. But of course he wouldn't kill him. Or anybody. Except maybe himself. Grant was right about that. An elaborate way to go about it, too.

Miller put his rifle next to Grant's and sat down across from him. He felt a chill on the wind. Night in the offing. Two crows cawed their way across the sky. They came low over the oak trees but saw the two of them and flew on. Miller and Grant watched them till they were out of sight, then out of earshot. A long time when you're really listening.

"Sorry I said that stuff, Miller."

"We better go. Night's coming on fast. Anyway, I deserved every word after this stunt. Can I ask for one thing though, one small favor? For our friendship—or for Maureena."

"If it's anything I can do."

"Take one day. Dawn to dusk. Sometime before you squeeze that trigger. Someplace quiet like this. One day alone with Grant. Play yourself back. And listen."

"I can do that."

"Your word?"

"I promise because I'll never see you again."

"I believe you. For the same reason."

It was dark when they made Sacramento. Miller sat in the car and watched Grant make a call in a booth with the glass broken out on two sides. In ten minutes somebody met them at a Shakee's Pizza parking lot. Miller made it a point not to notice much. Grant transferred the rifles wrapped in the rug, the cooler, and his pack. He slapped the fender of the Skylark.

"So long old car. This is my stop."

They gripped hands, a long awkward moment. The guy in the other car looked away.

"Good luck, brother," Grant said. He let go of Miller's hand.

"Same to you," Miller said.

After they left, Miller looked for a screwdriver and pliers in the glovebox. Under a pile of maps, he found three arms of the Leucadia starfish. Miller's and Maureena's had been there since

Fargo. The third one had to be Grant's. Miller picked it up. He believed that if Grant kept his word—to think this murder over, alone—he wouldn't do it. But who could be sure? Miller recalled his promises to Maureena in Seattle. He'd broken one when they said goodbye in Fargo. If he did nothing now, Grant's violence would be his, too, and another promise would be broken. He walked to the phone booth. Information gave him an after-hours number for the governor's office, and when a receptionist answered, Miller repeated the warning and the date twice and hung up. It took less than twenty seconds. Nobody could trace the call in that time.

Miller went back to the car and unbolted Grant's license plates and pulled the old ones out of the trunk. He sat on the pavement, thinking the last weeks through the best he could, staring at the four plates. Here, now. There, then. Blue and yellow. Red and white. The Bear State and the Beef State. He could have shuffled them. He was license-plate rich.

He stashed the California plates in the trunk and bolted the Nebraska ones back on.

38

Miller lay in the dark on the hideaway couch bed, staring at the living room ceiling in his mother's apartment. It was the same bed he had slept on in high school, the same streetlight shining through the same window. Even the thrum and whine of an occasional car or truck on Leavenworth Street a block away seemed unchanged.

It was 5 A.M. His mother was asleep in the bedroom at the end of the hall. Her alarm would go off in an hour. And if Miller hadn't lost track completely, it would be Friday.

He had driven into town after dark. Thirty-five numb hours behind the wheel, steadily reeling in Omaha along the unbroken asphalt thread of I-80, had proven only one thing to him—Maureena was gone. He had found Grant and retrieved the Skylark, but it made no real difference. As he stumbled up to the apartment house, he couldn't come up with more than the vaguest reason why he had just driven across half a continent. Something to do with license plates. License plates and rifles.

He dozed for an hour or two around midnight, but for hours now, he had been wide awake, lost in the past and the future. The past was nothing but numbers. Forty days now that Maureena had been dead. Thirteen years, seven months, and twenty-four days for his father. The future looked like blurred pieces of half-developed photographs. Here's a shot of Miller with Durham and Carlila in B.C., and here he is, returning to San Diego and finishing school. Here's one of him in Cuba, harvesting sugar cane, and here he is, back in Chicago, trying to track down Maureena's letters to him in jail.

Old friends, a paper degree, sugar for the revolution, letters from a dead girl. If he stared hard enough, he could begin to see that any one of them might result in a different Miller. He tried to flesh each of them out, ask them questions. Who are you? Who will you be? But it was as wooden and stiff as interviewing applicants for a job that didn't exit. Who was he kidding?

Sometime after he heard his mother's alarm and then the sounds of her getting ready for work, he crawled out of bed, straightened the blankets, got dressed, and fixed breakfast for the two of them. He lied and said the Skylark wasn't running well, so she called a cab as usual. After she left for work, he sprawled out on the couch and turned on the TV.

Channel 7 played reruns from the '50s most of the morning. *Dobie Gillis* and *The Rifleman* were the best. The local news at noon ran a national story, a follow-up on Altamont. It turned out that the Hells Angels had killed a black man near the stage while the Stones sang. They said it was the shadow side of Woodstock, the end of an era, blah, blah. The Omaha daily livestock exchange report followed. The futures on hog bellies and soybeans were both falling.

Miller reached for the World-Herald, looking for the TV schedule. He looked at the date on the paper, December Ninth. Twelve days before the first day of winter, sixteen shopping days left until Christmas, twenty-two days left in a decade. Maybe the future was only numbers, too. He found the TV schedule. At one o'clock, *Twilight Zone* was on twice in a row, and after that *Perry Mason*.

He made it through both *Zones* and most of *Mason*, but he nodded off in the final courtroom scene, with the camera making closeup rounds of the dead woman's suspicious friends and family while Raymond Burr bore down on a stammering witness.

 C3

Miller heard his mother mixing a drink in the kitchen. He listened to the Cabin Still bottle tip and pour. The clock said a quarter of seven. The TV was off.

He sat up on the bed and stared at the empty gray screen and knew immediately why he had come back to Omaha. He knew what he had to do. He reached for his boots.

"Are you awake, Miller?" Evelyn slurred her words just enough for Miller to guess she had had a few Friday night drinks with her friends after work.

"More or less," he said, yawning through all three words.

She came into the front room and sat on the edge of the bed.

"You feeling all right?"

He smiled. "Less or more."

"How do you like the new tree?"

He looked around. He had been in the room for almost twenty hours and hadn't even seen the new five-foot artificial white-flocked tree with red satin balls hanging on every branch.

"Sure. It's great."

"You don't like it."

"It's fine." He wiped his eyes. He bent and tied his bootlaces. "It's artificial. But it's fine."

"I didn't think you'd be here anyway. When you decided to leave on the train a month before Christmas, I thought you'd probably stay in California until second semester started."

"Well." He stood up.

"But of course, I am glad you're here. I know Christmas won't be easy for you this year. I know it's not the same, but I remember all too well the first Christmas after your father died."

Miller recoiled. He had no idea where to begin if he tried to pick at the ravel of just these few little lies—that he thought the tree was ugly, that he wasn't going to be here for Christmas, that he might not be going back to school, now or ever, that he hadn't really taken the train out of town, that he didn't know what she meant by "not the same." There was a slippery sound to her voice and a small clumsiness in her movements that told him it might be best to let them all go by.

"I have to go out," he said.

"But you've just barely arrived. Have you eaten dinner?"

"No. I'm not hungry. Or I'll grab something."

Suddenly her living room seemed like the most claustrophobic place in the world, and not the least because he knew a part of him had sought it out. Did he need to feel confinement? Did he go out of his way in search of prisons? Did he carry his own around with him all the time?

She swallowed the rest of her drink. The ice cubes clinked against the glass. "There's nothing I can ever do for you," she said. She stood and went back to the kitchen.

Miller heard her open the bottle again. This wasn't like her—drinking at home. Or was it? He realized how long he had been away.

"What do you mean by that?" he asked her through the wall.

"So what *are* your plans now?" She stayed in the kitchen.

"I don't have any."

Neither of them moved from their respective rooms. Miller sensed something building.

"Wonderful," she said. "Half the time I don't know what state you're in. What jail you'll be in. I thought you said you were going back to school. Now you show up in the middle of December and don't even know if you'll be here for Christmas?"

"The truth is, Mom, I don't care about Christmas right now. It's a long way off to me. It's just not on my mind."

"That's exactly what I'm trying to find out. You don't care about Christmas, or me, or your education, or getting a job. So tell me. What is on your mind?"

"What are you jumping on me for?"

"Don't you think if your father were alive, he might have jumped on you a lot sooner and harder than I ever have?"

It was a *what if* Miller was totally unprepared for, one she had hardly ever brought up, in any context, for any reason. Loren had died and they were alone, a thirty-five-year-old widow and an eight-year-old boy, and that was that. They had made the best of it and never spoken about what might have been.

"I have no idea about that," he said. "I just know I really don't want to be having this kind of talk right now. Especially when you're half-crocked."

"Sometimes people have to get half-crocked to tell the truth," she said.

Miller knew he should leave right then, just slip out the door and leave it open behind him, but he didn't. He looked down at his boots on the carpet. He spoke to her through the hallway.

"I don't think either of us is very good at truth," he said. "You couldn't even tell me about Maureena. You had to have your father do it."

"That's not fair, Miller, it's not fair. But if you have to bring it up, I didn't tell you about her because I was too angry at her. I was afraid what I might say."

Miller clicked the TV on and right back off twice. The aborted static-like sound of it starting and stopping pleased him somehow. He suddenly felt like kicking his boot through it.

"What right do you have to be angry at her?"

"Because she was a coward," she raised her voice and let the loud last word echo between rooms for a second. Then she continued even louder. "She was weak, she hurt you, and I hate her for it. I would never hurt you like she did."

Miller stood in the center of the room, shaking. He glared at the fake flocked tree in the corner of the room. It was grotesque. He focussed in on one satin ball until it was all he could see—a small blood-red globe with no countries.

"If she hurt anyone, it was herself," he said. "She lost a whole lifetime."

"You'd stand up for her, even though she deserted you," Evelyn said. "You never do appreciate the people who try to help you the most."

"As if you wouldn't stand up for dad." Now it was Miller's turn to let a word echo. Evelyn walked into the room and stood close to him. Her eyes were filmy and wide. Another drink swayed in her hand.

"Don't you dare try to compare my husband of so many years with your little teenage girlfriend," she said. "Your father died in an accident. A horrible tragic accident just when his life was finally turning around for him. For us."

"She was twenty-one," Miller said. "And they're both just as dead."

He wanted so badly to tell her what he knew, or thought he knew. He wanted to tell her about the dry pavement and the empty highway. He wanted to say it flat out—your husband killed himself. How could she have lived with it all these years and not even wondered?

"No, they're not," she said. "They're not the same the way you said. Your father lives on in you." She pointed at Miller. "You didn't have to go to war. You went to college. You have so many chances he never dreamed of. And then you throw them all away." She pursed her lips as if the words were dirty. "He'd be ashamed."

Miller felt his eyes water. "I shouldn't have come here," he said.

"Then get out." She turned her back on him, mumbling away toward the kitchen again. "You and that spineless girl. She let you sleep with her and wrapped you around her fingers from day one. That was the beginning of the end for you, kiddo. It's been all downhill."

Miller stood transfixed and furious by the door. What hell was this? And whose?

"I don't care if you're here or not for Christmas," she said. "I've been invited to Kansas City with Monty from work for the holidays. You don't like the tree anyway." She lowered the pitch of her voice to mock him. "It's artificial, but it's fine." She snorted. "And you're so damn real, aren't you?"

Miller stood ready to scream it at her. He could hear the words crash down the hall and into her life—dad's wreck was about as accidental as a Kamikaze. You've been living a lie a third of your life.

But the words wouldn't come. Instead he walked to the Christmas tree. He waved his arm and knocked it to the floor in one wide swoop. Red satin balls flew and bounced everywhere across the room. Bits of white flocking drifted onto the carpet like pieces of plastic snow. She came running back from the kitchen. She spilled her drink in the hall. It stained her dress.

"Miller. What have you done?"

He opened the door and held onto it.

"I'm going to see Maureena's grave," he said. "That's why I came back to this cold Godforsaken city. I have to tell my spineless girlfriend goodbye. At least it's something honest."

He pointed at the mess he had made of the tree and its decorations strewn across the floor.

"This is all a lie. That fake polyethylene monstrosity is a lie. How can anybody play Christmas when people are dying or killing everywhere you look? It's all a lie. The holidays, the flags, our lives. It's one big bloody dollar bill fudge bar on a stick. And I don't want to spend my whole life licking it."

He slammed the door behind him before it really registered that she had sat down on the bed crying. But he was too mad to care. He ran down the hall and then the steps. Before he was halfway to the Skylark, he knew how much too far he had gone and how easy it had been to get there, given her half-drunk push.

He felt guilt. Dark and heavy, burning down from behind and above on his shoulders, his neck. It was like something with many legs, alive and sick, needing to feed. But he kept right on walking. He recognized it. He almost liked it. At least it held him down.

39

Miller drove several blocks before he knew he was shaking and talking to himself. The road was a blur. He swerved to avoid a teenage kid jaywalking across Farnam in front of Mutual of Omaha. The kid flashed him the finger.

He pulled over at the next light and parked near the Blackstone Hotel. A Yellow Cab was sitting two cars away at the stand. Miller grabbed the toy Skylark off the dashboard and put it in his coat pocket as he walked toward the cab.

He sat down in the front seat. The cabbie had a pony tail and a thin beard. He turned down a portable tape player that was plugged into the cigarette lighter. Miller heard the wild drums of Santana's first album. He thought he smelled grass.

"Where can I take you?"

"You know Mount Calvary Cemetery on Center Street?"

"What about it?"

"That's where I want to go."

"They don't often keep graveyards open after dark." The cabbie smiled.

Miller reached for his wallet. He had an even hundred bucks left and held out a twenty.

"Please. Just take me where I ask until this runs out," he said. "Is that all right?"

"The customer's always right," the cabbie said. "Tell you what. I'll run awhile without the meter." He pointed at the box next to him. There was a picture of a little boy, two or three maybe, taped to the top of it above the red handle. "We'll both make out better. Sound okay?"

"Fine," Miller said. "You know Omaha?"

"Pretty well. I've been driving it seven months," he said. "I mustered out of the Air Force after four years at Offutt. I'm from Detroit, but I married an Omaha girl, so here I am. Anyway, this burg's laid out on a grid. What's to know?"

A gust of wind howled down Farnam Street. The stoplights hanging in the middle of the intersection swayed. The cab shook.

"Is it supposed to storm?" Miller finally noticed how cold it was. Winter wasn't paying any attention to the calendar, as usual.

"There's a big one brewing up north. They said it should be here sometime tomorrow."

They drove with the meter off. The cabbie turned his music back up. Miller thought of Durham and all his cabdriving stories. He imagined applying at the cab barn himself—yet another snapshot future.

When they pulled up at the closed gates of Mount Calvary, the cab's headlights cast thin black lines on the other side of the tall iron bars on the gate.

"Locked up for the night," the cabbie said. "I told you. S.O.P."

"Can you pull around on Gold Street, please."

Miller was trying to remember the Ocear family plot Maureena had shown him their first Christmas back from southern California together—both her father's parents and his brother who died as a child. And blank space. Room for Richard's growing family. The insurance agent left nothing to chance.

The pavement of Gold Street dwindled off into a one-lane dirt road that ran along the west edge of the cemetery. Miller directed the cabbie to a place far from a streetlight.

"How's the twenty holding up?" he asked.

"It's fine. But what now?"

Miller opened the door. "Now you wait and don't watch. I'll be back. If it takes too long, I'll pay you more. Sound fair?"

"No problemo," he said. "I don't know where you are, but I'm here. For an hour." He watched Miller step out and close the door.

Miller walked half a block back down the dirt road, climbed the fence, dropped to the ground, and stood among the tombstones. At the top of a rounded hill, he saw the silhouette of a huge vault, surrounded by trees. He walked up toward it, stepping carefully around and between the graves when he could see them.

From the hill, half the cemetery was in view. Miller searched from a memory he didn't want to be using. He walked south along a curving gravel lane through acres of graves, the city's essence, condensed and silent. He glimpsed a recent grave with a flat low stone. He recalled Maureena's words about Woody's grave at Holy Sepulchre—rumpled carpet. This one was bare dirt—no carpet at all. He slowed down and circled toward it over the frosted grass.

He didn't look down right away. The Ocear name was large and clear on the upright stone for her grandparents. He looked everywhere but at his feet. He was sure hers would be here, sure enough to climb the fence and steal through the graves, and yet at the same time he was trying to will it not to be. Not to be anywhere.

After he turned all the way around twice slowly, he did look down. A flattened oval mound of wilted, frosted flowers fanned out across the dirt. A carved stone protruded two inches from the frozen ground.

Maureena Ann Ocear
Beloved Daughter
September 22 1948 October 27 1969
An Angel Awaits Her Wings

Miller whispered the words once, twice, dozens of times, until his throat hurt and his ears burned. He lay down on his back next to the long rectangle of cold dirt that spread from the base of the stone. He stared up at the stars while he reached out and ran his fingers over the abyss of each stone letter.

He wanted more than anything he had ever wanted to speak to her then, to tell her about jail and St. Joe's and the train and Grant, and to talk with her about the terrible mistake of Fargo and the child that wasn't ever going to be and the wedding on the island that never was but should have been. He wanted to promise her that they could go back to the summer and escape on the ferry and ride in the Skylark and find a place where her parents would never find them and the war would never burn through. They would never leave each other and never make mistakes and never die apart like this. He wanted to tell her it was all right if she lived her whole life apart from him, with someone else, or no one else, or everyone else. As long as she would just promise to live, to live.

But if he told her anything, it was wordless. If he saw her at all, it was only in the sky and the stars. This stone and dirt was just a cold place with words only the ones who never really knew her might need. An Omaha place. Her parents' place.

He reached in his pocket for the little car. But instead he felt the two halves of his sand dollar, the broken pieces he had been carrying since Cook County. He remembered David Lindere's burnt black circle in the California sunshine and Maureena's flowers. He arranged the two pieces of the sand dollar next to each other on the ground, just below the stone.

CR

The cabbie was still there when Miller climbed back over the fence. The lights were off, and he was dozing with the windows rolled up. He straightened when Miller tapped on the glass.

Miller opened the door and sat down. When he felt the hot air from the heater fan, he realized how cold he was. His teeth chattered. He rubbed his hands together.

"You want some hot coffee?" The cabbie held up a thermos.

"Sure." The cabbie poured it and handed a cup to Miller. He held it between his hands, feeling the warmth. He took a slow sip. "One more stop?"

The cabbie checked his watch. "It's eight-forty. Say twenty minutes. Then I need to call in. I have to hit the real streets again." He looked right at Miller's eyes. "You okay, man?"

"Maybe."

The cabbie gazed out through the windows, staring all around, as if looking for someone.

"I like the jacket and the patch," he said, pointing at the peace sign on Miller's shoulder. "You want to smoke a joint?"

"Not tonight. But thanks."

"You mind?" He held up a half-smoked joint and a match.

"No, you go ahead."

He turned half around in the seat, leaning against his door. He lit up and took a hit and held it, smiling broadly.

"You seem pretty happy driving a cab," Miller said.

The man held up his hand and then exhaled slowly before he spoke.

"Well, I am. Not forever. But for now, it's not half bad, you know? You go till you don't want to go anymore, then you stop. You're your own boss. I need that right now after four years of Big Sam."

"Tell me something?"

He nodded as he inhaled again.

"That your boy?" Miller pointed at the picture on the meter box.

He exhaled and pinched the joint out. He smiled at the picture. "Zeke Junior. Yeah, he's the greatest. He's the reason."

"So, do you ever think about what you'll tell him about all this later?" Miller waved his hand around the cab and beyond.

"All this?"

"The times. The war. Picking up a guy like me and taking him to a graveyard and offering him weed. Omaha. Offutt." Miller pointed at the tape player. "Santana. All of it."

The cabbie pulled a cigarette pack out of his pocket and carefully slipped the long roach into it. He stared away from Miller into the dark cemetery behind the chainlink.

"You know," he said. "I haven't really thought about that. I have to get through it myself first, of course." He smiled. "But I'll tell him something." He waved his hand. "I'll tell him nobody really had a handle on it and it happened real fast."

He turned back to the steering wheel and laughed. He pointed at his boy's picture.

"Hell, by the time Zeke's old enough to really listen to me, I may have to make something up. I probably still won't have it figured out."

He put the cab in gear and turned the headlights back on.

"Why do you ask? You have a kid, too?"

"No," Miller said. "That's why I asked."

He pulled back onto the pavement. The lights of Center Street shone through the web of overhanging tree limbs.

"So where to next? Not another cemetery, I hope."

Miller told him the Ocears' address. The cabbie nodded. He turned out onto Center and then quickly right on 60th Street. Miller drank some more of the hot coffee.

When they turned onto the block, Miller half expected to see *For Sale* signs. Could they stay in that house? Keep using that garage?

But there were no signs. And no lights. It was just a plain brick house on an ordinary street. Miller thought he was ready to face them now. Maybe he would just listen. Maybe he would just tell them he was sorry he hadn't been here when it happened. Maybe he would just strangle them. Everything he could imagine was plausible. The cab pulled to a stop.

"We picking somebody up here?"

Miller opened the door and stepped out.

"I don't think so."

He walked up the steps to the front door and knocked. Nothing. No lights came on. He waited in the dark. Then he walked back down the front steps and moved down the side walkway toward the garage door.

Richard had replaced the broken door from January with an identical one. Miller looked through the narrow window. No car. The garage was empty. He couldn't see much beyond that in the dark. The taxi idled in front of the house. Miller cupped his hands above his eyes and leaned them on the window and looked harder.

He wanted in. Wasn't this where he belonged? The place where she vanished? He reached down and pulled on the garage door handle. He jiggled the lock back and forth.

"Ocears aren't home."

Miller jerked and whirled around. It was Wenshaw next door again. Always on the alert. The good neighbor.

"They're in Miami," he said, taking two steps across his front lawn toward Miller. "They have a security service watching the home though. And the Mrs. and me." He looked from Miller to the cab and back again.

"You from out of town? You a relative?"

Miller backed down the driveway toward the cab. They were both good questions.

"Just a friend," he said, opening the door. "Just in town for tonight."

"They go every year," Wenshaw said. "On business. We keep a weather eye peeled, if you know what I mean. It's that kind of neighborhood." He waved his arm around the silent tree-lined street. "I've got a phone number for them if it's really important."

He hadn't recognized Miller yet. And maybe he wouldn't—he didn't have his glasses on.

"No, just tell them I'm very sorry about their daughter."

Wenshaw shook his head back and forth slowly. He came a few steps down his walkway.

"Terrible thing," he said. "Terrible thing. No rhyme or reason. It's more than any parent should ever have to bear."

Miller sat down in the cab. For a second he imagined commandeering it and backing up all the way across the street into the neighbor's driveway and then taking a run at the garage door, crashing back into that silent stark space. But he sat perfectly still.

"Who should I say they missed?" Wenshaw asked.

"Someone who knew her in California," Miller said. "Goodnight."

He slammed the door. The cabbie drove away. Miller watched behind them as Wenshaw stood under the streetlight like a statue among the elm trees. The house and garage disappeared.

Zeke dropped Miller off back at the Blackstone, on his way downtown to answer a call at the Orpheum Theater. Before Miller left, he leaned back into the cab and they shook hands. Then Miller reached in his pocket and handed him the little Skylark.

"Thanks for the friendly driving," Miller said. "Something for the little guy, okay?"

Zeke smiled as he turned it in his hand. He stared over at the parked Skylark.

"Looks close to the original," he said. "I won't try to guess at what's on with you tonight, or why you're giving this up, but yeah, the boy will love this. Thanks. You take care, man."

Miller watched him drive away down Harney. He stood next to the Skylark and held out his hands. They were perfectly still. He felt as calm as he had in weeks.

He drove slowly back to his mother's place. Her lights were off, and he parked and went in. He heard someone's wash down in the basement, whirling around in a spin cycle. He knocked lightly on the door. When she didn't answer, he turned the knob. It was unlocked.

Miller tiptoed down the hall. She was asleep in her bed, breathing heavily. He went back to the kitchen and put the bourbon away. He washed her glass and filled the ice cube trays.

In the living room he picked up all the Christmas balls, one by one. He stood the tree upright and straightened out the branches that had bent in the fall. He searched out all the little metal hangers and reattached them to the satin balls and rehung them as close to the way they had been as he could imagine and then rearranged the folds of white felt around the base of the tree.

It was so quiet in the small apartment that Miller could hear his mother breathing in her sleep from the bedroom. He felt like an errant Santa Claus. He found some paper for a note and folded it like a card and wrote her name on the outside and set it under the tree.

Mom. I'm very sorry about the tree. Maybe we're not this angry at each other. Maybe it's us or the ones who went away. I think the KC trip sounds great. I don't know what I'm doing anymore and now I think maybe I never have. How can you tell? But I thought I believed in real things. I was wrong. The tree is pretty.

Love, Miller

Miller locked the door and pulled it shut. He went down the stairs to the front door and stepped outside. The wind was blowing much harder now, and the shallow puddles all across the front yard were skimmed with ice.

40

It was almost midnight when Miller pulled into Clay Center. He came in from the north on State Highway 14. The town sign said *Pop. 338*. Miller counted the outlines of a few houses, a gas station and store, a cluster of close small farms. It would have been the last little town, the last community, that his father ever saw. Miller looked at his odometer. The DMV accident report had said approximately four miles south of Clay Center. The town disappeared behind him. The countryside went dark again.

After three miles he slowed down. To the west an abandoned farmhouse sat atop the snowy crest of a hill like a dilapidated ark riding a white sea. Miller thought of his advice to Grant. To stop somewhere and play himself back. He turned off on the rutted farm lane.

He took a good run on the level and pulled on up the hill to the top and turned around and parked by the house. From up on the hill he could see the moon. It was a sliver shy of full and newly risen, balancing above the eastern horizon like a fat albino eye.

A coyote loped away from behind the barn as Miller stepped out of the car. It felt warmer behind the ragged old windbreaks. All the upstairs windows in the house were broken out, and an elm branch had split halfway off its tree and lay sprawled across one gable. The back door stood off its hinges. Someone had propped it over the doorway and angled a two-by-four brace between it and the broken boards of the small porch. Miller jostled it open and went inside.

What had once been someone's living room was empty except for two old box springs, a large ragged piece of foam bedroll, and a rocking chair with torn cane backing. The chair was next to a window with a bullet hole near the bottom. The pane was cracked in five jagged sections but still intact. Miller went back and propped the door closed, and then he sat down in the rocking chair and wrapped the old foam around his legs. He stared out the window.

It was closing in on a year now since Maureena's garage. Hundreds of days and over eleven months and thousands of miles. But which were important? Where were the clues? Miller tried to remember, rocking back and forth in the chair, gazing into the broad white face of the moon. The land around him unfolded and rolled out between the Little Blue and Big Blue rivers like the palm of a large rough hand.

At some point, much deeper into the night, snow flurries began to swirl and slash through the sky, driving in from the west. A low metallic moan rose and fell as the wind played across the ragged lip of an abandoned silo. Slowly at first, and then faster and faster, gray clouds sliced and feathered the moonlight. And then it was only a muted haze in the east.

Miller stood up carefully, testing his legs. He turned his back on the cracked window. He walked across the living room and then into the kitchen toward the door. Bits of broken glass and dried leaves crunched between his boots and the warped linoleum floor, the sounds so crisp and loud that he turned to look for someone walking behind him. But there was no one.

He moved the broken door again, went outside, and braced it back up the way he had found it. He looked around the run-down farm lot and then stepped off the porch. He reached the Skylark in four strides. Spring, summer, fall, winter. He whispered it to himself as he walked.

CW

At the pavement he turned south again. Farmland drifted away in every direction, slow brown swells crusted in white—beautiful, foreboding, even familiar—but he didn't get any kind of sign. He wondered if his father had had any hint at all, any sense of his life cresting or breaking like a wave above a sudden steep slant of beach.

In three more miles, he came to an intersection with a paved county road. Miller u-turned and doubled back, and then it dawned on him, spine-deep, below all thought. How he would finally find out. He would get tall. He would see over the walls. The maze would come clear. It had only been a one-door hallway all along.

Back at the farmhouse lane again, he pulled another u-turn. This time he ran through the gears, double-clutching, feeling nothing but speed and night. He caught fourth, pushed the pedal back down, and watched the speedometer needle rise. It was snowing harder, but the flakes weren't sticking to the pavement and the highway still looked dry. The needle passed eighty-five, as fast as Miller had ever had the Skylark. His grip relaxed until he had just one finger on each side of the wheel. Ninety. He was in the center of the road. Ninety-five.

The tone of the engine rose suddenly and changed pitch, and then there was a noise like a boulder on castiron. Miller jammed the clutch in and watched his hands on the wheel, steering into the skid, back and then forth. The engine clanked and the warning lights were all bright red. He eased onto the brake. The speedometer needle fell back in a quick arc as the car corrected left and right and again left one more time and then straightened out. Dark smoke blew from under the fenders, and lines of cracked paint spidered out from a gnarly star-shaped bump on the hood, as if someone had tried to beat their way out from the inside with a crowbar. When the speedometer dropped below twenty, Miller slowly let the clutch out and the Skylark slid over to the wrong side of the road, halfway into a shallow ditch, and stopped. The engine hissed and clicked and coughed. And then, it just hissed.

Miller turned the headlights off and stepped out in the snow with the door open in his hand. Fields of half-shattered corn lay on one side of the road and wind-slicked pasture stretched away on the other, both sides fenced off by five strands of barbwire, as if the highway were a prison. Next to a low wide wash, the skeleton of a dead cottonwood jabbed into the sky.

This might have been the place. Miller would never know.

But that was only the beginning. What he would never know was enough to fill a lifetime, enough, maybe, to carry him through a lifetime. Maureena, Loren, Evelyn, Miller—all the secrets kept and found and lost and half kept and half revealed. He would never know about his father's last moments, or if Maureena's key was on or off, or who had willed the Skylark through the garage door, or why it had blown itself out at just this time and place.

When he closed the car door, the interior light on the dash went off, the last light. Snow was sticking everywhere but on the hood, where it steamed as it melted. Miller grabbed his duffel bag, buttoned his jacket sleeves tight, tied the drawstring on his hood, and blew on his hands before he put his gloves on.

It felt like he was doing it for someone else that he was supposed to be good to. An old friend, deep inside his coat. Take care.

He started walking away, but turned around after less than a dozen steps. He went back and retrieved Maureena's letter from the glove compartment. He unfolded it and reread it in a single glance. He saw the phone number for British Columbia. Powdery snowflakes landed on her words. A letter from another century coated with dust. He blew the snow off the letter and folded it up small and slipped it inside his glove. He unsnapped the Skylark's top, pulled it down, and rolled it out across the back deck. Then he started walking north again.

൵

Miller's boots slapped like flat frozen bones against the pavement. It had already stopped snowing, or he had walked out of the squall, he didn't know which, but before long he began to see stars again, their faint light leaking through the bruise of a blueblack sky. At some point he glimpsed the far wink of headlights, cresting a knoll, disappearing and reappearing.

It seemed like a long time before the lights came up on him. It was a late-model Ford pickup with a camper topper. The driver stopped and rolled his window down and leaned out.

"I've seen better nights for a hike."

Miller stopped walking. He dropped his bag at his feet, but he still leaned to the right where the weight had been. He couldn't see the man's face clearly. He wasn't sure he could speak, or if the man would hear him if he did.

"Where you headed?"

Miller felt the letter, riding inside his glove. He cleared his throat. He said something that sounded pretty close to what he intended. "Canada."

"On this road?"

Miller looked down at the pavement. He didn't answer.

"How far have you walked?"

"I don't know."

"How far do you plan on walking?"

"I don't know."

"I see." A match flared behind the windshield, and the man lit a cigarette. In the quick yellow glow, Miller saw his face more clearly. He had a short dark beard and wore a brown farm cap and a sheepskin coat. He looked to be about twice Miller's age, maybe forty or so, somewhere in there. How did anyone survive for that long? Or maybe he wasn't that old. Miller couldn't tell. The man blew out a long stream of smoke.

"I'm not going anywhere close to Canada. I'm heading south to 136 and then east to Missouri. But, I could run you at least into Hebron. You might catch northbound traffic there."

Miller looked down the road in the direction of Clay Center. He wasn't even back as far as the old farmhouse. The main highway had to be another ten miles. He wasn't sure at all how cold he was, or if he even felt cold, and that didn't seem right. He walked around the front of the truck, pulling and skidding his bag along behind him.

The man leaned across and pushed open the door. "Good call. It has to be near zero out here, partner."

Miller steadied himself on the door. The warmth of the cab shoved at him like strong thick breath. After a minute he hefted his bag up and tipped it in and then climbed in after it very slowly without a word. Like an old man, like a refugee without the language.

ভথ

It must have been a squall, because they drove back into it, still close to where Miller had left it and still swirling white. The man gave Miller a wool blanket from behind the seat and told him to stretch out. He kept the truck steady at forty-five and talked slow and just as steady.

He said his name was Lydell Currey but everybody except his mother and the pastor at his church called him Dell and he was headed home to Hannibal, Missouri, the best little town and the best kept secret on the Mississippi River. It was a good twelve hours out yet, but he would take two days anyway, because he had several more stops ahead. He made this drive between North Platte and Hannibal several times a year on business, selling walnut woodcrafts from the family factory in Hannibal to small town retail stores and tourist shops.

He was still talking when they came up on the Skylark. The interior was completely covered in white now. Snow drifted in piles against the seat backs and clung to both sides of the windshield. Dell slowed almost to a stop.

"There's one I've not seen before, this side of a salvage yard anyway. A car full of snow."

"It was mine," Miller told him. "I blew it up."

"Do you want to stop?"

"No. It threw a rod, I think."

"You're just leaving it?"

"I'm done with it," Miller said.

"Too bad," Dell said. "It looks like a nice ride."

As they drove away, Miller pulled the blanket up close around himself and turned away and stared out his window. Dell kept talking, about Hannibal and his wife and kids and the small, but reliable, market for his walnut wood products. Miller didn't hear all of it and he didn't sleep and he didn't notice they were slowing down until they stopped.

"What's here?" he asked, straightening up and turning around.

"Hebron." Dell pointed at the sign. *Hebron Grocery and Feed Store.* There wasn't a car in sight, just rows of buildings that looked abandoned and useless.

"Nothing looks open," Miller said.

Dell pulled his sleeve back and looked at his watch. "They'll be open for me. And, they make some darn good wake-up." He fished a thermos up off the floor. "You want some?"

"No thanks," Miller said. "Have you seen a phone here before?"

"Ma Bell's finest," Dell said. He pointed right across the highway to a booth in front of an A & W Drive-in. There was ice on one side of the booth and for a moment all Miller could see was Maureena and then Durham, calling from California on South Thirteenth Street in Omaha.

Miller reached for the door handle and then turned back. He put his hand out.

"Thanks for the ride. I'm going to try a phone call and be on my way." He looked in Dell's eyes for the first time. Maybe he was older than forty. Miller pointed over his shoulder.

"I wasn't intending to be unfriendly. I'm pretty tired out tonight."

Dell pursed his lips and shook his head like there was nothing wrong at all, like he had seen something like this same night before and there was nothing about it in need of explanation. He shook Miller's hand and smiled.

"You're entirely welcome, partner. Everybody runs across some nights like that. I hope it can all work out for you."

☙

The booth had wire mesh in the glass. The door folded in half to open and shut, but it was jammed open. Miller unfolded Maureena's letter and called collect to the number in Canada.

Durham accepted the call as soon as he heard Miller's name.

"Miller? Is it really you, man? I was sleeping. Where are you?"

"Still in Nebraska," Miller said. "It's real tough to get out of in the winter."

"Oh man, you should see the snow *here*," Durham said. "God, it's so good to hear your voice, Miller. I talked to Drew when he helped me over the border. He said you were in Cook County Jail, but I sure hoped you'd be out of there by now. Sorry I lost touch. I really owe you."

"I'm just glad you slipped through, Steve. Forget the money."

"No way. Maureena saved me, man. I can fight fires next summer. That's how everybody gets through the year here. I'll send it then."

"You keep your fire money, Durham. Chalk it up as my bit to keep the army at least one soldier smaller."

"No, listen, you guys worked too hard. And it's Maureena's money, too."

He and Carlila hadn't heard. Like Grant, they had escaped to another planet, woken up in a whole other zone. And now Miller knew he couldn't cross over there. He couldn't go to them. They were in some separate past or future that Miller would never be able to find again.

"You haven't talked to your folks, Durham?"

"I can't, man. Since the bust, I stay completely incommunicado. I send them a letter whenever I can to let them know I'm alive. But I have to wait till somebody's going down to the States to post it. I'm invisible, Miller."

"Well look, the money's invisible, too, all right? Just forget the money. Tell me about you. Tell me about Carlila."

"She's copasetic. Hey, and so's her daughter."

"She had the baby?"

"A little girl. Almost a week ago. They're both great. Are you guys heading on up here? You can see her."

"No, I'm not sure what's next." Miller looked at the license plate on Dell's pickup across the road. "Missouri," he said, "I think."

"Missouri? As in somewhere between Iowa and nowhere? Oh man, you're going to have to put Maureena on the line for that one. I want to hear her say she's going to Missouri."

"Maureena's sleeping," Miller said. "She's asleep in the car." He stared through the mesh in the glass and knew it was the last time he would hear Durham's voice in a long time. Or maybe at all. "Look, Steve, this is person-to-person. It'll cost you way too much."

"Okay, but Miller, you keep in touch. We're like a family here, and it's so different being out of the States and all the war crap. All you have to remember is Turkey Flats, Edgewood, B.C. It's too easy to forget. Anytime you two need a place. Anytime."

"Thanks. It's good to know. Say love to Carlila for me."

"I will. And Leucadia. She named her Leucadia. Remember?"

"Perfect," Miller said, because he couldn't think of anything else. And because it was. "That's perfect. Goodbye, Durham."

"See you, Miller. Thanks again for the help. Keep the top down."

The receiver clicked. As Miller hung up, a pickup loaded high with hay bales rolled down the highway and stopped in front of a cafe just as someone inside pulled up the shades on the windows and turned the outside light on. Miller folded Maureena's letter until it wouldn't fold anymore. He pushed it down deep in the watch pocket of his jeans.

Across the highway, Dell came out of the Feed Store with his thermos of coffee, steaming. Miller stood out of the booth and walked toward him.

∞

Right outside of town they crossed the Little Blue River, and then in only a few more minutes, the Kansas state line. Miller lay under two blankets on the foam rubber bedroll inside the camper. The sliding windows between the cab and the camper were open, and Miller heard Dell whistling and felt the camper warming up a little. All he could smell was the dark oily scent of walnut. On both sides of him there were cardboard boxes stamped *Hannibal Walnut Works*. Two of the boxes were opened and half full of walnut bowls and pencil holders and coasters.

Miller stared at the ceiling of the camper, listening to the low thrum of the engine and the tune the driver whistled. It was very familiar, but he couldn't remember the name of the song. Not the song and then not the name of the driver. Neither one. Then in another blink he couldn't remember any names, not his own, or the people at the end of the phone a few miles back, or even the names of the dead people he was sure he had been chasing for a long time through the night.

He moved his eyes to the side and looked out the window at the starlight, scattered across the black sky now like a sweeping array of white wounds. The night drifted by in dark waves, and Miller gave up trying to remember. He let everything go, all the names and all the stars, and nothing changed, nothing broke. Finally his eyelids closed down, a fraction of an inch at a time, a slow double eclipse between Miller and everything he had seen so far. He was hugging and holding himself with his cold hands up under his arms as he drifted away beneath the borrowed blankets, and it was a feeling not far from prayer.

Let me sleep. Give me dreams.

It was all he wanted. Only in dreams would he ever find what had been lost and what strengthened. And when he awakened, perhaps he would remember more clearly. Or less clearly.

But differently, differently. He felt he could sleep for one, or ten, or thirty years, and still, never dream deep enough.

Phil Condon is author of *River Street: A Novella and Stories* (Southern Methodist University Press, 1994). His stories have appeared in the *Georgia Review, Sewanee Review, Manoa, New Letters, Shenandoah, Black Warrior Review, Epoch*, and *Prairie Schooner*. He received a creative writing fellowship from the NEA in 1993. He teaches Environmental Writing for the EVST program at the U. of Montana and lives in Missoula, with his wife, Celeste River. *Clay Center* is his first novel.